Dee Williams was born and brought up in Rotherhithe in East London where her father worked as a stevedore in Surrey Docks. Dee left school at fourteen, met her husband at sixteen and was married at twenty. After living abroad for some years, Dee moved to Hampshire to be close to her family. HOPES AND DREAMS is her thirteenth novel, following twelve hugely popular previous sagas set in Rotherhithe.

Hopes and Dreams

Dee Williams

headline

First published in 2002
by HEADLINE BOOK PUBLISHING

First published in paperback in 2003
by HEADLINE BOOK PUBLISHING

10 9 8 7 6 5 4 3 2 1

ISBN 0 7553 0097 1

Typeset in Times by
Letterpart Limited, Reigate, Surrey

Printed and bound in Great Britain by
Mackays of Chatham plc, Chatham, Kent

HEADLINE BOOK PUBLISHING
A division of Hodder Headline
338 Euston Road
LONDON NW1 3BH

www.headline.co.uk
www.hodderheadline.com

This is for my two bestest mates Gilda and Jean,
who nag me sometimes.
But I still love 'em.

And for Caroline, a truly great agent.

Chapter 1

1943

Dorothy Taylor, or Dolly Day Dream as she was known to all her friends, laughed when her best friend Penny put a corner of a paper bag over her nose to stop it from getting sunburned.

'Don't wanna finish up with a red nose again, do I?' said Penny. 'So – what are we doing tonight?'

Dolly and Penny were sitting on the coping that ran round the Taylors' windowsill. It was late August and a warm sunny Sunday afternoon. 'Could go to the pictures, I suppose.' The pictures were Dolly's answer to everything. She looked up at the barrage balloons glinting in the sunlight. 'I'm sick of this war. I'll be glad when it's all over and we get a decent night's sleep.'

Penny, with her eyes closed and facing the sun, said, 'To be in a soft bed all night would be nice. I'm really fed up with it as well.'

'So are a lot of people, Pen. We've been lucky so far – touch wood. We've still got our houses, not like some poor devils. And what about Reg and Tony? I wonder what they're doing on this lovely afternoon?'

'We don't know if it *is* a lovely afternoon where they are.

1

I can't stop thinking about him.' Penny sighed. 'I don't half miss my Reggie.'

Dolly looked at the ring on the third finger of her left hand. 'And I miss Tony,' she said, moving her hand so the tiny diamond sparkled in the sunlight.

Dolly, who would be eighteen in November, was three months younger than Penny, who only last week had celebrated her birthday. Unfortunately, it hadn't been much of an occasion, as gifts were so very hard to find. Thank goodness Dolly had managed to get her friend a pair of pillowcases for her bottom drawer.

The girls had lived next door to each other in Wood Street, Rotherhithe, all their lives and were more like sisters than friends. They went to the same school and to the same job when they left at fourteen. Dolly, who was an only child, lived with her mother at number twenty. Her father was in the Merchant Navy and for most of her life he had been at sea. She was always dreaming of going to the faraway places Jim Taylor had told her about. She wanted to see for herself the white, palm-fringed sandy beaches and dusky maidens padding about barefoot. Then there were the Egyptian pyramids . . . but most of all it was Hollywood and New York that fired her imagination. America was very high on her list of Must See One Day. She would sit in the darkened cinema and be transported. Before the war it had been wonderful, almost like Christmas whenever her dad came home loaded with presents from far-off lands. If she had been a boy, she would have worked on ships like he did, but at the moment it wasn't such a good idea, as the German submarines were sinking our ships. Every night she prayed he would be safe, although if superstitions were to be believed, Jim would never drown. Dolly had been born with a cowl over her head, and according to legend, any sailor who had a cowl in his pocket would never drown. Dolly idolised her father and loved it when people said she was the image of him, since with his dark hair and flashing brown eyes he was very handsome. Dolly gently touched her neat pageboy bob and smiled.

Penny sat up and took the paper cone off her nose. 'Did you show Tony's mum the letter you had from him yesterday?'

'No, I didn't,' said Dolly indignantly. 'I told her about it though.' She laughed. 'That was when I could get a word in edgeways.' Mrs Marchant, Tony's mother, was a kind enough woman but Dolly wasn't that keen on going to see her. As Tony used to say, she could talk for England if it ever came to it. Since she'd joined the WVS there wasn't any stopping her, rabbiting on about some of the poor people she met.

'Where does she reckon Tony and Reg might be?' Penny asked.

'Dunno. We were trying to work it out. Think it might be in the desert. We should have got some sort of code going before they went away.'

'Didn't have much time, did we?'

'Not really.'

'P'raps they could put a couple of grains of sand in the envelope, then we'd know.'

'Penny Watts, are you daft.'

Tony and Reggie, Penny's boyfriend, also lived in Wood Street. The four youngsters had been friends all their lives. The boys had been in the Army for eighteen months now, and so far had stayed together. However, apart from leave when they were first called up, the boys had remained overseas.

'What did Rose have to say about it?' Penny asked.

'You know Rose. She always wonders why I get more letters than they do. I told her it was 'cos I write more than they do.' Rose was Tony's sister. She wasn't very fond of Dolly, who she thought was silly and giggly – and that upset Tony. Unperturbed, Dolly told him she was marrying him, not his sister. 'I wonder where we'll go for our honeymoon. Hope it's some exotic place.'

Penny laughed. 'I bet we finish up in Brighton.'

'Brighton can be very nice.'

'I know, but with a name like Smith everybody will think me and Reg are having a dirty weekend.'

'It's a shame both their dads are dead.' Dolly knew Mr Smith had died after the First World War in the flu epidemic. Tony's father had been killed in that war.

'There's a lot of men about that age who never came back. Look at the two Miss Gregorys,' Penny said sombrely.

'Let's hope we don't have too many of those rotten telegrams down this street.'

Penny didn't reply; she just sat back again, closed her eyes and replaced the nose-cone.

Dolly looked at her friend. Penny was taller than her and had a great figure. She was very attractive with her long dark curly hair, which most days she wore piled up on her head like Betty Grable. Her eyes were wide and a lovely blue. Dolly had always admired Penny, but was never jealous of her. Her friend might have the looks but it was Dolly who had the better life. She had never wanted for anything. Her father, unlike Penny's, had been in work all her life, while her mother was a skilled dressmaker who took in work before the war. As material was in short supply now, she worked at the old shirt factory, where they made uniforms. Penny had two younger brothers who drove her mad, so most times she could be found at her friend's house, except at night when they shared the same air raid shelter. Dolly sat turning her engagement ring round and round her finger. Tony had lived almost at the end of the street at number ninety-eight. He was the only boy for her, and she knew he loved her very much.

When the girls left school at fourteen they went to work on the counter at Woolworth's. By the time they were seventeen, they had moved on to factory jobs, as they knew they would have to enlist when they reached eighteen and hoped the factory would make them exempt, since neither of them wanted to be away from home. Their hours were seven in the morning till six at night from Monday to Friday, and till one o'clock on Saturday. They were lucky they weren't put on the night-shift. The wireless didn't have great singalong music at night. Both knew they made covers for shells. Sometimes, to ease the monotony, they stuck their names and addresses on them and sent the boys lots of love and kisses. For the first time since they had left school and gone out to work, Penny and Dolly had money to spend. The trouble was, there wasn't a lot to spend it on. Clothes were on ration, as were sweets, so it was pictures and dancing and buying hit records when they were able to. They both loved the modern music and would practise their dance steps in Dolly's mum's front room to the sound of Glenn Miller, and any other record they were lucky enough to get their hands on. They'd spend hours playing their records on the wind-up gramophone and got very upset when any of them became broken. Most Saturday nights would see them quickstepping round the floor at the local dance hall in the arms of any men who happened to be around.

To most it came as no surprise that when Reggie and Tony got called up the girls wanted to get engaged. Everybody thought it was a good idea – all except for Dolly's mum Grace, who thought her daughter was too young.

Dolly looked up and down Wood Street, which was typical of most streets in Rotherhithe. At the end was the King's Arms pub, where the men who hadn't been called up and the older women sat and discussed the day's events, then if the raids got too bad they finished up in the cellar. In the middle was a grocery shop and dairy that was run by Mrs Dobson and her husband. Next to it was the draper's-cum-sweetshop. That was divided in half and they sold many other things as well. It had belonged to a Mr Gregory and his two daughters, but he had passed away before the war and now the spinster sisters looked after it. They were kind and friendly, and had both lost their fiancés in the First World War. These two shops were where the rest of the community swapped the horror and sorrowful stories from the night before. Those that still lived in Wood Street were a proud lot. Every day it upset Dolly to see how the rows of back-to-back terraced houses that had survived the bombing no longer had white doorsteps and gleaming door knockers, or fresh-looking lace curtains at the bay windows that used to sway in the gentle breeze. Over the years the glass had been blown out of most of the windows and until it was replaced they were boarded up with wood, lino, cardboard – anything that could be scrounged or pilfered from the bombsites.

'So, what's it to be?' asked Penny, sitting up again and interrupting Dolly's thoughts.

'Pictures. Next week there's that *Mrs Miniver* on.'

'I know, but we'd have to give up dancing on Saturday if we want to see it. The queue will be miles long by the time we finish work.'

'I know,' sighed Dolly. 'We could go straight from work.'

'Dunno, I'd be starving.'

'Could always take sandwiches.'

'What about a drink?'

'How about a bottle of tea?' The inside of the flask they used to have had been broken and couldn't be replaced.

Penny giggled and the paper cone fell off her nose. 'D'you remember the last time we did that?'

'You laughed just as you were having a drink and spat tea all over that woman in front. She wasn't very pleased.' Dolly was grinning.

'Couldn't help it, it was a funny film.'

'So that's settled. We'll go on Tuesday straight from work.'

'OK. But what about tonight?'

'We could go to the bug hut – I think Abbott and Costello are on.'

'All right. But I don't really like them.'

'Nor do I,' said Dolly, 'but it's better than staying in, waiting for the siren to go off. Let's hope there's not a big raid. My mum gets really upset when I don't come home, but as I told her, there ain't a lot of point missing the film 'cos by the time we've got home, the raid's all over.'

Dolly's mother, Grace, was a slim upright woman who was still attractive. She had kind grey eyes and wavy brown hair which had been cut short and was always held back with a pretty slide. Dolly often looked at her parents' wedding photo. They had been married in 1921, when they were both twenty-one. They were a lovely couple and their smiles told the world how much they loved each other.

In 1940, the first air raids on London had been devastating around Rotherhithe and the Surrey Docks area. Night after night, Dolly and her mother had to sit in next door's brick air raid shelter. The Taylors didn't have one as their

7

yard was too small, so they shared with the Watts. Most mornings it was a question of clearing up plaster from the ceilings and glass for those who still had windows. Everybody hoped the gas mains and water pipes hadn't been damaged yet again. The kettles were filled before the raids and the round paraffin stove that made pretty pictures on the ceiling had to be used to boil a kettle. It took forever, but nobody could think or work without their cuppa. The WVS ladies sometimes managed to get round with a van, but Dolly and her mum couldn't wait for them.

Dolly always went into Penny's when her mother was on fire-watching duties. Although she laughed when her mum put on her funny-looking grey tin hat, Dolly worried; she didn't like her being out in a raid. 'I bet Dad will have a good laugh when he sees you,' she said when her mother first brought it home.

'I bet he will. I don't think they're much good,' said Grace, having a good look at it. 'Just saves the bits of shrapnel and bricks from crowning me, I suppose.'

Dolly unconsciously crossed her fingers that her mum and dad would be safe. So far Wood Street hadn't had a direct hit and she didn't know anybody who had died in this war.

'Pen,' said Dolly, 'did you hear what Betty said about the Americans that are over here?'

'I couldn't catch all of it but she said something about them going to the Palais.'

'I can't believe Betty is going out with a Yank. She's so quiet! How did she meet him?'

'Bumped into him in the blackout, so she was saying.'

Dolly giggled. 'I can't imagine her standing in a doorway snogging.'

'These quiet ones are always the worst. She said they're

ever so smart, and when they dance with you and hold you tight, you don't get a scratchy uniform to nestle your cheek against.'

'Sounds rather nice, I reckon.'

'Dorothy Taylor, you mustn't talk like that. Remember, you're engaged to be married.'

Dolly grinned at her friend. 'I know, but there ain't no harm in looking.'

'We ain't seen any down at our local hop yet,' Penny said.

'Give 'em time. Mind you,' Dolly added dreamily, 'fancy being married to a tall dark handsome GI who'd whisk you away to America.'

'They're not all tall and dark. I bet some of 'em are short, fat and bald,' Penny chuckled.

'Trust you to shatter my dreams.'

'You shouldn't be thinking thoughts like that with your Tony away, fighting for his country.'

'No harm in dreaming.'

'Talking of dreams, I wish I had enough coupons for a new frock,' said Penny with a sigh. 'It's all right for you – your mum can always knock something up out of a bit of old curtaining.'

Dolly laughed. 'I don't mind the odd skirt made out of blackout material, but I wouldn't fancy something in any of the floral bits.'

Curtaining wasn't on coupons, but you needed dockets to get any, then only if you'd been bombed out or were getting married – and even then it was still hard to obtain. Before the war, Dolly had always been well dressed as her mother had always made her clothes.

'Mum was saying they might be making parachutes,' Dolly said. 'If they do, just think – if there's any offcuts, we might have some posh undies.'

'I bet everybody who works there hopes that. Young Edna was saying that if you go up the Cut, off Brick Lane, sometimes you can get a frock on the black market. It costs a bit more, but it's gotta be better than giving up your coupons. Especially if you ain't got any.'

'Trouble is, you can't try 'em on. What if they don't fit?'

Penny shrugged. 'Could always get me mum to alter it, I suppose. Mind you, she ain't as clever with a needle as your mum.'

'OK. Let's go there next Saturday then.'

'We might even be lucky and get some fully-fashioned stockings as well. Mum goes mad with me getting that gravy browning over the sheets.'

'I really fancy these new nylons everyone's on about.'

'So do I,' said Penny. 'Might have to be like Betty and chat up a Yank for those, though.'

'Now it's you thinking wicked thoughts.' Dolly sat up. 'I wonder what will be next on coupons?'

'Anything, as long as it's not love.'

They laughed.

Dolly knew that when Tony came home, love was something she'd get plenty of. If his letters were anything to go by, there definitely wouldn't be any shortage of *that*.

Chapter 2

Grace Taylor sat knitting and listening to the wireless. She was dreading the mournful sound of the siren starting up. She hated it when Dolly went off to the pictures, as she knew that if there was a raid, her daughter would stay till the end of the film and Grace would have to go in next door. As she counted her stitches, she gave a little sigh. She was making Dolly a jumper from an old one she'd unpicked. It would have to be short-sleeved, as the wool had been difficult to undo and it wouldn't run to long ones. Grace and Dolly were very close, and Grace longed for this war to end so they could be a family again. Jim had promised her he was going to retire from the Navy when this was all over, but what about Dolly? Would she get married when Tony came home? Grace knew she couldn't stop her daughter, but she was so young. Then she smiled to herself. She didn't have a lot of room to shout; after all, she was only twenty-one when she married Jim, and *her* mother had been against it. That was many years ago now. Her mother had passed away and Jim was the solid dependable type, even if he was away for long stretches at a time. If only they had had more children, but it wasn't to be. Grace was more restless than usual tonight as today she'd received a batch of letters from Jim. They were full of love for her and

11

Dolly. He missed them both so much and being tossed about on the high seas was no joke. She prayed he was safe and longed for the day when she would see him again.

Grace looked up at the clock. It was a warm evening; she put down her knitting and went to the back door to get a breath of fresh air. The last rays of sunshine could still be seen over the rooftops. At least they didn't have to waste precious coal on heating just yet.

Grace glanced next door at the large brick shelter that seemed to look so overbearing and ugly; even though she didn't like sitting in there, nothing was going to upset her tonight – she had her letters to read over and over again. In the shelter the only light was from the hurricane lamp and it was hard to read by and she couldn't follow her knitting pattern. Any sewing she tried to do put a strain on her eyes. Although Grace was grateful to Mrs Watts for letting them use the shelter to save them going to the public one, the boys – Billy who was ten and Jack thirteen – got on her nerves. They were loud and argumentative. Mrs Watts, Penny's mother, was always trying to keep them quiet and under control. It had been lovely when the boys were evacuated, but they soon came back saying they had been ill-treated – but was it because they couldn't get their own way? Mr Watts was in the Army and with Mrs Watts working and most of the schools closed down through lack of teachers, the boys were allowed to run riot.

In many ways Grace didn't mind being on fire-watching duty; at least she could go in the wardens' post for tea and sympathy and have long chats with her friend Mary.

The sound of the siren brought her back. She would wait a while before going in the shelter. Perhaps it was only a false alarm. If she had her way she would stay in the house, but she had to think of Dolly.

* * *

After spending part of the night in the shelter, the all clear went and Dolly and her mother picked up their bedding and made their weary way back indoors for a few precious hours' sleep in their own beds. Grace straightened up. Sitting in a deckchair trying to get a wink of sleep was killing her back.

Dolly didn't bother to take off the siren suit she wore in the shelter; she just tumbled into bed.

All too soon the alarm clock was jangling and it was time to get up.

'I'll be glad when we can lie in bed for days on end,' said Dolly as she wearily pushed the kitchen door open.

Grace smiled at her dishevelled daughter. 'It's got to end one day. We've still got water and gas today, so tea's made.'

'Thanks.'

A little later on, Dolly and Penny crossed the railway bridge and picked their way over hosepipes as they walked to work. For them, last night's raid hadn't been too bad.

A policeman came up to them as they turned the corner. 'Sorry, girls, you can't go down there. They're demolishing a house that's unstable. You've got to go round the other way.'

'Thanks,' said Penny. 'Good job we started out a bit earlier today.'

They stood and waited before crossing the road when they heard the clanging bell of an ambulance bearing down on them.

'Hopefully that's another person they've found alive,' said Dolly.

'Or it could be a baby's on its way.'

'I reckon people must be mad bringing kids into this world.'

'I thought you wanted kids,' said Penny.

13

'I do, but not till Tony comes home and this lot's over.'

'I should hope you do wait till Tony comes home, otherwise Rose will have something to say about that,' joked Penny.

Dolly laughed with her. 'That would certainly put the cat among the pigeons, that's for sure.'

As they heard the rumble of the building being demolished they stood and watched the cloud of dust and soot rise.

Dolly rubbed her nose. 'That dirt always makes me nose itch.' She turned to Penny as they continued to walk on. 'I'm glad we put our turbans on. My hair goes all sticky in the dust and dirt.' She pulled the brightly coloured scarf she had skilfully tied round her head, down over her ears.

'Wouldn't be so bad if we could get hold of some decent shampoo,' Penny complained. 'I had to wash me hair with soap the other night.'

'Whatever you do to your hair, it always looks nice,' Dolly said.

Penny smiled. 'Thanks. Mum's getting a bit fed up with me putting sugar water on me bits, but when I wear it up I have to keep those little ends up somehow.'

'As long as the bees don't come buzzing round.'

Penny laughed. 'Thank Gawd we don't get a lot of bees round Rotherhithe.'

Every morning when they turned into Linton Street, they were always surprised to see the factory was still in one piece as it was so near the railway lines. Before the war, paper bags were made there. Now the building's windows were sandbagged up, making it dark and depressing. The factory was freezing in the winter and roasting in the summer. Although the women and girls who worked there often had a moan, everybody knew they were helping the war effort.

The men who worked with them were too old to fight and didn't approve of young girls wearing trousers and doing men's work. Their job was to maintain the rows of machinery and supervise the girls, making sure they didn't chatter too much. As soon as the girls sat at their benches, Dolly and Penny began singing along with the wireless.

Jane, who worked alongside Dolly, was a few years older than her. Jane's husband was in the RAF. She didn't have any children and had been hoping to go into the Forces, but she had to look after her old invalid mother-in-law. It didn't help to know that the old dear disliked her intensely. Jane tucked a strand of her bleached hair back under her turban and shouted over to Dolly, 'You doing anything this Saturday?'

'Going shopping, why?'

'Betty was saying a lot of the Yanks are giving a party to the poor kids what have survived so far.'

'That's nice of 'em.' A few months ago, everyone had been shocked at the number of youngsters who had been maimed or worse, lost their lives in daylight raids. It had been the main topic of conversation for weeks. There was always someone who knew someone. It was very sad.

'D'you know where?'

'No. Could be the church hall. Betty said they might want volunteers to help. Would you and Pen like to go along?'

'Course. Find out where and when.'

'It'll have to be a Saturday or Sunday.'

'That's all right. Let's hope they bring along some goodies.'

'From what Betty was saying, they'll bring along more than enough.'

Betty worked on a big pressing machine further down the

15

room. Everybody knew she was going out with a Yank. Some didn't approve, but Dolly and Penny couldn't see any harm in it; after all, it wasn't as if she was engaged or even had a boyfriend. When they first found out about it they wanted to know how she had met him and bombarded her with questions. Betty told them that she had been up West and had literally bumped into him in the blackout. The GI was full of apologies, and after he'd picked her up off the pavement, he'd insisted on taking her to a café for a cup of tea. That was months ago, and they had been going out together ever since. She said she would be very upset when he got posted, but so far that hadn't happened.

At lunchtime Dolly and Penny sat in the canteen and listened to Betty telling them what her Chuck had told her about the forthcoming party.

'So, you gonna come and give a hand next Saturday afternoon?' she asked.

'I should say so,' said Penny.

'I thought we was going over the Cut?' said Dolly.

'That can wait. This sounds a lot more interesting. 'Sides, they might bring along some nylons for the helpers.'

Dolly laughed. 'I think you have to do a bit more than wait on tables to get a pair of those.'

'No, you don't,' said Betty with a huff in her voice. 'My Chuck don't want any of that.'

'Any of what?' asked Jane, who after examining the contents of her sandwich took a bite.

Betty blushed. 'You know.'

'What sort of a bloke is he if he don't want any of that?' asked Jane with her mouth full.

'Don't listen to her, Bet,' said Dolly. 'She's only jealous.'

'Too bloody right I am. Can't wait to have a bit of that,' said Jane, grinning. 'And I'd be willing to sell me soul or anything else for a pair of nylons.'

Penny laughed. 'I don't think it's your soul they're after.'

'They can have what they like if it means nylons and chocolate. Here, I don't know what they put in this,' said Jane, opening the rest of her sandwich. 'it tastes like sawdust.'

'Could be that,' said Penny. 'This bread looks as if it was around during the First World War.'

'And these grey potatoes look as if someone's walked over them,' said Dolly.

'Young lady,' said Jane in a posh voice, 'don't you know there's a war on?'

They were all still laughing when the hooter went for them to return to work.

'You didn't mean that, Jane, did you?' asked Betty.

'What?'

'You know. About how you'd sell your soul and that for some nylons.'

'Give me half a chance, I'd soon show you.'

'What about your husband?' asked Betty.

'While the cat's away and all that. Besides, what's he up to? And what he don't know won't hurt him.'

Dolly looked at Penny who only shrugged.

'What if someone told your ma-in-law?' said Betty.

'That's when I really would run away.'

'Come on, girls, let's have a little less chat and a bit more work. Those boys out there are relying on you.'

'Mr Freeman, we know we make shell-cases, but if we knew about the blokes what handled 'em, and where they might finish up – well, that might help us to get a bit more enthused,' said Jane.

'I'll ask Mr Churchill to drop you a line and tell you,' the foreman said sarkily.

'Thanks.'

Those who had overheard the exchange started laughing.

'I want a letter from him as well,' put in Penny.

'You'll all get your cards if you don't get a move on. Then you'll have to join up. Winnie ain't gonna put up with slackers – he's gonna win this war.'

On Saturday morning at the factory there was a buzz of excitement. Those who were going with Betty to help at the church hall in the afternoon were wearing turbans round their hair to hide their pipe-cleaner curlers.

'How many Yanks did Betty say was gonna be there?' asked Jane.

'She told Pen it was about ten, but it could be more. It depends if they can get off duty,' said Dolly.

'Gave meself a face pack last night,' said Jane.

'Where did you get that from?' asked Penny. 'I've been trying to get one for weeks.'

Jane touched the side of her nose. 'That young kid in the chemist likes me and he sees me all right. Got me some Ponds cold cream the other day.'

'Lucky old you,' said Penny.

'Mind you, I don't know how old that face pack was. I had to crush it with a rolling pin to get the lumps out.'

'Was it worth it?' asked Penny.

'I should say so.' Jane gently ran her hand over her cheek. 'Feel, it's as soft as a baby's bum. I only hope the bloke I finish up with appreciates all the trouble I took to get this.'

Dolly laughed. Despite the heavy work she enjoyed being with the girls here. 'I wonder if the kids will eat all what they bring?'

'I hope not,' said Jane. 'I fancy trying some of that peanut butter they talk about.'

18

'It's tinned fruit I have a longing for,' said Penny.

'D'you think they'd notice if we pinched a sandwich or two?' asked Jane.

'Shouldn't think so,' said Betty.

'So what about you, Dolly?' asked Jane. 'You drooling for anything?'

Dolly laughed. 'What I want the Yanks ain't got.'

'I bet they have,' Jane winked. 'And I bet they're just as keen to give it away.'

'No. I'm gonna wait for my Tony.'

'Let's hope he's gonna wait for you,' said Jane under her breath.

As they all started singing 'A Slow Boat to China', Dolly's thoughts went to Tony. She was thrilled by his letters telling her how much he loved her and missed her. If only this war would end soon, then she could get married and her dad would be home. There was so much to look forward to. She sighed. As her mum had said this morning: 'it's got to end one day.'

Chapter 3

'I can't wait to see inside. Betty was saying they're gonna put up decorations.' Dolly was talking to Penny and Jane as she pushed open the door of the church hall.

The girls stopped dead in their tracks as the noise hit them. The shouting was deafening.

'Look at all that food,' said Jane, trying to make herself heard. 'I'm surprised those trestle tables can stand all that weight.' She took a hesitant step further into the room.

The American servicemen were working hard trying to get the kids seated and under control. Most of the kids were wearing paper hats; Dolly laughed at some of the little ones, whose hats had fallen over their eyes, making it difficult for them to see. She also noted that a few of the bigger boys certainly didn't have any table manners; they were standing on chairs and leaning over the piles of food in front of them, grabbing what they could, and stuffing it in their mouths before someone took it away, or made them sit down.

'I ain't never seen so much food,' said Penny. 'They've got jellies and cakes – and look, those look like the hot dogs we see in the films.'

'What about all the bottles of drink stacked up over there,' said Dolly, pointing excitedly to a table on the other side of the room.

'Let's get in then,' said Penny, pushing Dolly forward.

'Careful where you walk. Seems a lot of it's finished up on the floor,' said Jane. 'Watch it!' she yelled at a couple of boys as they raced past her, pushing and shouting. They were having a fight with balloons they'd taken from the bunches that festooned the wall.

'Hi, girls. Have you come to give us a hand?' A tall ginger-haired young man came up to them.

Dolly's knees went weak. With his freckles and wide smile, to her he looked just like Van Johnson, one of the many film stars Dolly was in love with.

'We certainly have,' said Jane, putting her arm through his. 'Now, where do you want us to start, young man? By the way, me name's Jane.'

He laughed. 'I feel I should say, "Me Tarzan," but I won't. I'm Teddy.'

'I hope you're all lovely and cuddly then.'

'I can be.'

Dolly and Penny looked at each other as Jane and Teddy walked away.

'I'm so glad you're here,' said Betty, coming up to them and dragging another well-dressed American serviceman behind her. Her face was flushed. 'This is Chuck. Chuck, this is Dolly and Penny. I told you about them.'

'You sure did.' He held out his hand. 'Pleased to meet you both.' Chuck wasn't much taller than Betty, but where Betty was thin and pale-looking, he was tanned, broad and healthy-looking. 'It's great to see these kids enjoying themselves,' he said. 'Some of them have had a hell of a time and been through such a lot. We were hoping that some from the hospital might be able to join us – you know, those in wheelchairs and on crutches, but they couldn't spare the nurses to come with them.'

21

Dolly could see he was a very caring man and she knew what had attracted Betty to him.

'What do you want us to do, Bet?' asked Penny.

'If you go into the kitchen, there's some WVS ladies out there – they'll tell you what to do.'

In the kitchen a number of women were busy buttering bread and placing various fillings on the bread.

'We've come to help,' said Dolly.

One woman looked up. 'Hello, girls. Could you take some of those out?' She waved her knife at plates piled high with sandwiches waiting to be taken away and devoured.

Dolly and Penny took a plate in each hand and cautiously made their way into the main hall.

'Where shall we put these?' Dolly asked the nearest American.

'On the far table. I don't think those kids have had enough yet.'

Dolly and Penny made their way across the room as an American came up to them.

'Hi there. I'm Josh. Shall I take those?'

Dolly handed him the plates. She knew she was being silly, but she felt she was in a film with all these tall, well-dressed, good-looking young men hovering around her.

'I'm so glad you lovely ladies could come and give us a hand. You Limeys are so brave.' Josh had dark hair and flashing eyes. When he smiled, his teeth were very white against his tanned skin.

Dolly knew she had a fixed silly grin on her face.

Penny nudged her and brought her back to reality. 'Come on. Let's see if they want any more help in the kitchen.'

When they were out of earshot Penny turned on Dolly. 'For God's sake, pull yourself together and stop making such an exhibition of yourself,' she hissed.

'What're you talking about?' asked Dolly indignantly as she was being shoved into the kitchen.

'You're acting like a lovesick kid. Smiling up at that bloke and batting your eyelashes.'

'Don't talk daft. I wasn't!'

'You was and that one looks like an Eyetie to me.'

'He wouldn't be allowed in the American Army if he was Italian. Besides, I was only trying to be polite.'

'It's bad enough Jane making a fool of herself. Look at her, throwing herself at that bloke.'

'She's only trying to be friendly.'

'Trying to get nylons, if you ask me. We don't want them to think that all British girls are easy.'

'Don't be such a misery, Pen. Let yourself go a bit. Reg won't think any less of you if you enjoy yourself.' After that, Dolly was on her guard; she didn't want Penny to see what a good time she was having.

When the kids finally left, Dolly felt as if her feet had grown two sizes larger.

'I don't think I've ever worked so hard before,' said Penny as she stretched out on a chair that wasn't covered with food and drink.

'Thanks, girls. You've done a wonderful job this afternoon.' Teddy was still with Jane. 'Look, me and some of the boys are going back to the Rainbow Club later when we finish clearing up here. Would you two ladies like to come with us?'

Dolly wanted to jump up. 'The Rainbow Club? What, the one at Piccadilly?'

'That's the one.'

'We've heard about that!' She looked at her friend. 'What d'you think, Pen?'

23

'Could do, I suppose. How we gonna get there?'

'Don't worry, transport's been arranged.'

Dolly could have flung her arms round her friend. She was dying to go somewhere exciting like that. She loved Tony and was going to marry him – nothing would ever change that – but she still wanted to have fun.

Dolly and Penny couldn't believe it when they went into the club. They were taken into the dance hall, where the music coming from a juke box was very loud and inviting. Dolly no longer worried about her aching feet; all she wanted to do was join in and dance. Some of the girls were jitterbugging and being thrown about by their partners, and showing their knickers, but they looked as if they were having a good time. She gazed around at some of the women there. Their make-up and clothes looked as if they had stepped out of a fashion magazine. Besides them, she suddenly felt very dowdy in a frock her mother had made a while back.

'What if there's a raid?' Penny asked the young man who was sitting next to her.

'There's a basement,' he told her.

'Don't reckon we'd hear the siren in here then,' said Dolly.

'Don't worry, they warn us. You ladies been here before?'

'No,' said Penny. 'We've been helping some of the blokes this afternoon. They've been giving our local kids a party and they asked us along.'

'Good for you. This is a great place for us; we can get almost anything here. They try to bring us a bit of home.'

'Where're you from?' asked Penny.

'Chicago.'

'I've heard of that.'

'It's very different from England.'

'Do you like it over here?' asked Penny.

'Sure, it's great to see a bit of the world.'

Penny seemed to be getting on very well with her friend. Dolly was looking all about her when a young man asked her to dance. It was a slow Glenn Miller tune. Dolly closed her eyes; he was a wonderful dancer. She thought she'd died and gone to Hollywood.

'You like our music?' asked her partner, bringing her back to reality. He had a soft slow drawl.

'I should say so. This tune is really lovely.'

'Glenn's been here.'

'Glenn Miller? What – here? Glenn's been here in the flesh? In this club?'

He laughed. 'Yep. And his band.'

'That must have been wonderful.'

'It sure was. We get a lot of stars come here.'

'I'd love to see some of 'em,' drooled Dolly.

He smiled. 'By the way, the name's Joe.'

'I'm Dolly.'

'Hi, Dolly.' Joe wasn't as good-looking as some of the others, but he had a kind face. Big brown eyes were set deep in his tanned face, and his slicked-down dark hair shone under the lights. 'Why not give me your phone number and I'll give you a ring when he's here next.'

'We don't have a telephone.'

He held her at arm's length and grinned. 'I forgot. I don't know how you people manage to live without a phone.'

'We manage all right.' Dolly noted that Penny was also dancing and laughing with the guy she'd been sitting next to.

All evening Dolly and Penny danced and ate crisps which the Americans called chips. Penny's dancing partner was called Gus and all four of them laughed and joked about the way they spoke and called things by different names.

'We've had lessons on how to behave, and what not to say,' said Joe. 'I only hope I'm doing things right.'

'Seems fine to me,' said Dolly.

At ten o'clock Betty came up to Dolly and told her she was going home. 'You can stay if you like. This place is open all night.'

As much as she wanted to, Dolly knew she should go home too. 'I can just see me mum's face if I stayed out all night,' she sighed. 'Chuck taking you home?'

'No, he can't.'

'Look, me and Pen will come with you.'

'Thanks – I was hoping you'd say that. What about Jane?'

'She looks a bit busy, but I'll ask her.' Dolly went over to Jane and the shaking of heads told them that Jane wouldn't be coming with them.

As the three girls made their way home on the bus, Dolly was full of what a good time she'd had. 'I'd love to go there again,' she said happily. 'D'you know they had Glenn Miller there in the flesh – with his band an' all? Have you been there before, Betty?'

'A couple of times, but Chuck ain't all that keen on it. He says he'd rather spend time on his own with me.'

'Oh, that's really lovely, ain't it, Pen?'

Penny nodded.

'Chuck thinks he might be sent away soon.'

'No! I bet you'll miss him?'

'I will. Very much. You see, he's the only boy I've ever really been out with.'

'Does your mum like him?'

'Yes, she does.' Betty began playing with her handbag. 'Don't tell anyone, but he's asked me to marry him.'

'What?' screamed Dolly.

'Shh,' said Betty. 'Keep your voice down.'

'Sorry. So what did you say?'

'I said yes. He's got to get permission from his boss, then I have to have a medical and there's a lot of forms to fill in. I think it's quite a palaver, but it'll be worth it.'

Penny, who up till now had been very quiet, said, 'How d'you know he ain't married already?'

'Course he ain't, or his boss wouldn't let him get married, would he?' asked Dolly.

'No.'

'What does your mum say about it?'

'We ain't told her yet. I think me dad might be against it, but as he's away we're hoping it'll be all right if Mum gives her permission.'

'What will you do if she don't give you her consent?'

'I think she will. After all, I'll get a good allowance – but that's not why I want to marry Chuck,' she hastened to add. 'Besides, it'll be one mouth less to feed when I go to America.'

Dolly knew Betty came from a large family who, before the war, had been very poor. Now her father was in the Army things were a bit better for them. To have someone like Chuck interested in her must have turned Betty's world on its head. 'Do you want to go to America?' asked Dolly.

Betty nodded. 'But not till the war's over. Chuck said he wants to be the one to take me to see his folks.'

'Ahh, ain't that nice,' said Dolly. 'It makes him sound all, I dunno, all countrified.'

Although the bus had very subdued lighting, Dolly knew that Betty was smiling.

'Where does he live?' she asked.

'In the Blue Mountains.'

'Has he got a big family?' asked Penny.

27

'I think so. I've just written to them.'

'I'm really pleased for you, Bet,' said Dolly.

'Thanks. You will come to me wedding, won't you?'

'You're sure your mum will let you get married?' asked Penny.

'I think so. You will come, won't you?'

'Just try to keep us away,' said Dolly.

'You gonna have a white wedding?' asked Penny.

'Dunno. I ain't got enough coupons for a long frock. It'll have to be something I can wear again.'

'Can't you borrow one?' asked Dolly, really beginning to get excited about the wedding.

'Don't know anyone who's as skinny as me.'

'I'll ask around,' said Penny. 'Where will you hold the reception?'

'Chuck said I wasn't to worry about that. The Base will take care of that.'

'Lucky old you,' said Dolly, giving her friend's arm a squeeze. 'I bet you'll have a proper wedding cake, not one with a cardboard top.'

Penny rubbed the window and tried to peer through the green mess that was stuck to the glass. 'I think the next stop's ours. It's all different now a lot of the usual landmarks have disappeared.'

'Dolly, Pen – you won't tell the others, will you?' Betty said anxiously.

'Not if you don't want us to.'

'Thanks. I don't want Mum to hear about it till Chuck asks her – and you know what a blabbermouth Jane is.'

'She don't mean any harm. I think her mother-in-law is such a cow, that's why she says the things she does,' said Dolly.

'I was surprised when she said she was gonna stay a bit

28

longer with that Teddy,' said Betty.

'Why, do you know anything about him?' asked Penny in alarm.

'No.'

'What will her old man's mother say about that if she gets home late?' asked Dolly.

'Or not at all if there's a raid and she can't get home,' added Penny.

'Knowing Jane, that'll be her excuse,' said Betty.

'For Jane's sake, I hope he's all right,' said Dolly.

'Knowing Jane, I think she'll do just as she pleases,' said Penny.

When they left the bus Dolly looked up at the night sky and shuddered. The silver barrage balloons were bobbing about in the moonlight. 'It's such a clear night I expect we'll have an air raid later, then Jane can really blame getting home late on the Germans.'

They said goodnight to Betty, and as Dolly and Penny turned into Wood Street, as if on time, the siren began its wailing.

'Another night in the shelter,' said Penny.

'Looks like it,' said Dolly, gazing up at the searchlights sweeping the sky and lighting up the silver barrage balloons.

Chapter 4

On Monday, Dolly and Penny couldn't wait to get to work and find out if Jane had had a good time and whether she was going to see Teddy again.

'Wasn't that Rainbow Club smashing?' whispered Dolly as she stood behind Jane in the queue at the canteen. 'What was that Teddy like? Are you seeing him again?'

'I should say so,' said Jane as they shuffled along.

'What time did you get home on Saturday?' asked Penny as they sat at the table having their break.

Jane grinned. 'Didn't, did I? There was a raid, so we had to spend the night in the basement.'

'What did Ma-in-law have to say about that?' asked Betty.

'Not a lot. I told her I couldn't get back 'cos of the raid and she didn't argue – probably hoping I'd be killed or something, then her darling boy would be able to find someone who she did approve of.'

'Jane, that's a terrible thing to say.' Dolly looked shocked at that statement.

'So what did you do?' asked Penny, with her elbows on the table and both hands clasped round her cup, drinking her tea.

'Just sat and talked. Teddy's a very interesting bloke. He told me all about where he lives and his family.'

'Is he married?' asked Penny.

Jane shrugged. 'Dunno. I didn't ask. He lives in New York – it sounds a smashing place. Where does your bloke live, Bet?'

'Virginia.'

'Where's that?' asked Jane.

'Dunno. It's in the atlas. It sounds very nice.'

Jane took a mouthful of tea. 'I was talking to those two blokes you was with after you left. I nearly forgot, I've got a letter for both of you,' she said, plonking her cup down.

'Let's see them then,' said Dolly.

'You'll have to wait till we go home. I've left 'em in me handbag in the cloakroom and you know how grumpy old Freeman gets if we ask to get something out of there in work time. I don't know those blokes' names. Was too busy with keeping Teddy happy.'

'Joe and Gus,' said Penny slowly. 'Did they say what was in the note?'

'Something about wanting a date.'

Dolly nearly choked on the tea she was drinking. 'A date?'

'Yer. What's wrong with that?' asked Jane.

'We're both engaged,' said Penny. 'We can't go out with any Tom, Dick or Harry.'

'No, there definitely wasn't a Harry,' said Jane seriously, before bursting out laughing.

'Well, we can't go.'

'Pen, don't be such a stick in the mud,' Jane cried. 'You're only what – eighteen? Get out and enjoy yourself. I tell you something – those boys know how to show you a good time. You won't regret it – ain't that right, Bet?'

Betty nodded.

'What about you, Dolly? Are you game?'

Dolly looked at Penny. Although she would have loved to have gone out with Joe, she knew Penny wouldn't approve. 'I don't think so,' she said.

'Please yourself. I'll give you the note anyway. But I still think you're both mad to throw away such a smashing offer. It ain't as though they're asking you to marry 'em. I reckon they'll be moving on soon anyway.' Jane stood up. 'I'm just going for a pee. After all, we should all be like Bet here and be nice to these poor boys who are far away from home. I only hope someone is being nice to my old man.'

Dolly and Penny sat silently watching Jane walk away until the hooter went for them to get back to work.

All afternoon Dolly's thoughts were on Joe. What did the note say? Did he want to see her again? She would have liked to see him again, but knew that would be out of the question.

After work, Dolly tried to look uninterested when with a great flurry Jane opened her handbag and handed the letters to her and Penny.

'Well?' asked Jane. 'Do they want to take you out?'

'Gus does,' said Penny, quickly folding the letter and putting it in her pocket.

'And what about your bloke?' Jane asked Dolly.

'He ain't my bloke, and yes, for your information, he *does* want to see me again.'

'And?'

Dolly looked at Penny. 'I ain't gonna answer it. Anyway, I expect he'll be moving on.'

'Well, I certainly won't be going out with Gus,' said Penny. 'Ready for home then, Dolly?'

As the girls linked arms and walked away from Jane, she called after them, 'Well, I think you're both daft.'

'She don't know the meaning of the word loyalty,' said Penny when they were out of earshot.

'No,' said Dolly, wishing she could see Joe again. She really did enjoy his company. He was so different from Tony; he was exciting and he lived in America.

It was the following Saturday when the girls came out of the factory and there, leaning against the wall, were Joe and Gus. They were nonchalantly smoking and when they caught sight of the girls they quickly threw their cigarettes to the ground.

'Hi, there,' said Gus, walking towards them. 'Did Jane give you our notes?'

'I sure did, big boy,' said Jane, beaming.

Joe was behind Gus and grinning at Dolly. 'Jane told us where you worked and what time you finished.'

'Did she now?' said Penny, glaring at Jane.

Dolly was aware that as the other girls were leaving the factory they were giving the group a good looking over and some of them deliberately came up and said goodbye – even women she didn't really know. Dolly felt uncomfortable. She didn't want Joe to see her in her headscarf and overall.

'We wondered if you'd like to come to the movies with us tonight?' Gus put his arm round Penny's waist.

She brushed his hand away. 'I don't think so. Thank you.'

'Why not?'

'Me and Dolly are engaged to be married and we don't think it's right to be going out with Americans.'

Joe and Gus laughed.

'Sorry,' said Gus, holding up his arms. 'We only wanna take you to the movies. We don't wanna marry you.'

Dolly thought she would die, she felt so embarrassed.

'How about you, Dolly?' asked Joe in his soft American drawl.

'As Penny said, we're both engaged, so it ain't really right, is it?'

'I can't see that it can do any harm,' said Jane.

Dolly wanted to scream at Penny. She knew it wouldn't do any harm. Why couldn't Penny see that?

'Well, I think we should help these boys to enjoy their stay in our country,' said Jane. 'Me and Teddy are going to the flicks tonight. Might even see you both there. Bye.'

Penny put her arm through Dolly's. 'Come on, let's be going.'

Dolly looked over her shoulder at Joe. She would have loved to go out with him just as a friend, but knew Penny would never approve.

'Why won't you go out with Gus?' she asked rather peevishly. 'It ain't as if he's gonna be here for ever, is it? What if anything happened to them? At least we can say we helped make their stay in Britain happy.'

For a while Penny was silent.

'Don't answer me then,' said Dolly, getting huffy.

'I don't approve of what Jane's doing,' said Penny.

'She ain't doing any harm and is it really any of our business?'

'Suppose not.'

'We don't have to be like Jane – or Betty, come to that.'

'I know.'

'Well then, what is it?'

'Perhaps it's 'cos I'm frightened of getting fond of some-one else.'

'What?' screamed Dolly.

'Shut up. Everybody can hear you.'

'I can't believe what you just said. I thought you was the

one that . . . well.' Dolly stopped. She couldn't remind her friend that she was the one who had suggested they got engaged when the boys were going away. Now she was the one who didn't want to go out with Gus in case she fell for him. What was she thinking about?

Penny's thoughts were tumbling over each other as she walked home with Dolly. She would have liked to go out with Gus, as he was nice, but only as a friend. She did love Reg. Like Dolly with Tony, he was the only boy she'd ever been out with. Should she have been so eager to get engaged when he was called up? Had she been worried that Reg might have found someone else, then she would have been left on the shelf? Never in her wildest dreams did she imagine the Americans would join in the war and would open up a whole new lifestyle. And what if, as Dolly had said, something happened to Gus? No, she had to be true to Reg, it wasn't fair otherwise. Even if she was a bit tempted.

Reg came over and shook Tony's arm. Tony was sitting under a palm tree on an empty ammunition box, trying to keep out of the heat of the sun and he was busy reading Dolly's latest letter. They had been lucky; he and Reg had been together since they were called up.

'What is it?' asked Tony, looking up at Reg.

'Been watching Bill Kennedy.' Reg inclined his head towards another squaddie. 'He's just picked up his mail and after tearing his letter open, he quickly read it and walked away. By the look on his face it could be he's had some bad news.'

'I hope it's not a Dear John.' Tony put his letter down and stared across the barren sand. 'D'you know, that's something I always dread. I really can't see Dolly waiting for me.'

Reg sat down next to him. 'Why? What makes you say that? You two have grown up together like me and Pen. Always been together. Here, mate, you ain't getting cold feet thinking about the future, are you?'

Tony laughed. 'Cold feet is something we don't get here in this stinking desert.'

'That's true. So what does our Dolly have to say?'

'Not a lot really. I think they're having a lot of air raids.'

'So, what is it? Don't you think she'll wait for you?'

'Don't know really. You know what a dreamer she is, always going on about seeing the world. What if she joins up and goes off to some foreign climes and likes it so much she don't wanna come back?'

Reg laughed. 'Why's that? D'you like it here and don't wanna go back?'

'Don't talk so bloody daft. How can anybody like this place? I don't care if I never see another grain of sand in me life.'

Reg scratched his groin. 'I know what you mean – it gets everywhere. And I reckon I've eaten enough to fill a sand-bag. D'you think I should go and have a word with Bill?'

'Dunno. He might like to be on his own.'

'I'll go over and offer him a fag.'

Tony watched his friend walk over to Bill. They stood for a while chatting, and then went off towards their tent. Tony folded his letter from Dolly. He was always worried about her. Although they said they loved each other, they had been young and life had been good till he went into the Army. Was it wrong to make her wait till this was all over? What if he got injured? Would it be fair to tie her to a cripple for the rest of her days? Dolly loved life and he'd give anything just to hear her laughing. He wanted her so much, but she had said no on so many occasions. Was that part of her charm? She wasn't going to give in till they were married. He was never sure about Reg and Penny. From the knowing look Reg gave her at times they could have done it, but what the heck, that was their business. He wished he had done it with Dolly, so at least if he got killed he would have known what it was all about. What if he did get killed? So far he'd been lucky. Would she marry someone else? Tony looked at his letter. He would go and answer this one right away. With luck, tomorrow there might be another one from her.

As Tony lay on his bed, his thoughts went to his mother. He missed his mum's cooking. He hated this place, the Germans, the sun, the sand – everything. And in a funny way, he even missed his sister, although they never did see eye to eye. And he knew Rose didn't like Dolly. Was that because Dolly was pretty and full of life, and Rose, at twenty-six, had turned into a sour old spinster? As Rose was older than him they never did have a lot in common. After Peter, her fiancé, got killed on the day the war broke out – he was killed crossing the road to join the Army – she had changed. She was a nurse and hadn't been called up. He began to feel guilty. He shouldn't be hard on her; after all, she'd lost the love of her life. How would he feel if he lost Dolly? And what about the sights Rose had seen? Some of the bomb victims' injuries must have been horrific. He began to feel sorry for his sister. Perhaps one day she'd find someone else.

He ran his fingers through his short-cropped hair and his thoughts went back to Dolly. This would bring a smile to her face, when she saw this haircut. But he was glad it was short in this heat; it'd grow again when he was back in

Civvy Street. Will I still have brown knees by the time I get home? he wondered. The blokes had laughed when they first saw each other nude with just the white bits showing up in the dark. He grinned. At least Dolly would be able to find him in the dark. But where would they end up next? The job here was finished. There had been talk of Italy, and some had said they could be going to the jungle, but rumours buzzed about all the time. Since Pearl Harbour and the Yanks had joined in, they could be sent anywhere.

Tony lay back and closed his eyes. If he was lucky he would hear Dolly's laugh. Funny, he knew he loved her but whenever he told her it was always with a laugh or when he was trying to get her knickers off. How would they react when they were together again? They would be older and probably a lot wiser. He knew that when he kissed Dolly again it would be with all the love and passion he had been denied.

Chapter 5

It was the end of October and Dolly was excited at Betty's forthcoming wedding the following week, Saturday, the sixth of November. It had all been arranged very quickly, as Chuck was being sent overseas.

'I'm so pleased me mum said I could wear her wedding dress. I didn't think she still had it. It's been packed away for so long that we had to hang it on the line all weekend to get rid of the smell of moth balls.'

'It don't smell now, and it looks really lovely on you,' said Dolly, admiring Betty's dress.

Betty was standing on a chair and Grace was busy pinning up the hem.

'I'm ever so grateful to you, Mrs Taylor, for altering it. It feels really nice.'

'You'd better stand still otherwise I'll end up sticking the pins in you.'

'And what about Jane lending me her head-dress and veil,' said Betty excitedly. 'At least, it'll hide my straggly bit of hair. I don't know what Chuck sees in me.'

'It's 'cos you're a nice person. Don't worry, you'll look smashing and Penny said she'd do your hair. Oh Betty, I'm so thrilled for you!'

'What does your mother have to say about all this, Betty?'

Grace asked after removing the fine pins she used from her mouth.

'She was a bit upset it was going to be so quick. She was worried I might be . . .' Betty blushed and said, 'You know.'

Dolly laughed. 'I reckon all mums must think that.'

'But I'm not – me and Chuck ain't . . .' She stopped. 'Penny don't seem all that pleased about it,' she added.

'She can be a funny whatsname sometimes.'

'You didn't go out with that Joe then?'

Dolly shook her head at Betty.

'Who's this Joe then?' asked her mother, looking up.

Dolly felt she wanted to die. 'He was just one of the blokes I met at the Rainbow Club, after that party the Yanks gave for the kids. You know, I told you about it.'

'Oh yes. You didn't say you'd been out with one of them, though.'

'I ain't been out with him. I just said that, didn't I.'

'All right, don't get on your high horse,' said her mother, struggling to her feet. 'Right – I think that's it. It looks really lovely on you, Betty.'

Betty ran her hands over her slender hips, thrilled at the feel of the smooth satin. 'Thank you ever so much.'

Grace helped the bride-to-be down off the chair. 'Careful how you take it off. I don't want the pins sticking in you and you getting blood all over it.'

'Chuck's gonna be ever so surprised when he sees me walk down the aisle in this. He thinks I'm getting married in a suit. I'm glad it's gonna be in a church. He got a special licence, you know.'

'Well, I hope you'll both be very happy,' said Grace as she gathered up her sewing box. 'Bring it down and I'll start on the alterations right away.' Grace stood in the doorway and gazed at Betty for a moment or two before she left the room. She looked so young.

When Dolly and Betty were alone, Betty said, 'I'm ever so sorry if I put me foot in it just now.'

'That's all right.'

'Would your mum be upset if you went out with a Yank?'

Dolly shrugged. 'Don't know. She wasn't all that pleased when me and Tony got engaged.'

'Why?'

'Thought I was too young to be tied down.'

'Are you sorry you didn't go out with Joe?'

'A bit. It would be nice to go out with a bloke again, and to go dancing at that Rainbow Club. I thought that was smashing.'

'Perhaps you'll meet someone at me wedding.'

'I ain't really looking now, am I?'

'No, suppose not.' Betty carefully took off her wedding dress and put her frock back on. 'I love Chuck, I really do.' She began putting her dress on a coat hanger. She stopped. 'I get a bit worried.'

'What over?'

'Do you worry that Tony might not come back?'

'Yes, course I do. Come on now. We mustn't be miserable. We've got a lovely wedding to look forward to. Where are you spending your first night?'

'A hotel. Chuck's made all the arrangements.' Betty put the dress on the bed and hugged herself. 'I still think I'm dreaming. I can't believe I'll be getting married and then spending my wedding night in a hotel. Me, who's never been in a hotel before, let alone slept in one.'

Dolly laughed. 'Just as long as you remember to take your toothbrush and a posh nightie.'

Betty sat on the bed and stroked her dress. 'Me gran's

given me some coupons and the money to get one. Then I'll have to think about the things I want to take to America. Fancy *me* going to America. It's a long way away from Rotherhithe.'

'Are you worried?'

'A bit. I'll miss me mum and the kids.'

Dolly sat next to her. 'You've got a lot to look forward to.'

'I know. I'd better take this down to your mum. I'll see you later.' Betty carefully put the dress over her arm and went back downstairs.

After Betty left the house, Dolly watched her walk up Wood Street. She was thinking about her friend going to America. Would it be all that she hoped for?

Her mother was busy at her sewing machine when Dolly walked into the kitchen. Grace looked up and stopped treadling. 'This is going to look nice on her. She seems happy enough.'

'She is.'

'I bet her mother ain't all that pleased about her going all that way.'

Dolly shrugged. 'She can't keep her tied to her apron-strings for ever.'

'Suppose not, but I wouldn't like it. In fact I'll be very upset when you marry Tony and you'll still be living round this way.'

'We'll have to see where we finish up. Tony might have other ideas.'

'Yes, I suppose. What was Betty saying about you going out with a Yank?'

'Mum, I told you. I had a few dances with him at that Rainbow Club. I did tell you about it.'

'But you didn't go out with him?'

'No.'

'I wouldn't like to see you get mixed up with one of them. Remember that they're a long way from home and probably looking for love and affection. And let's face it, you're a bit of a dreamer.'

'Thanks,' Dolly went out into the scullery. 'All right if I make a cup of tea?'

'If you want.' Grace looked at her daughter. She was young, pretty and vulnerable. She could so easily be swept off her feet.

Dolly stood looking at the blue flame dancing round the kettle. Her thoughts were in a turmoil and although it was wicked, in some ways she wished she was Betty, marrying an American and going all that way to a new life.

What would happen when Tony came back? Would they still feel the same way about each other? They had both grown up a bit, over these past eighteen months. Would he still want to marry her? After all, in some ways getting engaged had just been a bit of a lark. She looked at the ring on her finger. They were very young at the time. Penny and Reg, and she and Tony, all pledging to be faithful – had it been wise? They didn't have a party, and Dolly knew her mother wasn't very happy about the engagement. But she did love Tony. When he kissed her she wanted to throw her clothes off and become part of him. Dolly grinned. Her mother would have forty fits if she knew what she was thinking.

On the way home from work the following evening Dolly and Penny went across the road and into the sweetshop.

'Hello girls,' said Miss Ada Gregory. 'And what can I get for you?' Ada was the older of the two sisters. They looked very much alike with their kind grey eyes and grey hair pulled back into a bun. Ada was plumper than her sister May, but they were both lovely ladies and everybody liked them.

'You on your own?' asked Dolly.

'Yes, May's having a little sleep.'

'Is she all right?' asked Penny.

'Yes, thank you. These raids and broken nights catch up with us old uns, you know. We ain't got the stamina you youngsters have, not any longer.'

Dolly smiled. She was fond of these two old ladies. They always had a kind word for everybody.

'Now, what can I get you both?'

'Don't suppose you have any confetti, by any chance?' asked Dolly, plonking herself down on the bentwood chair that stood next to the counter.

'No, sorry. We sold the last box back in the summer and we've not been able to get any more. Who's getting married?'

'A girl we work with,' said Penny.

'We'll have to make sure we get some in when you two get married. How are the boys?'

'Very well – we think,' sighed Dolly.

'It's very sad you young people have to be parted.' Ada looked away from them.

'Best be going. We'll have to sit and cut up lots of paper into tiny little bits.' Dolly stood up.

'I reckon we'll end up with a lot of blisters,' said Penny, laughing.

'Just a moment.' With that Miss Gregory disappeared out through the door at the back of the counter.

Within a few moments she was back in, brandishing a metal punch. 'Use this. You can punch out lots of little round bits with this; it'll look much nicer than cut-up paper.'

'Thanks. This'll be great,' said Dolly.

'We could even go into business,' Penny grinned. 'A lot of brides would pay for a bit of confetti.'

'I think you'll soon get fed up with it – it can be rather hard on the hands.' Ada beamed at them.

She reminded Dolly of a kindly old spinster out of a book. 'Thank you. We'll be over and tell you all about the wedding,' she promised.

'I'd like that.'

Dolly hastily looked round the church. The men in the smart American Army uniforms on the bridegroom's side were a stark contrast to everybody on Betty's side who, despite clothes rationing, had tried to dress up in their finest. Dolly noted there wasn't any sign of Joe.

The organ began playing and everybody stood up. Dolly smiled at the look on Chuck's face when he first caught sight of Betty. She looked lovely. Betty didn't have any bridesmaids in long frocks, as the clothing coupons wouldn't run to it. Her young sister Linda walked solemnly down the aisle behind Betty wearing a nice pink frock and hat. Betty was holding her uncle's arm. She had told Dolly and Penny how upset she was that it was her uncle and not her dad who was giving her away.

All through the ceremony Chuck, who had his arm round Betty's waist, didn't take his eyes off her. Dolly could see he loved her very much.

As they walked to the room where the reception was being held, Betty's mother came up to Dolly, Penny and Jane.

'Thank you all so much for helping my Betty. She looks lovely, don't she?'

'Yes, she does,' said Dolly.

'And you managed to get some confetti. You're good girls. I'll be sorry when she goes.' Betty's mother took a handkerchief from her handbag and dabbed at her nose. 'Don't suppose I'll ever see her again.'

Jane took her arm. 'Course you will. I bet when this war's over and after a few years, she'll be back to see you with all her kids in tow.'

'We'll have to wait and see. It'll cost a lot of money.'

After the first gasps of astonishment from the guests at all the food that was laid out at the reception, the usual speeches were made, with plenty of wisecracks from the groom's buddies.

The best man read out a telegram from Chuck's parents. Dolly saw him whisper to Betty and a huge grin spread across her face.

'I wonder what he's just said to her,' said Penny.

'I bet I can guess,' said Jane.

'I love your hat,' said Dolly.

Jane touched the black straw hat that was perched at a saucy angle at the front of her head. 'Wore this when I went on me honeymoon.'

'Where'd you go?' asked Penny.

'Blackpool.'

'Well, I hope I go somewhere more exotic than that,' said Dolly.

'You would,' said Penny.

'I can't get over that cake,' said Jane. 'Look at the size of it! Just think – Betty's not gonna want for anything now.' She laughed. 'Including nylons.'

The chatter and gaiety went on for hours, then the tables were cleared and to everyone's surprise an Army band began playing. It was loud and everybody started to dance. A lot more of Chuck's friends drifted in and to Dolly's delight, she caught sight of Joe who was with Teddy and Gus.

Her heart gave a little leap when he walked straight up to her and asked her to dance. Dolly also could see Gus talking to Penny.

'I didn't think you'd be here,' she told him.

'Had to wait till this evening to get off. Most of Chuck's buddies were able to come to the wedding. I must say, the bride looks great. She's a good friend of yours then?'

'I've only known her since we started at the factory together. Not like me and Penny; we live next door to each other and have been friends all our lives.'

'That must be great, living close to someone.'

'So where do you live?'

'Deansville.'

'Where's that? Is it anywhere near Hollywood?'

He laughed as he whirled her round in the quickstep. 'Nope.'

Dolly could see Penny and Gus were deep in conversation. If only he could persuade her to go out with him, then Dolly wouldn't feel so bad if Joe asked her again.

All evening Dolly joked and danced with Joe. He was charming and so polite.

'Dolly, could I take you out tomorrow?'

'I don't know.'

'I would really like it. Perhaps we could go somewhere quiet and talk. I'd love to tell you all about my ma, and where I live.'

'I'd like that, I really would.'

'OK. Can I come to your house and pick you up?'

'I don't think that would be very wise.'

'Why's that?'

'My mum wouldn't approve.'

'Oh dear.'

'But don't worry. I'll tell her I'm going out with . . .' She stopped. Dolly knew she couldn't say Penny as Penny wouldn't approve and wouldn't be used as an excuse. She began to feel angry. She wanted to go out with Joe. She wanted to sit and talk to him. She wanted to know more about America.

'Dolly. Dolly.' Joe took her hand. 'Come back. You'd gone off in a dream then.'

'Sorry. I was just trying to think of a way I could meet you.'

'Look, honey, I don't wanna get you in any trouble with your mom.'

Dolly heard Jane's laugh. That was it! She knew Jane wouldn't mind being used as an excuse. 'No, don't worry. I'll meet you at, shall we say, Marble Arch Underground? What time?'

'I can't get away till after lunch. Is four o'clock all right?'

Dolly smiled. 'Sounds lovely.'

All evening the noise and laughter had got louder as the drink was being downed. Betty looked worried at one stage when Dolly could see her uncle and his wife having a few words. Betty had told Dolly her mother was keeping an eye on them, as Uncle Tom liked a drink and Auntie Mary didn't approve. Betty said she was a bit concerned at what he might get up to.

When it suddenly went quiet Joe looked up and said, 'Looks like the band is going for a smoke. What's that old guy doing?'

The guests began crowding round the stage.

Dolly stood on a chair to see over everybody's head. 'That's Betty's uncle.' She was full of trepidation. What was he going to do? Then she began to laugh. 'He's gonna play the piano.'

Uncle Tom sat down, gave everybody a big grin and struck up with 'The Lambeth Walk'.

'What's that?' asked Joe, pointing to the dancers who had hurried on to the floor.

Dolly jumped down into Joe's arms. 'It's "The Lambeth Walk". Come on, I'll show you how to do it. We've got to join in.' She grabbed Joe's hand and pulled him onto the floor to join the others.

The Americans who were standing at the side looked amused, while those who had been dragged onto the floor were looking completely bewildered.

'The Lambeth Walk' was followed by 'The Palais Glide'. Everybody was singing at the top of their voices. Dolly thought she would explode with such complete happiness.

When they had finished the 'Knees up Mother Brown', they flopped into a chair next to Penny and Gus. All four were laughing and trying to get their breath back.

'Well, I guess that's something new,' said Gus, taking hold of Penny's hand. She looked at Dolly and quickly pulled her hand away.

'It sure was,' said Joe.

'I'll say this for you Limeys, you sure know how to enjoy yourselves despite being blown to pieces every night.'

Penny had told Dolly that Gus came from Chicago; he was dark and swarthy-looking. He had a loud twang in his voice and Dolly could almost imagine him being a gangster.

'That's why we make the most of it,' said Penny. 'We never know if we're gonna be here tomorrow.'

'Don't say that,' said Joe.

'Well, it's true. We've been lucky so far,' shrugged Dolly. She looked at Joe; he wasn't strikingly good-looking, but he had something. His soft voice, searching eyes and tanned face could melt any girl's heart. When he took hold of her hand, she didn't pull away.

Betty came up to the foursome. 'Are you enjoying yourselves?'

'I should say so,' said Penny. 'Your uncle's a bit of a card.'

'Auntie Mary don't think so. More so now he's having more to drink.'

'Our beer ain't as strong as yours. Do you know, the other night Joe and I went to one of your pubs, and I don't remember getting back to camp,' Gus told them all.

Joe grinned. 'Good job you've got me to look after you, buddy.'

'Just as long as it stays that way when we get shipped out.'

'Don't talk about things like that,' said Dolly quickly, looking at Betty. 'We're here to enjoy ourselves.'

'I can't believe that my Chuck done all this for me.' Betty's eyes were shining. She looked radiant. 'I never guessed in a million years I'd ever get married. And to have a reception like this. I feel I wanna cry, I'm so happy.'

Dolly jumped up and threw her arms round Betty. 'You deserve it. Here comes your husband.'

Betty giggled. 'My husband. Ain't that a lovely word?'

Chuck came up to them and pulling his wife to him, kissed her lightly on the lips. 'Sorry to drag you away, hon, but we've got to cut the cake.'

Dolly watched them walk away with their arms around each other and said a silent prayer. '*Please don't let there be a raid tonight. Let them spend their wedding night in bed and not in a shelter.*' They were so happy. But what did the future hold for them? For any of them, come to that?

Chapter 6

When Dolly emerged from Marble Arch Underground station she pulled her coat collar up round her ears and eagerly looked about for Joe. It was cold after the warmth of the Tube and she shuddered. Would he turn up? Yes, he wasn't the type to let her down. Although she felt full of guilt at deceiving her mother, she smiled to herself as she recalled last night. Jane had thought it funny to be asked to be used as an excuse.

'What you gonna say to Penny?' she'd asked when Dolly had managed to get her on her own at the reception.

'I don't know. Got any ideas?'

Jane had just shrugged. A while later, she came up to her, grinning all over her face. 'Guess what? Penny's just asked me to give her an alibi too, so she can go out with Gus. You two are a silly pair of cows and no mistake.'

As Dolly and Penny had walked home from the wedding last night, Dolly had said, 'So you're going out with Gus tomorrow then?'

Penny turned on her. 'Who told you?'

'Jane.'

'I'll kill her. I told her not to say anything.'

'Why?'

'Well, I feel awful after I'd carried on about you wanting to go out with that Joe.'

51

'Don't matter.'

'I'm really sorry, Dolly.'

'What made you change your mind? Was it the promise of nylons?'

'No, it ain't. I know I was a bit of a pain, and I didn't think it was right to go out with him, thought I'd be letting Reg down. But he's such a nice bloke and he said he was lonely. I felt sorry for him. It won't do any harm, will it? I was gonna tell you, honest.'

Dolly laughed. 'Don't worry about it. I'm seeing Joe tomorrow and I asked Jane if I could use her as an excuse.'

'You never?'

Dolly nodded. 'We are a daft pair. We shouldn't have secrets from each other. After all, we should be able to please ourselves what we do. We ain't kids, and going out with those two ain't gonna hurt anyone.'

'I know.'

'So where are you going?'

'Gus said we could go to the pictures. What about you?'

'Dunno. Joe said he wanted to tell me about his home, so we could just be going for a walk round Hyde Park.'

'It's a bit cold for that. What time you meeting him?'

'Four. Outside Marble Arch station. Where're you meeting Gus?'

'Leicester Square, at four.'

'That's good. At least we can go off together. I wonder if we might finish up in that Rainbow Club again?'

'Dunno.'

Earlier that afternoon, Dolly and Penny had walked to the bus stop together, but parted at the Underground. As Dolly didn't want to arouse too much suspicion from her mother, and after she left Penny, she went in the toilet and dabbed her precious Evening in Paris perfume behind her ears. She put a little of her Bourjois rouge on her cheeks and then applied the new Tangee lipstick that she and Penny had been lucky enough to get at Woolworth's last week. They had queued up for ages, but it had been worth it. She didn't want anyone she knew to see how much effort she was making to meet Joe.

As it was going to be dark when they got home, nobody would see if they didn't arrive back together. Dolly's biggest worry was that there might be an air raid, not because of the raid, but because her mother worried about her, and if Penny got home before her they would meet in the air raid shelter, then there could be trouble. But she wasn't going to think about that now; tonight she was just going to enjoy Joe's company.

Despite all the Allied Forces uniforms and various offers from a lot of servicemen, when she caught sight of Joe hurrying along the road, Dolly smiled broadly.

He bounded up to her. 'Sorry I'm late, hon.'

Dolly was taken aback when he kissed her cheek. 'That's all right, I ain't been here that long. Mind you,' she laughed, 'I've had a few offers and I've been told to move on. Some tart said I was cramping her style and I was pinching her pitch. Saucy mare.'

Joe laughed. 'I'm sorry I kept you waiting. Mind you, I'm not surprised she was worried – you look gorgeous.'

Dolly could feel herself blushing. 'Not like one of those, I hope.' She touched her cheek. Had she used too much make-up?

'No, of course not. So? What are we going to do?'

'I don't mind.'

'It's a bit cold to wander around. How about the movies?'

'All right. Don't often come up West to see a picture.'

53

Joe took hold of her elbow as they moved along to the cinema. He was so polite; Tony didn't do things like that. What made her suddenly think of Tony? Was it her guilty conscience?

'Do you get to go to the pictures very much where you live?' asked Dolly.

'Sometimes. Seen quite a few since I've been on the camp though.'

'I love the pictures. I'd love to go to America.'

'It's a great country. D'you like musicals?'

'I should say so.'

'Right, we'll go and see Rita Hayworth and Fred Astaire. That all right with you?'

'Yes, please.'

There was a queue to see *You Were Never Lovelier*, but it moved very quickly and soon they were settled upstairs in the expensive seats.

'I ain't ever been upstairs before,' whispered Dolly, looking around as the usherette showed them to two empty seats.

'Could do with some popcorn,' Joe whispered back.

'Don't get that over here; don't even get enough coupons to buy sweets to nibble.'

'I've taken care of that. Here – have a Hershey Bar.'

'What's that?'

'A chocolate bar.'

The woman in front turned round and shushed them. Dolly wanted to giggle.

Soon they were engrossed in the film. The music and dancing sent Dolly off into a dream. When the lights went up and she was brought back to reality, she looked around her. 'Thought I might see Penny in here.'

'I think Gus took her to the Empire.'

'Oh,' said Dolly.

'Did you want to go with her?'

'No. No. Course not.'

When the lights were dimmed again and the news came on, Joe sat forward. They were showing the fighting in Italy. As Dolly looked at the screen, she wondered where Tony was. Was he safe? Was she letting him down by sitting here with an American? But how long would Joe be around?

It was very dark when they came out of the cinema.

'How d'you fancy a bite to eat?' asked Joe.

'I'd love to.' She looked at her watch. 'I hope we don't have a raid tonight.'

'We'll have to stay in a shelter if Jerry does come over. It's all those folks sleeping down the subway that intrigues us. Some have certainly made themselves comfortable, and d'you know, one night we saw some of them were having a party.'

'I know. They have people riding on the trains going from station to station giving little shows.'

Joe shook his head. 'That's amazing. I even saw a couple of women pushing a tea urn up the platform.'

'As Mr Churchill says: "We've got to keep our spirits up".'

'I think you'll win this war drinking tea,' Joe joked.

'I hope so. Mind you, with it being on ration we do have to be careful.'

Joe was guiding her along the pavement. He stopped outside a Lyons teashop. 'Will this do?'

Dolly nodded. Joe took her arm and led her inside.

Dolly sat opposite and looked at him while he gave the waitress their order. He wasn't good-looking in a film star way, but he was nice to be with. He had dark hair and nice brown eyes and a very tiny dimple in his chin, a bit like Kirk Douglas. She smiled inwardly as she noticed the looks and tuts she got from older women, and the glance of envy from the younger ones.

When the waitress walked away, Joe leant across the table and held her hand. 'Thank you so much for coming out with me. It's really great to be with someone who ain't simply after candy or nylons or anything else us Yanks have got.'

Dolly smiled.

'You've also got the cutest smile,' he said gently. 'You're very pretty, you know that?'

Dolly blushed. 'Stop it. I ain't used to blokes talking to me like that.'

'Sorry. What about—'

'Tony,' said Dolly.

'This Tony: doesn't he tell you how cute you are?'

'No – well, yes, sometimes.'

They sat back when the waitress brought their tray over. As she set their tea and teacakes on the table Dolly thought about Tony. He only ever joked about her being a smashing looker. Why did she keep comparing him with Joe?

'Your Tony's a very lucky guy to have someone like you waiting for him,' Joe told her.

'What about you? Have you got a girlfriend back home?'

'No.'

'Where do you live, Joe?'

'A little place called Deansville.'

'Oh, yes, you said. And is it near Hollywood?'

Joe chuckled. 'No, it's on the other side of the States and about three or four hundred miles from New York.'

'My dad's told me all about New York, with its sky-scrapers. He's been there – he's in the Navy.'

'That's a tough job with all the German subs patrolling the seas. My pa died years ago. There's only me and Bob, he's my older brother. I feel sad I had to leave him to help Ma, but she's a tough old bird.'

'She wouldn't like you saying that.'

He smiled. 'We've got a small farm – well it's small compared to others in the States. Ma's been running it for years. We grow mostly wheat, although we have a few animals wandering about. I felt terrible leaving them. I miss the smell of the country and the fresh air. Living with dozens of guys ain't exactly my idea of fun.'

'So you don't travel about then?'

'No. I only saw New York when I sailed for England. It's a big city.'

'America's a big place.'

'It sure is.'

Dolly sat and looked at Joe. He sounded so alone and lonely. She wanted to hold him close.

'Dolly. We don't know how long we'll be in England, or even how long this trip will last. Is it all right if we meet again, just as friends?'

'I'd like that, I really would.'

He smiled. 'Thanks. It's really great to be able to talk to someone.'

'What about all your blokes at camp?'

'Most of the time they're all shouting their mouths off. Gus ain't so bad, but I'm not used to mixing with a lot of loudmouths.'

Joe himself was a very nice, quiet sort of bloke, and as she poured the tea, Dolly wondered if Penny was enjoying herself. Was Gus as pleasant and as well-mannered as Joe? He treated her like a lady. When he held open doors and pulled her chair out for her and generally fussed over her, she loved every minute of it.

'I wonder if Gus and Penny are getting on all right?'

'I should think so. He's a great guy.'

Dolly hoped Penny would be going out with him again, then she wouldn't feel so guilty.

With her elbows on the table she gave Joe a smile as she drank her tea. What would her mother say if she could see her now? It was just as well she couldn't, although as he said, they were just going to be friends. But could it develop – and did she want it to?

Chapter 7

When Dolly arrived home, she was pleased there hadn't been a raid that evening, and settling down in the armchair, she waited for her mother to come off fire-watching duty. Her thoughts went to Joe. He was very nice and polite and she had found she could talk easily to him. A knock on the door startled her. She knew it wasn't her mother, as she would use the key.

'Pen. What are you doing here?' Dolly asked after struggling with the blackout curtain that covered the front door.

'I was hoping you was home. Is your mum in?'

'No.'

'That's a relief. I just had to call to find out if you had a good time tonight?'

'Yes, I did. Did you?'

Penny nodded and sat in the armchair opposite Dolly. 'Gus is ever so nice. He lives in Chicago – he's going to bring me some pictures of his home and his girlfriend.'

'He's got a girlfriend?'

'Yes. He said he knew I was engaged so he thought we could be company for each other. What about Joe? Has he got a girlfriend?'

'No.'

'But he knows all about Tony?'

'Course he does. You told him, remember?'

'Are you going to see him again?'

'He has asked me to go out. What about Gus?'

'I'm seeing him next Saturday.'

'I'm seeing Joe. Perhaps we can go off together.'

'Be careful what you say. I don't want Mum or the boys to find out. You know what that pair are like. I wouldn't have any peace from 'em. They'd want all sorts of things if they knew I was seeing a Yank, including a tank if I could get one.'

Dolly laughed. 'Don't worry, I don't want Mum to find out either. You know how she was about me and Tony getting engaged. I reckon she'd have forty fits if she found out about Joe.'

'And after all, we are just being friendly with 'em,' said Penny.

They both looked up when they heard the front door shut.

'I'll be off. See you in the morning.' Penny stood up as Grace walked in.

'Hello, Penny. You just off?'

'Yes, Mrs Taylor.'

'You don't have to go on my account.'

'No, it's all right. It's getting late and we've got to get up for work in the morning. We should make the most of getting into bed, even if it might only be for a little while.'

'That's true. Goodnight.' Grace sat in the armchair. 'Glad to see the fire kept in. Did you girls have a good time?'

'Yes, we went up West to the pictures.'

'That was a bit extravagant. Was it a nice film?'

'It was a musical and it was lovely.'

'That's good. D'you fancy a cup of cocoa?'

'I'll make it. No sign of a raid then tonight?'

'No, thank goodness.' Grace sighed as she eased off her shoes and wiggled her toes in front of the fire. 'It's so cold standing about on rooftops. I'm glad I was on the early shift tonight. Don't like walking about in the small hours and I get so tired having to go straight to work in the morning.'

'I wish you didn't have to do fire-watching duty.'

'So do I, but the government has other ideas.' Grace shivered. 'It's really bitter out there tonight.'

'You ought to get yourself a siren suit.'

'Like the one Churchill wears, you mean?'

'I admit they ain't that glamorous, but they keep you warm.'

'I might splash out and get one now the winter's here. I wonder how your dad keeps warm at sea? It was very different when he was on the posh ships.' Grace picked up the poker and staring into the fire, gave it a gentle poke.

'I'll see to the cocoa.' Dolly left her mother with her thoughts.

Grace was wondering why the girls had gone up the West End to the pictures. It wasn't something they normally did. It was too expensive and besides, the films came round this way soon enough. Had they been out with the Americans? Dolly hadn't said a great deal about who was at the wedding. There must have been a lot of the bridegroom's mates there. Would she tell her mother if she had been out with one? Oh well. It was no good worrying about it. If there was anything to tell, Dolly would soon let her know. Grace shuddered and pulled her cardigan tighter round her. Her thoughts went to Jim. She remembered when they snuggled up in bed to keep warm on cold winter nights. She knew he didn't like her doing fire-watching duty and being out in the raids, but she had to, she didn't have any choice.

She sighed. She wanted Jim near her now. She wanted to smell that lovely manly salty smell he had about him. She wanted his arms around her. She wanted him to make love to her. He was a very passionate man. Every time he came home it was like being on honeymoon all over again. She remembered how a year or two after Dolly was born she had desperately wanted another baby. Dolly was very special and she loved her daughter very much, but what about when she got married and left home? Would it be too late to think of another baby when this war was over? Would Jim be different? How had this war affected him?

As soon as Dolly and Penny walked into the factory on Monday morning, Jane came hurrying over to them.

'Well?' she asked. 'Did you go out with 'em?'

'Yes.' Dolly grinned at Penny.

'So where did you go?'

'We went to the pictures.'

'And?'

'And what?' asked Penny.

'Just wanted to know if you had a good time?'

'Yes, thanks,' said Dolly, tucking the ends of her hair under her turban. 'Did you go out with Teddy?'

Jane grinned. 'I should say so.' She looked around her and moved closer. 'Teddy had the Jeep and when we left the wedding we found this dear little pub in the country.'

'And?' said Penny cheekily.

'We stayed the night.'

'What?' screamed Dolly.

'Shh. Keep your voice down. Look out, here comes old Freeman.'

Although the girls wanted to hear more, they had to make their way towards the bench and start the day's work.

All morning they worked and sang along with the wireless. At lunchtime Dolly and Penny couldn't wait to hear more of Jane's weekend.

'What did you tell your ma-in-law when you got home?' asked Penny.

'I told her I'd stayed with a friend, which in a way was true. He *is* a friend.'

Dolly looked at Jane. How could she be unfaithful to her husband? What if she found she was having a baby?

'Is he married?' asked Penny.

'Don't know – didn't ask. And before you say anything, what I do is me own business. The only reason I'm telling you is 'cos I daresay Teddy will tell your two blokes. Are you seeing 'em again?'

Dolly nodded. 'Yes. Next Saturday.'

'Any idea where they're taking you?'

'No,' said Penny. 'Are you going out with Teddy?'

'I should say so. But I don't know where.' Jane looked all wistful. 'I wonder what our Bet's up to? I daresay she's having the time of her life. Did she say where they're staying?'

'She didn't know,' said Dolly. 'She'll be back tomorrow so she'll tell us then.'

'Only two days' honeymoon, that's a bloody shame,' said Jane.

'That's all the time Chuck could get off,' said Dolly.

'Remember, he is in the Army,' Penny added.

Jane laughed. 'You sound just like that song.'

The following morning Dolly eagerly looked round for Betty but she wasn't at her machine.

'I wonder where she is?' asked Dolly when they were having their usual lunchtime gossip.

'Probably can't get out of bed, lucky cow,' Jane joked.

'But Chuck had to get back yesterday. I hope nothing's happened to her.'

'Stop worrying, Dolly. He might have wangled another day's leave and she's spending it with him.'

'I hope so.' Dolly wasn't so sure. Chuck had to get back to camp and Betty would want to come home; she wasn't used to going places on her own. Had they been somewhere and got caught up in a raid? That was always the first thing people thought about when someone didn't turn up. Had they finished up in hospital or something much worse? Dolly tried to put her fears at the back of her mind.

Jane tutted. 'For goodness sake, Dolly, stop worrying. I expect she's having the time of her life.'

Dolly hoped so.

The following day there was still no sign of their friend.

'Pen, when we finish tonight, fancy coming round to Bet's house with me?'

'For Christ's sake, Dolly, leave it out!' Jane snapped. 'The last thing she wants is you fussing about where she is.'

'Suppose so. But it ain't like Betty to be away. She knows her money will be short.' Dolly was very concerned. All she could think of was that her friend might be injured somewhere, or even something worse.

'She don't have to worry too much about money now she gets an American Army allowance,' Jane reminded her.

When Jane left the table Dolly whispered, 'I don't care what she says – I'm going round Bet's. You coming with me, Pen?'

'OK.'

As soon as the girls finished work that evening they hurried round to Betty's house. Although Jane had thought

Dolly was worrying about nothing, Penny was willing to go with her, as she too was concerned for their friend.

They were silent as they turned into the street where Betty lived. Even before the bombing it had been a very rundown area. In the dark the battered buildings looked eerie as the moon flitted behind the clouds; they stood upright, looking like a row of bad teeth. Rubble was still lying in the road even though it was weeks since the last raid round that way. The girls carefully picked their way over it. Penny shone her torch on a door, looking for the number.

'Keep that torch down, Pen, otherwise you'll have some bloke shouting at us.'

'Got to find number forty-four, ain't I?'

'This is number twenty.'

'Then there's some missing.'

'This is it,' said Dolly. She knocked on the door. 'I hope somebody's home.'

'You can never tell now, with every house blacked out,' said Penny, standing back and stamping her feet to get warm.

After a lot of movement behind the closed door, it suddenly opened.

'Yes. Who is it?'

'It's me, Dolly, and Penny. Is Betty all right?'

'Come in, girls.' Dolly recognised Betty's mother's voice. 'It's this bloody blackout. Takes ages to get it just right. I'm terrified of showing a light. The Warden round this way can't wait to pounce on you.'

The girls inched their way into the passage and stood still till the blackout curtain was in place to Betty's mother's satisfaction, then she turned on the light.

The passage was full of bits and bobs. A two-wheeled rusty old bike was leaning against the wall. Next to it was a battered old doll's pram and then there was a bassinet full of bedding.

'That's ready to take along to the shelter, we ain't got one of our own.' She pointed to the pram. 'Every time the siren goes we all have to traipse along to the public one. It's a bloody nuisance, I can tell you. Now, what can I do for you?'

'Is Betty home?' asked Dolly.

Her friend's mother looked shocked. 'Course, you don't know, do you?'

Dolly and Penny looked at each other.

Dolly could feel the colour drain from her face. 'What's happened?'

'You'd better come into the kitchen. It's warmer in there.'

They squeezed along the narrow passage and past all the paraphernalia, following the older woman into the kitchen. Linda was the only one the girls really knew by name, although they had seen the other three girls and two boys at the wedding. They were all sitting round a huge table that took up most of the room. They looked up when the girls walked in.

'Hello, Dolly and Penny,' said Linda. 'Shame about Chuck, ain't it?'

'What's happened?' Dolly was almost beside herself with concern.

'Don't yer know?' asked Linda.

Both Dolly and Penny shook their heads.

'He's been sent away. All the blokes in his lot have got their marching orders. Betty went over to the camp to see him off.'

'When did they go?' asked Penny.

'Last night. She should be back soon. In fact, I thought that was her, when you knocked,' said Betty's mother. 'It's such a shame. He was hoping they would have a few more months over here.'

'Do you know where they're being sent?' asked Dolly.

'No. He reckons it'll be abroad somewhere. Would you like a cup of tea?'

'No, thank you. We'd better be going. Our mums get worried if we're late,' said Dolly.

'I can understand that. Betty'll be in tomorrow. I hope that foreman don't start carrying on to her. She don't want any of that, not on top of what's happened.'

'I expect Mr Freeman will be understanding,' said Penny.

As soon as they were outside Dolly took her small pencil torch from her handbag.

'Well,' said Penny disappointedly. 'That puts paid to our date next Saturday.'

'Yes. Wait till Jane finds out, she's gonna be livid.'

Both Dolly and Penny were silent as they walked home, but both were busy with their thoughts. Going out with an American had been fun. Dolly wished it could have lasted for a lot longer.

'Do you think we'll ever hear from them again?' asked Penny drearily.

'Don't know. Shouldn't think so. Does Gus know where you live?'

'No, I didn't give him me address. Did you give Joe yours?'

'No. I didn't think they'd be gone so quick.'

'Thank goodness it's our bus,' said Penny as a red double-decker came round the corner. 'Didn't fancy staying out here in the cold for too long.'

As they sat on the bus Dolly's thoughts went to Betty. Fancy only being married for three days and then your husband is sent away. That was something she certainly wasn't going to do. To get married in wartime was a mug's game.

Chapter 8

While Dolly was queuing to clock on the following morning, she was pleased to see Betty waiting a bit further back.

'We heard about Chuck,' she said, going up to her friend.

'I know. Mum said you'd been round. Thanks for being worried about me.'

'Well, when someone's been away and then they don't turn up, you always fear the worst.'

'That's true. Where's Penny?'

'She's gone on ahead. You're really gonna miss your Chuck.'

'Yes. We thought we'd have a bit more time together,' Betty said sadly as they made their way into the factory. 'You know Joe, Gus and Teddy have all gone off as well?'

Dolly nodded. 'We guessed that.'

'Where's Teddy gone?' asked Jane, coming up behind them.

'Been moved,' said Betty. 'Chuck thinks they might be sent abroad.'

'That's just my luck,' sighed Jane. 'Find meself one that's a bit of all right and he gets sent away. Seems like I'll have to go out looking again.'

Betty shrugged and let Jane pass them, then she said

softly, 'I wish she wouldn't talk like that. It makes us all sound the same.'

'Your Chuck don't think like that. He thinks the world of you.'

A faint smile lifted Betty's sad face. 'I know, I'm very lucky. Dolly, I don't know what I'll do if anything happens to Chuck.'

Dolly took her arm. 'He'll be all right.'

'I wanted to start a family, but Chuck wouldn't hear of it.'

'Why's that?'

'He didn't think it was right, him not being with me all the time.'

Dolly smiled at her friend. She was pleased Chuck sounded such a great guy.

'I really hope I'm gonna have a baby,' Betty added.

'Do you really? Would you want one knowing we could all . . .' Dolly stopped. She didn't want to say any more.

'At least I'd have something of him if anything happened to him.'

'You mustn't talk like that. Chuck is a survivor. He'll be back here whisking you up in his arms and taking you off to America before you know it.'

'I hope so. I really do hope so.'

Although Dolly was sad she wouldn't be seeing Joe, she knew she still had Tony. Tonight she would write him a long, loving letter.

All day they had been busy and it hadn't given Joe much time to think about anything else. Moving camp was always chaotic and it was dark by the time all their gear was loaded and they were on the way, to God only knew where – Him and the Commander, of course. They all guessed it must be abroad as they had finished their training weeks ago and they had been lucky, they'd had a couple of months being stationed near London so he had seen sights he had only read about. As Joe sat in the back of the truck, his thoughts went to Dolly. She was a lovely girl, and although he knew she was engaged to Tony he couldn't help thinking about her. She was like a breath of fresh air that had come into his life, even if it was only for a short time. She was happy and easy to be with. He leaned his head back against the canvas side of the lorry as it bumped over the roads. If only he had taken her address, he could write to her. It would be lovely to have some mail to look forward to; anything from home took so long to get here. He wanted to keep in touch with Dolly, but only as friends, if that was what she wanted. He glanced around at the grim faces. Gus had his head on his chest – was he trying to sleep? Chuck looked anxious: he didn't want to leave Betty, but that was the name of the game. This was war and they'd come over here to fight. *Fight*. That word filled him with fear. He didn't want to fight anybody; it was against his nature. Where were they going?

At the end of the week Betty came into work waving two letters. She rushed up to Penny and Dolly. 'These are for you. They're from Gus and Joe. They've sent you an address you can write to – that's if you want to. Will you?'

Dolly took her letter and casually said, 'Might do.' It was hard trying to keep the excitement out of her voice. 'What about you, Pen?'

'Could do, I suppose. There ain't no harm in it, is there? It'll be just like having a penfriend.'

'They'll be ever so pleased. Chuck said they all look forward to letters.'

'Did I get one?' asked Jane.

'No, sorry,' said Betty.

Jane gave a shrug. 'Ah well, better luck next time.'

'Did Chuck say where they were?' asked Dolly.

'No, but reading between the lines I think they must still be in England.' Betty looked sad. 'I wish I could see him.'

'I know how you feel. I feel that way about Tony,' said Dolly. 'It seems forever since I last saw him and when I don't get any letters for a few weeks I worry no end.'

'We all do,' said Penny, still looking at the letter from Gus she was holding.

'Come on, girls!' shouted Mr Freeman. 'This won't help the war effort.'

The girls moved to their benches, each with their own thoughts.

It was two weeks later. Dolly's eighteenth birthday had come and gone. There hadn't been any celebration, not like in years gone by when every birthday was an excuse for a party, and jelly and cakes were the order of the day. Grace was upset that her daughter had had to do without a card from her dad and Tony. She herself had given her the money and coupons for a new pair of shoes. At the beginning of the week she'd had a word with a girl in Dolcis who thought they might be having some stock in on Saturday. Grace smiled when she remembered Dolly's face when she'd come bursting in.

'You was right, they did have some stock in. Guess what? I queued for ages, and I prayed they'd have my size when I got served – and look.' With a great flurry she'd brought out a pair of black suede high-heeled shoes. Dolly had held them close. 'Thanks, Mum.' She'd kissed her mother's cheek and Grace had smiled, thinking how odd it was for her daughter to get so excited over a simple pair of shoes.

Dolly had already left for work when Grace picked up a letter from the front door mat. It had an Army look about it, and it was addressed to Dolly. She turned it over slowly. It wasn't from Tony; she didn't recognise the handwriting. Who was writing to her daughter? Could it be a late birthday card? Surely not. Grace looked at the letter and propped it up on the mantelpiece against the clock. She would have to wait till tonight to find out. Dolly had been very cagey these past few weeks. Had she met someone? Surely she would have told her mother if it was an innocent meeting. Was it an American? Grace said a silent prayer. *'Please don't let her get involved with a Yank.'*

Dolly rushed to the mantelpiece when she walked into the kitchen and saw a letter for her leaning against the clock. Like her mother she turned it over before opening it, but she recognised the handwriting instantly. It was the same as the note she'd had from Joe. It was lovely, not scraggly like Tony's. She couldn't believe he had answered her letter so quickly. Had she been wrong in putting her address on it? No. After all, he was just a friend – surely her mother would accept that. There was only a page. Joe told her that he couldn't say where he was and that he was sorry he had missed her and didn't get a chance to say goodbye.

> I hope you will continue to write to me as letters
> from home take such a while to catch up with us.
>   From your friend, Joe.

There was no loving message or any kisses. Dolly looked at the clock. Her mother would be home soon. She must know this wasn't from Tony. Dolly would have to come clean and tell her about Joe. But what was there to tell? She could read this letter; Dolly hadn't got anything to hide. Grace would be upset about her having lied about the pictures, but she'd get over it. After all, there wasn't any harm in her having a penfriend, was there?

'Was that a birthday card from some admirer?' asked Grace.

'No,' Dolly said nonchalantly.

'So, who was the letter from?' asked Grace, when Dolly wasn't forthcoming with the information. She'd finished the cup of tea Dolly had given her when she walked in, now she sat back and waited.

'It was from an American I met at Betty's wedding.'

'Was that the one she was talking about when she came for a fitting for her wedding dress?'

Dolly looked away. 'Yes.'

'But I thought you said you hadn't been out with him. So why is he writing to you?'

Dolly couldn't believe her mother had remembered that conversation almost word for word. 'I hadn't been out with him then. I saw him again at Betty's wedding and me and Pen just went to the pictures with them, that's all. Did I have to ask your permission then?' Dolly asked petulantly.

'There's no need to get uppity with me, young lady. I'm only interested in your welfare, that's all. I thought we were more grown-up than to have secrets from each other.' Grace picked up her cup and saucer and took it into the scullery.

Dolly followed her mother; she was full of guilt. 'I'm sorry. It's just that I didn't think you would approve.'

'Well, I don't. Are you meeting him again?'

Dolly shook her head. 'No. He's been posted away. He might be sent abroad. He just said he'd like someone to write to, that's all.'

'Does he know about Tony?'

Dolly nodded. 'Course.'

'Where does he live?'

'America.'

'I gathered that. Has he got a girlfriend?'

'No.' Dolly felt she was being given the third degree. 'And we're just penfriends, that's all. So is Pen. She's writing to Gus.'

Grace knew she shouldn't keep on at her daughter but she did worry about her. After all, she was the only one she had and her happiness was the only thing that mattered.

Christmas was on them, but nobody could get very enthusiastic with all the shortages. The only good thing was, the raids had eased and the extra day off meant they might be able to catch up on some much-needed sleep. Dolly was finding it hard to get presents. It seemed the only shop you didn't have to spend your coupons in was the chemist. But did Penny and her mum really want cough sweets or chilblain ointment? Dolly smiled to herself. Would Wintergreen rub be very welcome? Perhaps she could ask the Misses Gregory to put some chocolates by for her, and just hope she had enough coupons. If Joe was still around, that wouldn't have been a problem. Dolly was thrilled when she managed to get Penny a Harry James record, and even gave up some of her precious clothing coupons for a pair of fully-fashioned stockings for her mother.

Penny had also been scouring the shops trying to buy something for her brothers. She finished up in the pawnshop and managed to buy them a wind-up tin car. For Dolly she got a Glenn Miller record, and she gave her mother a scarf.

★ ★ ★

The New Year saw the weather worsen. The RAF was bombing Berlin and the Germans were being pushed up Italy. Dolly wondered if Tony was in that offensive.

As the weeks went on, Dolly was pleased that Joe answered her letters so promptly. For a while she knew his unit had been in Britain. Then his letters, like Tony's, had become erratic, so she guessed he'd been sent abroad. Joe's handwriting was lovely and his letters so interesting. He told her about his family, where he lived and his ambitions. She found she had no difficulty answering and eagerly looked forward to the postman. Dolly knew her mother was concerned about the number of letters she got from Joe, but Grace said nothing. When a letter from Tony arrived, somehow it was a bit flat. It wasn't his fault – she knew all about Rotherhithe and Wood Street, and that wasn't nearly as exciting as America.

Dolly knew Joe was twenty-two and worked on the land. He had never known his father as he was killed in a traffic accident when he was two. His mother worked hard, acquiring land as it became available. Joe said she was a strong woman. He was very fond of his family and especially his older brother Bob. Joe told her about the dances they had at the local hop and the type of music he liked.

She'd asked about the girls and did he have a girlfriend. His reply was that there had been a few but not now; none of them wrote to him and none were as pretty as Dolly. Dolly blushed when she read that line.

It was the end of March and the letters suddenly stopped. Although Penny hadn't had as many as Dolly, she was still concerned about Gus.

Betty was beside herself with worry. 'I know they've been where the fighting is. I just feel something's wrong. Chuck writes to me every day and I haven't had a letter in ages.'

'Perhaps they ain't got time to write,' Dolly said reasonably.

'I only hope you're right,' said Betty.

'We'll probably get a load together. That happens with Tony's letters sometimes.'

'I only hope you're right,' repeated Betty, more quietly this time.

As the weeks went on Betty was becoming more and more morose and she was beginning to look ill.

'I don't know what she's worrying about,' Jane said one day when Betty told her she wanted to sit on her own. She looked across at Betty and said to Dolly and Penny, 'She's getting to be a right misery.'

'She's worried,' said Penny.

'Sitting on her own ain't gonna help her,' Dolly commented, looking over at her friend.

'I'm sure she's getting herself in a state over nothing,' said Jane, taking a long drag on her cigarette. 'As his next of kin she'll hear soon enough if anything's happened to him. It's obvious. If he's stuck behind a gun he can't say, "Hang on, Sarge, I've just got to write to me missus".'

'But they must get some free time,' Dolly argued.

'Not if they're trekking through a jungle or tramping through the desert. The only free time they're likely to get is if they finish up in hospital.'

'You're a right Jonah, ain't you,' said Penny.

'No, just being realistic.' Jane ground her cigarette into the ashtray and walked away.

'She's only jealous 'cos that Teddy didn't write to her,' said Dolly.

'And she ain't got nothing to worry about with her old man sitting behind a desk in Scotland,' said Penny.

'She would have if he'd caught her with someone else.'

'Would he?' asked Penny. 'For all we know, he may be playing the field as well.'

A month later Grace opened the door to the postman.

'Sorry, missus, these have been Returned to Sender.' The postman handed her a bundle of letters.

Grace took in a breath and was relieved to see it wasn't her handwriting. She always dreaded getting her letters back, as it might mean something had happened to Jim's ship.

'Sorry,' said the postman again as he turned away. He knew that letters being returned was always bad news.

Grace quickly read the address. It was the American.

That evening when Dolly arrived home she sat looking at the bundle of letters that rested on the table. She was frightened to turn them over. Was it Tony or Joe? Slowly, she picked them up and read the address. It was her letters to Joe. They had been returned, unopened.

Chapter 9

Dolly felt very sad; she had to talk to someone, so putting her letters to one side, she went next door into Penny's.

'You don't look very happy. What's up?' Penny asked when she opened the door to her friend.

'It's Joe. All the letters I wrote since January have come back unopened.'

'Come in the front room. We don't want those boys to hear us.'

'You ain't had yours back, then?'

'No, but then I don't write as many as you,' said Penny.

'Gus never said anything about Joe in his letters?'

'No, but then you know I ain't had a letter for ages.'

'I wonder if Betty has got her letters back?' asked Dolly.

'Dunno. Joe might only be injured and can't write.'

'But my letters would have caught up with him.'

Penny knew that was true. So many wives and lovers talked about letters that were returned. Sometimes their men were injured and couldn't write, while others finished up as prisoners of war. That always took longer for their loved ones to make contact. Penny didn't know what to say to Dolly. She knew she was very keen on Joe even if she was engaged to Tony. 'I'm sure you'll hear if anything's happened to him.'

'How?'

'I don't suppose you've got his mum's address?'

'No.'

'Perhaps I'll get a letter from Gus – he'll tell me.'

That brought a smile to Dolly's troubled face. 'Yes, course he will.'

They chatted for a while longer then Dolly said she had to get back as her mum would be home soon.

Penny was worried about Dolly; she seemed to be very concerned about Joe. Was she getting too fond of him? She spoke about him far more these days than she did about Tony. But then that was Dolly, and he was an American and exciting.

Although Grace knew the answer, she still had to comment when Dolly walked in. 'I see your letters to that Joe have come back?'

Dolly nodded.

'I'm sorry, love. I know how much you looked forward to hearing from him.'

'Penny said she'll write to Gus to try and find out what's happened to him, but she ain't heard from him for ages.'

Grace was surprised at the hurt that was in Dolly's voice. Did this young man mean more to her than she let on? 'What about Betty? Her husband's in the same unit.'

Dolly nodded. 'The same – she ain't heard from him for a long while.'

'I expect if they're fighting somewhere they don't get time to write.'

'I know that.' In some ways Dolly was eager to get to work. At least she might be able to find out what had happened to Joe from Betty. Had *her* letters been returned?

★ ★ ★

When Betty wasn't at work the following morning, Dolly feared the worst.

'Pen, I'm going round to Betty's tonight. D'you fancy coming with me?'

'Dunno. Do you think she might reckon we're making a bit of a fuss again?'

'Course not. Look how pleased she was when she knew we'd been round there before.'

'She could just be having a day off.'

'I don't think so. She ain't like that.'

'I know. But this time . . .' Penny stopped. She didn't want to say that this time there might be a real reason for her absence.

'Well, I'm going.'

'OK, I'll come with you.'

Dolly smiled. 'Thanks. We won't say nothing to Jane, you know what she's like.'

It was still light when Dolly and Penny turned into Betty's street. It looked very different from when they were last there. The bomb damage had been cleared away, leaving great empty spaces that seemed to be full of kids laughing and playing. There were even signs that some of the weeds' little green shoots were trying to push their way through the broken paving slabs and concrete.

Once more Dolly found herself knocking on Betty's front door. For some reason, this time a great feeling of foreboding came sweeping over her.

When Betty's mother opened the door and saw them on the doorstep, Dolly knew from her expression and her sudden bursting into tears, that her fears had been well founded.

She clutched the girls to her ample bosom. 'Come in, girls. She's beside herself,' she sobbed. 'He's been killed.

She's only been married a few months, now she's a widow. It ain't fair.'

Dolly's hand flew to her mouth. 'Killed? I'm so sorry.'

'Poor Bet,' said Penny softly. 'She loved him so much.'

'I know,' said Betty's mother. 'She won't leave her room. Go up and have a word with her. Try to get her to come down. She's gonna make herself ill. She won't eat, she just sits crying all the time.'

Dolly pasted a warm watery smile on her lips. She quickly looked at Penny, who was staring straight ahead.

'She's in the bedroom,' sniffed Betty's mum. 'Up the stairs and it's the door on the right. See if she'll talk to you. And perhaps you can persuade her to have a drop of the broth I've got simmering.'

'I'll try,' said Dolly.

Slowly the girls climbed the wooden stairs, trying hard to suppress the sound their high heels made on the bare boards. At the top Dolly gave a little knock on the closed door. There was no reply. She knocked again, this time a little harder. Nothing.

Penny gave a small cough. 'Betty, it's me and Dolly. We've come to see you.'

'Go away.'

'No, we won't,' said Dolly with more force than she anticipated. She pushed open the door and for a moment or two stood in the doorway, letting her eyes get adjusted to the gloom.

Betty was standing in front of the window that still had the blackout curtain pulled halfway across. She had her back to them. 'I told you to go away. You can't help me, no one can – or have you just come here to gloat?'

Dolly stood, open-mouthed and it was Penny who spoke first.

'How can you say such a thing? We was worried about you when you didn't come to work.'

'Well, now you know. So sling your hook and go and tell them that poor old Betty's a loser again.'

Once Dolly's eyes had got used to the gloom she looked round the room. There was only one small bed, and a mattress and bedding on the floor. There was no other furniture. Clothes were hanging round the wall from the picture rail; there were no pictures.

'Betty,' said Dolly, stepping over the mattress, 'we've come round to see how you are. You're our friend, and we don't like seeing you unhappy.'

'So how you gonna make it better, then? Go on – answer me that. You gonna bring him back?' She turned and thrust the photo she was holding at Dolly. 'I love him so much.'

Dolly could see it was a photo of Betty's wedding. The newlyweds were happy and laughing together. Quickly Betty cuddled it close to her again.

Dolly's eyes travelled to her friend's face. It was red and puffy. Her once laughing eyes were just two small swollen slits. Her fine wispy hair was untidy and clung to her head. Dolly's heart went out to her; she walked over and, putting her arms round Betty, held her friend tight, letting her own tears fall.

Penny looked around the room and then at Dolly and Betty. Fear welled up inside her. How would she feel if anything happened to Reg? This brought it home to her just how vulnerable he was, and just how much she loved him. She said a silent prayer for his safe return so they could be together for the rest of their lives.

As Dolly stood holding Betty, her thoughts went to Joe. Would she ever find out what had happened to him? Was he still alive?

★ ★ ★

They finally managed to persuade Betty to leave her room. Downstairs she sat at the kitchen table and slowly spooned in the broth. The smell of it was making Dolly's mouth water, and although Betty's mother had offered them some, both girls declined.

'We really ought to be going,' said Dolly. She gave Betty's mum a slight smile. 'Me mum will be home and wonder where I've got to.'

'I understand. I'll see you out.' At the door she touched Dolly's arm. 'Thank you both for coming round. Now she's downstairs we might be able to talk.'

As they walked up the road Penny said, 'It suddenly hits home, don't it?'

'What d'you mean?'

'Well, here we are almost forgetting our blokes overseas and they could be – well, anywhere.'

'I ain't forgot Tony. I worry about him.'

Penny didn't answer. For she guessed that Joe was the one her friend had uppermost in her mind.

A week later Betty came back to work. It was strange how everyone tried to avoid her. Everyone except Dolly and Penny, that was. Even Jane couldn't bring herself to speak to her. Dolly said that was because of her guilty conscience. She must have felt it. After all, her husband wasn't in any danger – or was she genuinely upset about Teddy being out on a battlefield somewhere?

Weeks went past and Dolly hadn't heard any news about Joe. She knew she would have to forget him, but it was hard. She also knew it was wrong, but he was the one that she dreamed about.

It was a warm April evening and as Dolly and Penny left

the cinema, Penny put her arm through Dolly's. 'As it's a nice night, let's walk home.'

'OK.'

'That was a good film.' They had been to see *The Human Comedy*.

'I really like that Van Johnson,' said Dolly.

'You like all the film stars.'

'I know. Daft, ain't I?'

Penny suddenly stopped. 'Look. Look! There's Rose walking in front and she's arm in arm with a bloke and he ain't in uniform. Did you know she was seeing someone?'

'No, I didn't.' Dolly was hanging back. 'I ain't seen Mrs Marchant for a few weeks now, she's always out doing her good works.' She gave a little giggle.

'Let's catch Rose up.'

'No. Don't!'

'Why?'

'I don't want her to think I'm spying on her.'

'She can't think that. She must have been to the pictures. She's being a bit brazen about it. I wonder who he is – and why ain't he in uniform?'

To most people, every man who wasn't in the Forces was either a scrounger or a 'conchy' – a conscientious objector.

'He might be a doctor at the hospital. With a bit of luck he could give her something to make her a bit better-tempered.'

'Well, you'll have to go and see Tony's mum and find out who he is.'

'Yes, I will. I should go and see her anyway, I'll go tomorrow – that's if she's home. I like to pop in now and again.'

As they continued walking behind Rose, Dolly was surprised to see her go into a pub.

'They look very cosy,' said Penny.

'Yes. But let's face it, she does need someone in her life.'

The following night Dolly popped into Tony's mum.

'Hello there, love, ain't seen you for a while. Suppose it's because we're both so busy.'

Dolly always felt guilty at not going along to Tony's mum more often, even if she did only live at the top of the street. But although she was a kind-hearted woman who worked for the WVS, Dolly found her such hard work to talk to. Mrs Marchant was always on about the poor folk she visited and the terrible conditions some of them lived in.

'Did I see Rose the other night at the Odeon?' asked Dolly when Tony's mum stopped for breath.

'You might have done. She said she was going to the pictures. I think she went with a young man.'

Dolly grinned. 'Our Rose got a boyfriend then?'

'I don't think you can call him a boyfriend, dear. He's just a friend she works with and goes out with sometimes. Now I was telling you about this poor young lady that's got four youngsters, all under four. The poor thing's rushed off her feet. And what with one thing and another, thank goodness the raids have eased up, the job she had dragging them all down the shelter. She was saying how long it took her to get them ready: the eldest would run away. My dear, she's got her work cut out, has that one, and her middle one's a bit of a handful . . .'

Dolly was letting all this go over her head. She wasn't going to find out any more about Rose and her mysterious manfriend, and decided it was time to go home.

It was a few weeks later when Dolly got home from work and found a letter propped up against the clock. It was from America, but it wasn't in Joe's writing. She quickly tore it open.

She looked at the address. It was from Bob, Joe's older brother. She quickly folded the letter without reading it, her hands shaking. She didn't want to know the contents. Was Bob going to tell her Joe was dead? But she had to find out – and how had he got her address? Slowly she read through it. It appeared Joe had been in hospital. He couldn't write to Dolly as he had been moved about so many times and had lost all his kit and her address. He also believed that her letters had never caught up with him. Fortunately, just after he met Dolly, he had written to his brother and told Bob all about her, saying that if anything happened to him he should get in touch with Dolly in London.

> When we heard about Joe I decided to write to you. He is now on the mend and I have sent him your address so you should be hearing from him very soon. He was not badly injured – well, not enough to get him out of the Army, but he thinks he may end up with a desk job somewhere in England. I know he was very fond of you.

Her heart skipped a beat. *He was fond of her.*

Dolly knew her face was wreathed in smiles. He was alive. He was back here in England. He was fond of her! Those words thrilled her and she knew she was fond of him. She couldn't wait for a letter telling her she was going to see him again. Her thoughts quickly went to Tony. Why didn't she feel this way about him? Was that because he had been around all her life? Was she being silly? Was it the glamour that was attracting her to Joe?

Chapter 10

It was the last Sunday in April and as it was a still, pleasant evening, Dolly and Penny were sitting on the coping that ran all along the small concrete area fronting the houses. Before the war they'd had iron railings set in the top, and a gate, but those had long since gone to help the war effort. Dolly liked to think they could be part of a plane by now, flying high in the sky and helping to shoot down the enemy.

Dolly and Penny were chatting and casually watching Penny's brothers playing marbles in the street. They had been laughing at both boys' pudding-basin haircuts.

'Who did it?' asked Dolly.

'Me mum. I'm surprised you didn't hear our Jack hollering. You would have thought he was being murdered. Mum done it 'cos he's going for an interview for a job. That'll make him buck his ideas up.'

'Where's he going?'

'The garage in Broad Street.'

'Fancy, little Jack going out to work.'

'Don't let him hear you calling him little.'

'No, well he ain't that little now, is he?'

Penny was pleased she'd managed to steer the conversation away from Dolly telling her about the letter she'd had from Joe's brother. She didn't want to hear that she had written to his family, it was all wrong. Christ, she'd only seen the bloke a couple of times and here she was getting pally with his family! What was wrong with her?

'He says Joe's coming back to England and I should be hearing from him soon,' said Dolly, getting the conversation back to where she wanted.

'Dolly, do you think more of Joe than of Tony?'

'No, I don't. It's just that Joe's nice and—'

'And Tony ain't.'

'Course he is. You know that. But Joe is more exciting.'

'You've only met him a couple of times, you know nothing about him. He could be married.'

'He ain't. Don't forget I've written to his brother and he told me all about him and the family.'

'Well, I still think it's wrong.'

Dolly sat back. She wasn't sure of her feelings for Joe. What would they be if and when he returned? Would he like her? And what about Tony? She didn't want to hurt him. She loved him as well – but it was a different kind of love. Tony didn't have the same sophistication that Joe had. With Tony it had always been groping and giggling, but they had both grown up since those silly heady days. She was so confused. Was it possible to love two people at the same time? It must be. After all, mums love all their kids the same.

Suddenly Jack, who was at the end of Wood Street, called out, 'Hi mister. Got any gum, chum?'

Both Penny and Dolly's heads shot up. The evening sun was in their eyes but Dolly could clearly make out the man who was walking towards them. It was Joe. Dolly jumped up. All her fears and uncertainty vanished and she ran towards him, threw her arms round him and held him close.

Penny stood back and watched them kiss long and hard.

When they parted, Dolly's eyes were shining. She took hold of both Joe's hands and looked at him. 'You've lost a lot of weight.'

'I know.'

Penny was standing close to Dolly. 'Hello, Joe.'

'Joe. You remember Penny, don't you?'

'Sure. Hi. How you keeping?'

'I'm fine. How about you?'

'Not too bad.'

''Ere, Dolly. This your bloke?' asked Jack, who was pushing his younger brother out of the way.

Dolly blushed. She suddenly realised that she'd shown everyone down this end of the street her feelings for Joe. Feelings that she hadn't been sure of herself and had been trying to hide. But the joy of seeing him again had suddenly banished all that. 'No,' she said nonchalantly. 'He's just a good friend that I'm pleased to see.'

'Didn't look like it the way yer was slobbering all over him. What's Tony gonna say?' He grinned and hitched up his trousers.

Dolly felt embarrassed and was glad that Joe had come down the opposite end of Wood Street and had not passed in front of Tony's mum's house. It would be just her luck for Mrs Marchant or Rose to be looking out of the window.

'Here, kid. Here's a chocolate bar.'

'Cor, thanks. Sis, you wanna get yerself a Yank.'

'Joe, how did you get here? And how long have you been in England?' Dolly asked, steering him through her gateway.

He held his hand up. 'Whoa. One question at a time. I came to see you.'

'I was so worried when all your letters came back. Why didn't you write when you got over here?'

'Sorry, hon, but everything was so chaotic; all our gear,

including letters, got left behind. We never knew where we were going to finish up, so when we got back in hospital I wrote home. My folks knew I was laid up. Bob wrote me and told me he'd heard from you and gave me your address. As I had some leave due, I thought I wouldn't wait to write and find out if you wanted to see me. I decided to call on you anyway. You don't mind, don't you?'

Dolly smiled and shook her head. Thrills ran through her when he squeezed her arm.

'Have you heard from Gus at all, Penny?'

'No.'

Joe sat on the coping next to Dolly. 'I guess you heard about poor Chuck.'

'Yes. Betty's not been the same since.'

'You don't know what happened to Gus, do you?' Penny asked nervously.

'He was taken prisoner.'

Penny's eyes filled with tears. 'I'm so sorry. He was such a nice bloke.'

'I know. I was one of the lucky ones. I wasn't up at the front that day.'

'Where were you?'

'In the goddamn jungle. I had a bad bout of dysentery and was in the sick bay – that's why I was only injured when the skirmish started. I was lucky, I managed to get away.'

'Was it bad?' asked Dolly.

He smiled at her. 'I survived. I'm pleased you wrote to my brother. I'll have to watch him, he reckons you sound a real nice girl.'

'He sounds a nice bloke.'

'He is.'

The front door opened and Grace came out. 'Dolly, I'm just going on duty . . .' She stopped and stared at the young man who had jumped to his feet.

'Joe, this is me mum.'

Joe held out his hand. 'I'm very pleased to meet you, Mrs Taylor. I've heard a lot about you.'

Grace let her hand linger in Joe's for a moment or two. 'And I've heard a lot about you. You're back in this country now, then?'

'Yes.'

'I'm glad you're safe and well.'

'Thank you, it's good to be back in England again.'

'I'm sure it is. Dolly, I must be off. Give Joe a cup of tea. I'll see you later.' Grace kissed her daughter's cheek. As she walked down the street the last thing she wanted was to go on duty and leave Dolly with this young man. The look her daughter had on her face was very worrying.

Dolly smiled at Joe. 'Me mum has to go fire-watching.'

'But it ain't dark.'

'I know, but it will be and she has to report for duty just the same. Would you like a cup of tea?'

'Why not.'

'What about you, Pen?' As much as Dolly wanted to be alone with Joe she knew she had to ask her friend.

'Could do, I suppose.'

Dolly was hoping Penny wouldn't realise she wasn't wanted. She wanted to tell her to buzz off, but knew she couldn't.

'Come on in,' said Dolly.

Penny sat herself at the table. 'So what was it like in the jungle?'

'Hot, sweaty, loud and horrible. The Japs are slimy wicked bastards. I'm sorry – I beg your pardon.'

'So was Gus taken prisoner by the Japs?'

Joe nodded. 'I did wonder if he'd managed to write to you.'

'Should think his family and girlfriend come before pen-pals.'

'I guess so.'

'How come they didn't send you back to America?' asked Dolly, putting the cups and saucers on the table.

'I was picked up by some Brits.'

'That was lucky.'

Penny wanted to find out more about Gus, but she could see by Dolly's expression that she wasn't going to talk about it.

'Everything all right, Grace?' asked her friend Mary after she'd signed the duty book and settled herself down with a cup of tea.

'No, not really.'

'Why? What is it? It ain't Jim?'

'No, thank God. It's Dolly.'

'Oh my God. Nothing's—'

Grace smiled. 'No, she's all right. Well, I hope she is. It's just me being an over-protective mum.'

'We can't help that.' Mary was a widow; she also had a daughter who was older than Dolly. She was in the Ack Ack and Mary worried about her constantly. Her son had been taken prisoner when Dunkirk fell, so she had had more than enough to cope with. 'So, what's young Dolly been up to?'

'Nothing. Well, up to now, that is. She's been writing to this Yank and today he's just shown up after being missing for months, and I'm afraid my Dolly thinks the sun shines . . .'

'I get the picture,' said Mary, interrupting. 'So where are they now?'

'I've had to leave them indoors.'

'What – on their own?'

Grace nodded.

'No wonder you're worried. What's he like?'

'Don't know. I've never met him before.'

'Oh dear.'

'Don't say it like that. What am I gonna do?'

'Can't do a lot – well, not till midnight and if he's still there when you get home, then I think your fears might be justified.'

'But my Dolly's engaged to Tony, a British bloke. I'm sure she wouldn't . . .'

Mary gave Grace a playful nudge. 'Come on now. From what I've heard about your Dolly, I reckon she's got her head screwed on all right.'

'I hope so.' But Grace still fretted. Dolly was such a dreamer. What if this Joe promised her all sorts of things? Would she forget about Tony? If only this bloody war was over. She would be at home, Jim would be there and so would Tony, and the bloody Yanks wouldn't be sniffing around their girls.

'Come on, love, let's be having you. It's our turn to walk round the roof.'

Sighing Grace picked up her tin hat and followed Mary.

Dolly made a big thing of glaring at Penny as she took the cups and saucers from the dresser. She then went into the scullery to collect the teapot. Why wouldn't Penny go? If only she could get her on her own, she'd tell her to go home. Was she worried that as soon as she left, Dolly would whip her knickers off and let Joe have his wicked way? Dolly grinned. Mind you, that was quite a thought.

'Joe, what time do you have to get back tonight?' asked Dolly, walking back into the kitchen.

'It's all right, I'm not going back to camp. I'm staying at the Rainbow Club tonight.'

'That's smashing. Have you got much leave?'

'A month's furlough, so perhaps we could go out and about. You can show me London – well, what's left of it.'

'I'd love to. But remember, I do have to work.'

'I know. But I can see you at weekends and perhaps I can take you out some evenings.'

'We have to get up early,' said Penny.

Dolly had been trying her best to ignore her friend.

Joe smiled at Penny. 'I promise not to keep her out late.'

Dolly wanted to hit her best friend.

They sat and talked for a while then Joe looked at the clock. 'I'm sorry, but I still get very tired. I lost a lot of weight and it somehow sapped my energy.'

'That's all right,' said Dolly. 'It's lovely to see you're safe and well.'

'Suppose I'd better be going as well,' said Penny. 'What time does your mum get home?'

'About half twelve.'

Penny grinned. She knew Grace would be pleased she had stayed here with Dolly. After all, Dolly could be such a silly cow, and who knows what might have happened if they'd been left alone.

At the front door Joe kissed Penny's cheek. 'It's lovely to see you again and if I hear anything about Gus, I'll let you know.'

'Thanks, Joe. Goodnight, Dolly. Let's hope we don't have a raid tonight.'

'Have you had many raids?' Joe asked, looking worried for them.

'Not lately, thank goodness,' said Dolly. 'It's great to stay in bed all night.'

When Penny walked away, Dolly held on to Joe's arm.

'I'm sorry Penny didn't go home,' she said softly. 'I was hoping we would be on our own.'

'So was I, Dolly. It's great to see you again. Can I meet you from work tomorrow? Perhaps we can go somewhere and talk.'

'OK.'

'There are a lot of things I want to say.'

Dolly felt herself go hot. He was standing with his arm round her waist. What was he going to say?

Penny lifted her bedroom window. 'Goodnight, you two.'

'Goodnight,' called Joe.

Dolly didn't answer. You wait till tomorrow, she thought crossly. I'll give you a piece of my mind.

Joe turned back to Dolly. 'I'm pleased you've been writing to my folks. They think you're a swell girl. Now I must go.' He bent down and kissed her lips with a long and lingering kiss. This was like no other kiss she'd ever had. She felt she was soaring towards the heavens. She loved him, truly loved him – but did he love her?

Dolly watched him walk up Wood Street. At the far end he turned and waved. When he disappeared round the corner Dolly went inside and closed the door behind her. She didn't want him to go.

Dreamlike, she got undressed and slipped into bed. She knew sleep wouldn't come easily as her mind was in turmoil. She also knew she was being daft, but she couldn't help it. She'd only met Joe a couple of times. Was there such a thing as love at first sight?

Tony had never had this effect on her.

Chapter 11

Grace pushed open her daughter's bedroom door and gave a quiet sigh of relief at seeing her lying in bed, alone. You are daft, she said to herself. If they had got up to anything, do you honestly think he would still be here? Grace made her way silently to her own bedroom.

Dolly didn't let on to her mother that she was still awake. The last thing she wanted was the third degree; she'd get that in the morning.

As they walked to work, Dolly was nagging Penny.

'You knew I wanted to be alone with Joe, so why did you hang around?'

''Cos I knew you'd be all daft and when he looked at you with those lovely brown eyes of his you would have let him have what I expect he'd come for.'

'He didn't come for that.'

'Don't you believe it.'

'Well if he did, you're only jealous.'

Penny stopped. 'Dolly, you're my best friend, we're more like sisters than friends. I don't want to see you hurt.'

Dolly stood beside Penny and looked at the ground. 'I won't get hurt,' she said softly, feeling full of guilt at going off at her friend.

'You will if he goes away and you never see him again, especially if he promises you the moon.'

'I don't think he will.'

'Dolly, you're such a dreamer. You think that everyone is as nice as you.'

Dolly was pleased her friend thought she was nice. 'Joe ain't like that. You've met him, he's a great guy.'

'I know. But he's a long way from home and I expect he's very lonely. Dolly, promise me you won't let him – you know. I'd hate it if you finished up expecting. What would your mum and dad say, that's without Tony?'

Dolly continued walking. 'So that's what you think. You think I'm like Jane. Well, I ain't. I intend to keep me knickers on. So you ain't got nothing to worry about, have you?'

They continued to walk to work in silence. Dolly had had her mother giving her almost the same lecture this morning. Why did everyone think that was all he wanted?

As soon as Dolly caught sight of Betty she rushed over to her. She took her arm and ushered her away from everybody else. Keeping her voice low she said, 'Bet, Joe came to see me yesterday. I'm going to meet him tonight outside work – would you like to come and have a word with him? He might be able to tell you a bit more about Chuck.'

The expression on Betty's face was one of complete astonishment. 'What did he say? How come he's here?'

'It seems he wasn't at the front at the time and managed to get back to England.'

'Come on girls, let's be having yer.' Mr Freeman was walking towards them.

'I'll talk to you at break-time,' said Dolly.

Betty walked away in a daze.

'What you been saying to her?' asked Jane.

'Just told her Joe's back in England and he come to see me yesterday.'

'Did he now. He don't happen to know what happened to Teddy, does he?'

Dolly shook her head.

'He don't know that much at all,' said Penny. 'He said he was laid up with the runs when all the trouble started.'

'Poor sod. So you've seen him an' all then?' asked Jane.

'Yes,' said Penny, looking pointedly at Dolly. 'Watch out, here's Freeman,' she added, sitting at her bench.

At lunchtime Dolly and Betty sat well away from Jane and Penny.

'Why can't they sit with us?' asked Jane.

'Me and Dolly have had a row.'

Jane laughed. 'What over?'

'Well, when Joe came round Dolly's house yesterday I stayed with 'em all evening.'

'You didn't! You rotten cow.'

'I know. But you should have seen the way Dolly was looking at him, and the look she gave me. For two pins I reckon she'd have thumped me and chucked me out.'

'Where was her mum?'

'Fire-watching.'

Jane very nearly spat her tea out when she laughed. 'No wonder she won't speak to you. I certainly would have chucked you out, that's for sure.'

Dolly looked over at Jane and Penny laughing. She knew they were laughing at her.

'So, what did he say about Chuck then?' asked Betty.

'Not a lot.'

'Do you think he might know something?' asked Betty.

'I don't know. Have a word with him when we see him.'

Tears filled Betty's eyes. 'I'd like to know if it was quick.

I'd hate to think of him lying there wounded and crying out in pain.'

Dolly touched her hand. 'Don't get your hopes up. After all, Joe was in hospital, but at least he might be able to tell you if Chuck went to the hospital.'

'Thanks, Dolly.' After she sat silently drinking her tea, Betty stood up and left Dolly sitting alone.

At the end of their shift Dolly took hold of Betty's arm and hurried her out of the factory.

'Ain't you gonna wait for Pen?'

'No.'

'Look, there he is,' said Betty.

'Quick, before Jane comes up and grabs him.'

'Hello Joe,' said Dolly giving him a beaming smile. 'You remember Betty?'

'Course. I'm so sorry about Chuck.'

'Joe, could we go and have a drink or something? Betty wants to know about Chuck.'

'Can't really tell her much, but we can go to that pub over the road if you like?'

'OK.'

Joe held on to Dolly's arm and propelled her across the road.

Dolly looked behind to see Penny and Jane standing watching them. Penny's face was like thunder. There was going to be a lot said tomorrow.

It was early and the pub was empty when they walked in. Dolly and Betty ordered a shandy.

When Joe sat down with them he said, 'Betty, I'm afraid I don't know too much.'

'Was he injured? Did he go to hospital?'

Joe shook his head. 'Not as far as I know. We all got split

up.' How could he tell her about those poor souls who had
survived the attack, and who died being rushed to the ships?
The terrain was awful and the journey a nightmare. The
screams of his fellow soldiers could be heard everywhere.
For days they were tossed about on the ocean and every day
somebody's body was pushed overboard.

'Would it have been quick?' asked Betty in a trembling
voice.

'Yes, it would have been very quick.' Nor could he tell her
that if Chuck had only been injured and the Japs had found
him, they would have finished him off quick. They were
very fond of using their bayonets.

'Thank you, Joe. I feel a lot better knowing he didn't
suffer.'

Joe felt guilty at not giving her the answers she wanted.
'He was a real nice guy. And I know it sounds heartless,
but at least you had some time together as husband and
wife.'

Betty gave him a weak smile. 'I know. But I would have
liked to have spent the rest of me life with him.'

Joe touched her hand.

She stood up. 'I best be going. Will you be around for
long?'

'I hope so, about a month. Although with all this talk
about a second front, you can never be sure. I could be
recalled.' He stood up and held Betty close. 'Look after
yourself.' He kissed her cheek.

'I will. Bye, Dolly. See you tomorrow.'

'Course.'

Dolly looked at them. He was such a caring man.

When Betty left Joe said, 'I hope I made things a little
easier for her.'

'I'm sure you did.'

'Chuck was a great buddy. I'm so glad they had a few days' happiness.'

'Me too. I've never seen Betty so happy. Pity it was so shortlived.'

'Yes. But that's war.'

'Are you likely to be called back?'

'Could be. Something big is happening. Dolly, I'm in love with you.'

Dolly blushed. 'You can't say that.'

'Why not? Dolly, will you marry me?'

Dolly sat looking at him. She was speechless.

'I'm sorry. I shouldn't have said . . .'

'No. It's not that. It's such a shock. I wasn't expecting that.'

'It was being in the thick of it. I wanted you so badly. You were the only one I could think about and if I get sent away . . .'

'Joe, I can't. I'm engaged to Tony.'

'I know. And I feel a right heel for stealing his girl. But all's fair in love and war. Besides, who knows which one of us is going to come out of all this in one piece.'

'Don't say that.'

'Dolly, do you like me?'

'Yes. Yes, I do.'

'But not enough to marry me?'

'I don't know. This is too sudden.' Dolly couldn't think straight.

'I'm sorry. I should have waited. But talking about Chuck has put everything into perspective.'

'You'll have to give me time to think about this.'

He grinned and grabbed her hand. 'So you're not turning me down completely?'

'Yes. Yes, I am,' she said hurriedly. Her mind was trying

to grasp the situation. What about Tony? What about her mum and dad? Half of her wanted to say yes, but she knew she shouldn't.

'I'm sorry,' Joe said again. 'I should at least have given you a sign or a hint of my thoughts. You know that I love you and want you to be there when I get back.'

Dolly couldn't think straight. 'Can we find somewhere to eat? I'm starving. I told me mum I would be home a bit later.'

Joe laughed. 'Is that the effect being proposed to has on you?'

'I don't know. I ain't ever been proposed to before.'

'What about Tony?'

'He didn't ask – well, not properly. We just thought it was a good idea as him and Reg was going away.' Dolly didn't want to say the four of them did it for a laugh at the time.

'Come on, let's find somewhere to eat.'

Dolly wasn't sure if he sounded angry. Did he think she would fall in his arms? Had she been sending out the wrong signals? But *were* they the wrong signals? She knew she loved him, but she also loved Tony. What a mess. Who could she confide in? Her mother and Penny certainly would have strong views on it.

The meal in a café was a very subdued affair. Normally they found plenty to talk about, but today they could only talk about mundane things. Dolly knew she had to give him an answer, but at the moment she didn't know what that would be. Half of her desperately wanted to say yes, but the other half told her to be sensible. What should she do?

When they got outside, Joe took her arm. 'I'm sorry. I didn't mean to upset you.'

'You haven't. It's just that I need time to think.'

'Are you turning me down?'

'No. I don't know.'

'I'm so sorry, hon.' He held her tight. 'I just want us to be happy and together for the rest of our lives, for however long that could be.'

Fear grabbed her. How long did any of them have? As she nestled in his arms her fears and doubts began to vanish.

'Joe, I don't want you to take me home. I'd rather go alone.'

'You gonna talk to you mom?'

'I don't know. I need time to think.'

'Can I see you tomorrow?'

'No. Let's leave it till Saturday.'

'OK. If you say so.'

'I'll have an answer for you then.'

He held her tight again. 'I pray it's the right one.'

Dolly couldn't answer him.

On the bus her mind buzzed frantically. She was always talking about going to America, going to see the world, but now the opportunity was arising she wasn't so sure. Did she really want to leave Rotherhithe, her mum and dad and Penny? And what about Tony? Was she being fair to him?

When Dolly pushed open the kitchen door her mother looked up. 'You're early. I didn't think you'd be home just yet, I ain't got any dinner for . . .' her voice trailed off. 'You all right? You look ever so peaky.'

'I'm all right.'

'Have you had something to eat?'

'Yes, me and Joe had egg and chips.'

'Have you and that Joe had a row?'

'No.' Dolly didn't want to say she'd just had a proposal of marriage. It would only cause trouble. Tonight she just wanted to be alone and think.

Grace eyed her daughter suspiciously. Something had definitely happened. Was he going away? Had he given her the elbow? That would be the best news she could have. She didn't want Dolly messing about with Yanks. 'I'll make us a cup of tea.'

'No, sit down. I'll do it.'

As Dolly stood in the scullery watching the blue flame dance round the kettle she felt she was in a dream. She had had no idea that Joe would propose. Should she go and talk to her mother? But Dolly knew what her reaction would be. It would be the same as Penny's. What about Betty? She desperately needed to talk to someone.

'Dolly,' called her mother, 'I'm just popping over to the Gregorys. I want to see what ciggies they've got.'

Dolly filled the teapot. 'I'll go.' She knew that the sisters were people she could talk to. Those two ladies were sensible and Dolly knew her confidences wouldn't be repeated.

She grabbed her bag and hurried across the road.

Chapter 12

The tinkling bell above the door brought Miss Ada Gregory from the back room.

'Hello, young Dolly. What can I do for you?'

Dolly looked round the sparsely stocked shop. When she was young and before the war, it had been like walking into an Aladdin's cave. The shelves were always filled with wonderful jars of brightly coloured sweets and the glass counter revealed the tempting display of chocolate bars underneath. Now just a few sweets were pathetically displayed and the chocolates boxes were empty, as were the packets on the cigarette shelf. 'Mum wants to know what ciggies you've got.'

Miss Gregory smiled. Her grey hair framed her round face. Her sad eyes lit up when she smiled and showed her innermost feelings. The sisters were warm, lovely ladies and Dolly had known them all her life.

'Your mother's lucky, we had a delivery today. She likes Park Drive. I can let her have two packets. We have to be fair to everybody.'

'Thanks.' Dolly handed over a half a crown. Then she looked at the door. 'Miss Gregory, can I ask you for some advice?'

The elderly woman gave a little laugh. 'My goodness, my

dear. I don't know what advice I could give you.'

'I need to talk to someone.'

Miss Gregory looked over the top of her half-glasses at Dolly and said seriously, 'I do hope you're not in any trouble. We did notice that a nice-looking young man called on you last Sunday. American, is he? You seemed very pleased to see him.'

Dolly blushed. She had almost forgotten how she had greeted Joe. 'It's him I want to talk about.'

'Oh dear. Don't you think it should be your mother you should be talking to?'

'Not really. You see, Mum has already made up her mind about Joe. That's his name.'

'My dear, I wouldn't like to say anything to upset your mother.'

'Please. *Please* let me talk to you.'

'I can see you're a little distressed. You'd better come through.'

Dolly went behind the counter and through into the living room, which was exactly how it had been when the ladies' parents were alive. It was as if time had stood still. Heavy large furniture took up most of the room. A green chenille cloth covered the round table and reached down to the floor. A bowl of artificial fruit stood in the middle. Dark pictures hung from the picture rail and the light that hung low over the table had a dark floral shade with a deep fringe and made everywhere dark and depressing.

'Sit down, dear.'

Dolly sat in one of the dark-coloured tapestry armchairs that stood either side of the fireplace. The range that had been well black-leaded for years shone and the grate was dazzling white. 'I'll just give May a call, in case someone comes in the shop. We don't want to be disturbed. May!' she called through the back door. 'Come in here.'

May came bustling in, she was younger and slimmer than her sister, although she had the same grey hair and sad eyes. 'What is it? I was just seeing to the potatoes. Hello, Dolly. What are you doing here?'

'Dolly has a little problem, May dear, and she wants some advice. Not that I'm sure I'm the right one to help her.'

'It's not your father or Tony, is it, love?' May asked immediately.

'No.'

'Thank goodness. Tony's such a lovely boy. We know how you must worry with him being abroad and in all this fighting.'

'May. Just be quiet for a moment and let Dolly tell us her problem.'

'Sorry,' said May.

Dolly looked at these two lovely ladies. 'You see, Joe has asked me to marry him.'

'Joe?' asked May.

'He's the American I've been seeing and writing to.'

'Was that the young man we saw arrive on Sunday?'

Dolly nodded. 'Yes. I've been writing to him and his family as well.'

'What, in America?' asked May.

Dolly nodded. 'You see, I know I'm engaged to Tony Marchant, but I really like Joe as well. I don't know what to do.'

Ada Gregory sat opposite Dolly. 'Do you love him?'

'I think so. But you see, I also love Tony. I don't know what to do.'

The shop bell tinkled.

'May, dear. Go and see who it is,' Ada said quietly.

'Don't tell anyone I'm here, will you?' Dolly panicked.

'Not if you don't want me to.' May left the room and pulled the door shut behind her.

'Now, Dolly. The only advice I can give you is for you to sit down and have a long talk with your mother. Try to keep in control and don't end up having an argument about it. And remember, at the end of the day it's your happiness that she will be worrying about. If you do marry this young man, I expect, God willing, that you will be off to America when all this trouble is over. So think about that. After all, you are their only child. You mean a lot to your mother, especially with your father away for long stretches.'

Dolly stood up. 'He says he's going to retire when the war ends.'

'That'll be nice.'

'Thank you for listening to me.'

'Not at all. And Dolly, it's you who will have to make the final decision. In the end you should let your heart rule your head. Remember, none of us lives for ever.'

As Dolly walked across the road she knew the time had come for her to have a proper talk with her mother.

Joe sat in the club. He had been sitting alone at the end of the bar holding the same drink for over an hour and the ice had melted long ago. All around him there was music, laughter and noise, but he wasn't listening. He had a problem that was filling his head and he had to sort it out. He'd been a fool to blurt out a marriage proposal to Dolly. He should have told her his feelings for her. He should have given her time to think about it. But did they have the luxury of time? When he'd found out that most of the men in his unit had been killed, taken prisoner or wounded, he knew that he wanted to be part of Dolly. The thought of loving her had kept him going.

Joe knew he'd made a hash of it. He should have led up to it gently, but he couldn't wait. He loved her and wanted to marry her. What would her answer be on Saturday? He was meant to marry her! He wanted some happiness before they were sent to Europe – and who knew what would happen then? He had seen how happy Chuck had been; at least he'd had some joy, even if it was shortlived. Joe knew his luck couldn't hold out for ever. And he wanted Dolly. He loved her so much; it would give him something to fight for.

Joe frowned. But was he being selfish? Was he being fair to Dolly – and what about Tony? He also saw the heartbreak that Betty was suffering. Should he just disappear from Dolly's life? After all, she did have Tony. He looked around at all the couples and wished with all his heart that Dolly was here with him, then he could tell her just how much he did love her. Very slowly he swirled his drink round and round in the glass, almost hypnotised as he sat staring into it, waiting for inspiration. If they did come out of this mess together, how would Dolly settle down back home? Farm life was so very different from London and from everything she was used to. And what about Ma? How would she react? Hell, they had to get to that stage first. He threw the last of his drink down his throat and went to bed.

'You took your time,' said Grace when Dolly walked in.

'Been talking to Miss Gregory.'

'Did they have any ciggies?'

Dolly put the two packets of Park Drive on the table. 'Mum, can I talk to you?'

Grace looked at her daughter. 'Course you can.'

Dolly sat at the table. 'I don't know where to begin.'

It was the expression on her daughter's face that made Grace blurt out: 'Oh my God! You're not pregnant, are you?'

'No, I'm not. Why does everybody jump to the same conclusion?'

'You've not enlisted, have you?' Grace's voice was a little calmer.

'No, I ain't. I just promised Miss Gregory I wouldn't lose me temper, but I can see I'm gonna.' She stopped and saw the look on her mother's face.

'You went over and discussed whatever it is with them before talking to me?'

Dolly hung her head. 'I'm sorry, but I didn't know who to turn to.'

'Well, thanks. I thought we had a better understanding than that. I suppose you've discussed whatever it is with Penny as well. I'm only your mother so I'm bound to be the last to hear it. So come on, spit it out – what is it?'

Dolly was taken aback by the anger in her mother's voice. 'I ain't talked to Penny about this.' She knew now that any sympathy she might have got had disappeared. She began to play with the packets of cigarettes resting on the table. 'Mum, I know you don't like Joe.'

Grace froze. 'I don't know him,' she said, dreading what was coming next.

'Well, he's asked me to marry him.'

The silence was long. Finally, Grace asked: 'What did you say?'

'Nothing yet.'

'Do you want to?'

'I don't know.'

'Do you love him?'

'Yes.'

'But what about Tony?'

'I love him as well.' Tears began to fill Dolly's eyes.

'Well, I'm sorry, but you can't have two husbands. It's against the law in this country. Besides, you ain't old enough.'

'But, Mum . . .'

'You don't know anything about him.'

'I do.'

'How old is he?'

'He's twenty-two.'

Grace lit another cigarette from the one she'd been smoking. 'I'm sorry, but I'm definitely not giving my consent. So let that be the end of it.'

'But, Mum,' repeated Dolly. 'Why not?'

'You're too young to know your own mind. Or is it just the thought of going to America for free?'

'That's a rotten thing to say.' But Dolly couldn't truthfully answer that.

'So what did Miss Gregory have to say about it? I presume that's what you was talking about?' Grace was very angry.

'She told me to talk to *you*.'

'At least she's got some sense. Well, now you've got your answer.'

'We could always go to Gretna Green.'

Grace laughed. 'Don't talk such rot. Would he get permission to marry someone who's under age?'

'I don't know.' Dolly sat staring at her hands. She knew now she wanted to marry Joe, or was it more because her mother was so against it? Could he get permission to marry her?

'Dolly. Look, love, don't get upset. Don't let us fall out.'

Dolly stood up. 'What? After you've just said I can't be happy with the man I love.'

'Stop being so dramatic. You should be worrying about Tony. After all, he's hoping to come back and marry you.'

'I suppose if I'm still not twenty-one you wouldn't let me marry *him*?'

'Course I would. After all, I know him.'

'Well, don't bother yourself. I'd rather stay an old spinster like the Gregory sisters.' Dolly slammed the kitchen door as she walked out.

Grace sat back in the armchair. A tear ran down her cheek. Why did Dolly have to meet this bloke, and why did she have to fall for him? But was it him – or was it America? How could she reason with her daughter? If only Jim was here to help her with these decisions.

In her bedroom Dolly threw herself on the top of her bed. She was angry with her mother. Surely Grace could see that in this war both Tony and Joe could be killed, and she could be all alone for the rest of her life. Tears fell. She did want both of them, but what if Tony had changed? He'd seen a lot and could be a very different person from the boy she had kissed goodbye. She twisted her engagement ring round and round. If she was going to marry Joe it was time she removed it. She slipped off the bed and went to her dressing-table and took the little satin-lined ring-box from her special drawer. As she put it safely back inside she gave a sob. Why did life have to have so many ups and downs? She would need to write to Tony. She wouldn't say anything about getting married just yet, as she knew how much Dear John letters upset the fellers, and the last thing she wanted to do was hurt Tony. She was too fond of him to do that, but if she was going to marry Joe, he must hear it from her first.

What if she brought Joe home on Saturday afternoon and he asked her mother? Dolly rubbed her hand across her tear-stained cheeks and gave a little grin. Joe could charm the birds out of the trees, so perhaps he could work the same magic on Grace Taylor. Perhaps he could even get Mum to write to his mother, and then she would find out that he came from a nice family. After all, Joe's people would be worried about the kind of girl she was.

Chapter 13

On Tuesday morning when Penny knocked on the door, Dolly picked up her handbag and without bothering to call out goodbye to her mother, left the house and hurried along the road.

'Blimey, you're eager to get to work this morning.'

Dolly didn't answer.

'You all right?' asked Penny, falling in step beside her friend. 'You don't look happy.'

'I'm fine.'

'You and Joe ain't had a row, have you?'

'No.'

'You was in a bit of a hurry to whisk him away last night after work,' said Penny, tottering along on her high heels and trying to keep up with Dolly.

'I wanted Betty to talk to him.'

'Did he know anything about Chuck?'

'No, but I think he helped put her mind at rest. She was worried he might have suffered.'

'Look, I'm sorry I didn't leave you and Joe on your own Sunday and I'm sorry about taking the mick at work yesterday.'

'That's all right. I seem to be falling out with everybody lately.'

Penny stopped and clutched Dolly's arm. 'What? You *have* had a row with Joe, ain't you?'

Dolly brushed Penny's arm away. 'No.'

'So what is it then?'

'It's just me and Mum.'

'Oh dear, did you get home late last night?'

'No.'

'Oh come on, Dolly. Stop being such a misery. What have you and your mum fallen out over?'

'She won't give her consent for me to marry Joe.'

Penny stopped dead in her tracks. 'What?'

'I think you heard.'

'I think I did, but I don't believe it.'

'What don't you believe?'

'That you want to marry Joe.'

'Why not?'

Penny broke into a trot as her friend hurried on. 'Because you're engaged to marry Tony, that's why.'

'We can all change our minds.'

'Dolly. Think about this.'

'I have, all night.'

'Look, slow down a bit. Do you really want to marry him?'

'Yes.'

'So what you gonna do?'

'I don't know. And don't say anything to them at work. I don't want everybody to know about it.'

'Don't worry, I won't.' Penny's mind was going over and over the startling news. What was Dolly thinking of, talking about marrying Joe? 'How long a leave has he got?'

'A month. That's if he don't get recalled for this second front everyone's talking about.'

'I see. Is that why he's asked you to marry him?'

115

'I don't think so.'

'What if anything happens to him? Think about Betty.'

'I have, and that's made me more determined than ever. I want to be his wife, even if . . .' She couldn't finish the sentence.

Penny was worried about her friend. Did she want to marry Joe for the right reasons? And what about Tony? Why couldn't she see sense? 'Are you seeing Joe tonight?' she asked.

'No. I'm not seeing him until Saturday. Why?'

'At least he's giving you breathing space.'

'Yes, and I'm taking him home to talk to Mum, to see if he can make her see sense. So I don't want you coming in and spoiling it.'

Penny was hurt. All their lives they had been friends, even as children they hardly ever fell out; now there was this big gulf widening between them. Why did the bloody Yanks have to come into this war?

'Pen, what's wrong with Dolly?' asked Jane after she'd spent the lunch-break on her own.

'Dunno.'

'Her bloke ain't gone away, has he?'

'No.' Deep down Penny wished Joe *would* go away and soon, so that they could get their lives back to normal – well, as normal as you could be in wartime.

For the rest of the week Dolly wouldn't discuss Joe with Penny and she ignored her mother's attempts to talk about Joe, the reason being that she didn't want every conversation to end up in a shouting contest. She loved Penny and her mother too much to have this endless arguing. If only Grace would come round and give her consent. Couldn't she see how much Dolly wanted to marry him?

Grace tried hard to bridge the gap that had come between herself and her daughter, but at the same time she knew she would never give her consent to the marriage. 'Can we just talk sensibly about this problem?' she said once.

'I'm sorry. I haven't got a problem.'

'Dolly, please let's talk.'

'No, Mum. Not unless you've changed your mind.'

'I wish your father was here.'

'I bet you do, then you could blame all this on him.'

Grace sighed. She knew it was of no use. 'Are you going out tonight?'

'No.'

'When are you seeing . . .?' His name stuck in Grace's throat.

'Joe. His name's Joe.'

Grace looked away. It wasn't his fault, poor lad, that he'd fallen in love with her daughter.

'Not till Saturday.' Dolly wasn't going to tell her mother she was bringing him home as she might decide to go out.

Grace was frightened to ask too much, she didn't want to be told her daughter might be leaving home. What if the pair of them went to a hotel and Dolly found herself in the family way? Then Grace admonished herself for being over-dramatic and tried to forget the whole thing.

That night, Grace was having a great deal of difficulty sleeping. If only Jim was here! How she missed him, his arms lovingly round her, his tender kisses; he would soon have this sorry mess sorted out. She didn't want Dolly to hate her, they had always been so close. Should she give in? After all, they were at war, and if anything did happen to Joe, Dolly would never forgive her.

★ ★ ★

117

On Saturday afternoon after work Dolly was thrilled to see Joe waiting for her. She did have a little niggling doubt that he might have had second thoughts.

'You came,' she said breathlessly.

'You bet. I wanted to know if you've changed your mind and decided to marry me.'

Dolly smiled up at him.

'Have you?' he asked eagerly.

'You'll have to wait to find out.'

He put his arm round her and held her tight. 'That sounds promising. So where's it to be?'

'We're going home for you to meet my mother properly.'

He grinned. 'It's beginning to sound better and better. Can I kiss you?'

'No, you can't, not with everybody looking at us.'

'Hi, Penny. You coming our way?' asked Joe easily as Penny came up to them.

'Don't know, where are you going?'

'We're going to Dolly's house, so why not walk along with us?'

Penny was quickly recalling what Dolly had said about not interfering on Saturday. 'Is that all right, Dolly?' she tentatively asked.

'Course,' Dolly said cheerfully, holding on to Joe's arm.

Penny was suspicious. What had happened? Had Mrs Taylor given her consent and Dolly not told her?

Much to Penny's relief, Joe was keeping up the conversation all the way home. He seemed very happy and kissed Penny's cheek when they reached her house.

Dolly's hand was trembling as she pulled the key through the letterbox and opened the front door. What would be the outcome today? Was she doing the right thing?

'Hello, Mum,' she said, opening the kitchen door.

Grace was reading the paper. She looked up. Her face turned to thunder when she saw the American standing behind Dolly. She folded the paper. 'I'll put the kettle on,' she said heavily. Why hadn't Dolly warned her she was bringing him home? Grace knew that this was going to be a long and painful afternoon.

'Have a seat,' Dolly told Joe. 'I'm just going to have a word with Mum.' She closed the scullery door behind her.

Grace was standing next to the sink. 'What have you brought *him* here for?' she said tersely.

'Please, Mum. Hear me out. Don't let's start shouting.'

Grace turned her back on Dolly. 'Well, my girl?'

'I want you to talk to him, then you'll see what a nice bloke he is. Please, Mum, do this for me.'

'OK, but I won't change me mind.'

Dolly gave a sigh of relief. At least she was going to get the pair of them talking, whatever the outcome might be. When she walked back into the kitchen, Joe was studying a photograph of Dolly with her mother and father.

'This is a great picture. Your dad looks a nice guy.'

'He is. Joe, me mum won't let me marry you.'

He grinned and held her tight. 'So you do want to marry me?' He covered her face with kisses.

Dolly looked nervously at the scullery door. 'Stop it. Did you hear what I just said?'

'I sure did.'

'What we gonna do?'

'Why is your mom so against me?'

'Lots of reasons. For a start I'm engaged to Tony. Then there's the fact that you're an American, and she's worried I'm gonna go away. And lastly, she don't think I've known you long enough.'

He held her at arm's length and looked into her face. The

119

lovely face that belonged to the girl he loved and with whom he was determined to spend the rest of his life. 'When you say all that together, it does sound stupid, I guess, but Dolly, we don't have time to hang about waiting till things are just right. I love you and want you to be my wife.' He held her close. 'Do you think you could learn to love me?'

'Yes, I do. And I want to marry you.'

Joe kissed her long and hard.

Grace had opened the door just enough to hear what was being said. The couple were too engrossed with each other to notice her standing back from the doorway. Tears filled her eyes. She had wanted to throw him out, but as she stood silently listening to him, she could understand her daughter being in love with such a man who was four years older than her. He was more grown-up than Tony. But what about Tony? In these days life could be very short so should she stand in the way of their happiness? After all, Dolly could finish up a widow like Betty, and if they never married . . . if that happened. Dolly would hate her for the rest of her life for taking away a few precious weeks of happiness. Grace didn't know what to do; she crept back into the scullery and picked up the teapot. She made a bit of a thing when she rattled the door handle.

Dolly and Joe jumped apart.

'Dolly, get the cups. Sit down, young man.'

Joe quickly sat at the table.

'Now what's all this about wanting to marry my daughter – my *only* daughter, as it happens?'

Joe swallowed hard. 'I love her.'

'But you've only known her five minutes.'

Dolly groped for Joe's hand under the table and silently prayed.

'What about back home? Have you got a girlfriend?'

'No.'

'I'm sure your mother'll have something to say about all this nonsense.'

'It ain't nonsense, Mum!'

'Mrs Taylor, I am old enough to fight for my country, so I think I'm old enough to know who I want to spend the rest of my life with. And none of us knows how long that'll be.'

Dolly was trying hard to keep her temper under control. The gruelling interview went on for what seemed to her like hours, but every time Joe seemed to win her mother over.

Finally, Grace sat back and took the cigarette Joe offered her. 'You know I don't approve of you going out with her at all. Dolly, what are you going to say to Tony?'

'I don't know.'

'I've got to think long and hard about this. I wish your father was here.'

Dolly sat up.

'If I did come round to saying yes, I think you should give yourselves more time and wait a while before you get married.'

Dolly felt as if her mother had just burst her balloon. 'But Mum, we ain't *got* a lot of time!'

'That's all I'm gonna say. You know I don't want you to marry – Joe here, and I hope in time you will realise how silly all this has been and that you will remember your promise to Tony.'

Joe stood up. 'I'm sorry you feel this way about me, Mrs Taylor. I can't tell you how much I love your daughter. She's the only good thing that has come into my life lately, and if you don't give us your blessing then I'll take her to

Scotland, where I understand Dolly wouldn't need your consent.'

Dolly sat open-mouthed. He was willing to do this for her. Tears filled her eyes.

'Mum, I don't want to start my married life with you hating us!'

Grace walked to the door and took her coat from off the nail. 'That's all I've got to say,' she said in a choked voice. 'Now I have to go. I'm fire-watching tonight.'

As she closed the front door she was trembling? Why wasn't Jim here? What had she done?

When Grace arrived at the warden's post, Mary was reading the paper. She looked up. 'What are you doing here this time of the day?' she asked in surprise. 'You're not supposed to be here till tonight.'

'I know, but I had to get out.'

'Why? What's happened?'

Grace sank into the armchair and began telling Mary the whole saga.

When she had finished, Mary sat up. 'Well, I must say that's quite a problem.'

'What should I do?'

'Let's be practical about this. What if you don't give your consent and they go to Scotland? Dolly ain't gonna be happy about coming back home to live.'

'I don't think they will,' said Grace uneasily. 'I think they were just trying that on.'

'You can't be sure of that. What if they just make out they're married and go off somewhere? What if she finishes up in the family way?'

'Don't, Mary. Don't you think all this ain't gone through me mind?'

'Well, as the saying goes, the ball is in your court.'

'I know,' said Grace sadly. 'Thanks for letting me bend your ear. I'd better be going.'

'That's OK. I'll see you tonight.'

With a heavy heart Grace made her way home. She would have to tell them she'd forgotten there had been a change in the rota.

Chapter 14

Joe went to kiss Dolly when her mother left the house.

Dolly pushed him away. 'No, don't.'

'Why not?'

'I'm sorry, but it's Mum. I don't like this bad feeling between us – it upsets me. We've always been close.'

Joe held her at arm's length. 'Dolly, would you like me to go out of your life?'

'No. I love you, Joe, and want to marry you.' She sat down. 'This is all such a mess.'

'Is it because of Tony?'

'A bit.'

Joe sat next to her. 'I can understand your feelings, but I can't help you. You have to choose.'

She smiled at him. 'Will I like it in America?'

Joe gathered her in his arms and kissed her. When they broke away, he said, 'I'll go back to camp Monday and start the ball rolling. I have to get permission and I'll need a special licence. You know you have to have a medical? We may only be able to have a few days' honeymoon in Scotland. Is that OK?'

Dolly nodded, feeling frightened at the speed of it all. What had she done? She did love him, but to go against her mother's wishes . . . 'I'll get meself a nice suit,' she told him.

'I'll go down the Cut – I can buy something there without coupons. It'll cost a bit more, but that don't matter.'

'Are you sure this is what you want?'

'Yes.'

'Hallelujah!' he shouted. 'I sure am the luckiest guy alive!'

Dolly laughed. 'What about your mum? Do you think she'll approve of me?'

'I know she will. I shall write tonight and tell her.' In fact, Joe was a little concerned his mother might *not* approve, but what the hell – life was too short. Anything could happen. 'Come here, the future Mrs Walters.'

Dolly giggled. 'Mrs Dorothy Walters. Sounds rather nice.'

He put his arms round her and kissed her long and hard. 'I do love you, Dolly,' he whispered, kissing her ears. 'And I'm going to make you real happy. You'll never regret marrying me.'

'Hello, Mrs Taylor,' said Penny, walking across the road from the grocer's and falling in step beside Grace.

'Hello, Penny. You coming in?'

Penny looked sheepishly. 'I don't know, I'd better not.'

'I think you'd better.'

'But Dolly said . . .'

'I don't really care what Dolly said. *I'm* inviting you in.'

Penny walked with Grace along the road. 'Have you just come home from the Warden's post?' she asked, seeing Grace was carrying her tin hat.

'Yes.'

'I think Dolly would rather see you on your own, she don't want me hanging about.'

'What she wanted to ask me has all been said.'

Penny guessed from the look on Grace's face that the outcome wasn't what Dolly had wanted.

When they got into the kitchen, Joe and Dolly were busy writing and studying a map.

'Mum – I thought you was fire-watching?'

'I'd forgot they'd changed the rota.'

'Penny. What are you doing here?'

'I asked her to come in for a cup of tea.'

Dolly gave Penny a glaring look.

'Perhaps I'd better not stay,' her friend said nervously.

'Course you can. Sit down. Clear all this off the table, Dolly.'

'We don't want any tea. Me and Joe are going out. Come on, Joe.'

Joe shrugged and picked up his cap. 'Be seeing you all.'

'Sorry about that, Penny,' said Grace, sitting at the table. 'Did you know they want to get married?'

Penny nodded. 'Dolly did tell me.'

'Well, I won't give my consent.'

'I'm sorry to hear that.'

'Why? Do you want her to marry him?'

'No. But I don't want Dolly to do something she might regret for the rest of her life.'

'Does she honestly believe the grass is greener over the other side of the ocean?'

'I wouldn't think so.'

'We know nothing about him. He could be married.'

'I don't think he is,' said Penny.

'What about his family? They could be gangsters or hillbillies.'

Penny smiled. 'Dolly does write to them.'

'I know.'

'Look – she can be a bit of a dreamer at times.' Penny

was feeling very uncomfortable talking about her friend behind her back.

'That's what worries me. He said they could go to Scotland to get married.'

Penny sat up. 'What – Gretna Green? She wouldn't, would she?'

'I don't know. I don't know what to think any more. I wish Jim was here then I wouldn't have to make all these decisions.'

'I did try to talk her out of it.'

'I thought you might have.'

'It's Tony I'm worried about.'

'I know. What am I gonna do, Pen?'

'I don't know, Mrs Taylor. I honestly haven't a clue.'

'Where are we going?' asked Joe as they stood at the bus stop.

'I thought we might have a look round the Cut – we've still got time before they close up. You never know, I might see something I fancy.'

'What are we looking for?'

Dolly's eyes were shining with happiness. 'Something for me to wear for my wedding.'

'I thought it was unlucky for the groom to see the dress before the wedding.'

'It won't be a proper wedding dress, so I shouldn't think that matters.'

Joe bent down and kissed her cheek. 'I'll have to buy you something *very* special for your wedding night.'

A shiver went down Dolly's back. 'I can't wait,' she whispered. 'This is our bus.'

When they sat down, Dolly thought about what Joe had said earlier this afternoon. When he had suggested they go to a hotel for the night and she had said no, he hadn't pressed her, or got upset. Tony got annoyed when she wouldn't let him have his way, but Joe said he would wait, if that's what she wanted.

She sat holding his hand. 'How long d'you think it'll be before we can get married?'

'I should think that this time next week we could be on our way to Scotland. Is that all right with you? I don't want to waste any precious moments apart from you.'

'Well, yes. I should think that'll be all right.'

Dolly's mind was working busily. Next Saturday. Did she really want to be alone when she got married? She wanted her mum to be sitting in the church wearing a big hat. She had always promised Penny she would be her bridesmaid, and she had pictured herself walking down the aisle in a long frock holding her dad's arm. Dolly knew that couldn't be, but she did want her mum at least to be around.

Joe patted her hand. 'Don't look so sad.'

'Sorry. I was just thinking about shoes. I hope I can get an outfit to match the shoes Mum bought me for me birthday.' Dolly was also thinking about Tony; she would write to him straight away. She didn't want him hearing it from Reg or from Rose, his sister. News like this would soon get around.

Tony sat in the field hospital waiting for news about Reg. It had been a long hard battle and he was weary. When he found Reg lying in a foxhole writhing in agony, he didn't hesitate but slung him on his back and made straight for the field hospital. Now he had lost contact with his mates and was fed up with all this fighting. He wanted to go home. He wanted to see Dolly and hold her tight; he wanted to see his mum again. He put his head in his hands. What was wrong with this sodding world? Why couldn't they all just be left in peace, to live out their lives?

An Army nurse came up to Tony. 'Your mate's asking for you,' she told him.

'Is he gonna be all right?'

'Yes, it's just a small wound. We'll have him fighting fit in no time.' She smiled and moved away.

Tony admired these young women; they were up at the front line almost as much as the soldiers. Some of them had been killed. This was a bloody wicked war. He stood tall and walked into the ward.

''Ello there, mate. Skiving off as usual?' Tony grinned at his friend who was lying face down.

'Don't bloody well laugh, it ain't funny.'

'It is from where I'm standing. How many blokes do you know who've got a bit of shrapnel in their arse?'

'Look, I don't want you writing and telling Dolly,' Reg said in a muffled voice. 'I don't want to be a laughing stock. It's bad enough being in here with all these young nurses having a good look at me arse.'

'There's some blokes that'd pay a fortune to have a young girl rub cream into their important parts.'

'Well, I ain't one of 'em.' Reg began to laugh. 'Mind you, it is rather nice. And Tone, thanks for carrying me all the way back.'

'That's all right, mate. You'd do the same for me.'

'Let's hope it never comes to that.'

'Yeah.'

Tony sat talking to his friend for a while, but knew he had to find his regiment and get back to the front. He patted Reg's shoulder. 'Take care, mate. I promise I won't say a word to Dolly.'

As he left the hospital, Tony's thoughts were on Dolly. He

wanted her so badly. As soon as this lot was over they'd get married, he decided. He wanted to settle down and have a family. When he arrived here at the field hospital, someone had found him a bed and after a bath he had felt human again. Sleep was something he had been deprived of for nights on end, when he did sleep, his dreams were all of Dolly.

Tony leaned against the side of a truck and lit a cigarette. Reg had been lucky, if you could call it that. If the shrapnel had touched his spine he could have been paralysed for the rest of his life. What would happen if I finish up a cripple? Tony asked himself. Would Dolly still want me then? It wouldn't be fair to tie her down; she was too full of life. He had to try to stay fit and well. Tony smiled to himself. After all, she needed a man who could give her the love she wanted and deserved. After a few more puffs he threw his fag down and ground it into the soft earth with his boot. Then he knew he had to find someone to get him back to his regiment otherwise he could be reported as a deserter.

Dolly and Joe wandered round the Cut looking in the windows of the few shops that were open and those that had a window. The sign *Business As Usual* was painted in big letters on the wood of those that had recently lost all their glass. Shops which did have windows had little or nothing to show off. The butcher's had a lovely display of parsley and photos of meat products and very little else. One or two dress-shops had a man or woman standing in the doorway trying to find customers for what little they had in stock.

Dolly stood admiring a smart blue suit that was displayed in one of the shops.

'Hello, there, love,' said a small, dapper-looking man who

began hovering when they stopped to peer in his window. He came closer. 'Looking for something nice for when you go out with your boyfriend? Lovely fellers these Yanks, got plenty of money to show you young ladies a good time.'

'I ain't got any coupons,' said Dolly sadly.

'That's a pity. That would look very nice on you.' He pointed to the suit.

'Don't even know if it's my size.'

'I think it is. Besides, you can always try it on.'

'Ain't any point.' She put her arm through Joe's.

'Hang on, hon. Do you like it?' Joe asked.

'Don't know, but it ain't any good without coupons.'

The little man coughed discreetly. 'Let's go inside and you can look at it properly, miss. You can even try it on.'

A quarter of an hour later, Dolly and Joe walked out of the shop with the suit in a paper bag.

'He was a right old shark charging you all that,' she said disgustedly.

'But it looked great. You just had to have it.'

'Thanks.' She kissed his cheek. 'And we didn't have any coupons.'

'Not to worry. I want my bride to look gorgeous. Right, where to now?'

'Don't mind – pictures, a drink? Whatever you want to do.'

Joe stopped and held her tight. 'You know what I want to do.'

'No, Joe. I'm sorry, but I want to wait till we're married.'

'OK. If that's what you want.'

'Yes, I do. I'm sorry, but that's the way I am.' Deep down Dolly was worried that if she gave in to him, he might not want to marry her – then who would want second-hand goods?

131

'Right, it's the movies then.'

'Thanks.'

'Next week I hope I shall be having my wicked way. Is it cold in Scotland at this time of year?'

'I don't think so. It should be fine and bright. I love the spring, not that we see a lot of it round Rotherhithe way now they've dug up all the parks for allotments. The only flowers we see now are the wild ones growing on the bombsites.'

'Gee, honey, you'll love Deansville. We have fields of flowers over there.'

'I can't wait.' Dolly had looked at the atlas and Joe had pointed out where he lived. He had told her all about the folks who lived there and about the stores and the things they did. Dolly had bombarded him with questions.

They sat on the bus and Dolly held her suit close.

Joe laughed. 'Are you frightened someone's going to steal it?'

'A bit. I can't wait to wear it,' she said excitedly.

'Can you get a week off work?'

'I'll take it anyway.'

'Good. A week in Scotland away from all this will be really great.'

'Yes,' said Dolly softly. But it would also mean a week away from her mother. And what about when she went to America? She would be thousands of miles away from Grace then. But that wouldn't happen till the war was finished and all the danger would be over then. And besides, Dad would be home to take care of her.

Chapter 15

Dolly pushed open the front door and stood at the bottom of the stairs. It was getting late, would her mother be in bed? When she noticed the light under the kitchen door, she knew Grace must still be up. Should she go and show her her wedding suit? No it would only cause more problems. She decided to take it upstairs and tell her mother about it later.

Grace looked up when Dolly walked into the kitchen. She watched her take off her hat and coat. 'You're late. Has he gone?'

Dolly said, very deliberately emphasising his name, 'Yes, *Joe's* had to go back to camp.'

'Oh. I thought he was on leave?'

'He is. He had to go to get our papers sorted out and get permission to marry me.'

'Can he marry you as you're under age?'

'His officer said he didn't think that was an American problem. It was up to the bride's parents.'

'Did he now.'

'He's not wanted here, is he?'

'Look Dolly, I'm sorry. But I don't want you to marry him.'

'I gathered that.' Dolly sat in the armchair.

'Would you really go against my wishes and elope to Scotland?'

'Yes.'

Grace felt uncomfortable and couldn't think of anything to say that wouldn't cause more arguments. Why couldn't her daughter see that this was all wrong. 'Where have you been today?'

'Shopping and the pictures. Don't worry, we ain't been to some sleazy hotel so that he could have his wicked way.'

'Dolly, don't talk like that.'

'I can't help it, Mum.'

'Did you buy anything?'

'Yes. Mum, I want you to be at my wedding.'

'And I want me and your dad to be at your wedding when you marry Tony. I want to make your dress and be proud of you. I want all the neighbours to come out and give you all their good wishes.'

Dolly put her hands over her ears. 'Stop it. Stop it.' She began to cry.

'I'm sorry, love.'

'No, you're not. Can't you see how hard this is for me?' she sobbed. 'I never wanted to fall in love with someone else. Why did this war have to happen and Joe walk into my life?' She stood up. 'I'm going to bed.'

Grace leapt to her feet. 'Can't you see how hard this is for me as well?' She went to put her arms round Dolly, but her daughter quickly stepped back.

'Leave me alone.'

Grace sank back in the chair. 'Do you want some cocoa?' was all she could think of to say.

'No, thanks.' At the door Dolly turned. 'By the way, you might be interested to know I bought me suit for me wedding today.' With that statement she hurriedly left the room.

Grace sat open-mouthed. Tears filled her eyes. She was losing her daughter. What should she do? What would Jim do? Should she give in?

Upstairs Dolly looked at the suit hanging in her wardrobe. Like her mother she too had wanted a white wedding with all the trimmings, but it wasn't to be. She closed the door, got undressed and snuggled down in bed. Soon she would have Joe beside her with his arms round her holding her close and keeping her safe. The thought of him making love to her sent a shiver down her spine and any doubts she might have had about marrying him were quickly pushed to the back of her mind.

On Monday evening Joe was waiting outside the factory gate. Dolly ran into his open arms. He held her tight and kissed her. Dolly didn't care about the cat-calls and shouts she was getting. This was her future husband.

'Well?' she asked when they broke away.

'All the wheels have been set in motion.' He patted his jacket pocket. 'We've got a few forms to fill in, it's just a formality. So, young lady, it looks like it's Gretna Green for us.'

Penny had come up behind them. 'Hello, Joe.'

He put his arm round Dolly's waist. 'Hi, Penny. Well – are you going to congratulate us then?'

'Why? What for?'

'This gorgeous creature here and I are to be married.'

'But I thought . . .' Penny's face was full of consternation.

'We're going to Scotland. You can get married up there without your parents' consent,' Dolly informed her.

'Oh Dolly. What about your mum?'

Dolly didn't answer her.

As they walked home together Penny wanted to ask them

so many questions. She was hurt and upset that she wouldn't be with Dolly, her best mate, when she got married. She wouldn't be her bridesmaid. It wasn't fair. They had talked so many times about their weddings and who would get married first. Had it all been a silly childish dream?

Grace was sitting at the table when Dolly and Joe walked in. Dolly could see by the ashtray that her mother had smoked a few cigarettes.

'Hello,' said Grace light-heartedly. 'All right then?'

'Yes, thanks,' said Dolly offhandedly.

'Are you staying in tonight or are you going out?'

'We're staying in. I've got some forms to fill in if I'm getting married and I've got to see a doctor.'

Grace was filled with alarm. 'Why?'

'It's just a formality, Mrs Taylor.'

'They just want to make sure I'm alive,' joked Dolly, trying to ease the situation.

'So you're going ahead with this then?'

Joe put his hat on the chair. 'Mrs Taylor, I know you don't like me and I wish there was some way I could prove to you that I love Dolly so much that I want her to be my wife. When I'm stuck in some godforsaken place I want to think of her and know she's mine and waiting for me.'

'So does Tony,' was the cutting remark from Grace.

'It's no good, Joe. You ain't gonna convince her,' said Dolly.

'I'm real sorry about that. By the way, I've got some chocolate bars and a few tins of fruit and a couple of bars of soap for you. Dolly told me that soap's in short supply.' Joe put his gas-mask case on the table and began removing the gifts.

'I can't be bought, young man.'

Dolly was getting angry. 'Mum, stop being so nasty! What is it with you?'

'Nothing. Get yourselves something to eat. I've got to go fire-watching.'

'I hope you've got the right shift this time.'

'Yes, I have. Goodnight.' Grace collected her tin hat and walked down the street. Tears slipped down her cheeks. She was going to lose her daughter. If only Mary was on duty tonight, at least she would have a shoulder to cry on.

After Joe had left, Dolly sat and wrote to Tony. She knew she had to tell him before his mother or Rose found out. It was a hard letter to write and many pages were thrown away before she found the right words. Next she would have to tell Mrs Marchant before informing the neighbours. Why did life have to get so complicated?

The rest of the week Joe met Dolly after work and they usually went to a pub to discuss their wedding plans as the atmosphere at number twenty Wood Street was getting almost unbearable. Apart from the endless forms they had to fill in, everything was going well and they hoped that in another week, it would all be finalised. Joe was anxious about the wait, because all the while there was a real fear that he could be recalled. For Dolly, she hoped the delay would give her mother time to accept Joe.

'I can't believe you're going up north to get married,' said Betty when Dolly announced their plans. 'It sounds ever so romantic.'

'Yes, but what about when she gets back and he goes off? Her mum ain't gonna be best pleased with her,' said Penny.

'Will you stop being such a wet blanket,' Dolly said irritably. 'I've got enough to put up with at home.'

'Well, I still can't believe it,' said Jane. 'You sure you ain't up the spout?'

'No, I'm not.' Dolly was getting fed up with all the comments and she would be glad when next week was here and she and Joe would be on their way to Gretna Green.

All week Dolly had tried to see Tony's mum, but Mrs Marchant was always out doing her good deeds.

On Saturday lunchtime when Joe caught sight of Dolly leaving the factory, he rushed to meet her and waved a piece of paper at her. 'Here it is! This tells me I can marry Miss Dorothy Taylor.' He then picked her up and whirled her round and round.

Dolly was laughing with him. She felt her heart miss a beat. It was true. It was really going to happen. She was going to marry Joe. 'I suppose we'd better go and break the news to Mum.'

'When can we leave?' asked Joe.

'How much more time off have you got?'

'Nine days.'

'Nine days,' repeated Dolly. 'We can go on Tuesday. I have warned Mr Freeman, but I must tell him properly. I can't just go off like that.'

'That's my girl, always likes to do the right thing. I do love you.'

Dolly put her arm through Joe's and headed for home. She knew this would break her mother's heart, but Dolly would still be coming back home. It was just that she would be wearing a wedding ring.

That morning, Grace, who couldn't contain her curiosity any longer, opened Dolly's wardrobe door. She gasped as she put out her hand and touched her daughter's wedding suit. Tears filled her eyes. It was the most beautiful shade of blue and with Dolly's colouring it would look perfect. How could she not give in? Why was life so unfair?

When Dolly pushed open the kitchen door she was surprised to find the table was laid very nicely for three people. 'Mum?' she called out.

Grace came in from the scullery.

'Who's coming to tea?' asked Dolly.

'Joe is. Sit yourself down, young man.'

Joe shrugged at Dolly and did as he was told.

Grace disappeared into the scullery with Dolly close behind. 'What's going on?' she demanded.

'Nothing. I just thought it would be nice to get to know him – Joe.'

'Why?'

'Just go and sit with him. I'll bring the tea things in.'

Dolly went and sat next to Joe. 'I don't know what she's playing at.'

Joe took hold of her hand. 'Don't worry. Perhaps I'm for the third degree.' He grinned and held up his hands. 'I surrender.'

Dolly was laughing when Grace walked in. She smiled and sat down.

'First of all I must apologise for my behaviour.'

Dolly's mouth dropped open.

'So when are you going away?'

'Tuesday. We're off to Scotland and we've got a special licence. We can be married in a few days,' said Dolly softly.

'That's a bit quick.'

'I'm afraid we can't hang about,' said Joe. 'It looks like my lot could be shifted out real soon.' He took Dolly's hand and kissed it.

'I must admit I don't want you to marry my daughter.'

'You can't stop me, not now,' said Dolly.

'I know, and I've been giving this situation a lot of thought. As you both seem so determined to go ahead with this crazy idea, I've decided to give my consent.'

Dolly couldn't speak and for a few moments Joe too was speechless.

'Thank you, Mrs Taylor. I promise I'll look after Dolly and love her for the rest of my days.'

'You'd better.'

'Joe, does that mean we can be married here? Here in Rotherhithe?' Dolly's eyes were wide with excitement.

'Why not, hon. Mrs Taylor, you won't regret this day.'

'I hope not.'

Dolly went to her mother and with tears streaming down her face held her close. 'Thank you, Mum. I couldn't bear it if you wasn't at my wedding.'

'The same here,' said Grace. She was trying hard to keep the tears back.

Dolly sat down and wiped her eyes. 'What made you change your mind?'

'Your suit. It's very nice and such a lovely shade of blue, it should look perfect and I wanted to see you wearing it. Pity we ain't got time to get you all dolled up with a long white frock.'

'It doesn't matter, Mum. Thank you. I can't tell you how happy you've made me.'

Although Grace was trying to put a brave face on things, she had a very sad heart. This wasn't what she wanted for her daughter.

On Saturday morning, 20 May 1944, Dolly was standing alone in her bedroom. She was meeting Joe at eleven o'clock outside the register office. Penny and Betty were downstairs talking to her mother. What a contrast this was to Betty's wedding. She pushed back the tears. This was what she wanted. She wanted to marry Joe. He was the most exciting thing that had ever happened in her life and she loved him. She could hear her mother coming up the stairs. Dolly quickly looked in the mirror and adjusted her hat.

'Penny and Betty are downstairs,' said Grace, as she opened the bedroom door.

'I know, I could hear them.'

'You look very nice.'

'Thank you.'

'Dolly, are you . . .'

'Don't, Mum. Please don't upset me. This is my day, remember.'

Grace went and held her close. 'I just want you to be sure.'

'I am sure.'

When they left the house to get into the taxi, Penny's mum and her brothers, along with the two Miss Gregorys, were standing at the gate.

'All the best, Dolly love,' said Miss Ada.

'You look really lovely,' said Miss May.

'Good luck,' said Penny's mother, Mrs Watts.

'Thank you,' said Dolly as she quickly got into the taxi.

Everything had happened so fast and to everybody's surprise and shock. Penny and Betty were the only two friends who had been invited to the wedding.

Joe was standing at the top of the steps with the best man. As the taxi drew up he rushed down to meet his bride. He kissed her and held her close for a moment or two before turning to the man next to him.

'This is Guy,' said Joe, introducing his best man to Dolly.

Dolly smiled broadly. 'Thank you for coming.'

Guy nodded. 'My pleasure, ma'am.'

Guy passed Joe the corsage he was holding and as Joe pinned it onto Dolly's suit, he whispered, 'I love you.' He put his arm round her waist as they made their way into the register office.

After the ceremony they left for a meal in a hotel. There wasn't going to be a fancy reception or honeymoon, as Joe had to report back to camp on Monday. It seemed that everybody's leave had been cancelled.

When the other four members of the party left, the newlyweds were alone.

They went to their room and Joe took her in his arms and kissed her. 'You look gorgeous. I couldn't take my eyes off you. I was thinking that I can't believe that you belong to me.'

'I just wish these two days could go on for ever.'

Joe kissed her gently at first, then with a passion Dolly had never known before. She loved him and she knew he loved her. As they explored each other's bodies, they soared to heights of pleasure, and Dolly knew that she wanted to spend the rest of her life with Joe, making love.

Dolly had decided that after saying goodbye to Joe she would go straight back to work. There wasn't any point in staying at home.

'So that's why you had Friday off,' said Jane when Dolly went back to work on the Tuesday. 'Penny here was just telling me you got married Saturday. That true?'

'Yes.'

'Well, you're a dark horse and no mistake. You sure you ain't up the spout?'

'No, I'm not.'

'Leave it out, Jane,' said Penny. 'Can't you see she's upset?'

'Why, ain't he very good at it?'

'You and your big mouth. For your information, Joe's had to go back to camp. Looks like this second front could be starting real soon.'

'Sorry,' said Jane, walking away.

Everybody knew there was something in the air, and the Americans would be fighting alongside the British.

'I'm glad you asked me to your wedding,' said Betty, coming up to them and trying to ease the situation. 'I think Jane might be a bit put out about not being asked.'

'Well, it was very quick, and I just wanted my real friends there, but it was all right.' Dolly knew it wasn't all right. She had wanted a wedding like Betty's, with a proper wedding breakfast, not just Joe, his friend Guy who was his best man, someone she didn't even know, her mother, Betty and Penny in a restaurant, even if it was in a posh hotel. She wanted her dad to be there to hold her hand and give her away, and she wanted a honeymoon. In some ways she wished they had gone to Scotland; at least she would have had a change of scenery.

'Didn't she look nice,' said Penny to Betty.

'She looked really smashing,' said Betty.

'Thanks for coming. It must have been hard for you. And thanks for letting me borrow your hat,' said Dolly quickly. She noticed at the wedding that Betty had been trying to put a brave face on things. Had she been wrong to invite her? Was it too soon after her wedding and losing Chuck?

'That's all right. You had to have something borrowed.'

Dolly had been a bit superstitious about wearing Betty's hat; she prayed that her husband wouldn't have the same fate as Chuck.

'That was a lovely suit and such a lovely colour.'

'I only hope it ain't too long before I wear it again. I promised Joe I'd wear it when he comes home.'

There was a short uneasy silence. Then Betty said quietly, 'I wish you both all the happiness in the world.'

'Thanks,' said Dolly.

As she worked she thought about Joe. She loved him so much and to have his arms around her for the two nights they had spent in the hotel had been bliss. She desperately prayed that he would come back safe.

That evening when Dolly and Grace were having their tea there was a loud rat-a-tat-tat on the front door.

They looked at each other.

'I'll go,' said Grace.

Dolly sat listening and soon realised who it was who was doing the screaming and shouting. She hurried up the passage just as her mother was shutting the front door behind Rose and her mother.

'How could you?' yelled Rose when she caught sight of Dolly. Grace was gently easing her along the passage.

'What about my Tony?' sniffed Mrs Marchant.

When they reached the kitchen Grace told them to sit down.

'I'm surprised at you, Mrs Taylor, giving your consent.'

'I'm sorry, Mrs Marchant, I should have told you. I have tried to catch you in, but it all happened so quickly,' said Dolly.

'I suppose you're expecting?' sneered Rose, looking at Dolly's stomach.

'No, I'm not. Why does everyone think that?'

'Could be because it was done in such a hurry.'

'For your information, it was because Joe has had to go away.'

'And I suppose you couldn't wait to get your hands on his allowance? I've heard it's very good, much better than our poor blokes and their wives get.'

'Rose,' said Grace quietly. 'I think you've said enough.'

'I presume you're going to write and tell my brother that you've deserted him?' said Rose, ignoring Grace's request.

'I already have.'

'Well, that's one thing in your favour. I shall be writing to him myself tonight, my lady!'

'Dolly,' said Mrs Marchant, dabbing at her eyes. 'Why didn't you tell me? I felt such a fool hearing about it in the grocer's. Gawd knows what Tony's going to say.'

'I'm really sorry about that. I should have told you. I did come up a couple of times before but you were both out.'

'Would you like a cup of tea?' asked Grace.

'No, thanks all the same but I'm on duty tonight.' Mrs Marchant smiled reluctantly. 'I'm down the Underground seeing to the tea. Even though the raids have eased up, a lot of people still go down there. I think they like the company. It's almost like a second home for some of them. Come on, Rose.' She stood up wearily.

'I'll see you out,' said Grace and opened the kitchen door.

When she returned, she sighed, 'Well, we should have expected that.'

'I know. I feel awful not telling Mrs Marchant.' Dolly's face was pale.

'Let's hope your letter reaches Tony before that Rose gets her oar in.'

'Yes, I hope so too.' Dolly had written and told Tony all about Joe. She said how much she had been missing him, and when Joe came along she just fell in love. She hoped they would always be friends and that he would meet a nice girl one day.

Chapter 16

The fighting had eased and Tony and Reg were back behind the line waiting for new orders. Tony was lying on his back staring up at what was left of the once painted ceiling. He was taking a well-earned rest on a bunk in a house his regiment had commandeered. It upset him to see that so many beautiful houses had finished up as shells. What about back home? How many houses were still standing in Wood Street? Although Dolly kept him up to date with all that was happening, he knew she still had to keep some of the horrors from him through censorship and out of consideration for his peace of mind. He looked up when Reg popped his head round the door. His mate stood in the doorway sniffing the letters he was holding.

'Mail's caught up with us. And it smells good. Looks like it's your lucky day. You've got two from Dolly.'

Tony jumped up. He loved Dolly's letters; they were always full of what she'd being doing and where she'd been, although Tony had noticed that the last few hadn't been as loving as they usually were. 'Did you get any?' he asked Reg.

'A couple from me mum, she's a good old stick.'

Tony had known Mrs Smith all his life. She was a nice friendly woman who thought the world of her son. 'Nothing from Pen then?'

'Nah, she ain't as good as Dolly for writing.'

Tony tore open one of the envelopes and began reading.

'You all right, mate?' said Reg. 'You ain't arf gone a funny colour.'

Tony sat down heavily on his bunk. He looked up at Reg and said in utter disbelief, 'She's gone and got married.'

'What?' yelled Reg. 'Got married? Who the bloody hell to?'

'A Yank called Joe,' said Tony softly.

'A Yank?' Reg almost spat the word out as he sat next to Tony. 'How long has it been going on?'

Tony handed Reg the letter and lit a cigarette.

'You had no idea she was seeing this bloke?' asked Reg after reading Dolly's letter.

Tony shook his head. 'Unless there's something in this one.' He threw the unopened letter to the floor. 'Ain't no point in reading it.'

'Looks like she'll be going to America when this lot is all over,' said Reg.

'She always was a silly cow, a right dreamer, always talking about the places her dad'd been to and that she wanted to see,' Tony burst out bitterly. 'D'you reckon that why she's married him?'

'Dunno. Don't upset yourself.'

'Why not? I've got every right to upset meself as you so delicately put it. I'm not just upset, I'm bloody angry. How could she do this to me?'

'D'you know, I reckon that's why I ain't had a letter from Pen. She's frightened I'd hear about it first. Christ, I hope *she* ain't run off with some bloody Yank.'

'Shouldn't think so, she would have told you. Besides, Penny's a bit more sensible and loyal.'

'I hope so.'

'What am I gonna do?'

'Just forget her. There's plenty more fish in the sea.'

'I loved her. This bloody sodding war.' Tony banged his hand hard on the table. 'We could have been married be now if I'd still been home.'

Reg picked the other letter up off the floor and put it on the bed, then helped himself to one of Tony's fags. 'You gonna read this one?'

He shook his head. 'Waste of time.'

This was something every serviceman dreaded. Reg walked away. He couldn't find any words to comfort his friend.

6 June 1944 was the day everyone had been waiting for. D-Day. Dolly and the rest of the world listened to the wireless telling them that the second front had started. British and American troops had landed in France.

Dolly knew Joe had been kept in Britain for a while longer, and she prayed that he was still here. She knew he was in administration, so perhaps he was, although she had only had a couple of letters since he went back. He had warned her they could have a blanket on all mail.

Day after day the wireless told them how much progress was being made in France. When Dolly and Penny went to the pictures it was only the Pathé News that Dolly was interested in. Somewhere out there could be her beloved Joe. They had both written to his mother and brother telling them about the wedding. Dolly was still waiting for the reply.

It was later on that month that Dolly and Penny were walking home from the pictures when an unfamiliar sound filled the air. It was moonlight and they stopped to watch the dark object in the sky that had flames pouring out of its back.

Dolly clapped her hands. 'Look – they've shot down a plane.'

Penny too was grinning. 'A good job an' all. Mind you, I didn't know there was a raid on. Ain't heard no siren or ack ack guns.'

'No. They didn't put it up on the screen.'

As they watched, they began to realise that the object was too small for a plane. When the engine cut out they both knew this was no plane coming down. When it hit the ground and the explosion sent smoke billowing up, they were full of fear.

Grace was out fire-watching when Dolly got home, but as soon as she heard her mother return she jumped out of bed.

'Thank God you're all right,' said Dolly.

'I've been so worried about *you*, wondering which picture-house you went to.'

'What was that thing?' asked Dolly fearfully.

'It's a flying bomb.'

'What?'

'It seems Hitler's sending over a new menace.'

'But I thought the war was nearly over!'

'Oh, no, it's not. They were saying at the post tonight that Hitler's getting desperate.'

'We're not going to have more raids, are we?'

'Looks like it.'

The objects in the sky were a new source of fear; the flying bombs came to be known as doodlebugs and Hitler was sending them over thick and fast. When the engine cut out, the fear was apparent on everyone's face. They soon learned that if they counted after the engine stopped, the higher number they got to, the further away it was likely to drop.

In July the raids were beginning again in earnest and

once more it was back and forth to the shelters, gas mains cut and power lines down. Some mornings the paraffin stove had to be used again to boil a kettle and it took for ever. At the factory they had lookouts on the roof telling them that a doodlebug was heading their way and the girls had to rush off to shelter double quick.

'I'm getting fed up with this lark,' grumbled Jane when they had been down to the shelter three times that day.

'It's them things coming over in the night that put the wind up me,' said Penny.

'And it's those bloody ack ack guns that frighten the life out of *me*,' Jane shuddered. 'I'm sure we've got one that stands right outside our house at night.'

'I reckon they know there's a good-looking tart lives there,' said Penny.

''Ere, not so much of the tart,' laughed Jane.

'Dolly, you're very quiet,' said Betty. 'Is everything all right?'

She nodded. 'Mum had a letter from Dad yesterday. He ain't very happy about me getting married.'

'Don't suppose he is,' said Penny.

'What did Tony have to say about it? Have you heard from him?' Jane asked.

Dolly shook her head. 'Shouldn't think he'll write to me any more.'

'Well, you can't blame him,' said Penny.

Dolly felt full of guilt. She knew Tony wouldn't write to her any more, but Penny would keep her informed if anything happened to him or Reg.

The ground slowly lifted and a cloud of dust rose then settled, making them cough.

'Christ, that was close,' said Jane.

'Just think of the blast if the factory went up,' said Betty.

'Christ, you're a right wet blanket. D'you know,' said Jane, settling back, 'I've been thinking about joining up.'

'No!' said Penny. 'What in?'

'Quite fancy the Air Force. The uniform ain't half bad and there's some right good-looking blokes in that lot.'

'You've left it a bit late,' said Dolly. 'The war's nearly over.'

'Don't think it is,' said Jane. 'Not with this lot he's sending over. Hitler ain't gonna give in that easy.'

When the all clear went they filed out of the shelter till the next time.

Every day the news from abroad was getting better as the Army slowly gained ground on all fronts. Dolly had had a very short letter from Joe, and as it had mud on it, she suspected he could be over in France.

She had also received a letter from Bob, Joe's brother. He said how happy they were to hear that Joe had got married, although his Ma was upset she wasn't there. They were all looking forward to welcoming her to America when this war was over.

Dolly sat looking at the letter. America. It was a long way away. She would miss her parents, and would she like it over there? More importantly, would his family like her? And would she fit in? Joe had told her he lived on a farm, and Dolly couldn't see herself milking cows. She knew from the correspondence she'd had from the US Army and the dozens of forms she'd had to fill in, that all the wheels were being set in motion for her to go one day.

It was the middle of July. Dolly got out of bed. She wasn't feeling very well and had to run to the bathroom, where she was sick. She sat on the floor, breathing deeply. Thank goodness they had a bathroom; their landlord was good and had converted the small back bedroom into a bathroom, so they didn't have to go out in the cold to the lav. This had confirmed Dolly's fear. She was having a baby. She had missed two periods but put that down to the excitement of getting married and all the upset of the war and Joe going away. But now she knew for certain. She sat and counted the months on her fingers. February 1945 – she would be a mother next year in February. Was that what she wanted? If this war was over by then, would it put her to the back of the queue to go to America? Half of her was thrilled and the other half was full of anguish. She sat remembering what Betty had said, how much she wished she'd had a baby, something that was part of Chuck. Now Dolly had something that was part of Joe, but was it what she really wanted? And what about when Joe came home? She wanted him to herself, not to share him with a baby. Was that being selfish? They had talked about a family, but not till they were together and settled.

'You all right, love?' Grace was knocking on the door.

'Yes, I'll be out in a minute.' How long had her mother been outside the door? Had she heard her vomiting? What should she tell her? Should she wait till she had seen a doctor and was really sure? Dolly wiped her mouth and opened the door.

'You took your time. Your breakfast is on the table.' Grace said as Dolly hurried past her.

Dolly sat looking at the tea and toast. She didn't think she could stomach it.

When Grace walked into the kitchen she said, 'What's up with you? You ain't touched your breakfast.'

'I don't feel like it.' Dolly put on her coat and hat. ''Sides, I ain't really got time. I best be off.'

As Dolly closed the door Grace sat at the table with her worst fears filling her head. Was Dolly expecting? Had she heard her being sick, or was that all in her mind? She did look very pasty. God, she hoped not. Her daughter was still only eighteen and there was a war on. Why hadn't her husband been more considerate? What if anything happened to him? Who would look after poor Dolly? As Grace sat thinking, a slight smile slowly lifted her troubled face. Mind you, it'd be rather nice to be a grandmother. She wouldn't pry; she would wait till Dolly told her. But what if she went to America? She would never see her grandchild again. Grace got up from the table and quickly cleared the dirty crocks away. Tears filled her eyes. Life was so bloody cruel.

'You're very quiet,' said Penny as they walked to work.

'Sorry. I was deep in thought.'

'You all right? You look ever so pale.'

'Yes, I'm fine.'

Penny had known Dolly too long to see that she wasn't fine. What had happened? Had Tony written and been nasty? No, that wasn't Tony's way. But she knew there was something troubling her friend; perhaps the new in-laws didn't approve of their son marrying an English girl. 'Have you heard any more from Joe?' she asked lightly.

'No. I expect he's too busy to write.'

'I heard from Reg. He said Tony's very upset at your getting married.'

'I expect he is.'

'Dolly, for Christ's sake, what is it?'

'Here's our bus, come on.'

Penny wasn't going to let the subject drop. As soon as they sat down she said, 'I saw Tony's mum last night. She ain't very happy about this.'

'I know and I don't care. This is my life and I can do as I please.'

'All right, keep yer hair on. It's just that a lot of people are disappointed about it and they're worried that you might not have made the right decision.'

'Penny Watts, if you don't shut up, I'll go and sit on me own.'

'OK.' Penny knew she wasn't going to find out what was troubling her friend just at the moment and that was to be the end of this conversation for today. But Penny was determined to find out her friend's problem. If it was anything to do with that Yankee husband of hers, he'd have *her* to answer to!

Chapter 17

Joe was weary. Although he was in administration and back from the front line he was still in the thick of it. The noise from the planes, guns, men screaming and shouting out in pain was neverending. Sights he was being subjected to were sickening. He should be used to it after his stint in the jungle, but how can anyone get used to the stench of death and destruction? Bodies and the wounded, some barely alive, then there were men with limbs missing. God, it was a damn awful job. He had to collect nametags and list as many bodies as he could, ready to be sent back across the Channel. Some of them were so young and hadn't even stepped ashore.

He hadn't come over with the first wave; his was an office job. He looked around. At the moment this was his office, the back of a truck. He had to try and get a letter to Dolly. God, how he loved her and missed her. He sat thinking of the two wonderful nights he'd spent with her. When this lot was all over he'd take her to see the sights of New York. Perhaps they could even get to Niagara Falls – that's if Ma could spare him. Why had her letters not mentioned his marriage and Dolly? Was she still hoping he'd marry Sandra? Sandra knew he didn't think of her in that way; she was silly and giggly. No, no one but his dear,

dear Dolly could steal his heart and he was aching to see her again.

Joe was brought back to reality when someone started yelling for him. More bodies had been brought back from the front. They were in body bags, and as he tied the labels to the bags, he felt it was almost like delivering a parcel. This was a goddamn awful war, but the end must be in sight now.

Sunday morning Dolly knew the time had come for her to tell her mother she was expecting. Every morning for the past week she had been sick and every morning her mother had looked at her suspiciously and made her feel guilty. Dolly also knew she had to go and see the doctor. Expectant mothers were given green ration books to get certain extras, so now everybody would know.

Slowly Dolly made her way down the stairs. Her mother was sitting at the table.

'There's tea in the pot.'

'Thanks, I'll pour it out later.'

'You don't look very well, are you sure you're all right?'

'I'm having a baby,' said Dolly softly.

Grace put out her cigarette and said quietly, 'I guessed as much.'

'Is that all you can say?'

'What do you want me to say?'

'I thought you might be a bit pleased?'

'Why? I ain't gonna see it once you get over there, am I?'

Dolly shook her head.

'Do you want it?'

Dolly's head shot up. 'Course!'

'Won't it upset his family?'

'Why should it?'

'Well, will they want a baby cluttering up the place?'

'Mum, why are you being so horrible? Can't you see I'm upset that Joe won't be with me?'

Grace went to Dolly and held her close. 'I'm sorry, love. It's just that I don't want you to go away. I want me and your dad to be here when it's born. Course I'm thrilled at the thought of being a granny, but I want to be there when—' Grace stopped. What was the point – she shouldn't upset her daughter. She kissed Dolly's tear-stained cheek. 'Does Pen know?'

Dolly shook her head. 'I wanted to tell you first.'

Grace smiled. 'Thanks, that was nice of you. Have you been to see the doctor?'

'No,' croaked Dolly.

'We'll go together tomorrow – that's if you want me to come with you?'

Dolly gave her a watery smile. 'Yes, please. I'd like that.'

Grace gave her a hug. 'At least you'll get extra rations.' She was smiling, but her heart was heavy.

'I know. There'll be no way of keeping it a secret.'

'Do you want to?'

Dolly shook her head.

Soon the news of Dolly's forthcoming baby was all round the factory. Penny was over the moon when Dolly suggested she could be a Godmother. Betty offered her her congratulations, but Dolly could see her heart wasn't in it. Jane thought she was mad, and told her so. The two Miss Gregorys were happy for her, but Dolly knew they wished it had been Tony's.

The doodlebugs were coming over thick and fast now and everybody was getting very war-weary. When Dolly had a letter from Joe telling her how thrilled he was at the prospect of becoming a dad, that helped to lift some of her fears. If only he was around to hold her and make love to her.

In September there were some very strange explosions in London. They were told that gasometers had been blown up. It was a while before the government admitted that this was another new menace. V2 rockets just fell out of the sky without any noise or warning. People were very distressed about this latest development and wondered with all the fighting in France, why the end still wasn't in sight.

'Don't know why they can't find the sites. Thought our boys would know where they were and bomb 'em to kingdom come,' said Mr Freeman.

'They move 'em about,' said Jane, looking up from the newspaper. 'It says here they can move the sites.'

Dolly was impressed that she took time to read anything that was that interesting. Jane had changed since being turned down for the Forces. She told everybody it was because she had flat feet, but both Penny and Dolly suspected it was something else she had and it had quietened her down. She was no longer the same old Jane.

As the winter drew on, when Dolly looked in the mirror at her bump, she gently stroked it. Her baby was growing inside and she felt at ease with the idea. Even her mother had started knitting tiny garments. On cold winter nights they would sit huddled round the fire, listening to the wireless, talking and knitting and discussing babies' names. Dolly was pleased her mother was taking a real interest; they were becoming very close.

Joe's brother Bob, had written and told her how much they were looking forward to the baby. As Dolly read the letter she wondered why his mother never wrote to her. Was she disappointed Joe hadn't married an American?

In November, as Dolly was not going to celebrate her nineteenth birthday, Penny suggested they went up West to the pictures.

'Can't go to a dance, not with that sticking out,' she joked, pointing to Dolly's stomach.

'Wouldn't be able to get a bloke near me. Besides, I don't walk now, I waddle. No, I reckon the flicks would be great.'

As they wandered around the West End the two girls talked about when the lights would finally all go on again. Even though the war was still raging in Europe it seemed weird that the government had partly lifted the ban on the blackout. People could now see to read on the buses and trains at night. It was only the coast that still had to be completely blacked out.

'I can't wait to show Joe what London really looks like.'

'It's a bit battered, but it's still the best place in the world. Sorry, I didn't mean that. Well, you know what I mean.' Penny knew that Joe had promised to take Dolly to New York and even Niagara, if they had the time. Dolly said she had wondered about him saying if they had the time; perhaps the farm was a lot bigger than he let on.

'D'you fancy coming Christmas shopping next week?' asked Dolly.

'Got anywhere interesting in mind?'

'Not really. It's the same everywhere, there's nothing much in any of the shops.'

'OK. Shall we go straight from work?'

'Why not.'

The following Saturday Dolly wasn't feeling too well and she didn't fancy traipsing round the shops desperately trying to find some sort of present, so they decided to wait till the following week.

When they left work on Saturday they didn't want to go too far, so they settled on going to New Cross, which was just a bus ride away.

Dolly and Penny left the bus and were busy chatting away when suddenly their world exploded.

Grace looked around the front room. This was a cold damp room, but with Christmas coming along she thought she'd try and give it a bit of a spruce-up. Perhaps she could get the old paper chains out – they were looking a bit tatty but she might be able to do something with them. She wished Jim was here to look at the fairy lights, as they never worked at first. Every Christmas they'd had a tree with lights and baubles, but because of the war that had all stopped; it didn't seem right to have paper chains and lights. Next year would be different. Jim would be home God willing, and there would be the new baby to buy for. Her thoughts went to Dolly and she hoped that her daughter would be here for a while. She wanted to get to hold and love her grandchild, but would Dolly be around next Christmas?

Grace felt sad, but quickly admonished herself. She looked round the room, pleased with the new curtains she'd made and just hung. Thank goodness the government gave out dockets for the material after bomb damage; the last lot had been ripped to shreds when the windows were blown out. Perhaps she and Dolly could spend Christmas night in here. It'd be cosy with the fire and they could bring the wireless in. Even with a coal shortage Grace knew she could manage an extra fire for just one night. It would be nice to sit in a comfortable armchair for a change. Grace knew Dolly was finding it difficult to sit for too long in the wooden armchair in the kitchen. So with a duster, brush and pan, she set to. Suddenly there was an explosion. The sound filled her ears and the house rocked, and Grace could see the window slowly and visibly bend into the room. She jumped back expecting it to fall in, but to her great relief it stayed in one piece. When the soot fell from the chimney all over her clean hearth, she cursed. Now she had to clear this room up yet again. She then felt guilty; she knew that must have been a V2. Poor buggers. At least when one of them hit you, it was all over quick.

Grace went to the front door and like everybody else in Wood Street, stood looking at the pall of black smoke that had risen above the houses.

'Looks like it's over New Cross way,' said May Gregory.

Mrs Watts held on to Grace's arm. 'The girls! I'm sure Pen said they were going over that way shopping.'

Grace felt her knees buckle. 'No. I don't think they would have got there yet. You know what the buses are like. Besides, they may have changed their minds.'

'You all right, Mrs Taylor?' asked Miss Gregory.

'It's Penny and Dolly. We think they was going shopping over that way.'

'It might be a bit further over than New Cross. Distance can be very deceiving.'

'Mum, shall we go and look?' asked Billy, the younger of Penny's brothers.

'No, don't. You'll only get in the way. Besides, Jerry might send another one over.'

Grace sat on the coping wall, feeling bemused. She was trying to remember what Dolly had told her. Were they going somewhere else first? She suddenly stood up. 'I'm going over that way. If they get home before me, tell them to stay put.'

'Is that wise?' asked Ada Gregory, still looking towards the smoke.

'I can't sit here wondering. I'll call in at the Wardens' post first, just to find out where it fell.'

'Be careful,' said Mrs Watts.

As Grace hurried to New Cross her one thought was for Dolly. '*Please God*,' she silently prayed, '*don't let anything happen to her or her baby*.'

Chapter 18

Penny slowly opened her eyes. What was she doing, lying on the cold ground? She shuddered; she hurt all over. Her head was on one side and it hurt like hell. She couldn't see anything. She felt something wet and sticky on her face and ran her hand across her forehead; it was blood, her blood. What had happened? She was bewildered. Her eyes were smarting from all the dust and smoke; she seemed to be in the middle of a thick fog. Her lungs felt as if they were full of dust and she was having trouble breathing. Someone was moaning – she suddenly realised it was her. All around her came sound. There was a lot of noise. There was screaming, yelling, and crying. People seemed to be rushing about and shouting. Penny felt her head was going to explode. Where was she? What had happened? She vaguely remembered she was with Dolly. Dolly? Where was Dolly? Her mind was in a muddle. Penny struggled to sit up.

'You all right, gel?' shouted a warden as he hurried past.

'I think so.'

'If you can't walk I'll send someone over to look at you. The Red Cross should be here in a tick.'

Penny was trying to clear her head and get everything in focus. Despite the pain, she slowly got to her knees and looked around. It was carnage. Then after a moment or two she managed to get to her feet. Her legs felt all wobbly. Every bone in her body hurt. She felt as if she had been used as a punch bag. Where was Dolly? She began to stagger towards a heap of clothes. It was Dolly. She was lying very still. Tears filled Penny's eyes as she went down on her knees beside her friend. She wasn't moving. Penny gathered her up in her arms and wept. Her tears made clean streaks down her face as they fell onto Dolly.

The bus conductor rang the bell for the bus to go a couple of times, but it remained stationary.

'Bleeding drivers. What's up with him? Trouble is, it's all old blokes they've had to get off the scrapheap. D'you know,' he said, not talking to anyone in particular, 'last week one silly old sod got his bus stuck under a bridge – he thought he was driving a single decker.' With that he got off and walked to the front of the bus.

Grace sat frozen and watched him. When he returned he yelled out, 'Everybody off!'

'Why?' shouted someone from upstairs.

'That big bang we heard a while back was a bleeding rocket and it dropped not far from here. The police have closed the road up ahead.'

'What's gonna happen to us?' asked a little old lady.

''Fraid yer gotta walk, love.'

'Bleeding Hitler. He should have my bunions, then he wouldn't be so clever.' Tutting to herself she picked up her shopping bags and moved along the bus.

Grace waited till everyone was off then she spoke to the conductor. 'Did they say where it dropped?'

'No love, just told us the road was closed. Do you live round this way?'

She shook her head. 'No.'

'Think it's pretty bad by all accounts.'

She gave him a weak smile. 'Thanks.'

As she hurried along the road, Grace's mind was in turmoil. What if . . .? No, she wasn't even going to think like that. She was breathless and seemed to be half running and walking for miles. She knew she was getting nearer the scene as many others had joined her and were silently running with her. The fear on their faces told her how worried they all were. The clanging bells from ambulances and fire engines filled the air with their urgent noise as they raced along.

When they turned a corner, a crowd of people blocking her way confronted Grace.

'Excuse me,' she said, trying to push her way through.

'They won't let you through,' said a young woman holding a baby.

'But I've got to.'

'They won't let you,' repeated an old man who had a very worried look on his face. 'I've been pleading with 'em, but it's no use.'

'Who won't?' asked Grace.

'The police. Told 'em me missus is in that lot, but that don't make any difference.' He sniffed and wiped his eyes with his coat-sleeve.

'Was it a V2?' asked Grace.

He nodded. 'Hit Woolies, so they say. Bloody butcher. It'll be mostly women and kids in there.'

Grace stood silently. Was her Dolly in that lot? What could she do? She caught sight of a policeman and hurried over to him. 'Excuse me. Is there somewhere I can go to see if my daughter's safe?'

'Sorry love,' he said kindly. 'I can't tell you anything. Me orders are that nobody is allowed down there. You'll have to wait till they start pulling the bodies out.'

Grace wanted to be sick. She felt everything spinning.

'You all right, missus?'

'No.'

'Look, I'll call someone over.'

'No. No, don't. Don't stop anyone from helping the wounded. I'll be all right.'

'OK. But only if you're sure.'

'Thanks.' Grace just about managed to walk away and found a wall to sit on. She wanted to find a small hole and curl up in it.

Penny was rocking Dolly back and forth. A young woman came and squatted beside her. She went to ease Dolly away, but Penny hung on to her with all her might.

'Please, just let me look at her.'

'No. No! Don't take her away.' Tears were streaming down Penny's face.

'I'm not going to take her away. I just want to see how bad she is.'

'She's dead, I know she is. Look at all the blood.'

'Please let me look.'

Penny gradually let the young woman take Dolly into her arms. She brushed the bloodied hair from Dolly's chalk-white face. She then turned and looked at Penny. 'She's not dead, but she is badly concussed. I'll get someone to come and look at you both.'

'Will she die?'

'Not if we can help it. Tom, over here,' she called out to a man who hurried towards them.

He took Dolly's pulse.

'Is she gonna be all right?' asked Penny.

'I hope so. Her pulse is strong.' He pulled back her coat. 'Was she pregnant?'

Penny nodded. 'Yes,' she whispered.

He looked concerned. 'We've got to get her to hospital. Stretcher over here, Fred,' he called out. 'Careful with this one,' he said as he helped the other man to gently lift Dolly into the ambulance. Then he turned to Penny. 'You'd better come along as well, then we can get that head wound seen to.'

In the ambulance were other people; some were sitting with a cloth pressed to their faces to staunch the blood, or holding on to their broken arms. A woman whose face and hair were thick with dust was sitting wrapped in a blanket. She said all her clothes had been ripped off.

'Funny thing, blast,' said an older-looking nurse who was trying to keep her balance as the ambulance, with its bell clanging, went hurrying on its way.

Dolly had been laid out along the side. She too was covered with a blanket. The nurse smiled at Penny. 'Don't worry, love, we'll soon have her on her feet.'

Penny wasn't so sure. Dolly looked very bad. 'Was it a V2?' she asked.

The nurse was looking at Penny's head. 'Yes. It caught Woolworth's.'

'But we was miles away from there.'

'You were unlucky, you were in the line of the blast. This will just need a stitch or two.'

Penny looked at Dolly. 'Will she be all right?'

'I would think so.'

'What about her baby?'

'The doctor will see about that,' said the nurse as she moved to another patient.

Tears slowly fell from Penny's eyes. Why did this have to happen?

★ ★ ★

It was getting dark and Grace knew she wasn't doing any good sitting here. She suddenly felt cold and stiff. What if the girls were home? Dolly would be worried about her. As she passed all the people who were waiting for news her heart went out to them. So far her little world had been safe. They had been lucky, apart from the night in December a few years back when incendiaries rained down out of the sky and almost set light to the whole of London. Fortunately Grace hadn't been fire-watching that night as one had finished up in the bedroom that was only used as a workroom. The wardens had quickly put it out; although it did burn some needlework and linen. Since then they'd been lucky. Apart from the inconvenience of having no water and gas at times and going to the shelter at night and replacing the windows several times, it hadn't really affected them very much. When Jim and Tony finally came home, things would be just as they were before this terrible war. Grace suddenly realised what she was thinking. It wouldn't be Tony who was going to be part of Dolly's future world; it was Joe Walters, her husband.

What if anything happened to her? How would Joe react? And what about the baby? *Please God don't let her lose the baby.*

Chapter 19

Penny sat in the crowded corridor for what seemed like for ever; she was waiting to see the doctor who was with Dolly. She had to find out how her friend was. People with fear filling their faces were arriving looking for loved ones and still more patients were being brought in. There was so much noise and activity going on all round her. Nurses were hurrying from patient to patient. People were being helped into chairs and others were being brought in on stretchers. The groans and sounds of those crying out in pain were very distressing. Some looked so bad Penny doubted if they would make it through the night. She knew she was in the way but she couldn't leave; she *had* to know how her friend was. Was she badly injured? Penny had had the wound in her forehead cleaned, and two stitches held the deep gash together under the plaster. Although she felt groggy, she wasn't going to go too far away from Dolly. As soon as she had some news she would go home and tell Mrs Taylor.

Although she was waiting outside she could see into the ward where Dolly was. As soon as the curtain was pulled back from her bed, the doctor and nurse who were in deep conversation began to move towards the door. Penny hurried up to them. 'Is she gonna be all right? Dolly – Mrs Walters.'

The doctor turned. 'Mrs Walters is going to be fine. We're just moving her to maternity, but as far as we can see, nothing's broken.'

'Maternity?' queried Penny.

'Yes. Are you a relation?'

Penny shook her head. 'I'm her best friend.'

'I'm afraid she's going to lose the baby.'

'No!' cried out Penny. 'She can't!'

'I'm sorry,' said the doctor.

'She is conscious,' said the nurse, 'so you can go and sit with her for a while if you like, but not too long mind, she needs some rest.'

'Thank you.' Penny peered round the curtain. Dolly was very pale and still. 'Dolly. You awake?'

Dolly opened her eyes. 'Pen.' She started crying.

'It's all right. I'm here.'

'I'm bleeding. I've started. They've told me my baby's dead. I'm so frightened.'

'Of course you are, but everything will be all right.' Penny sat on the chair beside her friend's bed and held her hand.

'It's not. I'm gonna lose me baby. I wish Joe was here.'

'I know.' It upset Penny to see her friend so distressed. 'Try not to get in a state.'

'I can't help it.' She wiped her eyes on the sheet and looked at Penny. 'What happened to you?'

Penny forced a grin and lightly touched her head. 'The pavement come up and hit me. What about you? You got any other aches and pains?'

'I don't know. I think I've got a cut on me head. All I know is that I hurt all over and me baby's dead.'

'I'm ever so sorry. Are they sure it's dead?'

Dolly nodded. 'They can't hear its heartbeat and I've started labour. Even if it is still alive they don't think it will survive.' Tears ran from Dolly's eyes into her ears and with the flat of her hand she brushed them aside. 'I don't want this to happen. It hurts.' She screwed up her face and squeezed Penny's hand. 'I want me mum and Joe.'

Penny waited till the surge of pain left her friend then asked, 'Will Joe be able to get back?'

'I don't know. Pen, I just want him here so much.' Dolly brought her knees up again in pain.

'I know. But thank God we're alive.'

As the pain eased Dolly said, 'Sorry. What about you – any other injuries?'

'No. Just the bump on me head. Mind you, it might knock some sense in to me.'

'Joe'll be ever so disappointed. I've let him down.' The tears started again.

'Christ, it wasn't your fault! But you're safe and that's all that matters.'

'It ain't fair. I want him here.'

'I know you do.' Penny was a little upset that Dolly was thinking only of her baby and Joe and not about herself. 'You're young. You've got plenty of time to think about babies.'

'Suppose so, but it'll never be the same.'

'D'you know when they're gonna take you to maternity?'

'Soon. I'm ever so frightened.' She began to cry.

'You'll be all right.'

A trolley was being wheeled into the ward.

'Sorry,' the nurse said to Penny, 'but you must go now.'

'Don't leave me, Pen.'

'I must.' Penny glared at the nurse then took hold of Dolly's hand and gently patted it. 'Look, I'm going home to tell our mums what's happened. They'll be worried stiff. So don't worry. Your mum will be in as soon as she's allowed.'

'Thanks, Pen,' she sniffed and brushed her tears away.

Penny's head was throbbing as she made her way home. They had been lucky. There were a lot of injured people still being brought in. And what about the dead? She heard someone say that it could be over a hundred. A hundred killed. And Dolly has lost her baby. When would this nightmare end?

Penny went into her own mother first who hugged her tight when she saw her walk in.

'My God, look at the state of you, what's happened?' she asked when she saw Penny's dishevelled appearance and the plaster on her forehead. 'We've been so worried about you.'

Penny told her what had happened.

'She's lost her baby? The poor girl. I'll come with you into next door.'

Penny knocked on Grace's front door and immediately it flew open.

'Penny,' said Grace, looking beyond Penny and Mrs Watts. 'What happened? Where's Dolly?'

'Can we come in?' asked Penny.

Tears filled Grace's eyes. 'Course. Sorry, I thought Dolly might be with you. Is she all right?'

'She's in hospital. We were both caught in the blast from that rocket.'

'She's alive?'

Penny nodded.

'Is she badly injured?'

'Not too bad.'

'Shall I put the kettle on?' asked Mrs Watts.

'Yes, please. It's nearly boiled. What hospital is she in?'

'They took us to St Olaves.'

'I'll get me coat.'

'Mrs Taylor.'

Grace quickly sat down. She knew by Penny's tone that she was about to hear something horrible, something she didn't want to hear. 'Is she badly injured?' she asked again, hoarsely.

'No. But they think the baby's dead and she's in labour.'

Grace put her hand to her mouth. 'Oh no.'

The whistling kettle sent Mrs Watts hurrying into the scullery where she quickly filled the teapot and after placing it on the table, took the cups and saucers from off the dresser.

'Did you talk to her?' asked Grace, her voice wobbling with emotion.

'Yes. She's very upset.'

'I expect she is.'

Mrs Watts pushed a cup of tea in front of Grace.

'Will they let me see her?'

'Should think so.'

Grace lit a cigarette and slowly sipped her tea. She needed to pull herself together if she was to be of any use to Dolly.

Dolly looked at the nurses and doctors who were wearing masks and surrounding her bed. She was terrified. Her feet were up in stirrups. She hurt so much she wanted to die.

'Come on now, push.'

She didn't want to push. What was the point when there wasn't going to be a baby?

A nurse came and mopped her brow. 'Come on now, Mrs Walters, your baby can't help.'

'*Course it can't help, you silly cow!*' Dolly wanted to scream out. '*It's dead. It will never breathe, or run, or go to school. Its father will never see it.*' Tears ran down her face.

Why didn't they all go away and leave her alone? She wanted to die just like her baby.

Suddenly there was a huge pain, her body almost split in two, and she felt a great rush of something. The nurse quickly picked the child up and wrapping it in a cloth, immediately left the room. Dolly struggled to sit up but a hand pushed her back.

'It's all over, Mrs Walter.'

'What did I have?'

'A daughter.'

'Can I hold her?'

'No, I'm sorry.'

'Well, can I see her?'

'No, I'm sorry.'

'Why not?'

'It doesn't do.'

'A daughter – but she's mine. *Please* let me see her!' When her pleas were ignored Dolly wanted to argue but she lay back exhausted. She could only cry for her lost baby.

At the hospital there was still plenty of activity and chaos as Grace made her way to the desk. She was told what ward Dolly was in and when she caught sight of her daughter in the bed, her dark hair against the stark white pillowcases, she felt the tears stinging her eyes. She looked so peaceful; no one would guess the trauma she had been through. Grace held Dolly's hand and when she opened her eyes and saw her mother, she began to cry.

Grace held her tight and gently patted her back. 'There there,' she said, comforting her as she had when she was a child.

'Mum. It was horrible. What am I gonna do? I've lost me baby.'

'I know, love. I know.'

'What's Joe gonna say?' she sobbed. 'I've let him down. Him and his family was so looking forward to this baby. It was a little girl.'

Grace wiped her eyes. 'You're young. You've got plenty of time to make more babies.'

'Mum, it was awful. They wouldn't let me see her. I couldn't hold her. I wanted to see what she looked like. I want to tell Joe what she looked like.' Dolly's sobs were heartbreaking.

'At least it was over quick.'

'What if anything happens to Joe? I'll be like Betty.'

'Now stop upsetting yourself. Everything is gonna be all right.'

'How can it be?'

Grace didn't have an answer.

'I want Joe. I want to come home. I don't want to see everybody else with their babies.' Dolly lay back.

Grace was worried about her daughter. She looked drained. 'You must rest. Do you think there's any chance he might be able to get compassionate leave?'

'I don't know.'

As beds were so short, a week later Dolly was resting at home. She was aware that all the knitting for the baby had been discreetly put out of sight. Every evening Penny came and sat with her. Betty and Jane came to see her and the Misses Gregory somehow managed to find a box of chocolates. When Dolly asked them about the coupons, they told her they were theirs.

She had written to Joe and his family and she was waiting for a reply. Would they be very disappointed?

★ ★ ★

When Joe read the letter from Dolly telling him he wasn't going to be a father he was upset and angry. He had asked for leave on compassionate grounds, but was told in none too polite words that there was a war on. Even when he explained that his wife had been injured in a rocket attack and had lost their baby daughter, it still didn't help him. He needed to be with her, to help her through all the trauma she must be experiencing.

Many thoughts went through his mind of how he could get back to her. What if he wrote himself a sick note? He could get on the next boat. But when he looked at the injured lying at the side of the road waiting to get back to England and the hospital, he knew he could never do anything like that, not take up someone's place. Besides, Grace and Penny would look after her till he got back.

He wrote long loving letters to Dolly, telling her how much he loved her and wanted to be with her, and that they could make many more babies in the future.

He also found time to write to his mother. It was mostly Bob who wrote, but her last letter was all about what they were doing; she never mentioned anything about Dolly or their wedding or the baby. It upset Joe that she never said she would write to Dolly. What was wrong with her? He knew she didn't have a lot of time for the British, although he didn't know why. But he felt sure that once she met Dolly, his wife would win her over. Joe lay on his bunk waiting for more dead and injured to arrive. He lit a cigarette; he would give the world to be with his Dolly Day Dream right at this moment, just to hold her and to caress her lovely body gave him a warm feeling. They had the rest of their lives to make love and Joe knew he wasn't going to waste a minute of it.

★ ★ ★

Christmas had been a very low-key affair. Grace didn't put up the paper chains; she didn't have the heart. She tried to help her daughter but Dolly seemed to sink deeper and deeper into a state of depression.

Joe's letters were full of love and what they would be doing next Christmas. Dolly couldn't read his letters without tears spilling from her eyes. She was angry and miserable that he wasn't at her side.

One evening Penny was telling Dolly about the factory; it was then she made up her mind to go back to work.

'But you've only been home two weeks!' said Grace.

'I know, but I can't sit around here moping all day. I've got to go back to work. Look how it helped Betty.'

'I know, but it's different with you, you've had a baby.'

'I know that.'

Grace had so much sympathy for her daughter. 'I still think it's a bit soon, love.'

'At least I won't be standing all day.'

'Well, only if you're sure.'

'I've got to do something, I'm bored out of me mind staying in.'

'I expect you are. See how you feel on Monday then.'

Dolly was dreading walking into the factory, but when almost everybody came up and offered their sympathy, it helped to quell her fear.

Penny had told her how concerned they all were, and had brought her letters and magazines all the while she was at home.

Dolly could feel the tears well up when Betty held her close.

'Dolly, I'm so sorry. It must have been awful for you.'

'Yes. Yes, it was. Thank you for your letter, that was nice of you.'

'I remember how you were there to help me through my bad time.'

Then it was Jane's turn – Jane who was always full of jokes. Today she only smiled sadly at Dolly and patted the back of her hand. She didn't speak. Dolly swallowed hard at that gesture. Even Mr Freeman came and spoke kindly to her and told her how sorry he was to hear about her ordeal.

At the end of the day Dolly felt drained, but at least now the first day was over. Perhaps she could try to pick up the pieces of her life again.

For most people, 1945 started full of optimism. All over the world, everything seemed to be happening at breakneck speed. Every day some new ground was gained, but there were still casualties. The one that upset the residents of Wood Street most and made them realise the war was closer than ever, was the sad news about Penny's father. Mr Watts had been killed in Greece.

When Dolly heard the news she tried to comfort her friend as much as she could.

'It's the boys,' said Penny when she came and sat at Grace's table. 'What they gonna do without a dad? Mum's worried to death that they'll go right off the rails without him around.'

Dolly held her close. They were always there to comfort each other.

'We ain't even gonna have a grave we can visit,' Penny wept.

I know how you feel, thought Dolly. She didn't have a grave for her daughter.

'How's your mum taking it, love?' asked Grace.

'She seems to be bearing up in front of everybody through the day, but I can hear her crying at night.'

Dolly was worried about Joe. His letters were always loving and full of their future and she knew he was desperate to see her again, but her fear that he might be killed or injured was always in her mind. At night she dreamed of them together with their daughter. If only she had seen her baby and held her. She could have told him who she looked like, but she had nothing.

Grace desperately wanted Jim to come home. His letters were very erratic. Although the end was in sight, everybody still dreaded that buff-coloured telegram. What would she do if one came to her? Would Dolly still go to America and leave her alone? She hoped that was the one question she would never have to answer.

Chapter 20

As the year progressed, everybody knew that the long dreary days of war were at last coming to an end. In his letters Joe told Dolly how they were being swept along the front. He'd been through France; now he was on his way to Germany. His biggest worry was that when it was finally over, he and his fellow GIs might not get leave when they returned to England, but could be sent on to a transit camp and shipped back to America. Most of the guys were overjoyed about that, apart from those who had married British girls.

Dolly had been reading as much as she could about Americans and their funny ways. When Roosevelt died she knew how much that would upset Joe and the rest of his country. It was a shame he didn't live to see the end of the conflict.

The terrible scenes of the concentration camps being liberated filled the newspapers and newsreels. It left everyone feeling disgusted and angry. At the end of April, Hitler was found dead, so it was only a matter of time before peace would be declared.

Bunting was draped along the front of houses, flags were rescued from lofts and banners were being made from any spare scraps of material, to welcome the men back home.

Suddenly it was all over. Whole families took to the streets laughing and crying. Church bells were ringing out the good news. Street parties were hastily arranged and everybody was determined to enjoy themselves.

8 May 1945. It was officially all over.

'No more going in the shelters at night,' said Grace as she danced round and round the kitchen with Dolly after they'd heard the news on the wireless. 'Your father will be home, so will Joe. This is a wonderful day.' She stopped. 'To be truthful, there were times when I didn't think we'd make it.'

'Some didn't. I feel almost guilty at enjoying ourselves when Penny's dad won't ever be home,' said Dolly soberly.

'I know. We've been very lucky.'

The banging on the door sent Grace hurrying up the passage. 'Penny!' She threw her arms round the startled girl and waltzed around with her.

When Penny managed to break away she said as she walked into the kitchen, 'The grocer and the Miss Gregorys are sorting out the details for the street party we're having.'

For weeks the residents of Wood Street had been putting by any rations they could spare and saving sixpence a week towards a party. The grocer and the Gregory sisters had been keeping the books; now it was all coming into place.

'They're holding a meeting tonight to finalise everything,' said Penny. 'Can you both come?'

'I should say so. I can't believe it's really happened,' said Grace, still smiling.

'Yes, but don't forget it's not over with Japan yet,' cautioned Dolly.

'I know,' said Grace, 'but that's a long way away from us.'

Deep down Dolly was worried. There was still heavy fighting in that part of the world and she prayed that Joe wouldn't be sent there now the war in Europe was over.

'You should see some of the flags that have come out,' said Penny.

'What, already?' asked Grace. 'Where'd they get 'em from?'

'There's always some spiv around who's got a ready supply.'

'We'll have to see what we can find,' said Dolly.

'Your dad brought some home once, I'll look them out. They might be from a country I don't know, but that won't matter as long as they're colourful.'

On the day of the street party, Wood Street had been transformed. Chairs and trestle tables had been brought out of the church hall and set at one end of the road. Bunting was stretched across the road from house to house. Paper hats, food and drink appeared from nowhere. It was a huge success.

Dolly was talking to both the Gregory sisters. 'I don't know how you managed to do all this.'

'Mr and Mrs Dobson from the grocer's have been helping out with the food, and don't forget all our neighbours who have been giving up some of their rations. They also did the hard work putting up the trestles.' May stood back and looked along the tables. 'It all looks very nice.'

Penny's brother Billy had had so much to eat and drunk so much lemonade that he was sick. Penny had to take him inside to clean him up. Jack was looking very grown-up now he was at work. Mrs Watts sat on the coping wall and Dolly could see she was quietly crying. Dolly went and sat next to her.

'Try not to upset yourself,' Dolly said gently.

'I can't help thinking about their dad. He was such a nice man.'

'I know,' said Dolly, genuinely sorry.

'Who's gonna give Pen away when she gets married?'

'Have you or Mr Watts got a brother?'

She shook her head.

'What about Jack?'

'Don't think Pen would like that.'

'I could always ask me dad. I think he was a bit put out he wasn't here for my wedding.'

Mrs Watts wiped her eyes on the bottom of her pinny. 'That would be nice. I'm sure Pen will agree to that. After all, you are like family.'

After the food had been devoured, Mr Cooper's piano was brought out. Then the singing, dancing and drinking for the adults began. During a lull Dolly and Penny were sitting quietly on the coping wall reminiscing.

'I still can't believe it's all over,' said Dolly, holding on to her glass.

'A lot has happened over these past years.'

'I know. I've got married and lost a baby.'

'And I've lost a dad,' said Penny sadly.

Dolly put her glass down and went and hugged her friend. They both had tears in their eyes.

'Promise me that when you get to America you'll never stop writing to me,' said Penny as she wiped her eyes with the flat of her hand. 'Damn. I've smudged me mascara.'

Dolly laughed. 'I promise. And if you ever need me I'll do my best to come and see you.'

It was Penny's turn to laugh. 'What, all the way from America?'

'All the way from America,' repeated Dolly. 'Even if I have to stow away.'

Once more they hugged each other. Dolly knew that theirs was a friendship that would last a lifetime.

'I hope you get married before I go,' said Dolly as the music started up again and she sat watching her neighbours enjoying themselves.

'So do I. I wonder if Reg has changed much?'

'We've all changed. We've all had to grow up.'

'I guess so.'

'Rose seems to be enjoying herself,' said Dolly, inclining her head towards Rose who was doing the Hokey Cokey with her mother and a very handsome man.

'Fancy her getting engaged to that doctor. He's very good-looking.'

'I know. That was a surprise. Reg never said anything in his letters then.'

'You know Reg, he was never that good at letter-writing, not like you and Tony. I used to get more news about what was happening from you than from Reg.'

'But you love him though.'

'Yes,' said Penny with a smile.

'I did write to Tony for quite a while after I got married, but he never answered.'

'Well, you can't blame him, can you?'

'Suppose not. But I was hoping we could still be friends.'

'I think he was very hurt. You'll still be here when he comes home.'

'I should think so.'

'That's gonna be a bit awkward, ain't it?'

'Shouldn't be.'

'I don't want you two fighting at my wedding. Remember, you're gonna be me matron of honour and I expect Tony will be Reg's best man.'

'Don't worry, we'll behave ourselves. Your mum's worried about who's gonna give you away.'

'I know.'

'I suggested me dad.'

'Did you? That'd be great! D'you think he would?'

'I would think so. As I told your mum, he was disappointed he wasn't at my wedding.'

'Come on, you two,' shouted Grace. 'Old Fred's gonna play "The Lambeth Walk" again.' She dragged the girls up and pushed them into the middle of the road to join everybody else who was waiting for Fred to hit the keys of Mr Cooper's battered old upright piano. It didn't matter that some of the keys didn't work, everybody knew the words to the songs anyway.

The weeks were hurrying past, and soon it was Dolly and Joe's wedding anniversary. The letter she had from him was full of love and how much he missed her and longed to be with her. She could remember every moment of their wedding a year ago and their two days' honeymoon. She longed to be with him.

It was a warm June evening and Grace was sitting in the yard, feeling restless. She missed going to do her stint of fire-watching. She hadn't seen her pal Mary since they were all stood down, and she often wondered how she was getting on. It was strange – all the times they were together, she never found out where she lived. She also missed going to work. They had stopped making parachutes and the women were waiting for the factory to start up again, although the noise from the machines never really allowed any real friendships to develop. Everything was happening so fast. Would Jim mind her staying on at the factory when they started to make shirts again?

How long would it be before he was home? This war and what he'd been through must have changed him. All the time he was back and forth in peacetime, every homecoming was like another honeymoon. She loved him so much, but had he changed? They were both older now and they could have been grandparents. Grace sniffed back her tears. That was such a sad time for Dolly; fortunately, she was alive. But that didn't stop Grace's heart from breaking for her daughter's loss.

Dolly had been to the authorities to find out about her move to the States. She longed to see Joe again. She knew from his letters that he was hoping to be sent back to England and would try to get to see her, but he didn't know when or where. Bob, his brother, had written and told her they were looking forward to meeting her. She was nervous. Would she get there before Joe? At the Rainbow Club they were giving the 'GI brides' as they had become known, lessons on living in the States. When Dolly arrived with the hundreds of other women she felt a little daunted. What was it going to be like on the ship? Would she like America? When she looked at the picture of the late Glenn Miller she felt sad. They had never found his body in the Channel. It was through her love of his music here in this very place that she had found Joe and love. Now she was his wife and would go to America to begin a new life. She swallowed hard. What was in store for her?

There was much laughter as the women were told to remember that although the British and Americans spoke the same language, many words had different meanings.

'Our chips mean crisps and fries are chips. Gas is our name for petrol. And remember we drive on the *other* side of the road, so you have to look to the left. We don't want you getting killed the moment you step off the sidewalk.'

Dolly was smiling as she left. It was a good thing she saw

so many movies, as she now had to call them; at least most of it would come easy.

One by one the men who'd been called up began to return. Some looked well, while others looked sad, ill and afraid.

It was 1 August when Dolly came home from work and found her father sitting in the armchair. Her mother was positively glowing, while Jim Taylor looked older and tired.

'Dad!' she screamed out and rushed into his arms. He kissed her face all over.

'My baby, my baby,' he cried as he held her close. 'God knows I've missed you and your mother.'

'It's been a long while,' sniffed Dolly. 'And you look ever so well.'

He stood back to admire her. 'And you look all grown-up.'

'I have. I'm now a married woman.'

Jim Taylor visibly stiffened. 'So your mother wrote and told me.'

'You'll like Joe.'

'Will I?'

Dolly glanced at her mother who walked off into the scullery.

'What was wrong with Tony?'

'Nothing. But I fell in love with Joe.'

'Is it 'cos he's an American?' Jim settled himself back in his armchair and lit his pipe from one of the wooden spills that were in a coloured cardboard container beside the fireplace. It was a Christmas present Dolly had made one year when she was at school.

'No.'

He blew the smoke high into the air. 'It ain't all a land of milk and honey, you know. There's some pretty rough places, and some pretty rough blokes.'

'Dad, stop. I don't want us to get off on the wrong side. When you meet Joe, you'll realise what a smashing bloke he is.'

'I'm very angry with you and your mother. You know I won't forgive her for giving you permission to marry him.'

'Don't say that, Dad. Don't be angry with us.'

'Why couldn't you have waited? Got to know each other a bit longer?'

'We didn't want to. He was being sent abroad and we didn't know what tomorrow would bring. Don't let's get all aerated on your first night home.'

Jim puffed on his pipe. 'I'm sorry. And I was really upset to hear about the baby. Thank God you were all right.'

Dolly didn't answer. She hadn't thought her father would be like this, not after all this time.

'So what about Tony?' Jim went on to ask.

'What about him?'

'He ain't gonna be pleased about all this.'

'Dad, I have written and told him. These things happen in wartime.'

'I daresay they do.' He stood up. 'Well, let's hope you come to your senses before it's too late.'

'What d'you mean?'

'You can always get divorced and marry Tony. That's if he still wants you.'

Tears sprang from Dolly's eyes. 'But I don't want to marry Tony! Dad, don't.' That remark really upset her, but she put a brave face on. She didn't want any arguments on his first night home.

All evening they sat and talked. He told them the narrow escape they'd all had when his ship had been torpedoed.

'You didn't tell me,' said Grace.

'Wasn't a lot to tell. We was lucky. We got picked up by another ship, although they wasn't supposed to stop when they were in convoy.'

'What, you mean you had to carry on and leave men in the sea?'

Jim nodded. 'It was very hard at times when you could see the poor buggers yelling and screaming, clinging to bits of wreckage and you had to leave 'em.'

'Why?' asked Dolly white-faced. 'Why couldn't you stop?'

'Your ship would get left behind and you would be a sitting target for the U-boats. The way the Navy looked at it, it was better to leave a few to die rather than risk losing another shipload.'

'That's barbaric,' said Grace.

'That's war,' said Jim.

Dolly winced. This had been a wicked war. So many horrible things had happened.

Grace was over the moon now that Jim was safe with her. No more goodbyes. He told her he was going to stay home. How would he settle into a job on dry land? She decided they would cross that bridge together when the time came. The biggest worry to Grace now was how she would cope when she had to say goodbye to Dolly.

A week after Jim Taylor returned, the war in the Far East ended. The event that upset and frightened everybody was the dropping of the atomic bombs to end the Japanese conflict.

People stood in the street and read the paper. They were told that man had made a weapon that could wipe out the world. For weeks everybody spoke about it. In Britain, the bunting and street parties were once again out in force, but they didn't have quite the same impact.

At work everybody was worried. Would they lose their

jobs? What would they do now it was all over? The government wouldn't want shell-cases any more.

'What you gonna do, Betty?' asked Dolly.

'I'm still gonna go to the States. I've been saving up my widow's allowance. Chuck's folks want me to go over there. They've even sent me some money for my fare when the liners start to take civilian passengers again.'

'Ain't you the lucky one,' said Jane.

'What are you gonna do, Jane?' asked Dolly.

'I'm gonna divorce me old man and bugger off somewhere. Not sure where yet, but I think I might take meself off somewhere where it's warm.'

'That's a bit extreme,' said Penny.

'Why?' asked Betty.

'Got to take things a bit easy,' Jane shrugged.

'Why?' asked Dolly.

'S'pose I can tell you now we're all splitting up. I've got a slight shadow on me lung. It's nothing to worry about just yet, but who knows what will happen in the future.'

The three girls sat open-mouthed.

'Why didn't you say something before?' asked Penny.

'Didn't want you lot fussing round me. I go and see the quack every now and again. They are keeping their eye on me.'

'But why are you divorcing your husband?' asked Betty.

'He won't wanna be lumbered with me. Anyway, I reckon he's got a bit on the side. Still – good luck to him,' said Jane in her usual cheerful way.

'Is that why you couldn't go in the Forces?' asked Dolly.

Jane only nodded as she walked away.

On the way home that evening both Dolly and Penny's thoughts were about Jane.

'I knew she'd changed after she was turned down for the

Forces, but I can't believe she would keep something like that quiet,' said Penny.

'And going to divorce her husband,' said Dolly.

'I'm sure if he really loves her he'd want to stick by her.'

'I wonder if she'll tell him?'

'Don't know. It just goes to show, we don't really know people at all,' said Penny sadly.

Weeks later, Dolly had a letter from Joe saying he was being shipped back to America. All the married men were angry as they were confined to camp and couldn't get to see their wives. They had been sent to a camp near Liverpool and weren't allowed any leave. Joe said he was desperate to see Dolly but wouldn't be able to come to London to meet her. She was heartbroken.

'I want to go to Liverpool,' she told Penny.

'Do you know where he is?' asked her friend.

She shook her head. 'No. The address I've got to write to just says Liverpool.'

'So how would you know where to look?'

'I wouldn't. I could always get a taxi to the camp. They must know where the Americans have been sent.'

'Don't talk daft. Liverpool's a big place – it'll cost you a fortune. And besides, what's the point? He might have been moved out by now.'

Dolly was crying.

'What do your mum and dad have to say about it?' Penny asked.

'Mum said what you just did. Me dad won't even mention Joe's name. He's hoping he's got a wife and a dozen kids out there, then our marriage will be null and void.'

Penny felt sorry for Dolly. All her hopes and dreams were being shattered.

Joe's letters were long and loving. Dolly didn't have any doubts that he loved her. He said he couldn't wait for her to join him in America. She knew her name was on the list. But how long would she have to wait?

It was in October that Penny came banging on the door waving a letter.

'He's coming home! He's coming home!' she yelled when Dolly opened the door. 'Reg and Tony should be here at the end of the week.' She twirled Dolly round and round.

'I'm so pleased for you, Pen.'

Tony was coming home. What would happen now? Dolly wondered. What would her feelings be when she saw him again?

Chapter 21

It was Saturday and Dolly knew that Reg and Tony would be arriving home some time today. Penny had decided to take the morning off work as she wanted to be around to welcome Reg. Dolly was on her own as she walked home from work, and she suddenly felt very apprehensive as she turned into Wood Street. Last night she had seen the huge Welcome Home banners hanging from Reg and Tony's houses. Were they home? She hastened her step, as suddenly Wood Street seemed to go on for ever. The last thing she wanted was to bump into Tony in the street. What would she do? What could she say? She turned the plain gold band on her finger. She was married. If only Joe was here at her side, he would help her get through this. As she hurried past Tony's house she kept her gaze straight ahead. Was he looking out of the window? Would he want to speak to her?

'Dolly? That you?' called her mother from the scullery when Dolly walked into the kitchen.

'Yes, Mum.'

Grace came in wiping her hands on the bottom of her apron. 'Reg and Tony's home.'

'That's good. How do they look?'

'Great. Older and thinner, of course, but then I expect we all do.'

Dolly didn't have a reply so she asked, 'Where's Dad?'

'He's gone along to Reg's. Seems his mum wants to give him a welcome home and an engagement party for him and Penny, as she didn't have time before he left.'

'That'll be nice for them.'

'Been saving her rations for weeks, be all accounts. Your dad's gone along to give 'em a hand with moving some of the furniture. You've been invited.'

'What – tonight? It's a bit soon, ain't it? I would have thought she'd have given 'em a bit of a time to get used to being home first.'

'I think she's that happy and proud that Reg is back, that she wants everybody to know about it.'

'I can't go.'

'Whyever not?'

'Tony will be there.'

'Course he will. Those lads have been through a lot together.'

'Well, I can't go.'

'You'll have Penny coming in here and dragging you in.'

'I'd feel uncomfortable.'

'I'm not going to say a word.'

'I can't go in there as if nothing's happened.'

'Well, whose fault's that?'

'I'd rather have a talk to Tony when we're on our own. I don't want to upset Penny and Reg's day.'

'Please yourself.'

'They want us along about seven,' said Jim when he walked in. 'D'you know, Mrs Smith's worked really hard, even made 'em a cake and made a jolly fine job of it as well.'

'She's not going,' said Grace, inclining her head towards Dolly.

'Why?'

'Said she'd feel embarrassed 'cos Tony will be there.'

'Should have thought about that when you was ditching him.'

Dolly was not going to rise to the bait. 'You go and enjoy yourselves.'

'Don't worry, we will,' said her father.

'I told her it wasn't fair to Penny.'

'Too bloody right it ain't,' said her father.

'Look how she looked after you when you come out of hospital.'

'Mum, please don't. I'm going upstairs.'

In her room Dolly sat on the bed. She knew this business with Tony should be aired, but not at Penny's party. Should she go along and see him? She couldn't spend all the time hiding from him; she could wish him well. Dolly went to the small drawer in her dressing-table where she kept her precious things and took out the small black box that held in its red satin folds the engagement ring Tony had bought her before he went away. All the happy memories of those days came flooding back. The laughter, the silly games they played on one another and the kisses. Tony's kisses were different from Joe's, but they had always been warm and full of love. She looked at her left hand and her plain gold wedding ring. It had been put on her finger with so much love. Joe didn't have time to buy her an engagement ring, but promised her one as soon as they got to the States.

She had to see Tony to explain. It was something she had to do. Dolly ran down the stairs and without going into the kitchen for her coat, grabbed her cardigan from off the banisters and yelled out, 'Won't be long!'

This was something she had to do before her bravado left her. She ran up the road and knocked on Tony's door.

Rose opened the door. 'What do you want?'

'I'd like to talk to Tony.'

'You've got a nerve. I can tell you that he don't want to talk to you.'

Dolly felt deflated. Why hadn't Tony opened the door? 'Is he home?' she asked Rose.

'No.'

'I know you'll never forgive me, but I just want to see him to explain to him and tell him I'm sorry.'

'I bet you are.'

'Tell him I called.' Dolly sadly turned to walk away. Was he with Reg? Should she go along there? She glanced up at the bedroom window and could see Tony watching her. Why hadn't he made any attempt to move away from the window? He was still the handsome feller she'd fallen in love with all those years ago. She stood and looked at him for a moment or two, then slowly walked away. Tears began to fill her eyes. Why couldn't he be grown-up and sensible about all this and at least talk to her?

When she had almost reached her house she heard him call her name. She turned and looked back. 'Tony. I'm so sorry,' she said when he got closer.

He looked about him.

'Can I talk to you?' asked Dolly.

'Yer, all right. We can't stand here though.'

'I know.'

'Don't want everyone to think I've gone soft.'

'Does your mum and Rose know you're talking to me?'

He laughed. 'What's it to them? I am me own boss, you know.'

'Tony, let's walk to the park.'

'OK.'

Although it was early October it was a pleasantly warm, sunny afternoon. Dolly slipped her cardi round her shoulders.

They were silent as they made their way to the park.

'You look very well,' said Dolly, wanting to break the silence.

'So do you.'

'Thanks.'

'Would you like an ice cream?' asked Tony.

'Yes, please.'

She watched Tony go over to the stop-me-and-buy-one man on the bike. He walked back with two ices.

Dolly pulled back the cardboard and began to lick at the frozen triangle.

'Seems a lifetime ago since I had one of these,' said Tony, sucking on his ice.

'We ain't seen that many.'

'Could have done with these in the desert.'

'Have things been hard?'

'It wasn't easy. Shall we sit down?'

Dolly nodded.

They carried on eating and finally Dolly wiped her mouth on her handkerchief. 'Tony. What can I say?'

'Don't know that there's anything to say, not now.'

'I still want us to be friends.'

'How can we?'

'I was hoping we could be grown-up about this. You didn't answer any of the last letters I sent you. Did you get them?'

'I didn't want to write to a married woman.'

'I didn't want to fall in love with Joe.'

'You sure it wasn't the uniform and the thought of going

197

to the States? We all know what a dreamer you are.'

'It wasn't like that.'

'You ask Reg. I was very cut up about it.'

'I can't say any more than I'm sorry.'

'I really thought you'd be the one girl who'd wait for her bloke. I really did love you, Dolly.'

Dolly swallowed hard and looked down at her hands.

'I suppose I was daft to expect a pretty girl like you to wait for me.'

'I didn't want you to be angry.'

'Angry? I'll tell you, I was that bloody angry that for two pins if we'd been near the Germans I would have given meself up.'

Dolly could feel the tears rising. 'I'm so sorry, Tony.'

'Anyway, when I calmed down a bit I really thought perhaps it was wrong of me to expect you to wait for me. I could have been killed or injured or something, and after all, you're young and full of life. As you said, we should be grown-up about it. A lot's happened in these past few years and we've got to look ahead.'

'What are you doing to do?'

'Don't know. Don't know what job I'll finish up with. And it ain't even as if the demob suit's anything to write home about.'

'But I thought they had to keep your job open for you?'

'They did, but as there ain't a factory there any more, looks like I might finish up on the dole. Reg is all right. They'll be calling out for builders.'

Dolly casually touched his hand. 'I'm sure you'll find something.'

Tony looked down at her hand covering his. 'Dolly, I still love you. I was hoping I could tell you to sod off, but I can't. Your bloke's a very lucky feller.'

Dolly quickly pulled her hand away. 'Can we still be friends?'

'Dunno.'

'Please, for Penny and Reg's sake?'

'S'pose it'll be a bit awkward at their wedding. You going to their party tonight?'

She shook her head and her dark hair fell over her face. 'No. I don't want to embarrass you.'

'You won't embarrass me.' Tony gently pushed her hair back and let it trickle through his fingers. 'I've been dreaming of this.'

Dolly pulled back. 'Don't, Tony.'

'Sorry.' He quickly put his hand down. 'Pen will be very upset if you don't come tonight, you know.'

'I can't.'

'I promise I won't embarrass you. I might get pissed though. It's a good few years since me and Reg have had a real good drinking session. Please come.'

'I'll think about it. I heard Reg got wounded.'

'Yer, poor bugger.' Tony laughed. 'Shrapnel in his arse. Couldn't sit down for weeks.'

'He didn't tell Penny that.'

'Didn't want to upset her, I suppose.'

'But you was all right?'

'Yer. I hear that you two had a narrow escape with those rockets.'

'Yes, we did.'

'Heard you lost your baby, an' all.'

'Yes, I did,' Dolly whispered.

'Sorry to hear that. You know, you didn't have to marry him just 'cos you was, you know. I would have married you.'

'I wasn't expecting when I got married.'

'Oh. I thought you was.'

'I married Joe because I love him.'

'So when d'you reckon you'll be leaving us then?'

'Don't know. Tony, please take this.' She took the box containing his ring from the pocket of her cotton dress and put it in his hand.

'So this really is it then?'

'I'm afraid so.'

'I was hoping . . .' He opened the box and sat looking at the diamond sparkling in the sunlight.

'No. Don't say it.'

'You can keep it if you like.'

'No. I hope you might find someone else who will love you.'

'Dolly. There'll never be another like you.'

She shivered. 'I think we'd better be getting back.'

'You're right.'

They were very close when they stood up.

'Dolly, please come tonight. I'd like everybody to see we can be sensible about all this.'

She smiled. She would have liked to kiss him in a friendly way, but thought better of it. It might give out the wrong signals. 'Thanks, Tony.'

'Where have you been?' asked Grace when Dolly walked in.

'Been to see Tony.'

'And?'

'We had a long talk and I'm going tonight.'

'That's good. Penny would be very hurt if you didn't.'

'I know.' But Dolly was still very apprehensive about it.

'Did you give him his ring back?'

'Yes, I did.'

'What did he say?'

'Not a lot. I'm gonna put me hair in curlers.' Dolly went to her bedroom. Why was life so complicated? She was a little worried. She'd seen Tony drunk before. She sent up a silent prayer. '*Please, God, don't let him get silly and show himself and me up.*'

Chapter 22

As Dolly did her hair and made up her face, she was still very apprehensive about going to the party. She ran her hands over the top of her dressing-table. Like her, it bore scars of the war. Once, when the windows had been blown out, shards of glass had been embedded in its surface. In time, these would be polished out, but her baby would never be returned. With her elbows on her dressing-table, Dolly applied her lipstick, then while sitting looking in her mirror, her thoughts went to Tony. She had been pleasantly surprised how reasonable he'd been about her getting married, although it upset her when he said he still loved her. But that part of her life was now over; she had to move on. She stood up and smoothed her pink frock down over her hips. Although her heart wasn't really in it, she knew she looked good and longed for Joe to be with her tonight. But for now she had to make sure nothing would happen to upset Penny and Reg's evening.

'Dolly, are you ready yet?' called her mother from the bottom of the stairs.

'Just coming.'

'Hurry up, girl. We're wasting valuable drinking time, even if the beer is watered down,' said her father as she walked down the stairs.

'Dolly, you look very nice, don't she, Jim?'

'I should say so. In fact, you *both* look very nice, and I tell you something. I'm that proud of the both of you.'

Grace gave him a beaming smile and kissed his cheek.

Dolly also kissed his cheek. 'Thanks, Dad.' She was pleased that he didn't say very much about her being married these days. Was he hoping it would go away?

Reg lived at number two, the first house in Wood Street, and as they approached it they could hear the music and noise spilling out through the open windows and into the evening air. When Dolly and the family walked in through the open door, Penny came racing up to her.

She cuddled Dolly close. 'I was a bit worried you might not come,' she whispered in her friend's ear.

'What – after all we've been through together? It'll take more than Tony to keep me away.' Dolly held Penny at arm's length. 'You look positively gorgeous. I love your frock. It's new, ain't it?'

Penny did a little twirl. 'D'you like it? Me mum bought it for me as a surprise. And it fits.' She smoothed the soft, slightly gathered blue jersey wool down over her hips. It had short sleeves and a sweetheart neckline that was very flattering.

'It's lovely and so are you,' said Dolly fondly. She could see her friend was glowing with happiness.

'I'll get you a drink.'

'Got to have a word with Reg first. Where is he?'

'In the kitchen with all the booze as is the norm with blokes at parties.' Penny touched Dolly's arm. 'Dolly, Tony said you and him have had a talk.'

'Yes. We went to the park this afternoon. I've given him his ring back.'

'I thought you might have.'

'Hello there, you lovely-looking creature.' Reg came up to Dolly and after hugging her tight, kissed her cheek.

'Hello, Reg. It's lovely to see you again. You look well.'

'I ain't so bad.' He put his arm round Penny's waist. 'Ain't I the lucky one to have this gorgeous creature to come back to?'

Dolly felt uncomfortable as he bent down and kissed Penny's eager lips.

Penny pulled away. 'Reg!'

'Sorry, Dolly.'

'I'll get that drink,' said Penny.

'I didn't mean to upset you. I promised Pen here I wouldn't say anything about you and Tony.'

'That's all right, Reg. It's not a secret and we had a long talk this afternoon.'

'That's good. So how's married life then?'

'Didn't get a lot of time to really find out. Joe was sent out two days after we were married. He'll be back in the States soon.'

'So when you going?'

Dolly shrugged. 'Got to wait and see. There's a lot of us GI brides that are waiting to go.'

'It's a big step.'

'I know.'

Penny arrived with Dolly's drink as the front door was pushed open again and more people arrived. Penny went to greet them.

'Reg,' said Penny, beckoning him over.

'Whoops – and this is before we get married. Been told I've not to drink too much and I've got to mingle. It's really good to see you again. I'll talk to you later,' said Reg as he walked away.

Dolly went and sat on the stairs. She knew everybody who was here. These were her friends, workmates and neighbours; somehow Mrs Smith had even managed to invite some of their old school pals. Dolly didn't have an engagement party when she got engaged to Tony and she didn't even have a proper wedding reception when she married Joe. She always seemed to dip out on these things.

'All right then, girl?' asked her father as he stepped over her and made his way up the stairs to the toilet.

'Yes thanks, Dad.'

He patted her head. 'That's good. It's great to see these boys home again, safe and sound.'

Tears began to sting the back of her eyes. People were coming and going all around her and everyone was laughing. Dolly didn't want to be here. The noise was getting louder as more people arrived and the drink flowed. So far, she hadn't seen Tony; he was in the kitchen and every so often loud laughter would break out from that direction – probably after a dirty joke. She felt so alone and lonely; she desperately wanted Joe at her side.

When Betty walked through the front door Dolly felt she had a fellow companion.

'Hello, Dolly love. All right then?'

'Not too bad.'

'Have you seen Whatshisname?' Betty looked around her. 'You know, the bloke you was engaged to.'

'Tony. We had a long talk this afternoon. He's all right about it.'

'Good.' Betty settled herself next to Dolly on the stairs.

'I feel a bit like a fish out of water here,' said Dolly.

'I know what you mean. Seems like when you're married, people tend to avoid you.'

'You're not married – well, not now.'

'I know, but I still think of meself as married. Don't suppose I'll ever get married again.'

'Why not? You're only young, as people keep telling me when I get upset about the baby.'

'That must have been really awful.'

'Yes, it was. But I'm sure you'll find someone else.'

'Don't think so. Chuck was the first and last. Nobody could ever take his place.'

'You never know.'

'Here, what are you two old married women sitting gossiping about?' asked Penny as she leant over the banisters. 'You ain't even got a drink yet, Bet. Come and meet my Reg.' She took hold of Betty's hand and led her into the front room, leaving Dolly alone once again.

'Mind if I sit next to you?' Tony was at the bottom of the stairs holding a glass of beer and looking up at her.

'No, course not.'

'You look really nice,' said Tony as he put his foot on the first stair. He steadied himself and his beer and sat next to her.

'Thank you.'

'It's good to see so many of our old mates are still around.'

'Yes.'

'Dolly, are you sure you want to go to America?'

'Course.'

'Why?'

'I want to be with my husband.'

Tony drained his glass. 'You'll miss all these sort of get-togethers. They don't have parties over there, not like this, you know.'

'I don't suppose they do.'

'I don't think you really want to go.'

'Tony, please. I think you've had a drop too much to drink.'

'Trying to drown me sorrows. I always thought you was the girl for me, and I ain't gonna give you up without a fight.'

'Tony, I'm a married woman.'

'I don't care. I'll make you love me. You did once, you know.'

'Yes, I did. But that was a long while ago.'

'I bet you wish I'd got killed.'

'Don't say things like that! I never wanted any harm to come to you.'

'Ah. See? You still care.'

'Please, Tony. Go and see Reg.'

'I don't want to. I want to stay here with you.' He put his glass on the stair and pushing Dolly back, gripped her shoulders and kissed her full on the mouth. It was a hard, passionate kiss.

Dolly tried to pull away but Tony's hold was firm. He was in control.

'Aye aye. What's all this then?' said Reg as he came to the bottom of the stairs. 'You two look like you're enjoying yourselves.'

Dolly pulled away and stood up. She couldn't speak. She wasn't sure if it was anger, embarrassment or sympathy. She knew her lipstick had been smudged so she ran up to the bathroom.

She put the lid down and sat on the toilet. What was he thinking of? What if her mother or father had seen them? She knew she had to go home, but what excuse could she give Penny?

The door handle rattled and it was when someone was banging on the bathroom door shouting, 'Hurry up, I'm bursting out here,' that Dolly left the shelter of the bathroom.

'Oh, it's you, Dolly. I thought you'd fallen down the hole,' said Mrs Larner who was on the other side of the door. She lived next door to Reg. 'You all right?'

'Yes, thanks.'

'Good party this. Don't they make a smashing couple?'

'Yes, they do.'

'Can't wait for the wedding. Pity you and Tony ain't still together.'

Dolly didn't answer and went to move away.

Mrs Larner took hold of her arm. 'I know it ain't any of my business, but I reckon a lot of you girls are gonna be very disappointed when you get over there in America. It ain't all milk and honey like in the films, you know?'

'I don't suppose it is,' she said as she made her way down the stairs.

Tony was no longer sitting on the stairs, so without saying goodbye to anyone, Dolly quietly slipped away.

It was very warm in the house and the air full of cigarette smoke was making Dolly's eyes water. Outside, many of the guests were lolling about, sitting on the copings; some had even brought chairs out.

'Ain't you got a drink then, Doll?' asked someone as she made her way through the crowd that had gathered round the gate.

'No, thanks. Just fancy a bit of fresh air.'

She pushed past them and was making her way towards her house when she heard someone say, 'I thought she was bloody daft, marrying a Yank.'

They must have thought she was out of earshot, but the shrill voice carried on the still air. 'Some tarts'll do anything for a pair of nylons.'

Shrieks of laughter broke out.

'Think she had to get married,' someone replied. Drink always made people loud and loose with their tongues.

Dolly walked slowly on. She should have run away but she wanted to hear what people really thought of her. She recognised Meg Windsor's voice, someone she was at school with.

'I heard she was up the spout,' Meg said spitefully.

'Yer, but she managed to get rid of it,' someone replied.

'Then why did she stay with the bloke?'

'Dunno.'

'Christ, she ain't the only one who got herself in the pudding club. Most of the tarts I work with have got a kid locked away somewhere.'

'No!'

'And Meg, they ain't all white.'

'Is Doll's bloke white?'

'Dunno. Not many have seen him.'

'She's always been a silly cow. Never did see what Tone saw in her.'

'Here, Meg, d'you fancy Tony then?'

'Could be, given half a chance.'

'Well, now's your chance, with Dolly out of the running.'

'Dolly should've kept her legs shut,' said another.

'Bet Meg wouldn't even bother to put her knickers on.'

'Too bloody true,' sniggered Meg.

More great shrieks of laughter went up.

Dolly moved on. She knew Meg Windsor had always had a soft spot for Tony, but she was wrong for him. She only wanted a good time; she wasn't a homemaker. Tears were running down her cheeks. She wanted to get away from all this so much. She still cared about Tony and wanted him to be happy. How could they talk about her like that? How could they say that she got rid of her baby? Her baby. Dolly ached for Joe and her daughter. Tears ran down her face as she fumbled with the key.

Dolly went up to her bedroom. She didn't bother to switch the light on. She just wanted to lie and think of Joe. She was remembering his kisses. The way his hands gently caressed her body, the thrill when they made love. Tears filled her eyes. Would it be the same when she got to America? Then someone banging on the front door brought her out of her reverie.

Dolly looked out of the window. Tony was staring up. She quickly ducked behind the curtain. What did he want?

'Dolly, I know you're in there!' he yelled through the letterbox.

She stood trembling. What did he want?

'Come and open this door.'

'Go away!'

'Not till you promise me you won't go to America.'

At this, she had to laugh.

'Come on. Open this door!' he shouted.

'Go away, Tony. You've had too much to drink.'

'I know. But it ain't gonna stop me from saying what I want to.'

'Please, Tony. Go away!'

'No, I ain't. So you'd better come down and open the door.'

What could she do? She didn't want to be in the house alone with Tony, not after the way he'd kissed her in a house full of people and not while he was in this state of mind. She looked at her watch. It was only eleven o'clock. It would be hours before her parents came home.

Tony was still banging on the door as she went slowly down the stairs.

Chapter 23

From the moment they'd boarded the ship at Liverpool, the men had been packed together like sardines. For days Joe had wandered about the deck hoping to find some small place to be on his own for a bit of peace. Anywhere to get away from the music a lot of guys insisted on making while others were busy throwing up. The Atlantic was large and rough. God, he hoped Dolly wouldn't have to suffer like this. She must love him very much to give up everything to start a new life with a guy she'd only really known for a few weeks. Today as he shifted aimlessly about the deck, an air of excitement was rippling throughout the ship. Tomorrow they would be in New York. The sight of the Statue of Liberty was something that everybody on board had been dreaming about over these past war-torn years.

As he leaned on the rail and looked at the distant horizon, Joe's thoughts returned to Dolly. If only he'd had a chance to see her again before he left England. He wanted to tell her that he loved her so much, and losing the baby wasn't the end. They had each other and the rest of their lives to make babies. Their letters were always long and very loving; he desperately wanted to make love to her again. Like Dolly, it had been his first experience of sex. It had been wonderful; they had explored and learned together.

His brow furrowed. Would losing the baby make any difference? How would she settle in America? He had never told Dolly they could never have a home of their own; they would always have to live on the farm. Ma would see to that.

Did he want to go back to working the land, Joe asked himself? He'd seen so many places and like Dolly, he wanted to see more, but that wouldn't please Ma. She'd been very angry when he was drafted and in some weird way, pleased that Bob wasn't A1. All that seemed like a lifetime ago. It was for some like Chuck, who would never come back, and for Gus. What had being a POW been like? Would he ever be the same? Thank God Joe himself had come home in one piece. He would be home for this year's Thanksgiving and it would certainly have a lot more significance for many. He would go to the local hop. How would Sandra react to him getting married? They were never really sweethearts although Joe knew everybody wanted it that way, none more so than Ma. She wanted to see Bolton's stud farm and the Walters' land as one. It would certainly be a magnificent spread. Would everything still look the same? He knew Bob's girl Norma was still teaching in the primary school. Would his future son or daughter go there? Then his thoughts returned obsessively to Dolly. What was she doing at this very moment?

Dolly called through the front door for Tony to go away. She wasn't going to let him in.

'I ain't going nowhere,' he bawled.

'Please, Tony.'

'Why don't you want to talk to me?'

'Everything was said this afternoon.'

'I didn't tell you I loved you.'

'Yes, you did.'

'I do love you, you know.' Tony started singing at the top of his voice.

Dolly stood behind the door grinning to herself. She didn't recognise the song Tony was murdering and, being tipsy, he was slurring the words.

Dolly opened the door. Tony had a dreadful voice. 'Stop it,' she giggled. 'You'll have all the dogs howling and all the cats joining in.'

'See? I knew I could win you over with me wonderful voice.' He held onto the wall for support.

'No, Tony. I'm sorry.'

He went to push past her. 'Just let me come in for a little while.'

'Tony. I said no.'

He straightened up. 'I ain't gonna hurt you, Doll. I ain't like that. I love and respect you and I'd never hurt you or make you unhappy.'

'I know, but you're drunk.'

He grinned. 'Only a little bit.' He held up his finger and thumb to show her how much.

'I'll stand outside with you, then you can tell me all what you want to say.'

'I just want to say you don't really know this bloke you went and married, this Whatsisname?'

'Joe.'

'This Joe. What if he's a wife-beater? I'd never be a wife-beater, darling Dolly.'

'I know that.'

'What if he's a drunkard?'

'Tony, you're being very silly.'

'No, I ain't. What will he look like out of that flash uniform? Is he a city slicker or a hayseed?'

Dolly really couldn't answer that. 'I'll just get me cardi,' she said. As she went to close the door he put his foot in the way. 'Tony, don't.'

'You never let me make love to you before I went away.'

'And I certainly ain't gonna start now.' Dolly raised her voice and pushed him back.

He fell to the ground.

'Stop being so silly.'

He didn't move.

'Tony, Tony! Are you all right?' She knelt down beside him.

He grabbed her and kissed her despite her struggling to get free. They rolled together on the ground. When she finally managed to get free she sat up and slapped his face.

'Don't you ever do that again!' she said angrily.

Tony was smiling as he rubbed his cheek. 'I ain't sorry I kissed you. You used to like my kisses. And Dolly, remember this. If you ever come back I'll always be here for you.'

They sat on the concrete together.

'Don't say that. I don't want you to waste your life waiting for something that will never happen.'

'D'you remember how we used to sit on the floor of the bandstand, even when it was raining? Reg and Penny was round the other side. They were happy days.'

For a moment Dolly was back in time.

'Did you and Penny tell each other what we got up to?'

'We never got up to anything.'

'What about the night the button fell off your blouse?'

'It didn't fall off, it came off in the struggle.'

Tony laughed. 'Used to think about things like that when we was abroad. We had some good times together, didn't we?'

'Yes, we did.' Dolly struggled to her feet.

Tony also stood up. 'There'll never be another you. Cue for another song.'

Dolly laughed. 'Please don't start singing again. You could go and serenade Meg Windsor, she's got it bad for you.'

'Trouble is, I don't fancy her.'

'Goodnight, Tony.'

'Goodnight, my little princess.'

Dolly watched him swagger down the road. He was such a nice person and she did like him.

The next day, it was almost lunchtime before Wood Street came alive. Penny was the first person to call on Dolly.

'Did you have a good time last night?' asked Dolly as Penny made her way into the kitchen.

'I should say so. What about you? I didn't see you go.'

They sat at the table.

'No. I sneaked away when I saw everybody enjoying themselves.'

'Wasn't you, then?'

'Well yes. But it was a bit sad for me not having Joe there.'

'Oh Dolly, I'm so sorry. I should have guessed it would have been hard for you.'

'Not to worry. It was yours and Reg's night. What time did it finish?'

'Don't know. Reg was out for the count when I left. Didn't see the going of Tony. I was a bit worried that he might have been up here with you.'

'He did follow me – you should have heard him singing to me.'

'No! What did he want?'

Dolly laughed. 'It was the beer talking. He wanted me to give up Joe and marry him.'

Penny laughed with her. 'I can just see you doing that. Dolly, we've picked a date for our wedding.'

'When?'

'Well, as we shall be living with Reg's mum, we've decided to make it quite soon. There ain't much point in hanging about. And another thing, I don't know how long I'll be able to keep Reg at arm's length.'

Dolly grinned. 'I always thought you let Reg have his wicked way.'

'That's what he wanted everyone to think.'

Dolly reached across the table and touched Penny's hand. 'I'm really thrilled for you. So when's the great day to be?'

'I wanted to be a June bride.'

Dolly took a quick intake of breath. 'I might not be here.'

'That's what I thought, so we've decided on April.'

'I might not be here then.'

'I don't think we can bring it any more forward. I don't want to get married in the winter. Besides, we need time to get rations saved up for the food. We want to have it at home, the restaurants charge so much and we have to be out at eleven. I know we ain't gotta buy furniture, but there are some things of me own I'll want.'

Dolly could feel her tears welling up. Her friend was willing to put her first, just so that she could be at her wedding.

'Do you think your dad will give me away?'

'What about Jack?'

Penny smiled. 'I still look on him as me baby brother even if he is at work. No, I'd rather have your dad give me away.'

They could hear him walking down the passage.

'Can you ask him for me?' whispered Penny.

The kitchen door opened. 'God, my mouth feels like a sandpit,' groaned her father as he walked in. He wasn't wearing a shirt and his braces dangled round his knees; he also needed a shave. 'Good night last night, Pen.'

'Yes, it was.'

'Dad, Penny wants you to give her away when she marries Reg in April,' said Dolly.

Her father pulled Penny to her feet and held her tight. 'I'd be that honoured, love,' he said.

'Aye, aye. What's going on here?' asked Grace. She was wearing her dressing-gown; she too looked very dishevelled.

'Penny and Reg are getting married in April and she wants Dad to give her away,' said Dolly quickly. She was trying hard not to cry. She was so happy for her friend.

'Will you still be around?' Grace asked her daughter.

Dolly shrugged. 'I don't know.'

'I hope so,' said Penny. 'It wouldn't be the same without Dolly looking after me.'

They sat chatting about the wedding. Dolly wanted to be happy about it, but would she still be here?

After Penny left her father said, 'I'm dead chuffed Penny's asked me to give her away. I was that upset when you got married without me.'

'That's in the past, Dad. I'm married and that's the end of it.'

'I hope you'll still be here,' said Grace, trying to ease the situation.

'So do I.' But Dolly was also thinking that she hoped to be in America by next April.

'That was a great party last night,' said Grace. 'Did you enjoy yourself, Dolly?'

'It was all right.'

'I didn't see you leave.'

'I went outside for a breath of fresh air.'

'Still, I was surprised to see you in bed fast asleep when we got home, and we wasn't all that late, was we, Jim?'

'Dunno, love. Lost track of time.'

'I'm not surprised.'

That evening there was a knock on the door.

'Hello Tony,' said Grace when he walked in behind Jim.

'What do you want?' asked Dolly angrily.

'Dolly, where's your manners?' said her father.

'I came to say sorry,' said Tony, looking very sheepish.

'Sorry,' said Grace suspiciously. 'What for?'

'I think I made a bit of a fool of meself last night.'

Dolly didn't answer.

'Why, what did you do, son?' asked Jim.

'I came up to see Dolly.'

'And?' asked Grace sharply.

'Nothing,' said Dolly quickly. 'He just came up to sing to me. And it was awful, I can tell you.'

They all laughed.

'I did see you looked like you'd had a few drinks,' said Jim.

'Hark who's talking,' said Grace.

Tony smiled. Dolly looked at him. He was very handsome and his blue eyes crinkled when he smiled. He ran his fingers through his sandy-coloured hair and said sheepishly, 'Got a lot of years to make up. I finished up sleeping in Reg's garden. It was bloody cold and damp when I woke up.'

'Would you like a cup of tea, Tony?'

He looked across at Dolly. 'No, thanks all the same. I'd

better not. Rose ain't that pleased with the state I was in last night.'

'When's Rose gonna get married then?' asked Grace.

'Christmas.'

'Looks like Wood Street's gonna see a lot of weddings in the future,' said Jim as he tapped his pipe out in the fire.

'Yes,' said Grace softly.

Dolly knew what was going through her mind. Rose might have a quiet wedding, but Penny's would be a grand affair with bridesmaids, neighbours, the lot – not a bit like her daughter's hurried one.

Chapter 24

When the parachute factory announced they were going back to shirt-making, Grace decided to stay at home and try to start up her dressmaking business again. Although not many people could afford to have new clothes made because of the rationing and shortages, Grace was still able to make two dresses into one and turn a blanket into a coat, so she was able to keep her hand in. Jim was finding plenty of work clearing the bomb-sites and doing the odd job for Reg when he needed it, so with his pension they were comfortable. Grace did mention light-heartedly that she'd thought about having another baby when he was home. Jim thought that was very funny.

'Christ! What, start again with all those broken nights and shitty nappies? No, thank you. We can go out and enjoy ourselves now.'

The shell factory was running down its workers in order to get back to peaceful work. Married women weren't encouraged to stay. Jane had gone off hoping to work abroad. Betty went to work in the hospital and Mr Freeman and all the older men were being retired. A lot weren't happy about that. As Dolly was getting a good allowance she gave up work and concentrated on going to meetings to learn about the American way of life. The cooking was going to be something very different. With all the different cultures food was very varied and Dolly didn't like the idea of sweet things on the same plate as her dinner.

There was such a mixture of girls and women waiting to go to the States. Some had children and Dolly was envious of those who had young babies. She should have been looking forward to her daughter's first birthday. Every little girl seemed to remind her of her lost daughter. At the meetings the chatter was excitable, as everybody was full of enthusiasm and longing to be with their husbands.

Christmas was two weeks away and all the memories of last year came flooding back to Penny, Dolly and Grace.

The shops were as bare as ever and as Grace got the fairy lights out and sorted through the prewar paper chains, she sat in the front room and her mind went over and over what happened to Dolly and her lost baby. What sadness they had had at the time; it was as though Christmas never happened. This year she had Jim at her side, but it almost broke her heart to know this would be the last Christmas she would have her daughter around. It should have been a happy time; there should have been a baby to fuss over. All those who had come home were rejoicing, while at the same time there was the sadness for those who would never come home and those who had broken spirits as well as missing limbs.

Dolly was trying hard not to go over the past. Joe's letters were full of love and he told her everybody was looking forward to meeting her. He said there were a few changes around Deansville, a couple of the old men had died, and Norma, Bob's girl, had a few new pupils, but apart from that it was still the same place.

Penny was trying to forget the past, but she would never forget losing her father, and it filled her with sorrow as she tried to concentrate on her wedding. Every time the rumour went round that certain shops had something that might be useful, it would find Dolly and Penny queuing up for shoes or material. Grace was going to make the lovely brocade taffeta Penny had bought into her wedding dress, as her gift to Penny. Reg and his mother had been very generous, giving her a lot of their clothing coupons.

Dolly was worried when Penny said what colour dress she wanted for Dolly; she was going to be the only attendant.

'I think blue would be nice. If I get the material, your mum could use the same pattern she's using for my frock.'

'That sounds nice.'

'My mum's gonna lend me her head-dress, so that's the something old and borrowed taken care of. It's really ever so pretty. It's all that waxed orange blossom.'

Dolly was trying hard to work up some enthusiasm, but what if she was on her way to America in April? Should she let Penny waste her precious coupons? 'I've got a blue hankie you can have.'

'Well, that's it then. Me undies will be new.' Penny giggled. 'I'm getting a lovely nightie from me mum for Christmas.' She hugged herself. 'I'm so excited about this wedding.'

Dolly smiled. 'And so am I.'

'Reg wants us to go to Ramsgate for our honeymoon. I said it might be a bit cold, but he reckons he's got enough love to keep us both warm. Is this how you felt with Joe?'

Dolly nodded. 'It seems a long while ago now.'

'But think of when you see him again . . .'

'I never stop thinking about it.'

Dolly heard from Penny that Rose was having a quiet register office wedding, as her fiancé didn't like a fuss.

* * *

The week before Christmas a parcel arrived for Dolly. Grace and Jim stood and watched as she eagerly opened it. Joe had sent them tins of fruit and salmon, nail varnish, four pairs of nylons, chocolates and four bars of lovely perfumed soap. But it was the pretty box at the bottom of the parcel that brought tears to Dolly's eyes. Inside, the gift was beautifully wrapped in Christmas paper, and when she opened it she gasped. It contained French knickers and a matching slip in the palest peach silk, trimmed with lace. They were beautiful. 'Look!' she cried as she held them up then put them close to her cheek.

'They're ever so pretty,' said Grace as she gently handled the delicate material, 'and beautifully made.'

'I'll almost be afraid to wear them,' said Dolly, still drooling over her underwear.

'Look at these.' Grace held a bar of soap to her nose. 'I've almost forgotten what nice soap smells like. Have a whiff, Jim.' She stuffed a bar under his nose. 'And nylons.'

'You can have a pair, Mum,' said Dolly.

'I'll say that for him, he seems a thoughtful lad,' said Jim, rubbing his nose after having a bar of soap nearly poked up it.

When Penny saw Dolly's nylons and finery, she said, 'I'd love something like that for my honeymoon.'

'You'll have to wait till I get to America before I can send you something like this, but you can have one of these.' She handed Penny a bar of soap. 'I was going to give it to you for Christmas, but I couldn't wait.' Dolly had decided to give Penny a pair of nylons at Christmas.

'Wow. This is smashing.' She too sniffed at the tablet.

'It must be wonderful to walk into a shop and see things like this for sale. I wonder what the shops look like,' said Penny.

Jim was sitting quietly in the chair. 'New York has certainly got some wonderful shops. Look at the stuff I've brought back in the past.'

'I know,' said Grace. 'But I never got things like these.' She held up Dolly's delicate garments. 'This parcel must have cost him a few bob.'

'Didn't think you'd want that sort of thing. It weren't as though we was just married.' Jim chuckled. 'Mind you, you wouldn't find *me* going into one of those shops, I'd feel a right fool.'

'Joe didn't mind,' said Grace.

'Well, he's young, and young blokes are different. 'Sides, I didn't know your size. Anyway, you was always good at knocking up things for yourself, and I didn't know if what I bought you'd like, or if it would fit.'

Grace kissed the top of his head. 'Always the practical one, is my husband. But I love him.'

Dolly sat watching this happy scene. Her heart was filled with love for these three people as she saw them laughing and talking together. She knew she would miss all this so much.

Dolly wasn't going to use the underwear Joe had sent her; she was going to save it till she saw him again, on their second honeymoon.

The Taylors were all seated round the table, having finished their Christmas dinner, when Jim said softly, 'When I was at sea I dreamed of this moment. That's all I could think of — sitting here with you both, enjoying all this.' He waved his arms at the table and the paper chains that hung from the ceiling. 'I must admit there were times when I didn't think I would make it.'

Dolly could feel a tear running down her cheek. 'We've

waited a long while for this,' she sniffed.

Grace didn't speak. She got up and went into the scullery.

'Come and sit down, love,' called Jim. 'We'll do the washing-up later.'

When Grace didn't return Dolly followed her mother. To her surprise Grace was standing at the sink, looking out of the window. It was a grey afternoon and there wasn't anything to see. The house that backed on to them still had the upstairs windows boarded up, and next door's air raid shelter took away a lot of the light.

'Mum. Mum, are you all right?'

When Grace turned, Dolly could see tears shining on her cheeks. She went to her mother. 'What is it? What's wrong?'

'We've waited years for this Christmas, for all of us to be together and now it's gonna be the last. You won't ever be here again.'

Dolly held her mother tight; she had no words of comfort for her.

'What's going on out here?' Jim's voice faded away as he pushed the door open and saw his wife and daughter crying together. 'Dolly. Grace. What is it?'

Grace broke away and wiped her eyes and nose on the bottom of her pinny. 'I was just getting a bit upset about Dolly leaving us.'

Suddenly Jim looked sad. Dolly ran into his arms. 'I'm so sorry, Dad. I didn't want to fall in love with Joe. I didn't want to hurt you.'

Her father held her tight. 'It's all right, love. I was a bit hasty at first, but I know what it's like to fall in love. Remember, all I'm worried about is your happiness.' He looked over Dolly's shoulder and said to Grace, 'I've been thinking. Who knows, what with my connections, and when things get back to prewar, we might even be able to pay you a visit.'

'What, in America?' asked Grace in amazement.

'Why not?'

Dolly broke away from her father and wiped her cheeks with her hand.

'Do you really think the big liners will be going again?' asked Grace.

'They will after they've finished ferrying all the servicemen and their wives back and forth.'

Dolly was laughing. 'That makes me feel much better. I couldn't bear the thought of never seeing you again.'

Grace too was laughing. 'Dolly, you've made a right mess of your mascara.'

'I think this calls for a little celebration. Funnily enough, I've got a bottle of port put by for just this occasion,' Jim announced.

'I'll get the glasses,' said Dolly.

'Bugger the washing-up. Let's go in the front room – the fire's nice and cosy in there.' Grace thought about last year and how she'd been preparing for a fire in the front room, when the V2 fell. Although coal was still very short she knew she had to have a fire in the front room again. After all, it was Christmas.

Chapter 25

The start of 1946 was cold and miserable. Everybody seemed to spend all their time in queues grumbling. The war was over but with all the shortages, things were still as hard to get. The only good thing that Wood Street was getting excited about was Penny and Reg's forthcoming wedding. Any food coupons and points for tinned fruit that could be spared were being deposited at the grocer's in order to help Mrs Watts and Mrs Smith with the wedding breakfast. Mr Dobson had told them he'd even managed to get hold of a large tin of salmon. Everybody was happy that the reception was going to be held at Reg's house. They all said it would be more homely and less expensive and it could go on all night if need be. Dried fruit was also being put aside for the wedding cake. When the date had been announced Dolly had written to Joe asking for icing sugar as that was impossible to get, and of course anything else he could send over.

When at last the parcel arrived, Penny was over the moon at such luxuries. It contained icing sugar, dried fruit and nylons. Penny stood and watched in amazement as Dolly laid the gifts out on the table. 'It must have cost him a small fortune. I can't believe that you'll be able to walk into a shop and buy things like this one day.'

'Joe sends his love and wishes he could be here.'

'I bet you do as well?'

Dolly smiled. 'What do you think?'

Excitement was gathering as Dolly looked on as Penny's dress was slowly taking shape. It was lovely and Dolly thought how she would have loved to have had a dress like this. The blue dress she was going to be wearing was also being put together and Dolly loved it, she felt like a princess. Miss Ada Gregory had told Dolly they were trying to get a silver horseshoe for Penny to hold. They had seen some at the wholesalers but they had been snapped up quickly. She told her that she'd managed to get a few boxes of confetti and they'd been put under the counter ready for the great day. Dolly smiled when she remembered how she and Penny had got blisters as they sat night after night punching out paper for Betty's wedding. It didn't seem right that Betty was now a widow; they didn't see her at all these days as she worked long hours. Penny had promised to send her an invitation.

Before Christmas Dolly had been to the American office full of expectations, but she had been told they couldn't give her any idea when her name would come up. She knew she had to go to a transit camp and that the war brides were being sent over in rotation. She prayed it wouldn't be in alphabetical order, as that would mean she would be at the bottom of the list.

Her passport photograph caused a lot of laughs.

'Dolly, even when you become an American citizen, don't give up your British passport, will you,' said her father as he handed it back to her.

'No, Dad. I won't.'

To Dolly, everything was gathering momentum. Joe had written and said he would meet her in New York. He told her he would only be able to spend a few days away from the farm, but he'd be able to show her the sights. That really thrilled Dolly, but there was no mention of Niagara Falls. Perhaps he was keeping that as a surprise. She still thought it was wonderful that she would be having her honeymoon in New York. That was something only film stars did.

Dolly often saw Tony and was pleased that they always stopped and had a chat. He told her he was working with Reg. Reg was a builder so had plenty of work. Tony said he enjoyed working outside. 'Couldn't stand being cooped up in a factory all day, not now.'

Dolly had heard that Tony had been seen with Meg Windsor, but he never mentioned it to her. She really hoped that Meg was the right one for him. Dolly only wanted him to be happy.

It was the last week in February when Dolly received a letter from the American Embassy with more forms to fill in. There was also a letter telling her that her name was near the top of the list and she was to get ready to be sent to the transit camp.

She sat and read it over and over. This was it. Soon she would be on her way to America. Suddenly she had cold feet. Did she really want to go all that way and leave everybody she knew behind? What was in store for her? Did she want to live for a while on a farm? She was a town girl. And what about Penny's wedding? The first thing she did was write to Joe to find out if he had any idea when to expect her. Would she be stranded in New York till she contacted Joe? She decided when she'd filled in all these forms to go up to Town to see if she could find out when she could expect to be on her way.

Her parents were very quiet as Dolly sat at the table with

the papers all around her. She was pleased her father was helping her fill them in. He seemed to be resigned that his little girl was going to leave them and go off into the big wide world.

'Christ, they want to know everything about you. I reckon they'll be asking what you had for breakfast next.'

'They don't wanna know that, do they?' asked Grace as she put the jumper she was knitting for Dolly to one side. She had been told that New York could be very cold in the winter. She didn't know about Deansville.

'Course not,' said Dolly.

'Here, Grace – look at this.' Jim looked over the top of his glasses and held up one of the sheets of paper. 'It says here, have you got a criminal record? As if you'd tell 'em! Besides, what about all the criminals they've got over there? Here, girl, write down that you're Al Capone's moll,' he laughed. 'That'll give 'em something to mull over.'

'Jim, stop teasing the poor girl. Can't you see she's got enough on her mind without you being silly.'

'It's all right, Mum. I need a bit of a laugh answering some of these daft questions.'

Dolly hadn't told them her name was near the top of the list. Tomorrow she hoped to find out just how close her departure to the States was.

When she got to the building it seemed as if every war bride was also there crowding round the entrance. They were all ages and sizes. Some looked so young and some were quite old. She was asked what she wanted and when she told the soldier that she had brought her papers back, she was shown to a very large ornate room full of women. It was very noisy. The kids running around were wild and loud; it was chaotic.

For five hours she sat and waited. During that time she struck up a conversation with the girl sitting next to her, who was about the same age as Dolly.

'God, I hope it won't be like this on the boat. I'd feel like chucking some of these little sods overboard.'

Dolly laughed nervously.

'So where are you off to then?' asked the girl, whose name was Ann.

'It's a little place called Deansville.'

'I bet it ain't so little. Everything's big in America.'

They laughed together.

'What about you?' asked Dolly.

'I've got two days' journey on a train when we get to New York. My Danny lives out West. He can't meet me, so I've got to do it on me own. I'm ever so scared.'

They sat and talked about their hopes and dreams and expectations.

'I wish they had tea instead of all this coffee,' said Ann as she peered into her cup.

'I think it's something we'll have to get used to. My Joe reckoned we won the war through drinking tea.'

Ann smiled. 'He sounds a nice bloke.'

'He is,' said Dolly wistfully.

'Wouldn't it be smashing if we got on the same boat.'

'Yes, it would. Have you any idea when we can expect to go?'

'No. That's why I'm here. I hope they can give us some idea. Me dad was killed in the war and I'm trying to make arrangements for me sister to look after Mum, but she ain't that happy about it. Mum ain't all that well. I'm a bit worried about leaving her. It's awful knowing we're not gonna see 'em again, ain't it?'

Dolly nodded and swallowed the lump in her throat. 'I'm

supposed to be a matron of honour at my best friend's wedding. I'll feel rotten if we go before it happens. She used her coupons to get material for me frock, and if I'm not gonna be there, it'll be such a waste.'

'When's she getting married?'

'April.'

'That could be a bit dodgy.'

'I know. I would have loved to have had a white wedding like she's having, but we got married quickly.'

'Been married long?' asked Ann.

'Got married the May before last.'

'I got married then as well – a month before they went off on D-Day. I was so worried about my Danny. He was an air-gunner.'

'That was dangerous.'

'I know. Thank God he came through it.'

'My Joe was attached to the medical side.'

'I had a white wedding,' said Ann.

'Lucky you.'

'I borrowed one of the frocks Mrs Roosevelt had sent over.'

'I didn't know about that.'

'She had a lot of frocks sent over for us war brides. All you had to do was get 'em cleaned after. I'll tell you something; mine was real lovely and slinky. I felt like a film star.'

Dolly could almost imagine this petite blonde in a long white frock.

'I'm surprised your feller didn't tell you about 'em.'

'I don't think he knew.'

At last Dolly's name was called out and she went into another office. A very young-looking man in uniform was seated behind the desk. He looked at the papers in front of him.

'Mrs Walters. Have you filled in all the forms you were sent?'

'Yes.' She handed him all the papers.

'You didn't have to bring them personally you know. You could have posted them.'

'I know.'

'This won't push your name any further up the list.'

'I didn't bring them for that. I would just like some idea when I can expect to be going.'

'So do all those out there.' He waved his arm towards the door. 'Every day we have hundreds of them coming here asking the same question.'

Dolly was beginning to feel this was indeed a wasted journey.

He sat back and, twirling his pen round and round, looked at her. 'This is a big step for you women to take.'

'I know.'

'Life is very different in the States.'

Dolly didn't answer. She wanted to shout at him: 'Course it's different! You ain't been bombed and blasted and suffered all the rationing.' But what was the point. She knew they didn't want all these women coming to their country. But she had fallen in love. 'So you can't tell me when I can expect to leave my family?'

'No, I'm sorry. We are processing everything as fast as we can, but we still have a lot of our own boys to ship back home. And they do have priority.'

'Thank you. I can understand that.' Dolly stood up, so did he.

'I can only tell you that you'll be sent to a transit camp before you're taken to the docks.' He held out his hand. 'Good luck.'

'Thank you.'

Outside she went over to Ann.

'Any news?' the other girl asked.

'No. Let me have your address, and if and when I hear something, perhaps we could meet up again.'

'I'd like that,' said Ann. She hastily wrote down her name and address.

Dolly put the piece of paper in her handbag and left.

As she sat on the bus her thoughts went out to all the women in that room. They were being talked to as if they were some sort of cattle. Taken to a transit camp, then to the docks. Dolly felt she would have liked to parcel herself up and go as a special delivery. There must be places like this all over Britain. Would all of these women be happy? And what about the children? Some had never seen their fathers. How would their fathers react to them? In some ways it was a good thing her mother hadn't had her baby around to love and make a fuss of; that would have made it even harder to say goodbye.

Every day when Dolly heard the postman she was at the door immediately.

It was with very mixed feelings that as March moved slowly towards the close, Dolly knew that she would be here for Penny's wedding. In one way she was pleased, but it seemed a lifetime away from Joe.

She had read in the papers and seen on the newsreels that the first shipload of brides had left England and had arrived in New York. She sat on the edge of her seat as they caught sight of the Statue of Liberty. One day that would be her running down the gangway into Joe's open arms. But how much longer would she have to wait?

Chapter 26

Dolly picked up the official-looking letter from off the mat. It was addressed to her and she knew immediately from the crest who it was from. She glanced at the closed kitchen door and decided to take it upstairs to read. She sat on her bed; her hands trembled as she ran her fingers under the flap. Dolly knew this was what she'd been longing for. The thought that quickly sprang to mind was that next week was 20 April, Penny's wedding day. Would she still be here?

6 May. 6 May. The date seemed to jump off the page at her. She would be leaving Wood Street on 6 May, for ever. Would she be in America to spend her second wedding anniversary, 20 May, with her husband? She had been married almost two years, and in all that time she'd only spent two nights with him. Tears filled her eyes. She was going to be with Joe again. Had he changed? Would they feel the same? She sat staring at the letter, unable to take it in. This was something she'd been looking forward to and waiting for; now it was really going to happen. She wanted Joe here. She needed him here. She suddenly felt all alone.

'Dolly,' called her mother. 'Breakfast is on the table.'

Slowly she made her way downstairs.

'Was that the postman?' asked Grace.

Dolly nodded.

'Anything interesting?'

'Bloody hell – I don't believe it. Look at this,' said Jim, looking up from the newspaper he was reading. 'They're gonna ration bread now.'

'No!' said Grace. 'Let me look.'

Jim handed her the paper.

'I thought the war was over. We're worse off now than ever.' Grace put the teapot down. Her face was filled with anger. 'It says here we've got to help feed the Germans. I thought we won the bloody war! I bet the Germans wouldn't feed *us*.'

'Don't get upset, love,' said Jim.

Grace looked up. 'Upset? I am bloody well upset! I'm really fed up with all these shortages. I bet them up in Parliament don't go short. I bet their wives don't spend half their day stuck in queues and then getting sod all at the end.'

Dolly looked at her mother. She had never heard Grace get so angry or swear before – well, not very often. Things must be getting her down.

'It's been a hard time for you, love,' said Jim.

'Me and all the other ordinary housewives. Well, there's not a lot we can do about it, is there?' She turned to Dolly. 'What was in your letter, love?'

How could Dolly tell her? Her mother looked so upset. She would let her get over the thought of bread rationing first, but would there be something else round the corner before long?

'It was from Joe,' she lied.

'I bet he's getting a bit impatient,' said Jim.

Dolly smiled. 'Yes, he is.'

'It surely can't be much longer, can it?'

Dolly didn't answer her father.

'Sounds as if you want to get rid of her, Jim.'

'Don't ever say that, Gracie.'

'At least you won't have to spend half your life in queues, not where you're going.' Grace left the table.

Dolly's news could wait a few more days. But three weeks would come round very quick. One of the first things she would do was to write to Ann, the girl she'd met at the American Embassy who was going out there to meet her Danny. With a bit of luck they could be sailing together.

Dolly opened her eyes. Today was Penny's wedding day, and to her great relief, the sun was shining. Dolly looked at the frock hanging behind the door. Today she would be walking down the aisle behind Penny. A lump came to her throat; her own father would be holding her best friend's arm. Dolly knew it was going to be hard to keep her tears under control.

A few days ago when she told her parents the date she would be leaving, she knew her mother would cry, but she didn't expect tears from her father. The news had spread up and down Wood Street like wildfire. 'We can make our party your leaving do as well,' Reg had offered generously. Dolly knew today was going to be difficult, but it was her best friend's big day and nothing must get in the way of that.

Her mother was already up and busying herself in the kitchen when Dolly walked in.

'I promised Mrs Smith she could borrow a couple of my big bowls and some cutlery. Could you take 'em along to her? Tell her I'll bring the plates later on.'

'Course.'

Reg opened the door to Dolly. 'Come in. Have you seen Pen?' he asked.

'No, not yet.' Dolly laughed and kissed his cheek. 'Mind you, that might have been her running away with the coalman.'

'Don't jest about things like that.'

'Hello Dolly,' said Tony, coming down the stairs looking very dishevelled and bleary-eyed. 'Had to bring him home last night, talk about having a skinful.'

'And I bet you was the good boy who didn't touch a drop.'

He laughed. 'See? She knows more about me than I do.'

'Just as long as you both look presentable by two o'clock,' she said as she made her way to the kitchen.

'Don't worry, we will,' Reg yawned.

'All this looks lovely, Mrs Smith.'

'Had a lot of help from the neighbours. And all that stuff from that husband of yours. That was really nice of him.'

Dolly smiled. She was proud Joe had helped to make Penny's day. 'Mum said she'll bring the plates along in a while. I'd best be going.'

'See you in church,' said Reg, closing the front door behind her.

Dolly was fussing round Penny. She was just setting the head-dress on Penny's lovely curls when she looked in the mirror to check it was straight and saw that her friend had tears rolling down her cheeks.

'What is it? What's wrong? Here, you ain't got second thoughts, have you?'

Penny shook her head. 'It's just that I can't imagine what my life's gonna be like without you around.'

Dolly held her tight. 'You've got Reg now. Besides, this time next year there might be someone else who'll be taking up all your time.'

'Promise me you'll write often.'

'Course I will. Now come on, dry your eyes otherwise you'll make a right mess of your mascara.'

'I love you, Mrs Walters.'

'And I love you, Mrs Smith.'

To Dolly, it didn't feel right walking back down the aisle holding Tony's arm. She knew everybody was looking at them and could see a few were whispering to each other. She could almost hear the things they were saying: what a lovely couple they made and wasn't Dolly a silly cow not to be marrying him instead of breaking her mother and father's heart by going all that way away from them for good.

Outside the church the photos were being taken and Dolly was swept along with all the happy chaos. The laughter, good wishes and kisses that came from everybody were truly wonderful.

'Dolly, you look really very nice, doesn't she, May?' said Miss Ada to her sister.

'That horseshoe was lovely, I know Penny was really thrilled,' Dolly told them.

'You're gonna miss Penny when you go,' said Miss May kindly.

'Yes, I will.' She turned and hurried away.

When Dolly caught sight of Betty wandering about she called her over. 'I'm so pleased to see you. How are you? And how's the job?'

'You're still here then? I thought you might have gone by now.'

'No. I go next month.'

'Lucky old you. I'm still saving, and as soon as they start to run the liners for civilians, then I'll be off.'

'Are you coming back to the house?'

'No. I've got to go on duty.'

Dolly kissed her cheek. 'Keep in touch, won't you?'

'I will.'

Dolly saw her walk over to Penny. Penny also kissed her cheek and Dolly watched her leave. That could be the last time she would ever see her. Poor Betty with all her heartache, would she ever marry again? Dolly stood and observed the crowd milling about. This could be the last time she would see most of the people here, too.

After the buffet and the speeches, the piano was being put to good use; there were always plenty of old 'uns who could thump out a good tune.

Once again Dolly was sitting on the stairs taking it all in.

'Can I sit with you?' Tony was leaning over the banisters.

'Be my guest.' Dolly moved over.

'You look really nice.'

'Thank you.'

Tony sat beside Dolly. 'I think we've done this before,' he said, grinning.

'Yes, and if I remember right you followed me home and ended up getting a slap.'

Tony laughed. 'You know me, always did like to live dangerously. But honestly, I'm not really sorry about that.'

'Tony.'

He held up his hand. 'All right. I am sorry.'

Dolly smiled. 'Don't worry about it, it'll give me something to laugh about when I'm on the high seas.'

'Dolly, I know I shouldn't say this, but you know that I'll always be here . . .'

Dolly quickly put her hand over his mouth. 'Please, Tony. Don't say it. In a short while I'll be gone and you'll soon forget all about me and end up marrying Meg.'

He kissed her hand. 'I don't think so.'

'Time will tell. Now come on, let's go and have a knees-up. I don't think we'll be having too many of them where I'm going.' She grabbed his hand and took him into the front room.

It was late when the last of the guests left. Penny and Reg had left earlier and were on their way to Ramsgate. The bride's mother, Mrs Watts, was having trouble with Jack who was definitely the worse for drink. Billy, who was now as tall as his brother, was trying to help his mother get Jack to his feet.

'You sure you can manage?' asked Dolly.

'Yes, thanks. Been managing him all his life.' She gave a wave over her shoulder.

Dolly smiled as she stood and watched them weaving down the road. Then she went inside to help her mother with the clearing up. Her father was asleep in one chair and Tony in the other, both snoring their heads off. Meg Windsor had gone home with another couple, but not till after she'd given Tony a right old telling off for drinking too much. Not that he was taking a lot of notice, he was too drunk.

Dolly and Grace managed to haul Jim out of the chair.

'Come on, lover boy, time to go,' said Grace.

'All right,' he said, staggering to his feet. 'Good party, though, wasn't it?'

'Very,' said Grace.

'D'you know, that barrel's only just run out.'

'I'm glad to hear that.'

Despite the laughter, singing and dancing all along the road, Dolly and Grace managed to get him indoors.

'Right, I'm off to bed,' Grace sighed. 'And Jim, don't stay down here too long.'

'Don't worry, Mum, I'll make sure he gets up the stairs in one piece.'

'Thanks, love.' Grace held her daughter tight. Today had been a happy day. Grace knew there would never be another one like this. She had wanted to give Dolly a farewell party, but she had said no. Dolly was right; Grace had seen it would be too much for her. She had noted her sad face today when everybody had wished her well as she said goodbye to her friends and neighbours.

'Fancy a cuppa, Dad?' Dolly asked.

'Yes please, love.'

Dolly was quietly singing to herself in the scullery. In many ways this had been a happy and sad day, and she didn't want it to end.

When she took the tea things in Dolly was surprised to see her father sitting at the table writing a letter. 'What are you doing? Making out your last will and testament? Don't worry, Mum ain't that mad at you. She ain't gonna kill you.' Dolly sat next to him.

'This is for you.'

'It's a funny time to sit writing me a letter as I'm still here.'

'I ain't drunk. I've got to put all the things I feel in a letter and I have to do it when I've had a few to give me Dutch courage.'

'You are a daft old thing.'

He took hold of Dolly's hand. 'You know that I love you very much, we both do and we're very sorry to see you go.'

'Don't, Dad.' Dolly wiped the tears with her free hand.

'Dolly, I don't want you to read this till you're on the ship. Promise me.'

'I promise. What are you saying?' Dolly tried to make

light of it. 'What you trying to tell me – that you'll be glad to see the back of me?'

Jim quickly put his arm round her and held her close. There was a catch in his voice as he whispered, 'Don't ever say that. Remember, this will always be your home.'

'I know that, Dad.'

'And you'll always be my little girl.'

Dolly swallowed hard. 'Come on, Dad, let's have our tea and get to bed.'

'You go on up when you're ready. I'll be up in a mo.'

Dolly left her father sitting at the table. Although she was thrilled at the thought of seeing Joe again, the next two weeks were going to be the hardest of her life. She smiled at the thought of her father writing her a letter. It was something to look forward to when she was on the boat.

Chapter 27

As the train sped through the countryside, Dolly, who had managed to get a window seat, sat and gazed at the green fields and trees rushing past. Joe had never told her that much about the area where he lived. Was it flat or were there hills? There must be fields if he lived on a farm. He had told her they had a couple of horses, and the farm grew cereals. The guard pushing his way through the throng of people lining the corridor shouted that the next stop was Tidworth, the one Dolly had to get off at. She was nervous and apprehensive when she stepped off the train. Like the train bringing her here, the platform was milling with women and children. At the station she looked round for Ann. She had replied to Dolly's letter and to her joy she knew she was coming to this camp today.

The US Army put them in line and they were shepherded and herded like cattle, placed in buses and taken to the transit camp.

Although the weather was warm, the camp looked a cold, bleak place. When Dolly was told which dormitory she was in she went in search of Ann. When they caught sight of each other they hugged and held each other like long-lost friends. They both needed someone to talk to and a shoulder to cry on.

That evening they were given a 'welcome' speech. Dolly shuddered at the American Captain who said, 'You may not like the conditions here, but remember, no one asked you to come.'

'Christ,' said Ann, 'that really does make you feel welcome.'

Dolly guessed that the men looking after them resented them as well. After all, they too wanted to go home, not play nursemaid to a lot of women and kids.

Over the next few days they were physically examined, which was very embarrassing. Dolly was told that a few of the very young girls came out of the room the doctors were using crying and very upset. They said they had been made to take off their knickers and stand over a mirror that had been placed on the floor and a torch was shone on their private parts. Apparently the doctors were looking to see if they had VD. Dolly was fortunate, she had been examined by an older doctor and it didn't happen to her.

It took a few days for them to be numbered and labelled. As they looked at the labels attached to their coats, Dolly said to Ann that she felt like one of the evacuee kids. It wasn't long before they found themselves in buses and on their way to the docks, where once again they were herded, this time on to the ship. Dolly held on to her hat as she stood and looked up at the massive grey bulk in front of her. Her heart gave a little leap. This was it. She was leaving England, her home, her neighbours, Penny and her mum and dad. She was going to start a new life. It was too late now to question whether she had done the right thing or not.

Dolly and Ann were sharing a cabin with two others. Fortunately the other two women didn't have children. It was very cramped and they all tried to fit their few belongings into the small space.

Dolly hadn't wanted anybody at the docks to see her off, as she knew it was going to be hard to say goodbye. She and Penny had hugged and cried together. For days it seemed, everybody came to the house with their good wishes. Dolly had spent her last days saying emotional farewells and her sleepless nights, worrying. Now it was here, it was a big step to take. Dolly knew it was very hard for her mum and dad to keep cheerful, and it really upset her whenever she caught sight of her mother softly crying.

When Tony came to say goodbye he held her close and whispered that he would always be here for her. She let him gently kiss her lips.

The women all stood on the deck as the ship slowly moved away and there were many more tears. The ship left England with a lot of noise from its hooters, which seemed to go on for ever.

At last the crying was over and England had disappeared. They were at sea. Dolly knew now that she would be with Joe on their second wedding anniversary. What surprise had he in store for her? Had she changed? Had *he* changed? Dolly and Ann shared these secret fears.

The thing that thrilled everyone was the shop on board in which they were able to buy such luxuries as sweets, nail varnish and lipstick, which quickly helped to suppress their blues.

'If this is a taste of what we can get in America, I ain't half glad I come,' said Ann, trying out yet another colour nail varnish.

Dolly had been wandering about on deck. She thought about how her father had been at sea for all those years and the time he had been torpedoed – something that he'd kept to himself for a long while. There was no fear of that now the war was over. When she stared over the side, the sea looked a long way down, very cold and very uninviting. It must have been horrible to be tossed about in a small boat, waiting to be plucked from this with nothing round them but water. How they must have hoped and prayed they would be rescued. She gazed out at the horizon; the ocean was a very big empty place. Then Dolly suddenly remembered the letter her father had written her on the night Penny had got married. She had kept her promise and hadn't read it.

When she got to the cabin, Dolly was pleased to find it empty for once. She scrabbled around in her suitcase and sitting on her bunk, opened the envelope. To her utter amazement there were fifteen pounds inside the letter.

My very dear daughter,

I know you think I'm a little drunk, but what I've got to say is something I can't say to your face. Besides, your mum might kill me.

This money is for you to put aside and if you ever need to, use it to come home.

We love you so much and want you to be happy. Me and your mum are devastated that you are going to leave us. You have been all the world to us. Perhaps one day we will see you again.

Remember, if you need to come home, go to the docks in New York and ask for Nobby Clark. Keep this letter and money safe and don't ever mention it to your mother.

I love you very much.

From your ever-loving dad, XXX

Dolly sat and stared at the letter and the three large crisp, white five-pound notes in her hand. Where had her father got all this money from? It must have taken him years to save this, and now he had given it all to her. She should have read the letter before she left home and then she could have given it back to him. Was this his funny way of trying to be helpful? Dolly remembered that he was half-cut at the time he wrote this letter. She would never need the money for that purpose. Dolly smiled to herself. It could be used in years to come if she wanted to bring her children over for a holiday to see their grandparents. That was another dream she would have to hold on to. Of course, by then this poor old Nobby Clark would be well and truly retired.

Just then, Dolly heard somebody talking outside. She quickly put the money and letter in the envelope and stuffed it back in her case.

The sheer size of the ship had taken Dolly's breath away. As she strolled around, she wondered what it must have looked like before the war. It must have been so beautiful before all the luxury fixtures and fittings had been removed. If she stood and closed her eyes, she could almost hear the band playing and see the women in lovely evening dresses dancing with handsome men in black tie and tails. But this ship, like all the luxury liners, had for years been used to ferry troops about. Would her mum and dad ever get the chance to visit her when fare-paying passengers started using it again?

The women were told they were now American citizens and given more forms to fill in and sign. The noise went on day and night. Kids ran about and babies cried. Dolly was finding it hard to sleep and some nights, fights broke out between the women. All in all it was very disturbing. Dolly often listened to the conversations all around her. She was surprised at what some of the wives were expecting to find on the other side of the Atlantic.

Ann said she wasn't really sure what to expect. Her husband was now working in a factory in Chicago; he was hoping to find them an apartment. 'I only hope it's half decent,' she said as they walked round the deck.

They stood and looked out at the vast expanse of water. So far, the crossing hadn't been that bad although some had suffered from seasickness.

Dolly knew Joe lived on a farm. Deansville was a small place, with just a primary school, a gas station, a liquor store and a grocery store.

'That don't sound very exciting,' Ann commented. 'Being a townie, won't you miss all the shops and pictures?'

'I don't know. Joe said we have to go into town to get most things – clothes and the like. He said the upper-grade schools were there as well.'

'Was he telling you that bit so you'd know what school to send any kids you might have to?'

Dolly nodded. She hadn't told Ann about her stillborn daughter.

'Do you want kids?' the other girl persisted.

'Yes, very much,' Dolly said quietly.

'I wanna proper house before I commit myself. Don't fancy bringing up a kid in a flat.'

'We've got to stay at the farm for a while, but I hope we can find a little house before too long. Joe said they have some round and about. In Deansville everybody knows each other, apparently, and it is a very friendly place.'

'Let's hope we all fit in then.'

'I hope so.' Dolly knew that from now on, everything was going to be so very different from life in Rotherhithe. That night she stood on the deck and watched the moon shimmering on the water. Would she miss London that much? Only time would tell.

* * *

Five days later a buzz of excitement raced through the ship. The women and children all pushed and shoved each other as they hurried to get up on deck. The Statue of Liberty was in front of them. The cries, yells and screams were electrifying. Everybody was crowding on deck to get a better view. Many of the kids were crying as they were pushed to one side. The sight of the skyscrapers took Dolly's breath away. It was wonderful and so emotional, like something out of a film.

Slowly the big ship was being pulled and nudged by the small tugs milling round them as they made their way towards the docks. It took a while for the ship to berth and then came the long wait to get off. On deck Ann and Dolly kissed and hugged each other as they said their goodbyes. Soon they would be separated. Ann and the other brides who were moving on were going to be taken to another clearing-house before being dispatched to meet their husbands. Everybody was scanning the shore, trying to find their loved one. When somebody did catch sight of a waving hand they recognised, the cries and tears of happiness were infectious.

'Ain't you seen him yet?' asked Ann.

'No!' shouted Dolly, trying to make herself heard above the din.

Dolly looked and looked, but she still couldn't see Joe. He was a civilian now. What would he be wearing? Would she recognise him? Would he be here to meet her? All these wild thoughts were filling her head as the queue slowly snaked its way down the stairs and out onto the gangplank. She stood for a moment or two, trying to take in the scene before her. She was in awe of the tall skyscrapers. Why didn't they topple over? On the docks there was a lot of noise as the large cranes moved overhead. They picked up their loads as if they were tiny boxes and gently deposited them on the dockside.

Very carefully, Dolly walked down the gangplank and stepped on to American soil. She put her case on the ground as tears filled her eyes. As far back as she could remember, this had been her dream; now it had come true. She was here, she was really here. She was in America.

Some of the women who had spotted their husbands brushed past her, yelling out their names. It was chaotic and she continued to search the crowds.

Suddenly she heard her name being shouted out. She looked up, and there was her Joe rushing towards her. She dropped her case and ran into his open arms. Kisses rained down on her face and she kissed him back. They stood locked in each other's arms completely oblivious of everything around them.

When they finally broke away Dolly was smiling. Her face was wet with tears. 'I must look a mess,' she said, straightening her hat.

'You look absolutely gorgeous. You haven't changed a bit. God, I've missed you.' Joe kissed her again.

'I can't begin to tell you how much I've missed you and longed for this day.' She laughed. 'You've let your hair grow.' Dolly ran her fingers through his thick dark hair.

'Can do what I like now I'm out of the Army. Happy?'

Dolly nodded. Her eyes were sparkling. 'I want to pinch meself, just to make sure I ain't dreaming.'

Joe picked up her case and put his other arm round her waist. 'I can tell you, hon, that you sure ain't dreaming. God, I love you.'

'Where are we going?'

'I've booked a room in a hotel just off East Street. That's near to all the sights.'

'I'm so excited, I hope I'm not sick.'

Joe hailed a yellow cab and they were on their way.

The hotel was small and not one of the best, but Dolly didn't notice the ageing décor for as soon as they got to their room Joe was kissing her madly and passionately and had started undressing her. Dolly was eagerly helping him out of his clothes.

Lovemaking was over very quickly and they lay in each other's arms. Joe levered himself up on his elbow and began to run his fingers over her lips. 'I promise I'll take a bit longer next time.' He kissed her lips.

'When will the next time be?' asked Dolly dreamily.

'How about now?'

After the first excitement of being together, Dolly showed him the photos of Penny's wedding.

'Don't she look nice?' she said fondly.

'And what about you? You look really lovely.'

'Next week's our anniversary – we've been married two years.'

'I know, but we've only been together for less than two weeks. Any regrets?'

Dolly shook her head. 'None whatsoever.'

That evening they dressed and went on the town for dinner. It tickled Dolly that every time anyone heard her talking to Joe they stopped and asked her to say something.

'Don't get a lot of Limeys over here,' said Joe, grinning.

Dolly thought her neck would ache as she spent most of the time looking up. 'These buildings are so tall. How come they don't fall over?'

'It's the bedrock they're built on. I've been told they can go up even higher.'

In the restaurant Joe held her hand and gazed into her eyes.

After looking at the menu in amazement Dolly said, 'I can't believe you can get all this to eat over here.' She felt like a child turning this way and that, taking in everything, determined not to miss a single detail. She had so much to write and tell Penny and her mum and dad.

She started eagerly looking around at the other diners, noting how they all seemed to be well-dressed. Suddenly her utility clothes seemed drab and uninteresting.

'This is so posh,' she said shyly.

Joe smiled. 'I love your funny ways.'

'I can't wait to see everything. How long can we stay here in New York?'

'Only two days, I'm afraid.'

Dolly couldn't hide her disappointment. 'Only two days? Then are we going on to Niagara?' she added eagerly.

''Fraid not. Ma wasn't that happy at me spending these two days away.'

'But why?'

'There's always so much to do on the farm.'

Dolly wanted to get angry, but knew that wouldn't help. How dare her mother-in-law stop them from having more time together? After all, this was their belated honeymoon.

'When we've finished here we'll go up to the top of the Empire State Building,' promised Joe. 'It's the tallest building in the world.'

'What – in the dark?'

'Best time to see Manhattan.'

'I hope they've got a lift.'

He laughed. 'They've got two.'

Dolly stood silently in awe as she looked down on the lights of the buildings, the river and the cars. She wanted to cry she was so happy. Joe was standing behind her with both his arms round her holding her tight. The warm wind gently ruffled her hair. She felt she was in one of her dreams.

'It's so beautiful,' she whispered.

'Not as beautiful as you.' He kissed her neck.

Dolly closed her eyes and quickly opened them again. Yes, it was still there; she wasn't dreaming this time. 'I never want this moment to end.'

For two days they saw the sights and made love. Then to Dolly's great disappointment it was coming to the end. As she stood in the lobby waiting for Joe to settle the bill she began to wonder what sort of welcome she would get from his family. Well, she would know the day after tomorrow. They were stopping en route at a motel as Joe had told her that Deansville was about 300 miles away.

'I'll just put these in the trunk,' said Joe, stacking her cases in the car.

'Is this yours?' asked Dolly as she stood beside the Ford car. It was very different from those back home.

'Belongs to the farm. Everything is the farm's property.'

'Oh,' was all Dolly could think of to say. She hoped that didn't include her and Joe.

Dolly had never seen traffic like New York had, the honking horns, shouting and people waving their arms; she sat silent and terrified. Soon they were speeding out of the town and were on their way. Dolly was sad at leaving New

York. She turned for a last, lingering look. Then she touched Joe's arm; he smiled at her as she settled down. She sighed with contentment, aware that so many new and exciting things lay ahead of her.

Chapter 28

It was dark when they pulled into the motel. The bright red flashing arrow indicated where the office was located. Dolly sat in the car and waited for Joe to collect the key to their room.

'Number thirty-four,' he said, getting into the car and handing her the key.

Dolly counted the numbers on the wall of the terraced bungalows.

'There it is,' she said, pointing through the windscreen, noting as she did so that the whole place looked a bit run down and in need of a drop of paint.

Dolly was standing gazing out of the window when Joe came in the room from the bathroom. The moon was shining on the parked cars. He stood behind her and took her in his arms. 'This time tomorrow we shall be in our own bed,' he whispered.

Dolly turned and he kissed her. It was a kiss with the promise of what her future and the rest of her life as Mrs Walters was going to be.

The motel was built close to the road and was very noisy and hot. Joe apologised for the lack of air conditioning. Dolly didn't really know what he meant. Was he talking about a fan on the ceiling? She tossed and turned, unable to sleep. After listening to the traffic and watching the head-lights as they raced past the motel, she crept out of bed and went to the bathroom to splash some cold water on her face. She turned on the light, and there, on the floor, was the biggest thing she'd ever seen. It scurried across the floor. She screamed.

Joe was out of bed and at her side at once. 'What is it? What's wrong?'

Dolly couldn't speak. She stood shivering and pointed to the floor.

Joe laughed. 'It's only a roach.'

Dolly looked at him and jumped onto the bed.

'It's a cockroach. You'll have to get used to them,' he said calmly.

'Kill it! Kill it!' she yelled, dancing up and down on the bed.

'Killing this one won't help. I expect the place is crawling with 'em.'

'Let's go.' She was panicking.

'Honey, you'll have to get used to this sort of thing.'

'Have you got these at the farm?'

'Yep. We spray 'em now and again, just to keep them down, but those little fellers just come back again.'

Dolly sat on the bed with her nightie pulled over her knees and tucked round her feet. 'Can we go? Can we leave now?' She was nearly sobbing with fear.

'No. Relax, baby.'

'Well, I ain't gonna go to sleep. I don't fancy those things crawling all over me in the night.'

'They won't hurt you,' said Joe, climbing into bed.

'I'm sorry, Joe, but I just ain't staying here.'

'Come on, babe. Come in the bed and snuggle down with me. I'll protect you.'

Cautiously Dolly slid under the bedclothes. Suddenly she sat up and lifted the clothes high in the air.

'Dolly, what are you doing?'

'I'm looking to see if any are in the bed.'

Joe laughed. He pulled back the bedclothes. 'See? Everything's fine. Now come and settle down. We've got a long drive tomorrow.'

Dolly slid down and despite being hot she pulled the sheet up round her neck. She knew sleep wouldn't come and prayed for the morning. This was something he hadn't warned her about. In Rotherhithe some of the houses had bed bugs, and everyone knew you could splat them easily with a shoe. These big buggers didn't look as if you could kill them with anything other than a hammer.

Dolly was being shaken. 'Come on, my brave little lady. Time to get up.'

She quickly sat up. 'What is it? What's happening?'

'We've got to be on our way. We can stop a little later on for breakfast at a drugstore.'

Dolly looked down at the floor. 'Have they gone?'

'For now.' Joe was grinning. 'But shake your clothes and tip out your shoes, just in case one's hiding in 'em.'

Dolly's face was full of alarm. 'Will they?'

Joe came and lightly kissed her. 'No. I'm just teasing.'

'Oh you.' She pushed him away.

Then Joe was on the bed kissing her. 'I love you,' he said and began making love to her again.

The last thing on her mind at that moment was cockroaches.

'Not long now,' said Joe after they'd been driving for hours. He slowed the car down. 'That's our church.' They passed a tiny building that looked more like a wooden shack with a cross on the top. 'And this is where we come to do our main shop.'

Dolly eagerly looked at the shops. 'Is this Deansville?'

'Yep. Get most things here.'

Dolly couldn't see how. There were only a few stores and as far as she could see, only one clothes shop – although she did spot a hairdresser's. 'Can you walk here?'

Joe laughed. 'No. It's a couple of miles. Besides, nobody walks. There's always someone going to the bank or taking the kids to school; anyone will give you a lift.'

'You've got a cinema!' shouted Dolly in delight.

'Don't get a lot of time to come here myself.'

'Look, they've got an Errol Flynn film. We can come sometimes, can't we?' Dolly twisted and turned, trying to read the poster.

'Maybe.'

'It's lovely round here,' she said, looking over her shoulder as they left the few shops behind. Fields full of fresh green leaves had now spread out either side of them.

'Not too far now.'

A mile or so further on they passed a gas station and Joe hooted and waved. He slowed down again. 'That's Bill's place. And that's the grocery store.' He pointed to the other side of the road. 'Madge runs that. Then there's the primary school. Only got one classroom. Bob's girl Norma is the teacher. Behind that is the Mission Hall, that's where we have our weekly dance.'

'Are Bob and Norma engaged?'

'No, they're just walking out.'

'Is this Deansville as well?'

'It's all part of it.' Joe turned the car onto a dusty track. 'This is it. This is home.'

They bounced along, sending up a cloud of dust behind them.

Dolly's heart was racing. What kind of reception had they got in store for her? Would they give her a welcome party? Would there be a banner with her name on it? She prayed her mother-in-law would like her, even though she'd never replied to any of Dolly's letters.

A long, low, unimpressive building came into sight and Joe stopped the car in front of it. There was no banner stretched across the door.

Dolly got out and looked around. The air smelt sweet and fresh, so different from London and New York. She took a few very deep breaths.

Joe was busy getting the cases from the boot, which he had called the trunk. There were so many new words she had to learn. She mustn't call her handbag a bag; it was now a purse. She nervously patted her hair as she waited for someone to open the door that had a mesh fly-screen in front. To Dolly it was just like being in the pictures – she corrected her thoughts, *movies*. She was almost expecting the doors to fly open and a group to come out singing and dancing. Why hadn't anybody come out to greet them? They surely knew they were here.

Joe must have read her thoughts for he said as he opened the door and took the cases in, 'They're all up at the fields. They won't be back till later.'

'What about your mum – Ma?' Dolly quickly corrected herself.

'She's up there with 'em. She never stops working – always got to be with the boys. You wait till you see her riding. She's as good as any of the hired hands. You'll have to learn to ride a horse.'

'What – me?' Dolly was filled with alarm. 'No, thanks. I

wouldn't even go on a donkey at Southend.'

Joe laughed. 'We'll see, but I'm sure we can find you plenty to keep you occupied round here.'

Dolly wasn't sure what he meant by that.

She had been ushered into the room that had been Joe's; it was now to be theirs. It didn't have a lot of furniture, just a new double bed, a table and chest of drawers; the large built-in wardrobe took up most of one wall. Her few clothes would be lost in there. It did have a large fireplace, and to Dolly's delight, their very own bathroom. 'I can't believe this,' she said excitedly. 'Our very own bathroom! You wait till I tell 'em back home.'

'We've all got our own. Every time Ma has another room added she puts in a bathroom as well.'

Dolly was amazed that someone could just add a room on when they felt like it. Mrs Walters must be very well off.

'We'll get a few bits later to make it more homely. Didn't bother when it was just for me,' said Joe, interrupting her thoughts.

Dolly could see it had potential. There were two windows: one had a fabulous view out over the fields, while the other looked out onto the yard, as Joe had called it. Dolly smiled. It was nothing like the little square backyard they had at home.

Joe showed her round the house. It was single-storey, built in the shape of a horseshoe, and very large. She saw Ma's office, her bedroom, Bob's room and the winter living room with a huge open fire. It must be lovely and cosy when it was cold. Joe had warned her that they sometimes had bad winters. There were three other rooms, but they were just full of junk. Joe stood with his arm round her.

'Maybe one day we might be turning one of these rooms

into a nursery,' he whispered tenderly.

Dolly wanted to reply that she was hoping they would have their own place by the time babies came along.

Outside on the porch were some large, comfortable-looking armchairs. As they wandered back into the kitchen Joe told her this was the hub of the place. Her high heels echoed on the stone floor.

'Coffee?'

'Do you have any tea?'

'Sorry, you're in America now.'

Dolly would rather have had tea. Perhaps when she was settled she could buy herself some.

'Everything is talked over and discussed in here,' said Joe as they sat at the huge plain wooden table hugging a mug of coffee, which made Dolly shudder. It was bitter, nothing like the Camp Coffee back home. The range had a black pot on the top; something was bubbling in it, and it smelt savoury.

'Ma must have come back to put a stew on.' Joe lifted the lip and peered in the pot. 'Smells good.'

Dolly only nodded.

'When you've finished your coffee we'll have a walk round. I'll show you Peggy.'

'Peggy? Who's she?'

'One of the horses. We've only got two. Ma takes Suzy when she rides. Suzy can be a bit boisterous at times.'

Dolly felt very overdressed as she tripped around the stables in high heels. She didn't like the look of Peggy; the horse was big and snorted at her. If Joe reckons he's gonna get me up there, Dolly thought grimly, he's got another think coming.

The dust from a truck coming along the track caught their attention.

'Here comes Bob. Let's go and say hi.' Joe took her arm and led her round to the front of the house.

Bob, who was standing by the truck, was tall and lanky with a shock of dark hair. He was wearing a check shirt, a cowboy hat and blue denim trousers. He was very good-looking and with his tan he looked just like someone out of a film.

'Hi,' he called. 'You must be Dolly.' He kissed her cheek. 'Welcome.'

'Thank you,' said Dolly. 'I feel I know you already, seeing as how we were writing to each other.'

'True. Joe, the fence came down in Martha's top field. Ma's up there now, she sent me down to see if you were back. She said if you were, to go up right away to give 'em a hand.'

'OK. Dolly, you wait here, we shouldn't be that long. I'll just get changed.' With that Joe was gone.

'I must say, you're a lot prettier than your photos. They don't do you justice.'

Dolly blushed. 'Thank you. Is this field very far away?'

'Nope, not really.'

Dolly would have liked to go with them, but that obviously hadn't occurred to either Joe or Bob.

Joe was back, having changed into an outfit like Bob's.

As Dolly stood and watched the truck disappear, she suddenly felt very alone. It was her own fault, she should have asked to go with them. Should she take a look around? What if she saw a snake or something? After the encounter with the cockroach, Dolly decided it was safer to stay here. She walked back into the house and collected her writing pad; she would sit on the porch and write to her mum and dad.

★ ★ ★

The sound of a car door slamming and voices woke her. It was dusk, she must have dozed off. Where was she? She was disorientated.

Joe came over and kissed her cheek. 'Don't sit out here in the dark, hon. You should have turned the lights on. We do have electric lights, you know.'

'I'm sorry.'

Bob was laughing. 'Give the poor girl a chance to settle in, bro.'

Joe switched on the lights, which made Dolly squint.

'Right,' said a loud strong voice. 'Where is she?'

Dolly jumped to her feet. She could see a tall lean woman with a shock of grey hair and steely blue eyes coming towards her.

'So, *you're* my son's wife?' There was no kiss or warm handshake. 'I don't like to pussyfoot round people. Had to look after this place, myself and my boys for too long. So, young lady, I expect you to pull your weight. Everybody here has to work hard.'

Dolly was getting angry with this woman. Who did she think she was, talking to her like that? And why wasn't Joe sticking up for her? 'And I'm very pleased to meet you too,' said Dolly as sarcastically as she could.

Ma ignored the remark and went on, 'We might as well start as we mean to go on. I'm a straight-talking woman. I wanted my boy here to marry Sandra. Her father's got a ranch that joins us – he breeds horses. She's an only child so one day all that could have been Joe's. Still, it's not to be. Mr Roosevelt's fault, God rest his soul, for getting us in that damn war.'

Dolly wanted to say, 'What about when the Japs bombed Pearl Harbor?' but thought better of it.

'So you see I wasn't best pleased when he said he'd got

wed to a foreigner. Let's hope you fit in. Things might be different when babies come along. By the way, I was sorry to hear you lost your baby.'

Dolly felt as if she'd just been thwacked with a baseball bat, but give her time. There was no way she was going to be treated like a doormat.

Chapter 29

As they sat at the large table and had their evening meal, Dolly was disappointed that most of the chatter was about the fence, the rounding up of the cattle and what was to be done tomorrow. Only Bob was interested in asking her about England and New York.

'Got to make sure those cows don't get out again,' said Mrs Walters, not having said much to Dolly. Why couldn't she be like most Americans, friendly and welcoming?

Dolly was upset. Why wouldn't this woman try to like her and help her feel at home? 'Joe, can you show me round tomorrow?'

'Sorry, hon, too busy.'

'I think you'd better get yourself the right clothes before you start,' said Ma. 'Can't have you flitting around in those duds.'

'Where can I get them?'

'Wally's in Deansville,' came the reply.

'How do I get there?'

'You'll have to wait till someone takes you.'

'Joe, can you—?'

'He's too busy just now,' interrupted Ma.

As she sat there, Dolly was comparing Mrs Smith, Penny's new mother-in-law, with this forbidding character. What a contrast the two women were! What would Penny and her mother say about this woman?

Ma cleared away the dinner things and went into her office.

'You can give us a hand with the washing-up,' said Joe. 'That way you'll find out where everything goes.'

Dolly went to the sink. The kitchen had been fitted out with a very modern sink and draining board with fitted cupboards under and on one wall. Dolly was intrigued by the huge refrigerator that was almost as tall as her. It stood in one corner and she would dearly have liked to ask if the light stayed on when the door was closed. A dark green range was along one wall. It was all very up to date.

The telephone ringing startled her. Bob went into the hall. He came back after a while, saying, 'That was Norma. She's coming over to meet the new bride.'

Dolly smiled. She hoped this Norma would be a little more welcoming.

It wasn't long before they heard a car draw up, the door was pushed open and Norma came breezing in like a breath of fresh air. She came straight up to Dolly and without waiting to be introduced, hugged and kissed her warmly.

'Welcome to Deansville. Joe, you didn't tell us how pretty she is!' Norma took her arm and propelled her out onto the porch. 'These men don't say much. Bob, bring me out a cold beer. What about you, Dolly?'

'Yes, please.'

'I love the way you talk. D'you know you're the only GI bride round here, so don't be surprised if the local rag comes down to see you. The folks round here will want to know all about you.'

Dolly could see that laughing was something that came easily to Norma. Her pupils must love her; she wasn't a bit like any of Dolly's teachers. She was attractive and slim; her dark hair was tied back into a ponytail with the ends of the pale pink chiffon scarf hanging down her back. She too was wearing blue denim trousers, but Norma had them rolled up to her calf. Like Ma had said, this was something Dolly would have to get. She stood out like a sore thumb and felt very overdressed in her black skirt and the frilly blouse that her mother had made out of parachute silk.

Ma stayed in her office all the while they sat on the porch talking and laughing. Dolly was happy; this was the Joe she'd married.

'Did you like New York?' asked Norma.

'I thought it was wonderful. I would have liked to have spent more time there, but Joe had to get back.'

'Only been there once, but I want to go again. It's so busy and exciting,' said Norma.

'I've never been there,' said Bob.

'You ain't missing that much. It's all cars and people,' said Joe.

Norma patted Bob's leg. 'Don't worry, honey, I'll take you there one of these days.'

'Have you been to Niagara Falls?' asked Dolly.

'Nope,' said Bob. 'In fact, I ain't been anywhere.'

Dolly was surprised. 'I wanted to go to Niagara,' she said wistfully, 'but we didn't have time.'

'One day you'll get there,' said Norma.

'I hope so.'

'Look, come and see me after school tomorrow,' said Norma. 'We can have a coffee and a nice long chat.'

'I'd love to.'

'That OK, Joe? Or have you got something else in mind?'

'No, that's fine. I shall be up at Martha's field till late.'

'How will I get to you?' asked Dolly.

'Don't worry, I'll come and get you,' said Norma.

When Norma left, Joe said it was time for bed. Dolly was tired. It had been a long, full day.

When they were in bed, Dolly asked, 'Why don't your Ma like me?'

'She told you. She wanted me to marry Sandra.'

'You never told me about Sandra.'

'There was nothing to tell.'

'But you married me. She should accept that.'

'Yes, I know.'

'Why don't you stand up for yourself, and me?'

'Let's sort this out some other time. It's been a long day. We both need some sleep.' At that, Joe turned over and was soon fast asleep.

Dolly lay on her back thinking. Why did the boys jump at their mother's every word? Joe now had her for his wife and she should come first. He had been his old self when they were sitting outside. Dolly was determined this woman wasn't going to make her life a misery. Tomorrow she would have a long talk with Norma and try to find out if they could rent somewhere away from Ma. Dolly knew she would get on with Norma. It was Sandra she had to face next. What would *she* have to say to her? Whatever was said, Joe was hers – and nobody was going to take him away from Dolly Walters.

Dolly was startled when Joe's kiss woke her. She could see he was dressed for work.

'What time is it? Where're you going?'

'To work. We like to start early.'

Dolly eased herself up on her elbow. 'But what shall I do all day?'

'Ma will tell you. So long.' He kissed her again and left.

Dolly lay back. This wasn't how she'd imagined things would be. But what did she expect? He had to work. She turned over; she wasn't going to jump to it like everybody else seemed to do round here. She'd get up when she was good and ready.

The phone ringing and the banging on the door woke her.

'Dolly. Dolly! Can you get up? I've got to go to Deansville and there's a few things I'd like you to do.'

Dolly jumped out of bed. Ma was actually talking to her. She quickly put on her dressing-gown and opened the door. 'Good morning,' she said cheerfully.

'Good morning.' Ma walked towards the kitchen and Dolly padded behind her. 'Can you cook?'

Dolly nodded. 'Yes.'

'There's plenty of food in the icebox. The coffee's on. The boys are coming back about one for some lunch today. You can rustle them up something, not too heavy mind, just a sandwich will do, as I don't want them falling asleep this afternoon. I shall be back later. Got to go to the bank then I'll be off to the beauty parlour to get my hair done and I have to see some other folks. I shall be having lunch out, so don't worry about me.'

'Is there anything you would like me to do?'

'Not really. We can talk about what chores we can give you tonight.'

Dolly was hoping she would ask her to go to Deansville with her, but instead she rushed past her as Dolly stood on the porch and watched her go.

Ma got into the car and left in a cloud of dust. Dolly walked over to the fridge. She would dearly like a cuppa.

All morning Dolly explored her new home. She didn't go near the horses, and the chickens rushing around frightened the life out of her. This was so different from how she had thought life would be. Joe had told her he lived on a farm, but she really didn't know anything about farms. They didn't have a lot in Rotherhithe. Would she ever get used to this way of life? She had to, for she loved Joe, and wanted to be with him for ever.

She felt like a naughty girl when she ventured down to the road. She stood for a moment or two wondering which way to go when a van pulled up.

'Hi. You must be Joe's wife. How you settling in?'

'Fine, thank you.'

'Gee, I love the way you Limeys talk. That David Niven in the movies talks like you. By the way, I'm Fred, the mailman. I expect you'll be getting mail from home? I look forward to seeing the stamps. I'm a great stamp collector.'

Dolly smiled. 'I'll save them for you.'

'Gee, thanks.' He took a bundle of letters from off the front seat. 'These are for Ma. I think they're mostly bills. That's all the folks round here ever seem to get. I usually leave them mail in the box over there.' He pointed to a box on a pole.

'Shall I take them?'

'Thanks. Must be off. Bye.' He gave her a wave and was off.

Should she have asked for a lift into somewhere? Perhaps not this time. She looked at her watch. The boys would be back for their lunch soon, and then Norma would be here to collect her.

After Joe and Bob had gone back to the fields, Dolly sat on the porch waiting for Norma. As soon as she caught sight of her car she rushed to meet her.

'Jump in,' said Norma.

'Thank you. I'm looking forward to having a look round.'

'Not that much to see round this way. It's mostly land.'

With the window open Dolly could feel the cool breeze. She gave a long sigh.

Norma turned and smiled. 'You look a bit down. Having trouble with Ma?'

'She just doesn't seem to want to talk to me.'

'She's a funny woman – don't talk to many folks round here. She will never forgive Joe for marrying you, you know.'

Dolly ignored that, asking instead: 'D'you know why she don't talk that much to people then?'

'No, although it's been said she's never got over her husband going. She worshipped the ground he walked on.'

'Did you know him?'

'No, but my pa did. He said he wasn't all she made him out to be. He was a rodeo rider. She herself is an excellent rider. Dolly, I'm sorry, darlin', but I think you've got your work cut out trying to reason with her. Just play it all as it comes. She might be different when babies come along.'

'I hope we'll have moved away by then, then she won't have quite so much hold over Joe. Are there places to rent round here?'

Norma didn't reply to that question as she was busy turning the wheel and parking. 'Here we are at our local community. That's the gas station and the grocery store.'

'Joe pointed those out when we arrived.'

'This is the schoolhouse, where I teach my little charges. They are still only young when I get them, then after three years I send them off to Deansville. Come in and we'll have a coffee.'

'Norma, does the grocery store sell tea?'

'Don't know, but we could go over and ask Madge.'

Dolly was amazed at the lack of traffic. The small bell above the door rang when they walked in.

'Hi Madge, this is Dolly, Joe's wife.'

Madge, a jolly round-faced woman, rushed from behind the counter and held Dolly close. 'Welcome, my dear, welcome to Deansville. I've been dying to meet you.'

'Thank you,' said Dolly when she was finally released.

'How are you settling in?'

'Give the poor girl a chance, she only got here yesterday,' said Norma, helping herself to an apple from the box. After rubbing it on her trousers she took a large bite.

'Yes, of course.'

'Dolly here wants to know if you sell tea?'

'Don't get a lot of call for tea round these parts, but I do have a packet somewhere. I'll just go out back.'

Dolly was grinning and enjoying this relaxed attitude.

'Right, here we are.' Madge handed her a packet of Lipton's tea. 'Came all the way from England. One of the boys brought it back for me.'

'How much do I owe you?' asked Dolly.

Madge waved her arms. 'No, have it with my compliments. Looks like I'll have to start stocking it now you're here. They do say Britain won the war drinking tea.'

'I think we did,' said Dolly.

'Was it bad, being bombed?'

'It wasn't nice.'

'Did you lose anyone?'

'No, we was lucky.' Nobody had mentioned her baby. If they did know, it was something they weren't going to ask about.

'Come on, honey,' said Norma. 'I want to show you off to everybody.'

'Bye, and thank you, Madge.'

'My pleasure. Come and have a chat anytime.'

'Thanks.'

'Catch you later, Madge.' Outside, Norma said, 'Madge is great – but make sure you've plenty of time when you go into her store.'

'Thanks for the advice.'

Dolly was shown the schoolroom.

'I hope we have your babe in here one day.'

'So do I,' said Dolly. 'Perhaps then Ma might take a liking to me.' It looked as though Bob hadn't even told Norma about her baby. If he had, was she waiting for Dolly to broach the subject?

'I'll show you where we have our weekly dances.'

Norma pushed open the door into a large hall with a stage at the far end. The Stars and Stripes flag was draped across the back. Dolly was surprised to see how patriotic these people were. There were always flags flying.

'What's Sandra like?'

'Blonde and beautiful. And rich.'

'Does she work?' asked Dolly, wandering round the room.

'In the beauty parlour in Deansville.'

'That's where Ma's gone. I bet they'll have a right old gossip about me.'

'Don't worry about it.'

But Dolly did worry; she only wanted to be liked. 'I wouldn't have thought this Sandra needed to go to work if her father breeds horses.'

'She'd get very bored round here with nothing to do.'

'Suppose so.' Dolly was thinking that she too would like to get a job to stop her getting bored, but give it time, she'd only been here a day.

They walked to Norma's house and had coffee. Then it was time to go.

'Don't worry, I can walk back,' Dolly said.

'Walk? Nobody walks here.'

Dolly grinned. 'We don't have cars back home.'

'How did you manage?'

'Public transport. We have buses, trains and the Underground.'

'Underground, that's the subway. Things are very different here, we don't have buses. Here you'll have to learn to drive.'

'Joe said he wanted me to learn to ride a horse, but I said definitely no to that.'

Norma laughed. 'I don't blame you. You wouldn't get me up on one of those things. Come on, jump in.'

'I've only been here a day and I've certainly got plenty to write home about.'

Norma turned and smiled. 'I think you're gonna fit in very well.'

'I hope so. I really do hope so.'

Chapter 30

Although Dolly had only been at the farm for two days she was restless and bored with no one around. She missed having her mum and Penny to talk to, then there were the Miss Gregorys; she was always able to have a chat to them. Was she being unreasonable to expect more than this? There wasn't that much to explore in the area around the house and she didn't want to wander too far in case she got lost. Even sitting out in the lovely sunshine soon lost its appeal with no one to talk to.

Friday morning, as she watched Joe get ready for work, she said, 'Joe, when can you take me out?'

'For Pete's sake, Dolly, we've only been home a few days and you know we've got a lot to do at the moment! Ma's given you some jobs; just hang on for a while, just till we get this problem sorted.'

'Why is putting up a fence taking so long?'

'This fence goes on for miles and every inch has to be checked.'

Dolly knew she was sulking, but didn't care. It was true Ma had given her jobs to do, but cleaning the house, cooking the evening meal and feeding the bloody chickens and collecting the eggs wasn't exactly thrilling, and besides, she hated chickens.

She felt a bit miserable when she saw the letter on the chest of drawers. She had been writing to Penny, telling her about a silly little hen that was running around being chased by what Joe had called the grand cock. God, was that all she had to write about? After describing all the exciting things that had happened to her – the journey on the ship, New York and the drive here – and all about Deansville and the people, including Ma-in-law, this letter was getting to be very pathetic and hard going.

Joe came and sat on the bed. He put his arm round her. 'Tomorrow night we'll be going to the dance. So why don't you spend today making yourself look pretty? Remember, I shall be showing you off to all the folks round here.'

'Joe, you ready?' shouted Bob.

'Just coming.' Joe kissed her cheek and left.

Dolly smiled. So that was it. She had to spend all day tarting herself up so she could be paraded like a trophy. Slowly she got out of bed and went to the window. She caught sight of Ma riding away in the distance. 'She looks like Roy Roger's missus,' Dolly said out loud. 'Can't ever see me up on one of those. Perhaps I could learn to drive and then I could get a job – that'd keep me busy. Me driving a car, that'll be something to tell 'em back home.' She laughed. 'Listen to me, I'm talking to meself now.'

Saturday morning was the first time Joe was home and he took Dolly in the truck for a ride to show her round the Walters estate.

'Is this all yours?' she asked, peering through the windscreen as they bumped over fields and drove through pretty shallow streams.

'Yep. It all belongs to us Walters. Lock stock and barrel.'

'It's lovely.'

277

'This time of year it is, but it's pretty mean in the winter.'

'Does it get very cold?'

'Below freezing for a while.'

'Can't say I fancy that. Don't like the cold.'

'We do have a fire in every room, so it's real cosy inside.'

Dolly had noticed the huge pile of logs stacked up against the side of the stable. She thought about Christmas back home when they had to worry about coal rationing and she wondered if things had got any easier. 'You've got so much land.'

'We sure have. Well, that is what the bank don't have shares in at times.'

'Why does the bank have shares? Does the bank own much?'

'No, it's just that if we have a lean year and the crops don't yield as much as we hoped, and if Ma wants to add on or something, then she has to borrow and she uses the farm as collateral.'

'I see. Why don't you sell some land?'

'I don't think that's such a good idea. What would we live on?'

'The money.'

'It wouldn't last for ever. After all, there's four mouths to feed at the moment, and who knows how many more there'll be in the future?' He pulled on the steering wheel and joined a dirt track.

'Joe, do you get a wage?' asked Dolly tentatively.

'Course. But Ma banks most of our money. We don't need much here.'

'What if I want to buy some clothes or personal bits?'

He stopped the truck in front of a number of buildings and kissed her. 'Don't worry hon, I'll make sure you get an allowance.'

Dolly didn't like the sound of the word allowance. 'Is it possible I could find a job?'

'I don't think that's such a good idea at the moment. Besides, we are a bit out of the way here.'

'Perhaps I could learn to drive?'

'Don't know about that. We can't afford a car just yet and anyway, you're taking some of the pressure off Ma.'

'Did she have a woman give her a hand at the house?'

'Nope, did it all herself, although she had a lad come and see to the chickens.'

'What's happened to him?'

'Drafted. Had to go in the Army.'

'Why didn't Bob go in the Army?'

'Don't really know. Ma said it's to do with his flat feet.'

Dolly laughed. 'Is that all?' Bob at twenty-six was two years older than Joe.

'Come on, I've got something to show you. This is where we keep the dairy herd.' Joe took her into a huge smelly barn.

'Who milks the cows?'

'We have cow hands, but it is all done mechanically.'

Dolly wasn't going to ask the details. 'Where are the cows now?'

'Out on the top field.'

Dolly smiled as they wandered around hand in hand laughing and talking. This was how she wanted things to be. She loved it when they stopped and shared kisses. This was her Joe. This was the Joe she married.

The sun was warm and they left the truck behind and climbed up the hill.

Joe stood with his arm round her waist. 'See that line of trees in the distance?'

Dolly put her hand to her eyes to shield the sun. 'What,

over there?' she asked, pointing.

'Yep. Well, that's as far as our land goes in that direction.'

Dolly was amazed by how much land they owned and couldn't see how selling a few fields would be missed.

They stood gazing out onto the rolling fields. To Dolly, this was just bliss – to stand here with her husband's arms round her. 'It's so peaceful. How far that way do you own?'

'You can't see where it joins the Boltons' land.'

'Who're the Boltons?'

'Sandra and her pa. Her mother died years ago. Ma was devastated – they were very good friends.'

Dolly stiffened. 'So if you'd married Sandra, you'd have their land as well.'

'Eventually.'

'It wouldn't half be a big place.'

'Yes, it would. But it's not going to happen. I'm married to *you*.'

'Did you love Sandra?'

'No, not really. A bit like you with Tony, I suppose. We grew up together, but we weren't promised or anything like that.'

'Why doesn't Bob marry Sandra?'

He laughed. 'She's definitely not his type, she's too flighty.'

Dolly felt guilty at questioning Joe; after all, he never mentioned Tony. 'I'm sorry, but I can't help feeling a little bit jealous. I'm frightened of losing you.'

'You won't lose me, Dolly. I love you.'

'And I love you.'

He took hold of her face and kissed her lips. Gently at first, then with passion as he began to run his hands over her breasts.

They sat down as they kissed, their hands began

exploring and removing each other's clothes.

Dolly pulled away. 'Joe, we mustn't, not here. Someone might see us.'

'Don't worry, nobody comes up here.'

In a few moments they were rolling on the grass enjoying each other. Afterwards, as they lay in each other's arms, the sun warmed their naked bodies.

Dolly sat up and started giggling. 'I feel very naughty and itchy doing it here on the grass. What if someone saw us?'

'I told you, nobody comes up here. Dolly, I do love you and I want you to be happy. Just bear with it for a while. I'm sure everything will work out.'

Dolly kissed him. 'I love you and I do want it to work out. After all, I didn't come all this way for nothing. Joe, when we start a baby, can we find a place of our own?'

'Sure can, my love.' He pulled her back down and kissed her neck with gentle butterfly kisses and gradually went down her body, making Dolly tremble.

After a while he stood up and started to dress himself, as she lay back admiring his wonderful body.

'Come on, young lady.' He pulled her up.

In this wonderful setting, Dolly hoped that this was the time they had just made a baby.

Saturday night, Dolly was excited as along with Joe and Bob she made her way to the dance. She was surprised to see so many parked cars as they drove up to the hall.

'Where have all these people come from?' she asked.

'All locals,' said Bob.

'I ain't seen this many people around. Where do they all live and work?'

'Most of them live and work in Deansville and around

281

the farms,' said Joe, pushing open the door. The heat and noise hit them.

'I'll get the drinks,' yelled Bob.

Dolly stood and watched the band who seemed to be enjoying themselves as much as the couples on the floor. It was a fast number and all the couples were jiving. The girls were being thrown in the air, just like she'd seen at the Rainbow Club all those years ago.

'*Joe!*' squealed a flurry of pink topped off with blonde hair. She came and grabbed Joe and kissed him full on the lips. Giggling, she wiped off the bright red lipstick mark she'd left behind with her long fingernails. Dolly noted that her matching bright red painted nails were beautifully manicured. She put her arm through Joe's and turned to Dolly. 'Hello, you must be Dolly. I've heard all about you,' she said sweetly.

'And I've heard all about you.'

'Joe, she's lovely. And I *love* the way she talks.'

Dolly felt like saying, 'You can talk to me, but keep your eyes off my husband,' but decided against making any waves.

'Hello, Dolly.' Norma came up and kissed her cheek. 'Settling in OK?'

'Getting a bit used to it.'

'You two have met already?' asked Sandra, with her finely plucked eyebrows raised in astonishment.

'We sure have,' said Norma.

'But you've only been here a couple of days.'

'Norma came to the house to see me.'

'That was nice of her.'

'Yes, it was.'

The band struck up with a slow tune.

'My dance, I think,' said Sandra, taking Joe's hand. Smiling at Dolly she said, 'You don't mind, do you?'

Before Dolly could answer, Sandra was leading Joe onto the dance floor.

Dolly stood and watched as Sandra wrapped her arms round her husband's neck.

'How old is she?' Dolly asked Norma.

'She was twenty-one a while back. Joe was away.'

'She had a real humdinger of a party,' said Bob.

'Let's face it, her pa could afford it.'

'It's our wedding anniversary next Monday,' Dolly told them. 'We will have been married two years and this will be the first one we've been together.'

'Dolly, that's wonderful. I'll bake you a cake. Joe can bring you over for a drink, unless he has other ideas,' said Norma.

'I don't think so. Thanks, Norma, that'll be really lovely.' Dolly didn't expect anything from Ma. She looked across at Joe while he was dancing with Sandra. She knew this one was going to be trouble, but he belonged to her.

All evening Dolly danced with Joe or Bob. Although Sandra had joined them, between Dolly and Norma she was having trouble hogging the conversation. Then it was the last dance and before anyone could jump up, Sandra had Joe on his feet and was pulling him onto the dance floor. He looked over at Dolly and shrugged.

The lights went down and as Dolly sat there alone, she knew she was going to have to keep Sandra away from Joe. There was no doubt about it, the blonde was a man-eater and Joe was on her menu.

Joe, Bob and Dolly were sitting in the front of the truck and they were singing as they headed home. Bob told Dolly he couldn't take Norma home as he didn't have transport to get back.

'He could always take a horse,' said Joe.

'I couldn't see Suzy standing outside all evening. She'd probably kick the joint down,' laughed Bob.

'And that wouldn't make you very popular with Ma.'

'Why didn't you take the car? In fact, why didn't *we* take the car?' asked Dolly.

'Ma don't like us using it,' said Joe.

'Why?'

'She's worried we might smash it up,' said Bob.

It didn't look that new to Dolly. 'She let you take it to New York.'

Joe looked across at Bob.

'That was because Joe threatened to hire one, and that wouldn't have looked good in folks' eyes,' said Bob. 'Ma sets a lot of store about what folks round here think.'

Dolly settled herself down. Any ideas she had of learning to drive had just disappeared unless she could persuade Joe to buy his own car. She knew Ma wouldn't let her use hers and the boys used the truck every day.

'Did you enjoy yourself tonight, Dolly?' asked Bob.

'Yes, I did. I like Norma.'

'And she likes you.'

'Joe, Norma wants us to go over next Monday. She's gonna make us a cake for our anniversary. Ain't that nice of her?'

'That's great.'

'It'll be the first one we've spent together. I said I didn't think you'd any other plans.'

'No, that's fine.'

'Norma's a great girl,' said Bob. 'You'll have to go into town with her.'

'I'd love that. When does she go?'

'A couple of times a month.'

Neither of the boys asked her what she thought of Sandra, and Dolly didn't volunteer her thoughts.

They arrived home and Bob said they had to be quiet. Dolly didn't comment as she poured out coffee for the men and tea for herself. What was wrong with Ma? She was such a funny woman, thought Dolly as they passed her bedroom door on the way to their room.

After they had made love Joe turned over and was soon fast asleep. Dolly lay on her back and began reflecting on the past week that she had been here. Would she ever get used to this life? If they moved away, if they had a home of their own, things would be very different. Would Joe be able to find work? Was she being too hasty? Was she being fair? Perhaps when a baby was on the way, everything would look better and fall into place. She had to give it time. After all, this is what she had wanted.

Chapter 31

Monday was their wedding anniversary and Dolly was thrilled to think that this was the first one they would be sharing. She was also excited when she, Bob and Joe drew up outside Norma's that evening. She was introduced to Norma's dad, George, whom she liked instantly. He was a warm, happy man. Dolly could see where Norma got her charm from. Dolly was overcome when she saw what Norma had done for them. There were bowls of chips, which Dolly told them were called crisps at home. The cake Norma had made was a large gooey thing; Dolly was telling them about the wedding cakes that some of the brides in Britain had had to have. They were amazed that they had cardboard covers over them to look like icing.

'Just goes to show, we don't know how lucky we are,' said Norma. 'By the way, did the newspaper get in touch?'

Dolly laughed. 'Yes, the reporter there did. He was coming to see me, but he phoned the next day to say I'd been upstaged. It seems his boss knew a GI bride with a baby, so she had priority. He did ask if I had twins or something or whether I had been bombed.' Dolly quickly glanced at Joe who gave her a soft smile and held her hand.

'Sounds like *Roxie Heart*,' said George.

'Who's that?' asked Dolly.

'A film with Ginger Rogers in.'

'I did laugh at the telephone operator. She was asking me all sorts of questions.'

'You want to be careful what you say on the phone. Ethel loves to listen in – sometimes she even joins in the conversations,' Norma warned her light-heartedly.

'I gathered that,' said Dolly.

She was having such a wonderful time, then all too soon it was over. That night Dolly prayed that when their next anniversary was here, she and Joe would have a baby son or daughter to share it with them.

It was the end of the month and Dolly, wearing her new clothes, was looking in the mirror. 'Well Joe, what d'you think? Do I look like an American now?'

'I think you look great. Come here.' He kissed her. 'Now you've got the duds I think it's time you were introduced to Peggy.'

'No, thank you.'

'Why not?' he asked as they made their way outside.

It was a warm sunny Sunday and Joe chased her to the barn. They were playing about when Bob joined them.

'Dolly's going riding,' said Joe.

'Good for you. I'll get Peggy.'

She stood looking up at the horse. 'Please Joe, no.'

'Come on, Dolly, it's not that bad,' said Bob, laughing.

'Just think how proud they will be back home,' said Joe as he held the reins. 'Bob get that stool over here.'

Bob placed the stool at the side of the horse.

'It's such a long way up,' said Dolly.

'Now put your foot in there.' Joe held the stirrup.

Dolly nervously did as she was told and as she put her leg over the horse, Peggy shivered. Dolly screamed and slowly slid off the other side. She sat on the ground.

Bob and Joe were laughing.

'Come on, get back up,' said Joe, helping her to her feet.

'Never. Never. Never.'

'Ma'll be very disappointed.'

'I don't care about that. You ain't ever gonna get me up there on that thing.'

Bob quickly put his hands over the horse's ears. 'Shh. Don't let her hear you call her a thing.'

Dolly was giggling as she fell into Joe's arms.

Summer was slipping into autumn. It had been blustery and dull all day, and after sitting staring out of the window, Dolly decided to write to her parents. It was getting hard to find something interesting to write about as not a lot had really happened. Over the months she had told them about when she first went into town with Norma and bought herself denim trousers and a shirt, which made her feel as if she belonged even though she didn't get on with riding a horse. She told them about how Joe had almost got her on Peggy, but she was terrified and wouldn't be doing that again.

She also described her first shopping trips, which had been a whole new experience, plus the fact that everybody knew everybody else. In a way, that was a bit like home, except the shops were filled with everything she wanted and more, and things she had never seen.

The first time she went with Norma she found it hard to get out of the clothes shop, as everybody wanted to meet her. The comments on her hair, figure, and the way she talked were so complimentary and she loved it. She wrote that she was hoping to learn to drive, but they had to wait till they got their own car. Everybody drives a car over here, she told them. It's the only way to get about.

Dolly never mentioned to her mum and dad that when she went to get her hair done, she found Sandra a bit overpowering and felt intimidated – not that Sandra was ever anything other than charming. Dolly had told Penny all this and added that she thought it was one big act. The movie-house was something Dolly loved, and after a lot of persuading had managed to get Joe to take her at least once a month. Dolly sat back and chewed the end of her pen. When she thought about it, life wasn't too bad and it was only when she was here alone at the farm all day with no one to talk to that she felt lonely and her spirits fell. That was something she would never tell anyone back home. Ma was talking to her a little more now, but only to discuss what provisions they would need when she went to town, or anything to do with the house. She never took Dolly with her on her outings. She did say that she was pleased with the way Dolly did things. Dolly told Joe what his mother had said.

His reply was, 'I told you you would get on with her.'

Was this the closest Dolly was going to get to her? How she missed her mother's and Penny's laughs and chats, and sharing things between them. Dolly sensed she'd never get through the hard shell Ma had put around herself. But the worst thing for Dolly was that every month she was bitterly disappointed when she found she wasn't pregnant.

'Not to worry,' said Joe. 'We can keep trying.'

Dolly was thrilled when at long last she heard from Ann, and had an address to write to. They were now living in Chicago, but Ann wasn't happy. She hated living in an apartment in a noisy city. That made Dolly feel guilty, when here she was living on a farm surrounded by fields and beautiful views.

★ ★ ★

As the months moved on, Dolly had taken to strolling across the fields when she'd finished her chores. The farm had a coppice that wasn't too far away and it was used for chopping the firewood. The days were cooler now and the leaves were beginning to fall; Dolly loved the sound of them scrunching under her feet. She wrapped her coat round her and sat on a log. Her life was so empty without a baby. If her little daughter had lived, she would be running around now, filling everyone's life with joy. Today Dolly was feeling very sorry for herself and she let the tears trickle down her cheeks. The reason was that she'd had a letter from Penny – and that always made her feel sad. Penny told her how well Reg was doing – he was thinking of branching out and working for himself. Tony was going out with Meg Windsor but so far they hadn't got engaged. Some things were still on ration but they were getting a little easier. She had been over the moon with the nylons Dolly had sent her, and was interested in the cuttings from the magazines she had also sent her, showing the latest American fashions.

What else was there to write about? If only she could go to work or Joe would let them have their own home, then at least she could tell them that she was happy over here. At times she felt nothing more than a skivvy. She and Joe had had many words about it, but he told her he wasn't going to move till he was good and ready. She had been here for five months now and things didn't look as if they would ever change. Why wasn't she expecting? It had been so very easy before. Should she go and see a doctor? She stood up and kicked the leaves. Yes, that was it. She'd have a word with Joe first, but she knew she would have to wait for the right moment to tell him her plan.

★ ★ ★

It was Saturday evening, and as usual they were in the room getting ready to go to the dance. Dolly thought this might be a good time to tell him what she was going to do. 'Joe, is it all right if I go and see a doctor?'

He stopped brushing his hair; he turned from the mirror and looked anxious. 'Why do you want to see a doctor? You're not ill, are you?'

'No. But I thought I'd try and find out why I ain't expecting.'

'Don't start on that again. Not tonight.'

'But I thought I could find out if . . .'

'I told you, give it time. We've got years yet.'

'Joe, I'm twenty-one next month, and I would like to have children while I'm still young.'

'The trouble with you is that you're too headstrong. You don't hear Norma badgering Bob to get married and have kids.'

'But Joe, I thought you wanted kids? Besides, Norma says she wants to see the world a bit before she thinks about getting married.'

Joe exploded. 'What is it with you females? You always think the grass is greener on the other side of the fence. Well I can tell you it sure ain't!' He stormed out of their room.

Dolly sat on the bed in shock. Tonight she'd have a word with Norma and find out where the doctor was.

At the dance the atmosphere was very hostile between Joe and Dolly, and Norma, sensing it, asked what was wrong.

When they went to the restroom, Dolly said, 'Me and Joe have had words.'

'Thought as much. Do you want to talk about it?'

Dolly nodded. 'OK. The trouble is, I want to have a baby.'

'And he don't?'

'No, it's not like that. You see, I did have a baby but it was born dead.'

'Oh Dolly, no! I'm so very sorry.'

'I was caught in a bomb blast and the baby died. It was a little girl.'

Norma threw her arms round Dolly and held her tight. 'You poor thing.'

'I thought I'd go and see a doctor to try to find out why I haven't fallen, but Joe don't want me to.'

'Why?'

'He thinks it's because I haven't settled here, he thinks I'm too tense. Do you know of a doctor?'

'Sure.'

'I don't want Ma to know.'

'Why?'

'She already thinks I'm a failure. To her I can't ride a horse or have babies, so what else can I do to prove myself?'

'I see what you mean.' Norma thought a moment. 'I'll phone Doc Flynn and I can take you there on Monday, if that's what you want?'

'Thanks. Are you sure you don't mind?'

'Not at all. We girls should stick together.'

'Norma, do you want kids?'

'I'm not sure. Remember, I see enough of them all day. I also want to do a bit of travelling before I'm too old.'

'You're not that old.' Dolly knew Norma was three years older than her. 'What about Bob?'

'I like Bob, but he isn't really the man for me. I'm too independent and I like having my own way.'

Dolly wondered if Bob knew about this.

After a last look in the mirror, Dolly said, 'Don't say anything to Joe.'

'Course not.'

Sandra had also noted the hostile atmosphere and was quick to pick up on it. Dolly knew she was playing right into her hands, but what upset her more was that Joe was very willing to go along with it.

It was a strange evening and Dolly was glad when it was over. The journey home was very quiet and she went straight to bed.

Monday afternoon, Norma was outside hooting. Dolly ran down the steps and got into her car.

'Thanks.' She kissed Norma's cheek.

'It's all arranged, you're going to see Dr Flynn. He's a great bloke, a bit old-fashioned.'

'Thanks,' said Dolly again.

As they drove along Dolly was happy to let Norma do most of the talking and it wasn't long before she parked the car outside a nice-looking house.

'This is it. I'll go along to the coffee-house. See you later.'

Again Dolly's only reply was, 'Thanks.' She very gingerly knocked on the door. Almost at once it was pulled open and a round rosy woman stood there smiling.

'Hello. You must be Dolly Walters? Come on in.'

Dolly followed the woman into a large room. 'Flynn will be out in a moment. He's just finishing his afternoon tea.'

Dolly didn't dare ask if he was British. She couldn't imagine an American having afternoon tea. She sat for a few minutes thumbing through a magazine, then the door opened and the doctor came out. He was a short, grey-haired man.

'Good afternoon, young lady.' He certainly didn't have an English accent. 'Come this way.' He held the door open and Dolly walked into a treatment room. 'Now, what can I do for you?'

Dolly went into great detail about her problem.

'There's not a lot I can say. Your periods are regular?'

Dolly nodded.

'And you say you had a baby that was stillborn because of a bomb blast?'

Again Dolly nodded.

'There may be some damage, but that's something I can't tell you. Are you happy here?'

'Yes.'

'If you like I can arrange for you to go into hospital for further tests.'

'Hospital,' whispered Dolly.

'Yes. How will young Joe feel about that?'

'I don't know.'

'Well, you have a word with him and let me know so that I can arrange it. Don't give up hope. Remember, every day these clever scientists find a new cure for something or another. How are you really coping with life over here?'

'Not too bad.' She turned her head as she was finding it difficult to keep her tears at bay.

The doctor was quick to note her distress, and he went and put his arm round her shoulders in a fatherly way. 'I'm sure it will all work out fine for you. Just try to relax and enjoy life. After all, you're still young.'

Dolly buried her head in his shoulder and wept. After a while she dried her tears.

'Do you have any other problems?' Dr Flynn asked gently.

Dolly nodded.

'Do you want to talk about it?'

'If I can.'

'In that case, let me order some tea.' He switched on the intercom. 'Annie, more tea please.'

Dolly blew her nose. 'It makes a pleasant change to be offered tea. I thought all Americans only drank coffee.'

'I was born in Ireland and I came here as an infant. My parents only drank tea, so you see, tea was part of my life.'

The door opened and Annie put a tray on his desk. She gave Dolly a smile as she left.

'Lovely woman,' he said after she'd closed the door. 'Now young lady, if you want to talk, I'm ready to listen.'

Dolly sat and told him about her life and how unhappy she was at times. She went on to describe her relationship with Ma.

The doctor sat studying his fingers, but Dolly knew that he was listening very carefully.

'You mustn't be too hard on Jennie Walters,' he said finally. 'I've known her for a long time and she's had a hard life. She was hoping Joe would marry young Sandra Bolton – in fact, she'd set her heart on it. She was very upset when Sandra's mother died. I understand they were great friends. Then it was a shock when Joe married you.'

'I know that. But it was Joe's choice.'

The man leaned forward and tapped her hand. 'I'm sure it will all work out for you.'

Dolly began to cry again. 'I hope so. I ain't got me mum to run to over here,' she sniffed.

Dr Flynn looked at her with sympathy filling his face. 'It must be very hard for you, but I'm sure you'll be able to overcome this particular problem. You have a lovely smile and you're very brave coming all this way.'

Dolly gave him a slight smile. He might have lived in America for years, but he certainly hadn't lost any of his Irish charm.

She stood up and held out her hand. 'Thank you.'

He took hold of her hand. 'Remember, I'm always here if ever you feel you need a shoulder to cry on.'

'Thank you,' she said again.

Dolly shuddered as she went out into the brisk air. She caught sight of Norma sitting in the car.

'Well?' she asked as Dolly climbed in beside her. 'What happened?'

Once again Dolly's face crumpled. 'He can't tell me.'

'Why?'

'He says he can arrange for me to go to hospital for tests. What if I can't have babies? What if that bomb blast did something?'

'Oh, my dear Dolly.'

Between blowing her nose and wiping her eyes she managed to tell Norma what the doctor had said.

'Would you be able to book into the hospital for further tests?'

'I don't know if Joe will like that. Would it cost very much?'

'Is money that important?'

'It is when you ain't got any.'

'Surely Joe wouldn't object to paying out for something like this?'

'I don't know. But would Ma?'

'The boys don't get paid much, do they?'

'I don't think so, but I don't know how much exactly.'

'What about you?'

'I get a few dollars' allowance, but as Joe says, what is there round here to spend it on?'

'What if you want to buy something new, or a surprise for him?'

'I just ask.'

Norma started the engine. 'Well, that certainly wouldn't suit *me*.'

Dolly wanted to say that it didn't suit her either, but chose to stay silent.

All evening Dolly was waiting for the opportunity to talk to Joe alone. It wasn't till they were in their bedroom that she told him she had been to see Dr Flynn. She wanted his reaction before she told him anything else.

'Why? What's wrong?'

'I wanted to find out why I wasn't expecting.'

'You did what?'

Dolly repeated what she'd just told him.

'I don't believe this. You went behind my back – and to that quack Flynn? You wait till Ma hears about this. There'll be all hell to pay.'

'Why? It ain't none of her business.'

'It will be when he sends her the bill.'

'Can't you pay it?'

'What with? Did you have the decency to ask what he cost?'

Dolly shook her head.

'And what did he say?'

The thought of telling him about the hospital was now out of the question. 'He said to give it time.'

'That's what I keep saying. Pity you can't settle. Could have saved a few dollars with that bit of advice.'

Dolly crawled into bed, defeated.

Chapter 32

It was 1 November and Ma was just leaving when Joe, who had been down to collect the mail from the mailbox, walked back into the kitchen. 'Sorry, hon, none for you this time,' he said to Dolly as he handed Ma her letters.

'What's this?' Ma held up a sheet of paper.

Nobody said a word.

'Who's been to this Dr Flynn?'

'I have,' said Dolly.

'Why? Are you ill? Joe, why didn't you take her to our own doctor?'

'I didn't go with Joe.'

'What's wrong with you? You can't go running to the doc with every sniffle, you know. It costs money.'

Dolly looked at Joe. She was hoping he would say something, but he remained silent. 'I went to try to find out why I'm not expecting a baby.'

Ma sat down heavily at the table. 'Have you thought it could be your attitude to living here?'

'What?'

'You've not been happy here since the moment you stepped foot in this place. I've given you a home, I feed you, and this is all the thanks I get – more bills.'

Dolly was almost stamping her foot with rage. 'You ain't

298

made me a bit welcome. You don't talk to me. All you want me to do is look after you. I'm just a bloody unpaid servant, that's all I am.'

'Joe – see to your wife. I always knew these foreigners carried on and behaved like this. I'm off. Somebody has to work to pay these bills.' With that she threw the letters on the table. 'I'll see you boys up in the north field. We've got to get that soil turned over before the winter sets in.' She stormed out of the kitchen and slammed the door after her.

Bob looked from Dolly to Joe. 'Oh boy, it looks like you've really got her all riled up now.'

Joe picked up the bill. 'Five dollars. Who's gonna pay this?'

Dolly went to walk out of the kitchen. She stood in the doorway. 'Take it out of me allowance.' She too slammed the door after her.

Joe followed her into the bedroom. 'I told you not to go. Why couldn't we have discussed this?'

'What? Like we talk about everything? Like when are we gonna move away from here. Like why you won't buy a car and let me learn to drive so I can get a job? I never thought you'd be hanging onto your mother's apron-strings for ever.' Dolly had tears streaming down her face. 'In some ways it's a good thing our baby's not here. I wouldn't want her to be as unhappy as me.'

Joe was shocked at Dolly's outburst. 'Don't say things like that. Why can't you try to be happy here? You must be patient, you can't expect to have your own way all the time. I don't know what to do to make you happy.' He sat on the bed and put his head in his hands.

Dolly moved round to the other side of the bed and sat with her back to him. Silently she began to cry.

'Joe? Joe,' said Bob gently from the open doorway. 'Come

on, bro, we've gotta get up to that field otherwise there'll be hell to pay.'

Joe stood up and tried to place his hand on Dolly's shoulder but she brushed it away. 'We'll talk about this when I get back,' he said as he left the room.

Dolly flung herself on the bed and cried bitter, sad tears. All she wanted was a baby. Why did it have to be like this?

For the rest of the day Dolly was like the weather, dull and miserable. She was feeling very down and homesick. As soon as she knew Norma would be home she phoned her.

'Sorry, Dolly,' said Norma's dad, George. 'She's gone to one of her kids' birthday party. Shall I ask her to call you when she gets home?'

'No, don't worry. It ain't that important. Just wanted a chat, that's all, and to thank her for taking me trick and treating the other night. I ain't ever done that before and it was good fun. I'll catch her tomorrow at the dance.'

'Only if you're sure.'

'Thanks.'

'Dolly, look – why don't I come and get you. I could do with a bit of company and a chat.'

'All right.' She put the phone back. Why couldn't Ma be as nice as George? She sat waiting for the car to come up the track.

'It's years since I've been here,' George said, looking round after he'd kissed her cheek. 'You haven't by any chance got the coffee pot on?' he asked slyly.

Dolly grinned. 'I sure have.'

'You're beginning to sound like one of us.'

'I don't think so. D'you know, there's some folk round here I can't understand at all – they could be talking a foreign language.'

He laughed. 'I know what you mean.'

As he didn't seem to make any attempt to move Dolly settled herself down at the table with him.

'Dolly, I know it ain't any of my business, honey, but Norma's real worried about you. She said you ain't very happy here.'

Dolly smiled, trying hard to keep her tears at bay. 'That's very nice of her.'

'What's bothering you?'

'Ma don't like me.'

'Is that all? She don't like a lot of folks.'

'Why?'

'That's for her to tell you.'

'I know she wanted Joe to marry Sandra.'

'That's true.'

'How did her husband die? Joe only knows he was killed in an accident.'

George sat back. 'Rip Walters? He wasn't liked round these parts. He used to think he was the big I Am – see, he used to be a rodeo rider, so did Jennie when she was a young girl. She still is a good horsewoman. She often breaks in horses for Frank Bolton.'

'Is that why she wanted his place?'

'Should think so. When the Walters first settled here, they only had a small plot. Then the boys were born and a few years later, Rip was knocked off his horse by a Brit driving a fancy car. Jennie went to pieces.'

'No wonder she don't like me. Joe has never told me that.'

'He might not know all of it.' George stopped. 'I don't know if I should be telling you all of this. She didn't want folks to know that he liked a drink or two and that Rip was a bit of a waster. She's a very proud lady and don't want people to know her business. Jennie worked damn hard to get this spread.' He laughed reminiscently. 'Rip used to make a fine drop of liquor though in the Prohibition days. Had to keep quiet about it at the time as me and my wife were struggling teachers.'

Dolly knew that Norma's mom Rosemarie had passed away a few years ago with a bad heart. George sat up as if trying to shake the memory of his wife away. 'Folks round here tried to help Jennie, but even then she was a very independent woman. Well, to cut a long story short, she brought those boys up single-handed and worked hard. Bit by bit she bought up the surrounding land, and now they've got one of the biggest spreads around.'

Dolly sat entranced. This was certainly something to write home about.

'Dolly, I've told you this in confidence. If Joe or Jennie want you to know, I'm sure they'll tell you in time, but don't let on that you know.'

'No, I won't. And thanks – I feel I understand her a little better now. But why are the boys so frightened of her?'

'Could be that she holds the purse-strings. Uh-oh – look at the time. I'll have to be getting back. Sorry, I didn't take you back to our place.'

'That's all right. And thanks.'

He kissed her cheek and she stood and watched him drive away. So everybody was aware that Jennie Walters held the purse-strings. Now she knew a bit about Ma, would this make any difference to them?

As soon as Ma came in, Dolly looked at her with different eyes. Most of her life she had had to be a strong woman and Dolly could understand that she didn't want a Brit to take all this away from her boys – an outsider who wasn't going to help manage the farm. Dolly tried hard to be talkative when they all came in, but that evening the atmosphere was very taut as usual when they sat down to their meal. Both Joe and Bob also tried hard to ease the situation with talk about the fields and how the weather would shortly be closing in. As soon as Ma had gone to her study, Dolly went to their room. The log fire was blazing and with the new sofa that had been installed it was warm and cosy. Why had Ma made such a fuss over the five-dollar doctor's bill? After all, the Walters must have money: they had a nice home with all modern conveniences, and Joe had even bought this lovely sofa. Did she keep the boys short?

'Dolly, I'm sorry about this morning,' said Joe, coming into the room and sitting next to her. He put his arm round her shoulders.

'I didn't think it would cause so much fuss. Norma's dad came here this afternoon.'

'What did he want?'

'Just someone to talk to.' Dolly was going to be very careful how she approached this. 'He was telling me about your dad and how in the Prohibition he made booze.'

'Did he now. Well, he should have kept his mouth shut. Ma don't like all her past being dragged up, so don't you go saying anything.'

'I'm sorry.'

'Did he offer to take you to another doctor?'

'No. Joe, why are you so against me seeing a doctor?'

'Did he tell you that Ma has worked hard all her life and how she don't like to see money squandered?'

'He told me that she did work hard.'

'Good.'

Dolly knew it would be a while before she ever got round to asking about going to the hospital.

'It's over now, so don't let's hear any more about it.'

'But what about the bill?'

'I've given Ma the cash. Dolly, why didn't you wait for me to make the arrangements? You should have gone to our own doctor.'

'You didn't seem to want to take me. I just wanted to find out if something was wrong with me.'

Joe held her tight. 'There's nothing wrong with you. As Ma said, it could be that you're all tensed up. Don't worry, we'll have a baby one of these days. After all, we managed to do it before.'

'I hope so.' Dolly relaxed as Joe held her tight.

He began kissing her neck. She turned her head and his lips met hers. 'How about trying now?' he whispered.

Dolly nestled in his arms. It didn't matter how angry she got; Joe could always manage to win her round. 'That sounds like a very nice idea.'

Tuesday 19 November would be Dolly's twenty-first birthday.

'What are you going to get me?' Dolly had laughingly asked Joe the week before.

'I don't know. Is there anything you want?'

Dolly shook her head, although she wanted to say, 'A proper job, and meeting people'.

'You do know it's Thanksgiving on the Thursday?'

'Yes. What do you do about that?'

'We normally have a turkey. Can you cook a turkey?'

'Ain't ever even tasted one, let alone cooked one.'

'As it's only two days after your birthday we could have a double celebration.'

She smiled. 'That'll be nice. Do you get the day off work?'

'Oh yes. Ma is a stickler for us enjoying ourselves on that day. The whole of America will be celebrating Thanksgiving.'

Dolly was eagerly looking forward to spending the whole day with Joe – but how would Ma react?

It was early on Tuesday morning and Joe whispered, 'Are you awake?'

'Yes.'

Joe leant over and kissed Dolly. 'Happy Birthday.' He fished under the bed and handed her two envelopes.

Dolly sat up. 'This one is from Mum and Dad,' she said, tearing it open. Tears filled her eyes. She picked up the other one that had an English stamp. 'And this one is from Penny and Reg. How long have you had these?'

'A few days. I thought it would be better to hang on to them till today.' He fished under the bed again.

Dolly laughed. 'What are you hiding under there?'

'Happy Birthday,' he said again as he gave her a birthday card and a very small package that was wrapped in shiny silver paper and tied with pink ribbon that had long curly ends.

She was beaming as she opened the card and read the words. 'Joe, this is lovely. Thank you.' She picked up the small package. 'What is it?'

'Open it.'

Dolly undid the ribbon very carefully; it was so pretty she wanted to save it. She gasped when she opened the small red box. 'Joe! What can I say? It's lovely!'

'This is the engagement ring I promised you.'

Again tears filled her eyes but this time she let them fall as she looked at the daisy-shaped sapphire ring. 'It's lovely.' She quickly kissed him and handed him the ring, held out her left hand.

He slipped it on and kissed her fingers.

'Thank you. Oh, thank you.' Dolly held his face in her hands and kissed it all over. Then she sat back and turned her hand this way and that for the stones to catch the light. 'When did you get this? And how did you know my size?'

'I guessed.'

'Joe, I really do love you.'

'And I love you.' He kissed her long and hard. 'I wish I could stay here all day with you.'

'So do I.'

'I must get up.' He kissed her lightly again and rolled out of bed.

She watched him get dressed. This was her Joe, so kind and thoughtful. If only they could spend more time alone. There wasn't any talk of that happening. Dolly had looked in the Deansville real-estate office and had brought home some details about rentals. John, who worked there, had been very eager to show her round some properties.

'Joe's never said he was thinking of moving out,' the young man remarked.

'No. Please don't say anything, this is just a whim of mine.'

'I see.'

When Dolly showed Joe the details they were very quickly thrown in the trash bin with him saying, 'I don't want to waste my hard-earned cash on renting, when there's plenty of room here.'

Dolly tried to point out to Joe that they would be near to civilisation and she could go to work to help pay the rent, but that didn't go down at all well.

Every morning, to avoid any confrontation, Dolly always waited till after the others had left before she went into the kitchen. This morning she was surprised to see a birthday card from Bob and Ma wedged against the sugar bowl. It was in Bob's handwriting. There was also a box wrapped in the same paper and tied with the same ribbon as that which Joe had given her.

Dolly gave out a squeal of delight when she saw the silver charm bracelet inside. In a piece of tissue paper was one charm – the figures 21. She was busy admiring it when the phone rang. Dolly smiled, it was Norma wishing her a happy birthday.

'Thank you.'

'I'll drop in after school.'

'I'll look forward to that.'

They said their goodbyes. Dolly went about her day singing. Life wasn't so bad after all and perhaps she had been silly to want everything her own way.

That afternoon Norma raced up the steps and held Dolly tight. 'Happy Birthday. Here's a little gift for you.'

Again it was wrapped in the same paper and ribbon. Dolly laughed. Everybody must have been to the same shop.

'Thank you so much, Norma. This is so kind of you.' Dolly looked at the tiny charm. This one was of the Statue of Liberty. 'This is just great.'

'I knew you'd like a reminder. By the way, did you like the bracelet?'

'It's gorgeous. I'm not sure who bought it.'

'It was from Bob, and Ma bought the charm.'

'What? I didn't think she'd get me something like that.'

'Well, it was me that got everything. Bob asked me to.'

'What about my ring?'

'That was Joe, but we shopped at the same store.'

'Where was that?'

'It's way out. We ordered from their catalogue. Did your ring fit?'

Dolly waved her hand under Norma's nose. 'Yes, and it's

really lovely. Fancy Ma buying me a charm. I didn't think she liked me.'

'Well, there you go.'

They sat drinking tea and Dolly showed Norma her cards. Then Norma said she had to leave. 'I'll see you on Thursday,' she said.

'But I thought . . .'

'Don't worry, we'll all be going to the hall. They always have a barn dance on that evening.'

'I ain't ever been to a barn dance.'

'It's good fun. I'll see you there. By the way, wear your denims and a shirt. We don't dress up for that.' She kissed Dolly's cheek and left.

Dolly sat and looked at her gifts. She'd never expected anything like this. These were the most expensive gifts she'd ever had. Why make all that fuss about the doctor's bill and then give her this? Perhaps they were right and she was too tense. Dolly gently held the tiny charm in the palm of her hand. Was she being accepted at last?

Chapter 33

It was Thanksgiving and the smell of the turkey roasting filled the house. Ma had taken over the kitchen and it was Dolly's duty to prepare the veg. The boys had to see to the milking as the cowhands were going to be with their families.

'Cows don't know about Thanksgiving, or Christmas come to that,' said Joe when Dolly looked surprised at him putting on work-clothes.

All through the morning as the preparations went on, Dolly was telling Ma about the rations back home.

'How on earth did you manage?'

'It wasn't easy, but me mum did a good job.'

'I was surprised when Joe said he was sending food to you.'

'We was very grateful, especially when it was for my friend Penny's wedding.' Dolly was hoping this would lead into her talking about her and Joe's wedding, but it wasn't to be, as Ma said brusquely. 'Put the other glasses on the table.'

Dolly did as she was told.

When the table was full of food, Ma said Grace and they all tucked in.

Dolly sat back full. 'I ain't ever had a meal like that.

When I think of what we had back home, it makes me feel guilty.'

'It won't always be bad back there,' said Joe.

'I hope not. That was really lovely. Thank you,' said Dolly to Ma. 'Now you sit down, me and Joe will wash up.' Despite her trying to be nice, Dolly was still having an uphill struggle to be accepted.

'Been thinking about getting one of these new dishwashers,' said Ma.

'Why not,' said Bob.

'Got to see what price the seed is this year. That comes first.'

'Is money a problem?' Dolly asked Joe.

'Only when we don't get a good price for the grain, or we need new plant.'

'When we have a good year then we can have a few luxuries,' said Ma.

Dolly smiled as she moved over to the sink. The radio was on and she began softly singing.

'You sound happy,' said Joe, coming up behind her.

'I am. I've had a smashing meal and I've got a lovely husband.' She looked over at Ma who was deep in conversation with Bob as they pored over a catalogue. 'And I think I might just have been made a little bit welcome,' she whispered.

He grinned.

The barn dance was wonderful and Dolly was breathless when she sat back on the bales of hay, blissfully happy. While Bob and Joe were getting a drink she said to Sandra, 'We don't have things like this back home.'

'You don't? I thought everybody had barn dances.'

'No. I couldn't see the managers of the dance hall letting

us bring in bales of hay – that's if we knew where to get 'em. Don't see a lot of hay round Rotherhithe, only at the coal merchants.'

'What's a coal merchant?' asked Sandra, smiling up at Joe as she took a bottle of Coca-Cola from him and provocatively put the straw between her bright red lips.

'He's a bloke what delivers coal and babies.' Dolly could see she wasn't interested in what she was saying.

Sandra didn't reply.

'What did you just say?' asked Norma.

'Just wanted to see if she was listening to me, but obviously, she wasn't.'

'Forget it. Look, the band's just come back. Right everybody, on your feet.' Norma grabbed Bob and Joe.

Dolly was happy. This was how she had dreamed her life would be.

The following month the weather turned and it was bitterly cold. Overnight there had been a heavy snowfall and at first light everybody was up, as they knew they had to go out looking for stray cattle.

The banging on their bedroom door had woken Dolly from a deep sleep.

'What is it?' yelled Joe as he struggled into his clothes.

'Hurry up,' shouted Bob. 'We've got to go up to the fields.'

Dolly put on her dressing-gown and wandered into the kitchen. Bob and Ma were dressed ready to go out.

'Dolly, fill those flasks with coffee,' said Ma. 'We'll want hot soup when we get back. You boys both go over to Bolton's, he'll let you borrow one of his mares.' She turned to Dolly. 'Pity you haven't learned to ride, missy – we could have got a horse for you.' Then she went out to the stables.

Dolly grinned at Joe as she filled the flasks.

'We'll have you on a horse yet,' he teased her.

'I don't think so. Once was enough. Why can't you take the truck?'

'It'll be too deep.'

Dolly stood at the window and watched both Joe and Bob ride away on Peggy. She grinned; they looked like something out of a Western. She almost expected John Wayne to come riding up behind them.

Other than where the horse's hooves had churned up the snow, it looked very deep but beautiful. From her bedroom window that overlooked the fields, everything appeared peaceful and serene. She wished she had a camera to capture this and show them back home. Perhaps she could ask Joe for one for Christmas.

The phone ringing brought her back.

'Dolly, this is Norma. Have the boys left?'

'Yes. Why?'

'Just to tell you that the road's blocked.'

'Thanks, but they've gone to get another horse from Mr Bolton, they've not taken the truck.'

'That's fine. Must go.'

Dolly put the phone down. 'I suppose this is it,' she said aloud. 'This is winter. I wonder how long it will last?' Life was very different here. Perhaps Joe was right. Even if she had learned to drive there was no way she could get to work in conditions like these.

Although they celebrated Christmas, it didn't seem to have the same impact as Thanksgiving; perhaps that was because the snow was still deep and everybody was busy with the animals. By now Dolly had her camera and she was happy taking snaps. Even though the roads had been cleared and they could still get provisions, they couldn't use the truck to get over the fields. Dolly was beginning to realise what a hard life this must be for Ma, but no matter how Dolly tried, she still couldn't get through to her. Ma had made it very clear that she didn't want her around; it was Sandra she had wanted to be Joe's wife and Dolly knew she would never be accepted. Dolly still got upset that Joe never stood up for her, or said they would move away. Was he worried that he would finish up with nothing? She supposed that was the joy of having nothing, like her mum and dad – when you have nothing, then you've got nothing to lose.

1947 saw little change in the weather and Dolly had resigned herself that this was going to be her life from now on. She no longer talked about having a baby. Joe had said to give it time before they went to the hospital, but he didn't say how long. Dolly gave up the thought of going to work, or finding a place of their own. This was the reality and she had better learn to make the best of it.

The spring brought forth new growth and gave Dolly a purpose. Bottle-feeding the lambs that had been orphaned or abandoned was her biggest thrill. She brought them into the kitchen and marvelled at their sense of survival, and for the first time since she had arrived here, she was busy, happy and felt useful.

'We'll make a farmer's wife of you yet,' said Bob when he brought in another poor little thing that was barely alive.

Dolly chuckled. 'If my mate Penny could see me, she'd have a right laugh.' She was cuddling a lamb and trying to feed it. 'Here, they don't half pull.'

'You're doing a great job,' said Bob.

'It's a bit different from Rotherhithe.'

'Glad to see you're helping out,' said Ma, coming into the kitchen.

'I'm really enjoying this.'

Dolly knew that after lambing everything would go back to normal and she'd be at a loose end again.

Her letters from home always brought her great joy, but each one made her very homesick. There was always news about Reg and his business and how it was thriving. Tony was now working for him, but there was still no word of him marrying Meg Windsor. Dolly knew Penny's brothers were growing up. Jack had been called up for the Army and according to Penny, he wasn't that happy about it. Billy was apprenticed to Reg. Dolly thought about when the two lads had been young tearaways; now it seemed they had turned out great, which must have been a relief to both Penny and her mum.

So far there wasn't any news of Penny having a baby. '*Please don't let her have problems like me,*' was always in Dolly's prayers.

Dolly's life had settled into a routine. Her wedding anniversary came and went as spring drifted into summer and summer into autumn. Her birthday, Thanksgiving and Christmas were soon over and every year other charms were added to her bracelet. She could almost read her life here in America. It was as if it was hanging on a chain.

The winter of 1948 was as harsh as the last year's had been.

Dolly had resigned herself to being Joe's wife from England. Other than Norma, she hadn't made any friends, and she often felt lonely. The letters she received kept her in touch, but even those weren't as frequent as they used to be. Ann didn't write now. Her last letter was about her baby – she'd had a boy – also her mother had died and she was very homesick. Had Ann gone home? But who did she have back in England? She had never got on with her sister. How would Dolly feel if anything happened to her mum and dad?

Chapter 34

It was July 1949 and late in the afternoon. Dolly was sitting on the porch cooling off, and watching Joe walk back from the stable.

'This was in the mailbox,' he said, handing her a letter.

Dolly's brow furrowed as she took it from him. She didn't recognise the handwriting, but it had an English stamp.

'I guess it's from home,' said Joe as he went and sat opposite her.

Dolly thought he looked tired. These last three years had been hard for both of them. Joe knew she was unhappy, but could do little about it. Dolly missed all the chatter she used to have with Penny on their shopping trips, even if there hadn't been much in the shops. Then there were the pictures and dances. Here they only had the local hop once a week and as soon as they walked in, Sandra came and joined them. Although Dolly was part of their group she knew she wasn't wanted. She knew she didn't fit in.

Her biggest treat was going into Deansville with Norma, or when she went with Joe to see a movie. Having her hair done was a bit of an ordeal at first when she found out Sandra worked at the salon, but she'd managed to overcome that. However, there was always an atmosphere.

Dolly let her mind wander. It was her job to keep this

place clean. At times she felt like one of the hired helps who worked in the fields. Just lately, every letter she received from home made her increasingly homesick. More so now Penny was expecting in October. Thrilled at the news, Dolly had sent a parcel of baby clothes. She'd had such pleasure buying the tiny garments, but all the while she wished they had been for her own baby. She so desperately wanted to be with her friend to share her joy.

Dolly knew she had changed; now she was grown-up. Joe, too, had changed. At first he was loving and happy; he was still loving, but his mother had gradually worn him down and he often seemed distant and subservient. He wasn't the man Dolly had married. Ma with her strong will and opinions was tough, and quite capable of running this huge farm, although she did admit it had been hard while Joe was away, as she only had Bob and the hired help. Jennie Walters would ride roughshod over anybody who stood in her way; many of the hired hands were frightened of her but stayed on as jobs in this area were hard to get. Ma wanted the boys to expand their acreage. Dolly couldn't see why, as the Walters had more than enough land, but it was because she had promised her best friend, Sandra's mother, on her deathbed that they would marry. So why didn't she marry Bob off to her? Was it that Norma was more of a match for her?

After one bad row, just after Dolly had found out Penny was expecting, Joe had promised her they would look for their own house, but somehow Ma managed to talk him round and they stayed. Dolly was surprised at how easily Joe had settled into his mother's routine.

Dolly opened her letter. It was only one page and quickly scanning through it, she saw it was from Reg. Why was he writing to her?

Just a few lines to tell you that Pen ain't that well.
I know she'll be mad at me for telling you, but if
you don't get a letter soon, you'll wonder what's
up. It's just at the moment she don't feel well
enough to write, but she's hoping to get better
soon. Don't worry, everything's fine with the baby.

Hope you and Joe are all right. I've never been
known for me letter writing. You've not got any
news about a baby yet?

Take care.

Love, Reg and Pen. XXX

Dolly gasped and was filled with alarm. She read the letter
over again. What was wrong with Penny? Dolly had been
wondering why she hadn't heard from her friend for over a
month. She knew she'd been poorly right from the beginning of this pregnancy. She did worry when the letters
began to get a little sparse as they had always written
regularly to each other; it was Pen's and her mum and dad's
letters that brought her a little bit of home.

The comment about a baby always hurt. Dolly was never
sure Ma believed her when she told her how she'd lost her
daughter. Did she think it was done deliberately?

'Who's your letter from, hon?'

'Reg.'

'Why is he writing to you?'

Dolly handed him the letter. 'It's Penny. I'm really worried about her, Joe. She never normally complains. Look
how poorly she's been all the while she's been carrying. It
was only me mum telling me that I found that out.'

Joe read the letter and handed it back to her. 'Don't
worry. I'm sure she'll be fine. He was only telling you as he
knows what a flap you get into when you don't get a letter.'

'I hope so.' Then Dolly said to herself, 'I wish I could be with her helping her, like she helped me.'

At that moment, the dust from Bob's truck as he drove up the track to the house caught their attention.

Bob came bounding up the steps and onto the porch. 'Hi, sis. Is there a cold beer handy?'

Dolly went inside and took one from the huge fridge. 'Do you want one, Joe?' she called out.

'Sure.'

'Where's Ma?' asked Bob.

'In the office,' said Dolly, handing them both a beer.

'Going to the hop tomorrow night?' asked Bob, plonking himself down on a chair.

'Expect so.' Dolly wanted to say, 'Is there anything else round here other than work?' She thought about New York. The two days she and Joe had spent there had been wonderful. The shops, the view from the Empire State Building, the Statue of Liberty and the lovemaking. After a week on the boat she had been so glad to be on firm ground again. When she caught sight of Joe on the quay, all her worries about being in this New World had disappeared. She had been over the moon; those two days had flown past and had been all that she'd hoped for in America. That was three years ago now, but it seemed like a lifetime. Now she had to settle down to be part of this family, when all she'd wanted was to have Joe to herself.

'Come back, Dolly Day Dream,' Bob said gently. 'You were really gone then. Thinking about the green hills of England again?'

Dolly smiled without speaking.

'Look, Norma wanted to know if you fancy going into town tomorrow. She wants a new dress. How about it?'

Dolly's eyes lit up. 'That's very kind of her. I'd love to go.'

318

Although it was a very small town with just a handful of shops, it was away from this dust-hole for a few hours. Deansville was a dust-hole in the summer and freezing in the winter.

'OK. She'll be over about ten.'

'Thanks, Bob. Do you mind me going?' she asked Joe.

'It's fine by me, just as long as Ma don't mind.'

Dolly wanted to scream out, 'Bugger your Ma! I'm going whether she likes it or not!' But she knew she couldn't do that. Nobody ever shouted at Ma Walters.

'I'll go and write a couple of letters. That way I'll be able to post 'em tomorrow.'

Dolly went to their room. Over the years she had tried to add a few feminine touches, such as scatter cushions and pretty curtains, but in many ways it didn't look right and after a while she had lost heart. She stood at the window; she never tired of the view from this one. Dolly had tried hard to describe it to everybody back home and had sent many photos, and they all said how lucky she was. But was she? There were times when she felt her love for Joe was being sapped away. She went and sat at the table, picked up her pen and began to write. As usual all the memories of her past came flooding back. Her mum and dad. Penny and Reg. What wouldn't she give to be able to see them and hold them again? How about Tony? Penny said he was still courting Meg Windsor, but even after all this time there was no talk of wedding bells. He always asked after Dolly, apparently. A tear slowly trickled down her cheek. She was worried about Penny and she wanted to go home.

Joe watched Dolly walk away. He knew she was unhappy. He also knew he should stand up to his mother, but what good would it do? She had threatened to cut him off without a dime if he left. She didn't even want him to rent a few rooms, and Joe himself knew he could never be happy in a cramped apartment, not after all the freedom he had here. If only Dolly would accept this way of life. He knew it was very different from London, but everybody had to adapt. He hadn't liked being in the Army, had he? Then Joe felt a pang of guilt. He was only in the Army for a couple of years, but this was for life for Dolly. If only Ma would accept her! Joe had known he was going to have problems with his mother when he married Dolly – she had never answered his wife's letters and had made it very clear to Joe that she didn't want a Brit around her. It was a Brit who had killed her husband, after all. Joe had tried to explain that people have to move on. He took a drink from his beer and stared out at all they owned. He loved Dolly, but at the moment he couldn't see any end to their problems. Was it because he was weak? And where should his loyalty lie?

At ten the following morning, Norma drove up to the homestead.

'Hi,' she called out as she pushed open the fly screen. 'Are you ready, Dolly?'

Dolly had been ready for an hour or more. It was almost a month since she'd been to town. Ma never offered to take her when she went to the bank or the beauty parlour.

'Shouldn't be too long, Ma,' said Norma. 'Haven't got that much to buy. And it's not as though we've got that many stores to hunt round. One of these weekends I'm off to New York.'

'Don't like New York,' said Ma. 'Full of criminals.'

Norma laughed. As usual, she was brimming with life and vitality; everybody knew her and loved her. Dolly admired her so much. Today she was wearing tight trousers and her blue striped shirt was tied at her waist, making her look tall and slim. Her dark hair was pulled back into a pony tail which bounced about as she spoke.

'Right, let's be on our way. Tell Bob I'll see him tonight.'

Joe and Bob had left the house hours ago.

Norma was singing as they bumped along the dusty road. After a while she said, 'You're very quiet today, Dolly. Something on your mind?'

'No, not really.'

'You're not very happy here, are you?'

'No.'

'So what's got you down today?'

'I had a letter from my best friend's husband.'

'Is that Penny's husband Reg you've told me about?'

'Yes. Reg said she's not very well.'

'Oh, I'm sorry, hon. Can you phone her and see how she is?'

Dolly shook her head. 'We ain't got phones. I feel awful. When I lost my baby she was with me all the time.'

'She's not losing her baby, is she?'

'I hope not.'

'It must be awful for you, knowing you've been through that.'

'It is.' Dolly had told Norma all about Penny's forthcoming baby and about the one she'd lost.

When they reached the shops, at every one they went into, Norma was greeted like a long-lost soul.

In the only dress shop Norma was given half a dozen dresses to try on. After a while she came out of the changing room wearing a green dress with a stiff petticoat underneath. 'Well, Dolly, what d'ya think?'

'I think it's lovely.'

The shop assistant smiled and said as they always did, 'I just love the way you talk, Dolly.'

Dolly did not respond. She had heard all this so many times before.

'You going to the hop tonight, Norma?' the assistant asked.

'I should say so. That's why I've got this.' She twirled round.

'You'll be the belle of the ball.'

Dolly sat listening to this conversation. She wouldn't have called it a ball exactly, but it was a night out.

'What about you, Dolly, you having a new dress?' The shop assistant Lauren was flitting round her. Everybody here knew each other's name.

'I don't think so. Ain't had a lot of wear out of the last one I bought.'

Lauren came and sat next to Dolly on the padded seat that ran along under the window. 'Sandra came a few days ago and got a sweet little pale-blue number.'

The banging on the window caused Lauren to stop and wave to the passer-by.

'Sandra always looks nice,' Dolly admitted.

'She's certainly got the figure for it.'

'Who has?' asked Norma, coming out of the changing room.

'Sandra,' said Dolly.

Norma didn't comment.

Dolly felt a kind of gloom settling over her as Norma drove back to the farm. Her friend patted her knee. 'You know I'm very fond of you, honey, but I can see you're truly unhappy. Are you sure there's nothing I can do?'

Dolly shook her head as her tears slowly slid down her face.

Norma pulled to the side of the road and stopped the car. 'What is it?' she asked.

'I want to go home,' sniffed Dolly. She felt like a sad little girl.

'What – to England?'

Dolly nodded.

'I can understand you worrying about Penny, but I'm sure she'll be fine.'

'It ain't only that, it's Joe. I feel he's let me down.'

'Joe's a great guy, but I'm afraid he's tied to his mother's apron-strings.'

'He was so different in England. I would have thought that all that fighting would have made him stronger.'

'I think he likes the quiet life.'

'Norma, do you think you'll ever marry Bob?'

'I don't know. I don't want to become one of Ma's slaves.'

'Is that what you think has happened to me? But you're much stronger-willed than I am. I should have been more determined. Got myself a job, learned to drive, even made myself ride a horse.'

Norma chuckled. 'It's still not too late.'

'I think it is. You're happy here. Would you ever leave?'

'I don't want to stay round here all my life. I want to live a little, travel some. If Bob wants to come with me, that's all well and fine, but if not . . .' She gently touched Dolly's hand again. 'Time will tell.'

'Would he go with you?'

'I'm not sure. We have talked about it, but as you know, Ma has a lot of influence over her boys.'

'Why don't they move out, or find their own way?'

'I think they both like a quiet life, not just Joe.'

'Well, they've certainly got that.'

Norma smiled and started the engine again and they headed for home.

★ ★ ★

At the dance on Saturday, as usual Sandra grabbed Joe as soon as they walked in and took him onto the dance floor. Dolly sat alone at the table while Norma and Bob also danced. She looked round the room. It was so typically American. The flag was draped across the stage and the band, who were looking very smart, were doing all the actions that she'd seen the big bands do in films. Her dad would have had a laugh about this.

The music stopped and Sandra brought Joe back to the table. 'Here he is, all in one piece. I always bring him back safe and sound to his wifey, don't I, hon?' She kissed Joe's cheek, leaving her bright red lipstick mark, which he quickly wiped off. She laughed and sashayed away.

'She's sure on form tonight,' said Bob as he watched her walk across the room. 'She's still got the hots for you, bro.'

Joe looked embarrassed. 'Leave it out Bob.'

'She's always been after you,' said Norma. 'Bob, get me a Coke. How about you, Dolly?'

'Yes, please.'

That night in bed, as usual on Saturday nights, they made love. Tonight Dolly was restless. 'Joe?'

He propped himself up on his elbow. 'I know what you're gonna say.'

'No, you don't.'

'Is it about Sandra?'

'Well, yes. You've never really told me how you feel about her.'

'Yes, I have. To me she's the girl next door. We grew up together, like you and Tony.' He yawned and settled himself down again.

Dolly lay on her back and looked at the ceiling. 'Did you ever love her?'

There was a pause before he answered. 'No.'

'Joe, would you like me to leave you?'

'What?'

'Would you like me to go out of your life?'

'No.' Once again he propped himself up on his elbow. 'What I would like is for you to look like you're enjoying life.'

Dolly sat up. 'Enjoying life. Do you call this living? Even Norma thinks I'm a slave.'

'Norma would, she's a free spirit. Ma will never tame her.'

'But Ma has tamed me. Why have you changed so much? Where's the Joe that I married and gave up everything for?'

'He's gone off with the lively happy English girl I married.' He lay back down and turned away from her.

Dolly watched the curtains moving in the warm evening breeze and wished she could be like the wind and fly a million miles from here.

Chapter 35

It was late September and the heat of the summer was giving way to autumn. For three years Dolly had marvelled at the colours that came with the cooler weather. She was worried that Penny still hadn't written. Dolly had asked her mother for more details regarding Penny's illness. Grace had told her things weren't too bad and the doctors weren't worried about the baby, which was due this month – but that had been weeks ago. Had Penny had the baby yet? If only Dolly could talk to them on the phone! She felt so cut off over here.

Once again Norma had asked Dolly to go to town with her.

As they drove along the dusty road, Dolly asked, 'What are you buying this time?'

'I'm not – at least, I don't think I am. I'm hoping to sell.'

'That sounds interesting.'

'I'm going to find out how much I'll get for this.' She banged the steering wheel.

'You're thinking of getting a new car?'

'Maybe not new.'

'So, what posh model have you got in mind?'

'Don't know yet. It's got to be reliable. Dolly, I'm leaving Deansville.'

'What? When?'

'I've asked for a replacement at the school, then I'm off.'

Dolly's heart sank. 'Is Bob going with you?'

'I don't think so.'

'Does he know?'

'I told him I was thinking of going, but like most of them round this way, they don't think I mean it.'

'Norma, I shall miss you so much. You're the only person I can really talk to. What about your dad?'

'He's great, he's all for it, while I'm still young and free.'

'When are you thinking of going?'

'As soon as they can get a replacement. It could be a month or even two, who knows.'

'So why are you selling your car?'

'I'm going to New York and this old thing wouldn't be able to tackle that journey.'

Dolly knew that Norma had a good eight hours' journey to New York, and not always on decent roads. She thought back to her own journey from New York. It had seemed to go on for ever. But with Joe at her side she didn't care. Life had been good in those days; she didn't realise then how things would turn out. Had she been expecting too much? Oh well; she wasn't called Dolly Day Dream for nothing.

The two women wandered round the used-car lot listening to the owner's spiel. Dolly's thoughts were, 'God, these Americans can certainly spin a line.' Fortunately Norma knew the man and wouldn't stand for any nonsense. It had been exciting helping her to choose a new car and the journey home was great fun. This car had a radio, and a radio was something that everyone round here enjoyed. It kept them in touch with what was happening in the world and, of course, they could hear all the latest dance numbers played by the big bands. The music had Dolly and Norma singing all the way back.

When they arrived at the farm the boys came out and gave Norma's car the onceover.

'This sure is a dandy little thing,' said Bob, sitting in the driver's seat.

'So where are you off to then, Norma?' asked Joe.

'First stop will be New York; from then on, who knows?'

'You're leaving Deansville?' asked Joe.

'I sure am.'

Bob laughed. 'You won't go, hon. Not when it comes down to it. What about your pa?'

'For your information, young man,' she touched Bob's cheek, 'my pa is all for it. He thinks I should go out and see what's in this big wide world while I'm still young and able.'

Bob was speechless.

'It's not all that good out there,' Joe said soberly, thinking of the war.

'That's for me to see for myself. Right, I'm off home.' Norma accelerated away down the track in a cloud of dust.

Joe put his arm round his brother's shoulders. 'Looks like you'll have to marry her if you want to keep her here.'

Dolly stood, quietly taking all this in.

'She won't go,' said Bob confidently.

'I think she will,' said Dolly, looking at the dust trail Norma had left behind.

The following week Dolly had a letter. It was from her mother but there was also one from her father. Normally he just added a postscript to Grace's.

Grace told her that Penny had had a daughter. They were going to call her Gail Dorothy. Dolly was having trouble reading the words because of her tears. Penny was doing as well as could be expected. What did that mean? What was wrong with Penny? What were they hiding from her? The rest of the letter was about the baby and how Reg was over the moon. There was nothing to say why Penny hadn't written to her. Dolly knew something was wrong. Somehow she could feel it. Why wouldn't they tell her?

Her father's letter was very different. He was worried that in her last letter she had sounded very down. Was Joe treating her all right? He reminded her of what he'd said before she left. And to remember that the offer would always be there.

As Joe's truck came up the track, Dolly quickly put her father's letter in her pocket. She didn't want him to see it. She had never told him about the money Jim had given her all those years ago. In fact, she had almost forgotten about it herself.

'It's warm work out there today and Bob's not pulling his weight,' Joe said tiredly. 'Ma back from town yet?'

'No. I had a letter from Mum. She said Penny's had a little girl.'

'That's great news. Is she all right?'

'I don't know. I'm really worried about her. Why don't she write?'

'Of course you're worried, but she's probably busy. Is the baby OK?'

Dolly nodded.

Joe went to her and put his arms round her. 'It must be hard for you, especially her having a daughter.'

'Yes, yes it is.' Dolly wiped her tears away with the back of her hand.

Joe held her close. 'You know, I'm sure that us not having kids was meant to be.'

That didn't help Dolly's longing.

★ ★ ★

Autumn was really coming in now and some days the cold winds that were seeping across the open farmland gave a taste of what was to come. The fields had been stripped and ploughed and the few animals had been moved to winter pasture. As the leaves fell from the trees, everything began to look very bleak. Many days Dolly went and sat in the coppice. This was one place in which she felt at peace.

At the usual Saturday hop Norma was sitting next to Dolly and looking very pensive. While Joe was dancing with Sandra and Bob was at the bar, Norma said softly, 'They think they've got a replacement for me at the school.'

Dolly looked at her, alarmed. 'When? When are you leaving?'

'Not sure yet.'

'Have you told Bob?'

Norma shook her head. 'No. I'm going to wait till I know for sure. That way he won't have time to talk me out of it.'

'Do you think he will?'

'He doesn't really think I'll go through with it, but when he realises I mean it, I think he'll try to stop me. But my mind's made up. Pa's going to help me. He's been saving up all these years – he knew I'd be off one day.'

'Will you worry about him?'

'Course, but I can phone, and as long as I keep money back ready to come home, everything will be fine.'

'Norma, I'm gonna miss you so much.' Dolly felt like crying, but didn't want to show herself up; she knew she had been very privileged to be the first to be told the news.

Norma looked round. 'Bob's coming back. Don't say anything.'

'Course not.'

All evening Dolly was thinking about Norma leaving.

That night, when they got back, she remembered again the letter her father gave her when she left England. It had been put right away when she first arrived here, as she didn't think she would ever need his help. What Norma had said about *her* father had made her want to read it again. It would have to wait till she was alone.

It wasn't until Monday that the opportunity came, and as soon as everybody had left, Dolly took the letter from the very bottom of the drawer.

> Remember, if you need to come home, go to the docks in New York and ask for Nobby Clark. Keep this letter and money safe and don't ever mention it to your mother.
> I love you very much.
> From your ever-loving dad, XXX

Dolly sat and stared at the letter. Memories of Penny's wedding came flooding back. The way Jim had sat at the table and written this letter. She gently fingered the five-pound notes. She remembered when her father had slipped this letter into her hand and whispered to her to keep it safe. Tears ran down her face when she thought about reading it on the ship, on the voyage that was to be the start of an exciting new life. Why hadn't she ever told Joe about this letter or the money? Was it because at the back of her mind in all those happy carefree days she knew she'd never leave him? Was she keeping it for a surprise holiday one day? At first she had asked him to take her to Niagara, but he always made excuses.

Dolly put on her coat and decided to walk to the school. It was a long walk and she'd never learned to drive. Ma always said it wasn't necessary, like it wasn't necessary for her to find a job. Why was that? Was she frightened that Dolly would have too much freedom and go off? Walking wasn't really a problem as there was always someone coming along the road willing to give her a lift. She just had to see Norma.

Grace sat holding Gail, Penny's baby. 'She's so lovely,' she said, looking up at Reg.

'I know.' Reg sat next to Grace and looked at her. 'What am I gonna do?' He sounded broken.

'I don't know love.'

'Both the grans are great, but what about when she gets older and starts to run rings round 'em? I don't want a spoilt brat for a kid.'

'She won't be spoilt. There's a lot of difference between being loved and being spoilt.'

'I wish Dolly was here.'

'Don't we all, son.'

'I don't suppose we'll ever see her again.'

'Please don't say that.' Grace put Gail over her shoulder and gently patted her back. 'That's better,' she said when the baby gave out a loud burp.

'Dolly always sounds very happy over there,' said Reg.

'Yes, she does. What time will your mum be back?'

'Visiting time is only for half an hour, so her and Pen's mum should be back soon.'

'I was surprised they let you have Gail home,' Grace said.

'I think they felt I needed to get used to the idea of having a baby around. They know she'll have plenty of back-up. Besides, Pen will be home next week.'

Grace gently kissed Gail's forehead and put her back in her cot.

'Thanks for coming up, Mrs Taylor.'

'It's my pleasure. She's such a dear. Now, you're sure everything's all right?'

Reg nodded.

'Remember, I'll always help out, so call me any time.'

'Thanks. Good job she sleeps through the night. I dunno how I'd manage if she kept me awake. We've got so much work on at the moment. Tony's great. Even young Billy's making himself really useful and he's willing to learn. We're doing a lot of jobs on our own now. It's better being the boss. Mind you, Gawd knows how we'll manage if we have a bad winter.' He stopped and turned away from Grace and said in a muffled voice, 'Penny used to do the books, you know. God, I miss her being around so much.'

Grace went to him and held him. 'Everybody in this street feels for you, son. You'll never be alone and if you want any help with your books, Jim said he'd give you a hand.'

'I might keep him to that.'

Grace looked in the cot. 'She's gone off now. Her night bottle's made up ready. I'll pop in tomorrow to ask how Penny is. Good night, Reg.' Grace kissed his cheek and left.

As she walked home her mind was turning over. What would Dolly say if she knew what had happened to Penny?

'Everything OK?' asked Jim when Grace walked in.

'Yes,' she said as she took off her hat and coat. 'Least-ways, as well as can be expected.'

'Such a bloody shame. Two smashing kids with a lovely baby as well.'

'I know. Thank God they live here. At least everybody's trying to help them out. Jim, do you think you could give Reg a hand with his books?'

'Course, any time.' Jim, who was sitting in the armchair,

looked up. 'I keep thinking about Dolly.'

'I know. So do I.'

'Who would she have if . . .'

'Don't even think about anything like that.'

'She seems happy enough over there, thank the Lord.'

'Jim, we'll have to tell her one day. She's getting worried as to why Penny don't write.'

'I know – but how can we? Those two were as thick as thieves. More like sisters than friends.'

'I know.' Grace sat opposite Jim. How could she write and tell her daughter that her best friend had got polio. Thank God it was caught in time and she wasn't in an iron lung. But she was paralysed from the waist down and would probably have to spend the rest of her life in a wheelchair. Life was so bloody unfair at times.

Chapter 36

Dolly pulled her coat tighter round her as she made her way along the road. She had only been walking a few minutes when Old Harry, as he was known to everyone, drew up alongside her. Harry lived down the road.

'Hello there, young Dolly – and where are you off to?' he yelled out of the truck window.

'I was just on my way to see Norma at the school.'

'You walking?'

'Yes.'

'You could have phoned or let Joe drive you over there.'

'It ain't that far and a walk will do me good.'

'Would have thought you'd have learned to drive by now, girly.'

Dolly smiled. 'Perhaps one day.' She wasn't going to tell him the reason she didn't drive.

'You Brits are a funny lot. You sure you wouldn't like a ride?' He leaned out and looked up at the sky. 'Looks like it could rain.'

'Well, all right then.'

'Jump in.'

'Thanks, Harry.' Dolly climbed in beside him. The truck was a typical workman's vehicle. Empty cigarette packets were screwed up and strewn over the dash and newspapers were scattered all over the seat.

'So what d'you think about our Norma going?' he asked.

The news had spread like wildfire. Everybody was devastated; they didn't want the young woman to leave.

'It'll be hard on the kids,' Dolly sighed. 'They really love her.'

'Don't we all. I think her old pa will be upset too. Still, I expect your pa didn't like the idea of you coming over here either?'

'He was a bit upset.'

'I tell you, honey, if any of my kids wanted to up sticks, I'd tie them to a chair first.'

'But you'll have to let Young Harry go when he's drafted.'

'That's a different thing. That's for his country.'

Dolly knew the Americans had a great sense of loyalty towards their country.

When they arrived outside the school Dolly jumped out of the truck. 'Thanks, Harry,' she called out.

'My pleasure.'

Dolly stood and watched him drive away. Everybody was so kind here and had accepted her; everyone except Sandra and Ma Walters. She waited till the kids came tumbling out before she ventured into the classroom.

Norma was cleaning the blackboard. 'Dolly,' she called out when she caught sight of her. 'What are you doing here?'

'I've come to talk to you.'

'You could have phoned. How did you get here? Is Joe outside?'

Dolly shook her head. 'Old Harry gave me a lift.'

'Take a seat, I'll be through in just a moment.'

Dolly squeezed herself into one of the tiny seats.

'You know they're going to give me a farewell party at the hall on Saturday?'

'Yes.'

'You don't sound very thrilled about it.' Norma put the sponge away and tidied her desk. 'Right. I'm ready.'

'I hear the new teacher starts tomorrow.'

'Yes, that gives her a few days for me to show her everything.'

'Do you know the exact date you're leaving here?'

'Yes,' she said softly. 'I'm off on Monday.'

Dolly stopped in her tracks. 'Next week? You can't. It's too soon.' She felt panicky.

Norma looked surprised. 'If I leave it any later, the roads could be snowed under, you know what the winters are like. Then it'll be spring and then – well, time goes so fast, I'm afraid I might change my mind. Come home for a coffee and then I'll run you back.'

'Thanks.'

Norma's house was only a couple of blocks from the school and as they drew near Dolly took her arm. 'Is your pa home?'

'No,' she smiled. 'What is it? You and Pa are as thick as thieves.'

'I know. I like chatting to him, but right now I want to talk to you on your own.'

Inside Dolly decided to say nothing until Norma was seated.

As she pushed a mug of coffee in front of Dolly, Norma asked, 'Now, what's on your mind?'

'I want to come with you to New York. I'm going home.'

Norma slowly put her mug down on the table. 'You're what?'

'I think you heard.'

'Yes, but why?'

'I don't fit in and I'm so unhappy.'

337

'You're going to leave Joe?'

'Yes.'

'My God. Does he know?'

Dolly shook her head. 'I've only just decided. Well, a couple of days ago.'

'What will Ma say?'

'Good riddance probably.'

'Don't you love Joe any more?'

'I don't really know. I know it's all my fault. Perhaps I was expecting too much. It was so different when we were on our own. Now I feel his mother has taken the heart out of him and she's doing the same to me. He ain't the Joe I married.'

'We all change.'

'I know. I did so want to be happy here, but I also want to see my mum and dad, and Penny. I know something's happened to her, I just know it.' Dolly let her tears fall.

Norma came and put her arm round Dolly's shoulder. 'You need to talk this over with Joe first. I'm not doing anything that will hurt any member of this community. Remember, my pa still lives here and one day I'll have to come back to Deansville.'

'I understand,' Dolly told her.

On the way back Norma said, 'Dolly, you realise it'll cost you to go back?'

Dolly nodded. 'My dad gave me some money when I left home. I never thought I'd have to use it for this. I'd always hoped it would be for a holiday. I wanted me and Joe to go away. I have also managed to save a few dollars from my allowance.'

'Your allowance? That sounds archaic.'

'It is. Norma, I must go home, it's where I want to be.'

Norma stopped the car at the bottom of the track.

'D'you mind if I don't come in? I don't want to seem a coward, but I don't want them to think I encouraged you.'

Dolly kissed her cheek. 'Thanks.'

That evening Dolly sat mulling over her plans. She had to tell Joe, but when would be the best time? When would they be alone?

That night when they were in the bedroom, Joe was in bed and Dolly went and sat on his side.

'What's the problem, hon? You've been very quiet all evening.'

'Joe. I'm going home.'

He laughed. 'You are home.'

'No. Back to England.'

He quickly sat up. 'What did you say?'

'I'm going home.'

'When? How?'

'I'm going to New York with Norma.'

He lay back and laughed again; this time it was a cynical laugh. 'And where are you getting the money from?'

'My dad.'

'Hold on a minute. Your dad's sent you the money to go back?'

'He gave it to me when I left England.'

'You've had it all this time and you never told me?'

'I didn't think I'd ever need it.'

'But now you do?'

Dolly didn't answer.

'So you're going with Norma? Does she know?'

'I asked her today.'

'Have you two been planning this?'

'No, Norma didn't know. It wasn't till she said she was going that I thought about it.'

He jumped out of bed. 'You can't go. You can't leave me! I won't let you! You're my wife and I need you here.'

'No, you don't. I was just a trophy you brought home from the war. Your mother has made it very plain she doesn't like me. And you don't want to move away or get a place of our own. You're quite happy here.'

'You know I can't move away, Ma needs me here.'

'Exactly.' Dolly was trembling as she got into bed. She wasn't really sure this was happening. It was almost like a bad dream.

'Dolly, I love you. I don't want you to go.' Joe went to hold her.

'I must, Joe. I've got to take this opportunity to get to New York. It may never come again.'

'Don't you love me?'

'I don't know. You've changed.'

'And so have you. You used to be full of fun and always laughing.'

'What have I got to laugh about here? If we had moved on I would have a job and when you came home at night we would be alone.'

'I want to live here. I don't want to be cooped up in some little room. This is a great place, we've got everything we want.'

Dolly wanted to say, 'Everything but our privacy.' They couldn't even have a good row or make love whenever they fancied it, but she knew Joe didn't see it that way.

Joe turned away from her. 'Wait till Ma hears about this.'

Dolly knew that it would be the best news his mother would have had since she arrived.

Saturday night was Norma's leaving party and even Ma was going. Dolly decided she wouldn't go.

'But why?' asked Joe bitterly. 'Everybody knows you're leaving with Norma.'

'It's Norma's party.'

'I don't understand you.'

'As you said, it's Norma's party and I don't want to spoil it for her.'

'Please yourself,' said Joe as he slammed out of the room.

As they were all getting ready the atmosphere was very strained.

Bob took Dolly to one side. 'Please come. Norma's going to be very disappointed.'

Dolly smiled. 'She'll understand.'

When they left Dolly was glad to be alone and began her packing. As she put her things in her case she felt very sad. This had been her life. Everything she had could be fitted in this case. She sat on the bed and shed tears. Where did it all go wrong? She looked at her wedding photo and thought about the one of her mum and dad. All the years she had looked at that, they were happy. Had she been expecting too much? She pushed the case under the bed. She didn't want any more arguments tonight.

It was late when Dolly heard the truck stop outside. The laughter and loud voices told her that Joe was definitely the worse for drink. When he climbed into bed, Dolly remained perfectly still. She didn't want to talk to him as whatever he said it still wouldn't change her mind.

His snoring was loud and intrusive and she was finding it difficult to sleep. She wandered into the kitchen and was surprised to see Bob sitting at the table drinking coffee.

'Couldn't sleep,' he said, looking up when Dolly entered.

'Nor me,' she said, pouring herself a cup of coffee and sitting opposite him.

'I wish you weren't going.'

341

'I've got to. I won't get another chance.'

'It was a great party. You should have come.'

'No, I couldn't. How was Joe?'

'He's really cut up about it.'

'What about Sandra?'

'What can I say?'

'I wish it hadn't ended like this,' said Dolly, stirring her coffee round and round.

'How are you going to pay for this trip?'

'I have got some money.'

'Is it enough?'

Dolly shrugged.

'Wait here.' Bob left the room. In a few minutes he was back. He held out some money that was folded in half. 'Here, take this. It ain't much but it might help.'

'I can't take your money.'

'You can. I'm really sorry you're leaving.'

'Please, Bob. Take it back.' She stood up and held out the money.

'No, have it as a gift.'

'I can't.'

'I'm sorry Norma's leaving but she'll be back one day. If she ain't married then I hope she'll marry me – and Dolly, I've learned a valuable lesson about how to treat a wife.'

'Don't be hard on Joe.'

Bob put his arms round Dolly and held her tight. 'I'll never forget you.'

Dolly pulled away from him and went into her room. She didn't count the money. She would put it in an envelope and leave it behind.

The following Monday it was very early when Dolly took her suitcase out onto the porch. She was upset that nobody was around. She had stood at the window and watched Ma drive off – Dolly knew she would be gone for most of the day. The boys had also left. Last night Bob had said goodbye and wished her well. On Sunday Joe had asked her to change her mind, but he hadn't pleaded or become upset. How different things had been when she first arrived here. Dolly knew that having got this far, she couldn't change her mind.

All weekend the arguments had been long and hard, and when Ma said her son might as well divorce Dolly and marry Sandra, and Joe didn't object, that was the last straw. She knew her marriage was over.

When Norma arrived to collect her, it was with very mixed feelings that she loaded her luggage into the trunk.

She looked up when Joe's truck came racing towards the house. He jumped out. 'Dolly! Please don't go.'

'I must. I've got nothing to stay for.'

'I thought you loved me?'

'I did, I do. Joe, can't you see I'm a townie? I miss the people. I'm not cut out to ride a horse or work on a farm.'

'Is that what this is all about?'

'I know it's my fault. I wanted to live away from Ma, but you've made it very clear that you won't move.'

'You know I won't. Why can't you be satisfied? You've got a good home here.'

'I'm sorry, Joe. I've got to go back. I'll write.'

He turned away. 'Don't bother.'

Tears ran down Dolly's cheeks. She wanted to rush to him, to hold him close. He didn't offer her any money.

The journey to New York was long, and apart from the radio, it was quiet. Norma had said she didn't want to stop over on the way. Dolly's heart gave a little flutter when they passed the motel where she and Joe had stopped for the night. She remembered the way they had made love, and grinned when she recalled her first encounter with a cockroach. That night the moon had been very bright in a very dark sky, and as she'd looked out of the window with Joe's arms round her, she had been so happy and looking forward to a lifetime with him. Now it was over.

Dolly thought about how determined she'd been to marry Joe, against her mother's wishes. Why had she been so headstrong?

'Will you have time to see some of the sights with me?' asked Norma, interrupting Dolly's thoughts.

'I don't know. I'd like to find out when the next boat leaves for England and the cost.'

'We'll do that first, then find a hotel. I'm so glad you came along with me.'

'I ain't been very good company.'

'Well, I have seen you a whole lot happier. You know, you should have come to the party Pa gave me.'

'I couldn't. Was Sandra enjoying herself?'

'What do you think?'

'I bet she was pleased to hear I was leaving.'

'Let's say she wasn't shedding any tears.'

It was dusk when the skyscrapers and their twinkling lights in the far distance came into view. The sight gave Dolly a thrill. These past three years had seemed like a dream; now she was back in New York.

Norma was as bright and excited as Dolly at the view. 'It's years since I've been here!'

'It's a lovely sight,' breathed Dolly.

'I agree. Look, it's very late and I'm tired from all the driving. What say we find a motel round about here for the night and start our sightseeing tomorrow after we've been to the docks?'

'Course.' They had been on the road for eight hours.

The motel was small and a bit rundown, but it was cheap and Norma insisted on paying. The next morning they slowly made their way through Manhattan's noise and traffic.

When they turned into the docks, Norma announced, 'Here we are. I'll park up and we can go in together.'

At the desk Dolly was directed to the booking office. She asked to see Nobby Clark and wasn't surprised to be told he had retired. She explained what she wanted and was told to wait.

The young man returned with some papers. 'Have you got your passport?'

Dolly put it on the desk.

'Do you want first class?'

'No, it's got to be the cheapest.'

'That'll be tourist.'

'How much?' Dolly crossed her fingers behind her back. What if she didn't have enough money? What would happen to her, stranded in New York?

'The *Argentina* leaves at the end of the week for Southampton. Tourist class, one way, will cost one hundred and fifty dollars.'

Dolly gasped.

'I assume you do have the fare?'

'I'll have to go to the bank and change my money.'

'Everything OK?' asked Norma, when Dolly came out looking pale.

'Norma, I ain't got enough money. I've got fifteen pounds – that's only sixty dollars. I need another ninety dollars.'

'What are you going to do?'

'I don't know. I'll have to get a job and save.'

'I wish I could help.'

'No, no. You've done enough.'

'Let's find a room then perhaps we can sort this out.'

Dolly felt so unhappy. All her dreams of going home had been dashed. She should have kept the money Bob offered. How long would it take her to save enough?

As they passed a shop window Dolly stopped. In it was a display of jewellery. 'Norma, look.'

'You can't afford any of that.'

'I know, but see, they buy jewellery. I could sell my bracelet.'

Norma looked at her. 'Doesn't it have a lot of memories?'

'Yes. But to me at the moment, money is more important. Let's go in and ask.' Dolly stopped. 'I won't let him have my Statue of Liberty that you bought me. To me that is America.'

Norma hugged Dolly. 'I wish things had worked out for you.'

'So do I.'

Inside the shop a well-dressed older man came up to them. 'Can I help you?'

'Do you buy jewellery?'

'Only if it's worth selling on.'

Dolly took off her bracelet. 'How much will you give me for this?'

He took it and carefully looked at the charms. 'It is silver. And you do have a lot of charms. I expect they have a sentimental value.'

'I only want the Statue of Liberty.'

'I see. I can give you ten dollars.'

'What?' shouted Norma. 'The bracelet alone cost that.

346

Come on, Dolly. I'm not letting you give it away, there must be other stores.' She went to snatch it away from him.

'Hold it, lady. What say I make it fifteen?'

'Twenty,' said Dolly, suddenly feeling very confident.

'OK.'

'How much for this?' Dolly took off her engagement ring.

'Dolly, you can't.'

'I must.'

'I'll give you twenty for this.' He was looking at it through an eyeglass. 'But no more.'

'All right.'

Outside the shop Norma asked, 'How much more do you need?'

'Fifty dollars.'

'Fifty dollars,' repeated Norma. 'Do you have anything else to sell?'

Dolly smiled. 'No, only me body.'

'Don't jest about things like that. Let's go back to the docks and see if that feller has any suggestions.'

'Like what?'

'They must have cleaners on board. Would you mind doing a bit of cleaning?'

To Norma's amazement Dolly flung her arms round her neck. 'I'll do anything. That's a wonderful idea!'

In the office Dolly told the young man her story.

'You're lucky, not many go that way, it's mostly people coming here.' He told her what office to go to.

Dolly was nervous as she sat waiting. At last she was called.

The young man in uniform gave her a rundown for the job. 'We do need cleaners. You only get a few dollars salary, but you do get your food. You have to share a cabin and you can keep any tips you receive. We only employ on a temporary basis. I presume you only want to go the one way?'

Dolly nodded. She couldn't believe her luck.

'What a pity you sold your ring and bracelet,' said Norma as they made their way back to the hotel.

'That's all part of my past now. Besides, I shall need money to get to London.'

'You going to let your folks know?'

'I shall be there as quick as any letter.' Dolly beamed.

'They sure going to be surprised.'

'Yes, they sure are.'

Norma was going to stay a week and although she tried to enjoy herself, Dolly was a little apprehensive at returning to some of the places she'd visited with Joe. Memories came flooding back; the excitement she'd felt on looking out over New York from the top of the Empire State Building, was still there. Grand Central Station still impressed her, and she loved the boat-ride out to Staten Island to climb up the Statue of Liberty. She felt sad that she wasn't with Joe this time, but deep down she knew it would never have worked out. He would never leave his home and mother.

Norma had insisted on paying for the hotel room, saying it would have been the same charge if she had been on her own.

When it was time for Dolly to leave, Norma said she wanted to see her off, so after Dolly had been shown to the cabin she was sharing with another cleaner, she went up on deck to wave goodbye. Dolly would miss Norma; she had been a true friend. She planned on going to Washington next, as she was determined to see as much of America as she could.

'You will write to me?' Dolly said tearfully as they hugged.

'Yes, I promise.'

On deck Dolly managed to pick out Norma far below and she started to wave. The music was blaring out and streamers were thrown from the ship. Dolly could feel her tears. The ship's hooter made her jump. It was all over. Her great big adventure was over and she was on her way back home. What had happened to her hopes and dreams? What was in store for her? And why did she feel so apprehensive about Penny?

Dolly made her way back to her cabin with a heavy heart. Where had it all gone wrong?

'Hello, I'm Sally.' The older woman smiled at Dolly and held out her hand.

'Dolly,' she said, brushing away her tears.

'I hope it isn't going to be too rough.'

Dolly smiled. 'So do I.'

'You're British?'

'Yes.'

'Didn't it work out?'

Dolly shook her head. 'Can I ask why you're going to England?'

Sally sat on the bed and gave Dolly a photograph. 'This is my boy, Paul. He was killed in France and I want to see his grave. You see, my husband has been very ill and when he died a few months ago,' she stopped and swallowed hard. 'Sorry. We didn't have a lot of money and I was told this was a good way to get across the Atlantic. I have to see Paul's grave before I die. He was my only child.'

'I'm very sorry,' said Dolly, handing back the picture of a very handsome young man.

'I presume you're going home?'

'Yes.'

'I'm sorry.'

Dolly smiled. 'These things happen.'

'Yes, they do.' Sally put the picture on the small table. 'I'm glad we're going to be working together, even if it is only for five days.'

'So am I.' To Dolly, Sally appeared a nice woman. At least she would have some company to help the days and nights pass.

Chapter 37

It was early evening and Reg was in the downstairs front room looking out of the window; he was deep in thought. Tomorrow was a big day, but how would they cope? How would Penny cope? He knew he had to count his blessings. As she was always telling him, it was only her legs that had been affected, not her brain or her arms. Reg had done what he could in the house to make things as easy as possible for her. He had made a ramp to take her wheelchair through the front door and this room had been converted into their bedroom. A bunch of flowers stood on the table – his mum, bless her, had made it as nice and bright as she could. One of the good things about these old houses was that they had wide doorways. The old outside lav had been converted, but what about on days like today, when the cold wind whistled all around. And what about when it rained? 'I'll have to make a shelter for her to go under,' he said to himself.

Reg sat on the bed and held his head in his hands. He felt so useless. He loved Penny so much. Then there was his beautiful new daughter. Penny wanted to do things for her, but it was hard. What had his dear Penny done to deserve this? She hadn't said too much. She hadn't got angry or screamed out, 'Why me?' She was more concerned about her baby. She had begged everybody not to write and tell Dolly what had happened. Penny was worried at how she would react. She was concerned that Dolly might even think of coming back. Penny said she needed to be home to think about it before she wrote to her.

Reg continued staring out of the window. A short while ago he'd seen his mother pushing his daughter's bassinet across the road and going into the sweetshop. He let a smile lift his troubled face; she would be a little while in there while the two ladies cooed and gooed over Gail. She had spent the afternoon with Penny's mum. Thank God they lived in Wood Street; everybody had been so kind and helpful. Reg was very apprehensive at the thought of Penny coming home tomorrow. How would they manage? At least the old van they had would help. He could take her out in the summer. He could even take her to town next month, that's if she felt up to it and wanted to do any Christmas shopping.

Both mums had been marvellous, but what about in years to come, when Gail was running rings round them? Penny had been so very brave, but how would she feel when she was at home all day and wasn't able to do all the things she wanted to do for her daughter? And when Gail started school, who would take her backwards and forwards? There were so many problems in front of them.

Penny sat staring out of the window. Tomorrow she was going home. How would she cope? Putting on a brave face had been easy in the hospital, but what about when she had to look after Gail? Her beautiful baby Gail. In many ways she was so lucky; she had her mother and Reg's mum around, and her dear Reg. She loved him so much. Penny always knew he was a kind and considerate man, but he had been through so much. I will have to learn to be independent; our mothers won't be around for ever, she thought. Penny closed her eyes. If only Dolly was here. God, how she missed her. God. If there was one up in the sky, why was He so cruel? He took Dolly's baby and now he'd taken the use of her legs. In time they would give her callipers and with or without God's help she was going to learn to walk on them. If Dolly was here she would help her. Penny knew she had to write and tell her. She had made everybody promise they would let her be the one, and now the time had come. She knew from Dolly's last letter that she guessed something was wrong.

'Mrs Smith? Penny?'

Penny opened her eyes.

'Are you all right?' asked the young nurse.

'Yes, thank you, just day dreaming.'

'You won't have a lot of time for that when you get home.'

'I know.'

'Your husband was telling us what he'd done to convert your house. He's very clever.'

Penny smiled. 'I know.'

It was a cold morning and drizzling with rain when the liner reached Southampton. It had been a very different crossing this time. A cleaner's job with people being seasick had made the journey long and unpleasant. Dolly shuddered. She would hate to do this job all the time. At least she had managed to buy some of the wonderful gifts on board with the money she had saved from not paying her fare.

Sally and Dolly held each other tight.

'Thank you,' said Sally. 'You've been a great travelling companion.'

'We ain't really seen a lot of each other,' said Dolly as she struggled with her case.

'I know, but our little chats have been great. I wish you all the best, my dear, and I hope you find your friend well.'

'So do I. And I hope you find everything you're looking for.'

Sally kissed Dolly's cheek as they both made their way on deck.

Dolly stood and watched as the docks below her bustled with activity. She was back home. This was England. How would her parents greet her? Would her mother say, 'I told you so'? Would she be able to get a job? At night while on board her mind had been going over and over the sort of welcome she'd get. She couldn't wait to see Penny again and catch up with all the gossip and scandal and go shopping up West. God, how she'd missed them all!

Dolly had so many mixed feelings as she made her way down the gangplank. She was pleased to be home, but she was also sorry her marriage hadn't worked out. She had loved Joe. She held back her tears when she saw people run to their loved ones; the hugging and kissing reminded her of when Joe had met her. That had been such a happy time.

Although it was a dark miserable afternoon when Dolly finally turned into Wood Street, she still couldn't believe she was here. She put her suitcase on the ground and let her eyes take it all in. Her heart was beating rapidly with excitement as she stood for a moment or two and stared at all the houses and thought about the people she knew behind the closed doors. A wave of emotion swept over her. In just a few short years so much had happened. The houses had been repaired; some had even been painted. Lights were shining through the windows; all had glass in them now. She smiled at so many odd-coloured roof tiles that had been used to patch up all the damaged roofs; to her everything was looking nice and bright. Dolly was pleased there wasn't anyone about to stop and talk and so delay her getting home. She picked up her case and made her way along to number twenty.

She pulled the key through the letterbox and walked in.

'Hello,' she called out. 'Is anyone home?'

The kitchen door burst open and her mother stood in the doorway. The light behind her framed her, and Dolly thought she looked thinner.

'Mum!' she cried out. 'It's me!' Dolly dropped her case and ran to her mother with open arms. No words were spoken, only their sobs broke the silence.

It took a while before the weeping subsided and Grace began bombarding her daughter with questions.

'How? When? Why?'

Dolly took off her hat and coat.

'I can't believe this. I can't believe you're home,' said her mother, hugging her again.

Dolly smiled and wiped away her tears. 'Can I have a decent cup of tea?'

'Course. Why didn't you tell us you was coming home? Is Joe with you?'

Dolly shook her head. 'Didn't have time.'

'Why? What was the hurry then?'

'I'll tell you when Dad gets home. Nothing's changed,' she said, looking round the room. 'How is Dad?'

'He'll be back soon. He's working. Sometimes he helps Reg and Tony. They've got their own business now and it's growing fast.'

'That's good.'

'Yes, it is. Reg is talking about taking on more blokes, but you don't want to hear about that. Come and sit down and tell me all about why you're here and on your own.'

Dolly sat in the chair. This was it. She was home.

'Dolly, what's happened between you and Joe? Have you left him?'

She nodded. 'It's a bit of a long story.'

'Did he hit you?'

Dolly gave a silly little laugh. 'No. Joe was very kind.'

'So what was the trouble?'

'His ma, I suppose. I'm dying to see Penny's new baby. Is she lovely?' asked Dolly, wanting to change the subject. She preferred to wait till her father was home. She didn't want to go over and over the reason she was here. In many ways it was too painful.

Grace turned away and put the cups on the table. 'Course she's lovely.'

'I bet old Pen's as proud as punch. As soon as I've had me tea I'll pop up and see her.'

'Dolly. You didn't get my last letter then?'

'No. Why, is something wrong?' Fear filled Dolly. 'Is she all right?'

Grace shook her head. 'She wouldn't let us tell you, but I just had to. I see now I was too late.'

Tears filled Dolly's eyes. 'She's not . . .? What is it?' she whispered.

'She's in a wheelchair. She caught polio.'

Dolly slumped in the armchair and cried, 'No, no, not my Pen?' Weeks of pent-up emotion spilled out. She was home, but it wasn't going to be the happy carefree homecoming she had dreamed of. Suddenly she became angry with herself as guilt filled her. There she was, thinking of herself again.

Grace put an arm round her daughter. 'I still can't believe I'm holding you.'

Dolly choked back a sob. 'I must go and see Penny.'

'I'll come up with you if you like. Reg has tried to make things as easy as possible for her, but it's very hard.'

Dolly questioned her mother further about Penny and was told that she was very cheerful and settling in very well. She'd been home a couple of weeks now. 'She'll be really pleased to see you.'

'Who's left that case in the middle of the passage? I very nearly broke me blooming neck over it.' The kitchen door was flung open.

'Hello, Dad.'

Jim stood in the doorway, his face full of disbelief. 'Dolly!' He rushed to her and held her close. 'Dolly, it's you.'

Once again Dolly dissolved in tears.

When they parted, Jim asked, 'Where's Joe? Is he with you?'

'No. I'm afraid you've got to put up with me. I'm home for good. We're going to get a divorce.'

'Divorce,' whispered her mother. 'You didn't say that.'

'Oh no. Why?' asked her father.

'It didn't work out. It was mostly because of his mother. She didn't like me, and Joe wouldn't leave the farm.'

'I'm really sorry, love.'

'How did you manage to save for your fare home?' asked Grace. 'Did Joe give you the money?'

Dolly looked at her father. 'Dad gave me the money.'

'Where? When?'

'When she left I gave her a few quid, told her to look after it and use it only if she needed to.'

'I'm so glad you did.' She kissed her father's cheek.

'You crafty old bugger. You never told me,' Grace said.

'Well, I didn't see the point. I didn't think she'd ever need it. I thought she might come home with Joe and our grandkids one day.'

Dolly didn't answer that. She wasn't going to tell them that she had had to work her passage home – well, not yet anyway.

'It's lovely to have you back though, sweetheart.' Jim held her close again.

'And it's good to be back. I missed you all so much.'

'I think you'd better tell us what happened,' said Grace.

Dolly briefly told them about Joe, the farm and his ma, but she didn't want to dwell on it too much.

'Why didn't you tell us all this?' said Grace.

'I didn't want to worry you. Besides, I always thought it would get better.'

'She sounds a bit of a cow,' said Jim.

'She didn't like me, that's for sure.'

'How did you get to New York?'

'Norma, the local schoolteacher, was going – so that's what made up me mind.'

After many questions, Dolly said, 'I'd like to go along to Penny now. Is that all right?'

Jim looked at Grace. 'Does she know?'

Grace nodded.

'It's a bloody shame, just as those boys were getting on so well with the business. She's a brave little lass though. Always got a smile for everybody.' Jim went and hung his jacket behind the door.

'I'll come with you. I'll just get me coat,' said Grace. 'Jim, I'll do dinner when I get back. I'm all sixes and sevens.'

'Don't worry. Take as long as you like. I'll make meself a cuppa.'

It was with a heavy heart that Dolly went along to number two Wood Street. What could she say? What would she see? Her dear Penny in a wheelchair. It didn't bear thinking about.

Grace knocked on the front door and pushed it open. It was always left on the latch these days. 'It's only me,' she called out as they made their way down the passage.

The last time Dolly had been in this house was at Penny's and Reg's party when she sat on the stairs with Tony. So much had happened since then.

The kitchen door opened and Mrs Smith said, 'Come in, Grace. Penny's just putting Baby in her cot, she'll be out in a tick.'

Dolly followed her mother.

'Dolly!' said Mrs Smith, her voice full of disbelief. 'What are you doing here?'

'Mum, she's gone and dirtied her . . .' Penny was filling the doorway with her wheelchair. 'Dolly!' she screamed out.

Dolly rushed to her and, falling to her knees, held her best friend close. They hugged and kissed each other's wet cheeks, laughing and crying together.

'What are you doing here?'

For Dolly there was more explaining to do. When she'd finished, she said, 'That's enough about me, I'll tell you more later on. Now where's this baby?'

'Follow me.'

Dolly was amazed at how clever Penny was at man-oeuvring herself. When she went to put her hands on the wheelchair handles, Mrs Smith quickly shook her head.

'I can't believe this, you being here,' said Penny over her shoulder as they went into the front room. 'I never thought it would happen. You always sounded so happy. Mum, I nearly forgot, Gail needs her nappy changed.'

'I'll just see to her,' said Mrs Smith, easing herself past Penny.

Dolly watched her put a clean nappy on Gail.

'She's gorgeous. Can I hold her?' asked Dolly.

Penny nodded. Her eyes filled with tears as she watched Dolly carefully lift her daughter from her cot and hold her tight.

Dolly couldn't keep back her tears either. She thought of her own daughter, the tiny dead baby she had never got to hold or see. As Dolly's tears fell on Gail's face it caused her to blink. She gently kissed Gail's soft cheek. 'She's so lovely.'

'I'll be going on home,' said Grace tactfully as she and Mrs Smith left the room.

'Now,' said Dolly, sitting on the bed and nodding towards the wheelchair. 'When did all this happen?'

'I was six months gone and had been to the pictures – that's where they think I picked it up from. It started with what I thought was flu. It very quickly got worse and the doctor sent me to the hospital, where they found out it was polio. I'll tell you, Dolly, I was scared stiff. I thought about you and how you lost your baby at six months and I honestly thought we must be cursed. I did go the full term, then I had to have a Caesarean. They kept me in till Reg sorted out this place and they knew I'd be able to cope. Thank goodness we've got this new health service, I dread to think what all this would have cost. I was so frightened. That's why I didn't write.'

Dolly sniffed back her tears.

'When they told me it would be just my legs affected, I know it sounds daft, but I was over the moon. The thought of going into an iron lung – well, that would have finished me off. They hope later on that I might be able to wear callipers. It'll take a bit of effort to learn to walk with them, but now I've got you here to help me.' She stopped. 'Oh Dolly, it's wonderful to have you back.'

Dolly flung her arms round her friend's neck. 'And I'm so glad to be here.'

They were sitting in the kitchen laughing and talking when Reg came in.

For a moment or two he stood in the doorway, his eyes like saucers. 'Dolly? Is that really you?'

Dolly handed the baby to Penny as he rushed to her and they held each other tight.

Dolly shed more tears and she brushed them from her eyes. 'I bet I look in a right state. All me mascara's smudged.'

'You look lovely,' said Penny. 'Reg, I've put your dinner in the oven. I thought you wouldn't mind waiting a bit.'

'Course not, love. She's so bloody independent,' he said to Dolly.

Penny turned and poked her tongue out at him. Dolly couldn't believe how well Penny was managing.

'You didn't mind me holding her all this time, did you?' Dolly was kissing the tiny fingers that were wrapped round her big finger.

'Course not. That's what godmothers are for,' said Penny. 'Has she been christened?'

'No,' said Penny. 'It's been a bit difficult. But you will be her godmother, won't you?'

'Need you ask? I'm so happy to be home.'

'And I'm so glad we waited. Now you're here we can start making arrangements.' Penny's eyes were shining. 'I can't believe you're here. I'm afraid I'm gonna wake up and find it was all a dream.'

'I am here, and I intend to stay.'

'Talking of staying, I wish you'd stay for a bit of dinner, Dolly,' said Mrs Smith. 'Your mum said not to worry about rushing back.'

'No, thanks all the same. I'd better be on my way. We've got a lot to catch up on.'

'I'll take the little 'un,' said Reg.

'She's had her bottle,' Penny told him. 'He's so good with her,' she said happily when Reg left the room.

'I can see that. Look Pen, I'll come tomorrow. Is there any time that I might be in the way?'

'Don't talk daft. You're more than welcome any time. We too have got a lot to catch up on.'

'I'll see you out,' said Reg, coming back into the kitchen.

At the door Dolly kissed his cheek. She couldn't speak. Words wouldn't come.

As she walked back, her thoughts were with Penny. She seemed so happy and had a smile for everyone. Dolly was filled with guilt. In America, she had had everything – a home, her health and a husband who, in his own way, loved her. Why was she always striving for new pastures? Would she ever settle down? She knew now that Penny needed her and she would do all she could to help her and her baby.

Chapter 38

For the next two days Dolly was in a whirl as neighbours kept coming round to see if it was true, that she was really home. She told them how she had fed the lambs and chickens, and how she'd even sat on a horse once.

Betty was the one person who hadn't called and Dolly did wonder if she should go to see her. She felt guilty that she hadn't made her marriage work when she knew how much Betty had loved Chuck and how desperate she had been to get to America. Was she still intending to go there one day? Perhaps she had already left.

Everybody wanted to know what her life in America was like. Ada and May Gregory were very intrigued when Dolly went into their shop and told them about the things they sold over there.

Dolly spent as much time as she could with Penny. Dolly knew she got cross with her whenever she rushed to help her.

'I can manage,' Penny said, when she was trying to bath Gail. 'It's only me legs that don't work.'

Mrs Smith took Dolly to one side. 'Let her get on with it. She needs to do these things for herself.'

'I'm frightened she'll drop her.'

Mrs Smith smiled. 'Oh no, she won't, and she won't

thank you for trying to help, neither. I found *that* out meself weeks ago.'

It was Friday evening when Dolly was sitting in with Penny that Reg came in, followed by Tony.

'Hello, Dolly.' He came and kissed her cheek. 'Reg said you was back. It didn't work out then?'

'No. How are you, Tony?' Dolly could see he had changed; he appeared taller and more sure of himself. 'You look very well.'

'I'm fine. It's all this work – keeps us fit. Me and Reg are doing all right.'

'I'm glad to hear that.'

'You gonna stay round this way now?'

'I would think so.'

'Tony, fancy a cuppa?' asked Reg.

'I should say so.' Tony turned to Dolly. 'Been sawing up old floorboards all day trying to make a new floor in this bloke's house, and that sawdust gets right down your throat. We've got so much work lined up that Reg is even thinking of taking on another bloke.'

'So you've settled down then?' Dolly knew this was a silly conversation, but they both felt ill at ease. 'Not married yet, then?'

'Been trying to get him settled with Meg Windsor for ages,' said Penny, 'but he don't wanna know.'

'I thought you liked her?' said Dolly.

'She's all right.'

Penny laughed. 'Poor girl's wild about him.'

'Give over, Pen,' said Reg. 'You're making him blush.'

'Best be going,' said Tony, finishing off his tea. 'See you in the morning, Reg.'

Dolly watched him leave; Reg went with him to the door.

* * *

Tony walked down the road. He couldn't put his feelings into words. When he'd seen Dolly, all the things he'd thought of saying had gone. All these years he'd tried to forget her, but he couldn't. When he first heard she was home he wanted to run to her and tell her he would wait for ever for her. But life wasn't like the films. Here she was, back in his life – but would she want him? It had been a long while and she had loved her husband at one time. Would she ever get over Joe? And could she have any feelings left for her old sweetheart?

'He ain't changed all that much, has he?' said Penny to Dolly.

'No.'

'Still fancy him?'

'Penny Smith. Wash your mouth out.'

'Only asking. That's one good thing about being in this chair, you can say what you like and nobody's gonna clock you one.'

Gail, who was in the bedroom, began crying.

'It's somebody's tea-time,' said Penny.

'Shall I go and get her?' asked Dolly.

'No, Reg will bring her in. He likes to spend as much time with her as he can. Dolly, fancy coming shopping with me one day?'

Dolly looked at her in surprise.

'Don't worry. Reg has made a ramp for his van so he will drop us off and we can have a look round the shops together. I can get you a birthday present as well. Mind you, there are some shops where I won't be able to get in through the door, but you can always do the running about for me.'

Dolly felt her heart would burst. She and Penny were

going shopping together. That was something she'd missed so much.

'Not been able to get you much all the time you was away. I still ain't seen this bracelet you've been on about.'

'I ain't got it any more. I had to sell it and me engagement ring when I thought I'd have to pay for me passage home.'

'No! So why did you buy all this make-up stuff for me, and your mum? Did it cost you a lot to come home?'

'Not in the end. You see, I worked me passage. I ain't told Mum and Dad yet, so don't let on, will you?'

'Course not, but why?'

'I want Dad to think he helped me – well, he did in a way, but I don't want them to know, not just yet.'

'So what was your job on the boat? A posh waitress?'

Dolly laughed. 'No such luck. I was a cleaner.'

'Cleaner!' yelled Penny. 'Not the bogs?'

'Yes, and a lot of 'em was seasick.'

'Yuk. That'll teach you to go running off to far-off places.'

'Not any more. I'm really looking forward to Christmas.'

'So am I. I'll never forget that Christmas when . . .' Penny stopped. She gave Dolly a weak smile. 'Sorry. We've had a few ups and downs, me and you.'

Dolly could only nod.

'Funny you didn't have another baby.'

'I know. His mother reckoned it was 'cos I wouldn't settle down. And before you say anything, Penny Smith, it wasn't for the want of trying.'

Penny smiled. 'Now about this shopping trip. My mum will look after Gail. She's always looking for an excuse to have her to herself.'

When Reg came back, Penny announced, 'It's all settled, love. Me and Dolly's going shopping.'

'That's really great.'

'When's best for you?'

'I can always fit any day or time round you, my love.' He bent down and kissed his wife's cheek.

Dolly couldn't remember having so much fun shopping. At times it was difficult getting Penny into shops, but it was all done in a light-hearted way. Now they were sitting in a café waiting for Reg.

'I've really enjoyed myself today,' said Penny.

'Not as much as me. I really missed all this laughing and wandering round the shops.'

'It's good to get out. Only wish I could go dancing.'

Dolly, her elbows on the table, clutched her cup and said, 'We did have a lot of laughs back then, didn't we?'

'We sure did.'

'In Deansville we went to a dance every Saturday night.'

'Lucky old you.'

'They were good and they've got some great bands over there.'

'What about when we went to the Rainbow Club,' said Penny.

'That's where it all started. It seems like a lifetime ago.'

'Are you really going to get a divorce? There's no chance Joe might come here for you?'

Dolly put her cup down. 'No. His ma really does rule the roost.'

'So what are you gonna do?'

Dolly shrugged. 'Did you ever hear from Betty?'

'Yes, she's a Ward Sister working up North now.'

'Good for her. I wonder if she'll ever get to the States?'

'Dunno. So what about you? Have you got any plans?'

'First thing is I've got to find meself a job.'

'That shouldn't be hard. There's plenty of work about. What do you fancy doing?'

'Don't really know.' Just then, Dolly saw Reg drive up. 'Right – time to go.'

When they were settled in the van, Penny said, 'Dolly's gonna be looking for a job, got any ideas?'

'Now the business is building up I might be wanting an office girl. How d'you fancy that?' Reg asked her.

'I can't type.'

'You can learn,' said Penny.

'I'll have to think about that.' Dolly was afraid that working with Tony might make things a bit awkward.

'Reg, I've been thinking,' his wife piped up.

Reg laughed. 'That sounds expensive. What now?'

'I think we should have Gail christened after Christmas. It'll be a lovely way to start the New Year.'

'Now that sounds a really smashing idea. I'll find out when the best Sunday will be, then see to all the arrangements.'

Dolly was so pleased to be here, sharing all this.

As Christmas was fast approaching, Dolly and Penny went shopping again. This was how Dolly remembered things before the war. What with the Christmas trees and shops decorated with twinkling fairy lights, it felt almost magical. Some things were still hard to get but gradually goods were beginning to appear in the shops.

On Christmas morning Dolly went to see Penny with presents for her and her family.

'Only got you some ciggies, Reg,' she told him. 'After all, what can you buy a man who has his own successful business?'

Penny was opening the lovely shawl Dolly had got for

Gail. 'This is beautiful – it's so fine.'

'I thought you'd like it.'

'And look at my gloves. They'll be really useful.'

'I noticed how your hands got dirty and they looked cold.'

'Come here,' said Penny. 'Let me give you a kiss.'

Dolly bent down and held Penny tight. It took all her strength to stop herself from crying. Penny gave Dolly a brush and comb set, which was lovely. Laughter was filling the kitchen.

'Mum and Billy are spending Christmas with us. You wait till you see our Billy and Jack. Billy thinks he's a man now he works with Reg, and Jack's grown so tall. He's a bit upset he ain't home for Christmas.'

'Does he like the Army?'

Penny shook her head. 'You know Jack. He don't like taking orders.'

After a drop of port to toast the season's greetings Dolly went home to spend the rest of the day with her family.

All day her mind kept drifting back to Joe. Although she had sent him a Christmas card, she hadn't received one from him. Dolly wondered if he ever thought about her. She couldn't believe that after the years they had been together he would forget about the good times. She was pleased to have received a card from Norma telling her how much she was enjoying herself on her travels; she was making her way down the coast to Florida. After dinner as they sat in the front room, Dolly was staring at the fire, and all the happy times in America came flooding back. There had been some good times. The carol singing and the party afterwards. The Thanksgiving dinners, the trick and treating with the children from Norma's school. They had all been part of her life once; now that was all over.

'So,' said her mother, bringing her thoughts back. 'They're having young Gail christened on the first.'

'Yes. Penny feels they want to start the New Year with something good. They're having a party and you've been invited.'

'I should hope so,' said Jim. 'After all, I gave her mother away, even if she wasn't mine to give away.'

'That was such a lovely wedding,' Grace said quietly.

Dolly knew she had never really forgiven her for her wedding.

'What shall we buy the little mite?' asked Jim.

'It has to be something silver,' said Dolly. 'I'll have a look round in the week.'

'Any thoughts about a job yet, love?'

'Grace, don't go and spoil the poor girl's Christmas. She don't have to worry about that.'

'I do, Dad. I can't live off you for ever.'

'I don't mean for ever, but at the moment you're busy keeping Penny company.'

'What about the job Reg offered you?' Grace said.

'I've been thinking about that, Mum, but in some ways it might be a bit awkward, seeing Tony all the time.'

'Why? You still got a soft spot for him then?' asked Grace.

'Mum, for goodness sake.'

'Why should it worry you?' asked Jim. 'He don't spend much time in the office. Besides, he's going out with that Meg.'

'I know. Look, don't let's talk about it now – how about a game of Monopoly?'

'Now that *is* a good idea,' said Jim.

'I'll go and get it,' said Grace.

'And bring that bottle of port in with you. I think we

should all have another drink, what say you, love?'

Dolly laughed. 'I say yes – after all, it *is* Christmas.'

Two days after Christmas Dolly received a letter from Joe's solicitor informing her that he had started divorce proceedings on the grounds of desertion.

Dolly cried when she showed her mother the letter.

'But this is what you wanted, isn't it?' Grace said gently.

'I don't know. I think so. But it's so final,' she sniffed.

'Yes, it is. There's no turning back, not now.'

Dolly sat and thought about all that had happened. She would always remember the good times; it was just a pity they didn't last.

It was very cold on New Year's Day 1950, but as everybody was well wrapped up, nobody cared about the weather.

Dolly was godmother and Tony was Gail's godfather. They stood together at the font making their promises. Most of the neighbours came to the church with a variety of gifts and good wishes.

As Dolly gently rocked Gail she looked at Penny, who seemed very solemn. What was going through her mind? When she caught sight of Dolly looking at her she gave her a beaming smile. Dolly swallowed hard. Meg Windsor was also in the church. Dolly had to admit she looked lovely in the latest fashion, a New Look coat and a neat little hat.

That afternoon saw them all back at Reg's house. The laughter was so good to hear.

'You was looking very serious in church,' said Dolly to Penny.

'I was thinking about when we got married. Who'd have thought I'd be stuck in a wheelchair at me daughter's christening?'

'And who'd have thought I'd be back here and getting divorced?'

Penny smiled and put her hand out to Dolly. 'Well, I'm glad you're here.'

'And I'm glad to be here. You're very lucky to have Gail. She's a lovely baby.'

'I know. Dolly, what are you going to do with your life now?'

'To start with, I'm gonna work for your old man.'

'Then what?'

'I'm just gonna take one step at a time.'

'I don't think Tony will ever marry Meg.'

'Now don't start on that again.'

'He would have done it by now, you know, if he wasn't still carrying a torch for you.'

'Penny, marriage is the last thing on my mind.'

'Give it time,' said Penny as she turned her wheelchair round and went away.

Dolly sat on the stairs and thought about Joe. Had she been too hasty marrying him? Was it the thought of going to America that had helped make up her mind? No, she had loved him, and they had been happy once. She swallowed hard. It was well and truly over now. She was thankful her mother had never said, 'I told you so.' She had been headstrong and wouldn't listen to Grace. But how different would it have been if her baby had lived, or there had been another baby? She was older and a lot wiser now, but all in all, it had been quite an experience.

In the evening the drink was flowing, and when old Mrs Chapman sat down at the piano, the singing began. Wood Street loved a singsong and any excuse would do.

Dolly was sitting on the stairs when Tony came and sat

next to her. 'Seems we've been here before,' he said, putting his pint on the stairs.

'That feels like a lifetime ago.'

'It was. You haven't changed, you know, Dolly.'

'I hope not. But I am a lot wiser now.'

'I'm really sorry things didn't work out for you.'

'Thanks, Tony.'

'I see you ain't wearing your wedding ring.'

'You don't miss much, do you? Joe's divorcing me.'

'Are you upset about it?'

'A bit. After all, it should have been for life.'

'That's the way it goes these days.'

'I suppose so.'

'Was it that bad?'

'No, not really. I should have knuckled under and accepted being a farmer's wife.'

He laughed. 'I can't see you milking a cow.'

'You haven't got yourself hitched yet, then?'

'No. Dolly . . .'

'So what are you two up to?' asked Meg Windsor as she leaned over the banisters.

'Just talking about old times,' said Dolly.

'Well, that's all right then. Tony, come and talk to me.'

'Later. I just want to have a word with Dolly.'

'Why? You'll be seeing her at work. I hear she's gonna join your firm.'

'She'll be in the office.'

'I could have done that job.'

'I don't think so.'

'Are you trying to say I'm thick?'

Dolly stood up. 'I don't think you could be as thick as me. I ain't done a lot of office work before.'

'So why has she got the job?'

373

'I think it was more Penny's doing,' said Dolly.

'I see. Well, just remember this – he's my bloke.'

Dolly grinned. She remembered how she felt about Sandra eyeing Joe.

Tony stood up. 'Meg, I wanna talk to you outside.' He took her arm and almost marched her into the yard.

Meg turned and beamed at Dolly. 'I love it when he's masterful.'

Dolly sat back down and Grace came and sat next to her. 'What was all that about?' her mother asked.

'Meg's worried I only got the job with Reg because I know Penny.'

'Well, it's true.'

Dolly laughed. 'Course it is. And she ain't very happy about it.'

'Why?'

'She thinks I've got designs on Tony.' As Dolly said those words she began to think back to what Penny had said.

'Well?' asked her mother. 'Have you?'

'No.'

'Are you sure?'

'Course I'm sure.'

'Don't break his heart again, love.'

'I wouldn't do that, Mum. Christ, I'm just coming out of one broken marriage, I certainly won't be rushing into another.'

'That's all right then.'

When her mother left her sitting alone Dolly started to think. She did like Tony – she'd always liked him – but she had *loved* Joe. Now that was all over. Could she feel the same way about Tony? She didn't want to walk into his life again if it wasn't for the right reason. It wasn't fair to him, or to Meg.

When it was time to leave and everybody was saying goodnight, Tony came up to Dolly.

'I'll see you tomorrow at work,' he said.

'Yes, yes of course.'

He came closer and whispered, 'Dolly, could you stay here for a bit, just till I've taken Meg home?'

'Why?'

'I want to talk to you.'

'Can't you—'

'Right, I'm ready,' said Meg, coming up and grabbing Tony's arm. 'See you around,' she said to Dolly. With that they walked away.

'You coming, love?' asked her father as her parents made their way out of the house.

Dolly stood in the passage for a while hesitating. If she left now, what would it tell Tony? But if she stayed and waited for him, what would it lead to?

'Get a move on, Dolly, it's cold out here,' called her mother.

'You go on. I'll stay for a bit and help Mrs Smith.'

'I think everything's been done.'

'I'll be along in a tick.'

Penny wheeled her way into the passage. 'I can't wait to try these calliper things.'

'Do you know when you're gonna get 'em?'

'No. They said it was gonna be hard work trying to walk again.'

'Remember I shall be here to help you.'

'Come and give us a cuddle.'

Dolly bent down and held Penny.

'I always knew you'd come back to help me,' whispered Penny. 'Now, you going home?'

'I'm waiting for Tony.'

'He's gone. He's taking Meg home.'

'I know. He asked me to wait for him.'

'I see.'

'Don't say it like that.'

'Look, Dolly. You know he never got over losing you. So don't go breaking his heart again.'

'That's what my mum said.'

'Is Tony why you've come back?'

'No. I fell out of love with Joe. He wasn't the same bloke I married.' Dolly sat on the stairs. 'I don't want to do anything stupid. I've made enough mistakes in my life. I don't want to hurt Tony any more.'

'I'm glad to hear that,' said Tony as he pushed open the front door.

'Look, if you two don't mind I'm off to bed. Reg has already gone, so don't make too much noise, will you? Goodnight.'

They both kissed Penny and watched her manoeuvre her chair into the bedroom.

Dolly sat back on the stairs. 'Well Tony, what was it you wanted to say?'

He sat next to her. 'I know how you felt about Joe and I'm truly sorry for both of you that it didn't work out. But Dolly, I've never stopped loving you.'

Dolly went to speak but he put up his hand to stop her.

'Let me finish. I've carefully rehearsed this all the way back here.'

'What if I had gone home?'

'I don't know. As I said, I've never stopped loving you – that's why I could never have married Meg. She's not a patch on you.'

'You mustn't say that. She would make you very happy.'

'I don't think so. Well, anyway, what I want to say is that

I'm quite willing to wait awhile, and if you feel you could love me again, I'd be the happiest bloke around.'

'Tony, stop. I can't. I need time to think.'

'I know that. But I can wait. After all, I've waited all these years.'

'What if I meet someone and he sweeps me off me feet?' she joked. 'You know what a dreamer I am.' Then Dolly added, 'Tony, I don't think I can have children.'

'I don't care.'

'Not now you don't, but what about in the future?'

'Dolly, I have loved you ever since we were kids. I always told you I would wait for you.'

'I know.' She smiled. 'Thank you. But give me time.'

'Time is something we have plenty of now.'

'I'm so lucky to have you wait for me.'

Tony kissed her; it was different from the silly kisses they had shared a long while ago. This was a kiss full of hope. Deep down Dolly knew what her answer would be one day. She wasn't going to rush into anything again, as this time it would definitely be for ever.

Now you can buy any of these other bestselling books by **Dee Williams** from your bookshop or *direct from her publisher*.

FREE P&P AND UK DELIVERY
(Overseas and Ireland £3.50 per book)

Forgive and Forget	£5.99
Sorrows and Smiles	£5.99
Wishes and Tears	£5.99
Katie's Kitchen	£5.99
Maggie's Market	£5.99
Ellie of Elmleigh Square	£6.99
Sally of Sefton Grove	£6.99
Hannah of Hope Street	£5.99
Annie of Albert Mews	£6.99
Polly of Penns Place	£6.99
Carrie of Culver Road	£6.99

TO ORDER SIMPLY CALL THIS NUMBER

01235 400 414

or visit our website: www.madaboutbooks.com

Prices and availability subject to change without notice.